DEEPWATER DEATH TRAP

Bill Brown looked up to the control room's ceiling as a shrill, metallic screech suddenly filled the compartment.

"Sounds like we're rubbing up against a mine-mooring cable!" the sonar technician warned.

Brown glanced at Chris Slaughter. "As far as the CAPTOR is concerned, we're friendly. It's not set to detonate as long as we don't snag it."

As the sickening screech intensified, the sonarman called out, "The cable appears ___ ___ ck in the crease of our port hydropl___ ___ down whatever it's attach___ ___

Brown ___ ___ ___at should be risked. Th___ ___ ___ an untested one.

"Mr. Foa___ ___ hydroplane, full rise!"

"But at th___ ___ we could breach!" the helmsman said. He was used to taking orders only from his OOD.

Brown turned to Slaughter for support. Slaughter said, "Just do it, Mr. Foard!"

As the helmsman yanked back on the contol column, Slaughter turned to the veteran submariner and said, "I just hope to God you're right, Bill!"

RICHARD P. HENRICK
SEA OF DEATH

ZEBRA BOOKS
KENSINGTON PUBLISHING CORP.

ZEBRA BOOKS

are published by

Kensington Publishing Corp.
475 Park Avenue South
New York, NY 10016

First printing: May, 1992

Printed in the United States of America

Special thanks to Steven Kram and Chris Godsick of the William Morris Agency, and Captain Michael T. Sherman, U.S. Navy, for their guidance and inspiration. The author would also like to acknowledge the invaluable assistance of Karen Launsby, head librarian of the Incarnate Word Hospital, St. Louis, Missouri, who helped unravel the mysteries of Bacillus anthracis.

"The Japanese people forever renounce war as a sovereign right of the nation. . . . In order to accomplish this aim, land, sea, and air forces, as well as other war potential, will never be maintained. The right of belligerency of the state will not be recognized."

— Article IX of Japan's Post-World War II constitution

"But my heart's leaning was for death, and night, and blood."

— Yukio Mishima, *Confessions of a Mask*

One

A single narrow footpath led down to the beach. In the gathering darkness, Airman First Class Vic Taylor initiated his patrol with a minimum of enthusiasm. As far as he was concerned, he had already done his day's work for Uncle Sam, in the form of his regular, nine-hour duty stint. This current assignment was beyond the call of duty. Yet since he lacked the nerve to express his displeasure directly to Sergeant Hawkins, there was nothing he could do about it but count the hours left until his relief arrived.

The sound of crashing surf came from nearby, and the tall, muscular Texan looked toward the sea. The ocean was unusually calm. Lit by the last glow of twilight, this portion of the East China Sea had a mirror-like sheen to it. The deep green of the water was interspersed with a set of evenly spaced, frothing-white breakers. Its call was almost hypnotic, and Taylor inhaled a deep breath of clean air, ripe with the scent of nutrient-filled waters.

Above the sea's surface, the heavens were ablaze, their fiery hues enriched by slashes of deep blue, indigo, and violet. The evening star twinkled like a jewel, while a sharply outlined, scythe-shaped crescent moon took form close by. Though this was certainly no

Texas sunset, Taylor enjoyed it nonetheless.

Until the gut-wrenching, roaring whine of jet engines diverted his attention. He turned away from the sea, in time to see the entire eastern horizon seem to fill with the massive form of the B-52 Stratofortress that had just taken off from the nearby air base. This awe-inspiring sight thrilled the young airman, who breathlessly watched as the sleek bomber flew overhead, all the while steadily gaining altitude.

He looked on as the aircraft's landing gear retracted, then followed the B-52 as it disappeared into the last remnants of the sunset. While wondering what mission the plane's crew had been sent off on, he scanned the southern portion of the adjoining beach. Dark clumps of uprooted kelp littered the sand, along with a variety of driftwood and the usual flotsam and jetsam. A good mile distant, the lights of the village of Kadena beckoned. As he visualized that collection of ramshackle structures, he spotted an intruder headed his way on foot.

Taylor's gut tightened as he loudly shouted. "Halt and identify yourself!"

The figure kept approaching, oblivious to his challenge, and Taylor nervously unstrapped his M-16.

"I said halt and identify yourself!" he repeated.

Again his command met with no response, and Taylor proceeded to ram a 5.56mm cartridge into his rifle's chamber. He was in the process of drawing a bead on the intruder when the stranger spoke out in a high-pitched voice.

"Don't shoot, Taylor-san! It's me, Etsumi!"

With this revelation, Taylor instantly lowered the barrel of his rifle and exhaled a long breath of relief. A wide grin turned the corners of his mouth as he got his first clear view of this unexpected visitor.

She was dressed in a tight, black miniskirt and

skimpy halter top. This simple outfit amply displayed her large, perfectly formed breasts and shapely legs. Taylor found it hard to believe that he had known this gorgeous creature barely a week now. They'd met at Mama San's, a smoke-filled, dimly lit bar less than a quarter of a mile from the base's main gate. Over an ice-cold brew they had become instant friends. Less than two hours later, they were lovers as well.

As she continued her approach, Taylor admiringly appraised her doll-like face. Her long, dark hair was cut in bangs that framed a pair of big, dark eyes set above highly etched cheekbones, a small nose, and a delicate mouth.

"Well, just look what the tide washed in," greeted Taylor, whose tone turned serious. "Now what in the hell are you doing out here, Little Bit? You know I'm on duty and this beach is strictly off limits."

Etsumi looked like a small girl as she reached the tall Texan's side and responded warily. "I'm sorry, Taylor-san. But I was feeling so lonely, and I just had to come out here to see you again."

Taylor's tone remained firm. "You know the rules, Little Bit. No hanky-panky while I'm doing my thing for Uncle Sam. So scat, before Sergeant Hawkins finds us together and busts me but good."

Disappointment etched Etsumi's face as she flirtatiously batted her eyes, took a cautious step forward, and softly cooed. "And I so wanted to feel you deep inside of me. Will your precious Uncle Sam at least allow me a single kiss after I walked all the way from Kadena?"

Not waiting for an answer, Etsumi sensuously rubbed her body up against Taylor's and gently cupped his crotch.

"Jesus, Little Bit! Can't you at least wait until my shift's over?" the Texan vainly protested. He was fight-

9

ing a losing battle to restrain his rising desire.

Etsumi responded by guiding his free hand to her heaving breast and smothering him with a series of deep, passionate kisses.

Five hundred yards off the beachside security perimeter, a periscope broke the water's surface. Without a moment's hesitation, the oblong viewing lens turned due eastward and initiated a quick survey of the relatively small portion of Okinawa's western shoreline visible in the distance.

Sixty-five feet below, from the equipment-packed control room of the diesel-powered, Romeo-class submarine *Katana,* Captain Satsugai Okura stood intently draped over the vessel's main attack scope. With the practiced ease of a veteran, the *Katana's* commanding officer scanned the wide beach, whose sandy surface was littered with long ribbons of glistening kelp. A breakwater lay to the south, formed from a series of massive boulders. While beyond the barbed wire-tipped, chain-link security fence that stretched the length of the beach flickered the lights of a distant town.

Okura concentrated on the breakwater, paying particular attention to the spot where it intersected the beach. He increased the lens's magnification tenfold and expertly fine-tuned the focus. Shortly thereafter, he spotted a single M-16 rifle propped up against one of the boulders. His pulse quickened, and fighting the urge to share this discovery with the rest of the crew, he excitedly scanned the adjoining beach.

Lying naked on the sand, less than ten feet away from the abandoned M-16, were a pair of copulating lovers. Okura grinned, then watched the two go at it for a full minute before backing away from the periscope and snapping shut its folding arms.

"Down scope!" he ordered.

The cylinder slid back down into its storage well with a hiss, and Okura turned forward to face the *Katana*'s helm. Here two alert planesmen were seated before their airplanelike steering columns. Standing immediately beside them, monitoring the complex of main-vent levers and air-induction valves was the bearded figure of Chief Mikio, the sub's diving officer.

"Chief, prepare to surface," instructed Okura.

The diving officer answered without glancing away from his instruments. "The *Katana* is ready when you are, Captain."

Okura quickly scanned the half-dozen manned stations set alongside the diving console. From these various positions, the sub was navigated and its weapons fired. Of particular interest to him was the sonar station, where a young, crew-cut technician appeared totally absorbed in the sounds being relayed into his ears by the bulky headphones that he wore. Okura walked over to the sonarman and addressed him while gently massaging his neck.

"I hope that's not the signature of another submarine or surface ship that's got you so absorbed, Saigo."

The sonar operator looked up from his monitor screen and eagerly replied. "Captain, our hydrophones are picking up only the mating sounds of a bunch of amorous shrimp."

"This appears to be a night filled with lust, Saigo," said the captain with a cryptic wink. "Now let's see if our special passengers are ready to earn their keep."

Okura reached out for a bulkhead-mounted telephone and spoke into the handset's transmitter. "Number two, is the team ready?"

The amplified voice of Senior Lieutenant Fukashigi answered. "The squad has assembled in the forward

11

torpedo room and is awaiting your orders to disembark, Captain."

"Understood, Number Two," said Okura. "We're on our way topside."

The captain hung up the handset, turned toward the helm and firmly ordered. "For the glory of the Emperor, surface the boat!"

Chief Mikio addressed his console, and the control room filled with the roar of venting ballast. At the same time, the planesmen pulled back on their steering columns and the *Katana's* bow angled sharply upward.

Fighting the slope of the deck, Okura returned to the periscope well. He was in the midst of a hurried three-hundred-and-sixty-degree scan, when Chief Mikio's gruff voice sounded.

"We've cleared the surface, Captain. Shall I pass on the all clear to the torpedo room, to open the forward access hatch?"

"That's affirmative, Chief," replied Okura as he turned the scope due eastward, and surveyed that portion of water between the *Katana* and the distant beach.

"Captain, sonar reports a surface contact, bearing two-one-zero, relative rough range forty-eight hundred yards!" exclaimed Saigo. "It sounds like it could be a small patrol boat that's in the process of rounding Naha Point."

Okura instantly swung the periscope to bearing two-one-zero and increased the lens's magnification to maximum. It didn't take him long to spot a dim red light just visible on the horizon.

"Shall I inform the senior lieutenant to pull back the squad and then put the *Katana* under, Captain?" asked the diving officer.

"By all means, no!" replied Okura. "We should have the all clear any second now. Just be ready to pull the plug the moment we get the word."

With a deft movement of his right hand, Okura decreased the lens's amplification and swung the periscope back to that portion of the sea separating the *Katana* from the shoreline. The calm waters were still clear as Saigo shouted out the latest update.

"Captain, sonar reports that the surface contact continues to close. Relative rough range is down to forty-five hundred yards."

This was followed by the concerned voice of Chief Mikio. "If it's indeed a patrol boat, we should be just about within their radar range, Captain."

Well aware of this disturbing fact, Okura backed away from the scope and impatiently looked up to the bulkhead-mounted clock. Their mission's ultimate success depended upon total secrecy. Detection by the surface vessel's radar would compromise this all-important factor, and Okura knew that he couldn't afford to keep the *Katana* in its current position any longer. He was in the process of reaching out for the telephone handset to inform his executive officer of this decision when the unit activated with a growling buzz. Okura, quick to answer it, listened as Senior Lieutenant Fukashigi relayed the report he had been waiting for.

"Captain, the team is free of the boat and the access hatch has been sealed!"

Okura's reaction was immediate. "Take us down, Chief! Dive! Dive!"

The control room reverberated with the raucous cry of the diving alarm and the sound of onrushing ballast. As the hull began to angle downward, Okura hurried back to the periscope. He anxiously peered through the lens, which filled with a close-up view of five wet-suited individuals smoothly paddling toward shore in a black rubber raft.

13

* * *

Airman First Class Vic Taylor felt like he had died and gone to heaven. For the past quarter of an hour, positioned atop him, Etsumi had made love like a woman possessed. She was wet and tight, and displayed a rising passion that seemed to have no bounds.

Sprawled out on his back on the moist sand, Taylor returned her urgent kisses while stroking the smooth, hot skin of her constantly plunging buttocks. No words were needed to express his own desire. With no thought to duty, the Texan concentrated solely on satisfying his lover's desperate needs.

Soothed by the gentle sound of the crashing surf, Taylor was further aroused by a series of deep French kisses. His lover's tongue touched his own, then probed his lips and mouth with sensual fierceness. This was accompanied by a wild, grinding of her hips, hinting that her need would soon be satisfied.

Taylor's stiff, nine-inch manhood plunged deep into Etsumi's hot depths. Time after glorious time, she took his all, until his rhythm was further intensified by the first hint of rising seed. Etsumi sensed this excitement and momentarily pressed her hips forward and halted all movement. Taylor assumed that she wanted him to hold back, so that they could share the pleasures of orgasm together. With all the self-control he could muster, he did so. And after a brief rest, they were able to resume intercourse without the Texan having to worry about leaving his lover unfulfilled.

A spirited rhythm was once more established, only to be interrupted by a distant, metallic clanging noise. This alien racket immediately diverted Taylor's attention. He broke off the deep kiss he had been submerged in and looked out into the black night.

"What in the hell was that?" he queried.

"It's nothing, cowboy," said Etsumi breathlessly. "So please, don't quit now. I'm so close I could burst any second."

Heedless of this request, Taylor pushed Etsumi away, the erotic spell that had captivated him now broken. As he struggled to stand and pull up his pants, she vainly protested.

"Don't be such an old lady. There's nothing out there but the wind and the sea."

"That's easy enough for you to say, Little Bit. But if that's the sarge, he'll throw me in the brig and then lose the key."

Taylor was doing his best to brush the sand from his chest and arms when the clanging noise was repeated. It appeared to be emanating from the direction of the sea, and sounded louder.

Not bothering to put on his shirt, Taylor turned toward the breakwater, where he had left his rifle. As he pivoted, Etsumi grabbed his arm and whined.

"Taylor-san! What's gotten into you?"

The Texan violently yanked himself free and, not bothering to reply, sprinted for his weapon. Raw, heart-pounding fear guided his steps as he spotted the M-16 propped up against a rounded boulder, only a few feet distant. Well aware of his sworn duty and his exposed position, he desperately extended his hand. His fingers made contact with the cool metal barrel. Yet his relief was short-lived, for a mysterious figure materialized out of the blackness and kicked the rifle out of his grasp.

Taylor turned to face this stranger. The man's tight-fitting black attire included a hood which revealed only a pair of dark, cruel eyes that had a frightening, almost demonic quality.

As a student of the martial arts, Taylor had no trouble identifying this figure as a Ninja warrior.

15

Though he prayed this was but a realistic exercise by his own security forces, he inwardly knew otherwise. And his gut conclusion was confirmed when the Ninja lunged forward with a lightning quick parry, spun Taylor around, and proceeded to snap his neck like it was a mere twig.

As soon as the Texan collapsed onto the sand in a twitching heap, Etsumi approached the rocks of the breakwater. Dressed now in her skimpy miniskirt and halter top, she faced the hooded figure responsible for killing her lover, coolly addressing him.

"My work here is now completed. Yours has just begun. For the glory of the Emperor, may your mission be a successful one."

The Ninja bowed in response, as did his four similarly outfitted brethren who now joined him. Only as the men silently turned to proceed inland did Etsumi spot the long metallic cylinder strapped to the back of each Ninja.

Two

A lone Bell UH-1 Huey helicopter soared northward over the rugged central highlands of Laos. Seated beside the open hatchway, Dr. Miriam Kromer gazed out at the passing landscape. Since leaving Bangkok three hours ago, the lush, solid green jungle canopy had given way to jagged, boulder-strewn hills. Gone were the rice paddies and fields filled with water buffalo. In their place was a desolate, inhospitable terrain, conspicuously void of human inhabitants.

This was the thirty-two-year-old toxicologist's first visit to Southeast Asia. She had studied the area extensively while in college, and had jumped at the chance to experience it firsthand when offered this assignment a week ago. So far, she wasn't the least bit disappointed.

She had spent the first two days of her trip in Bangkok, as the guest of the US embassy. Thailand's capital city was a bustling, exciting place. Not only was it a modern, thriving commercial center, but it was also filled with dozens of magnificent temples and fascinating museums.

Miriam had especially enjoyed visiting the Chapel of the Emerald Buddha: Built in 1785 and situated within the walls of the Royal Palace, its noteworthy

17

treasures included a stunning jasper image of Buddha that was reputed to be more than six hundred years old.

And just yesterday afternoon she had explored the city's numerous canals. Bangkok was situated on both banks of the Chao Phraya river. This site was a natural flood plain, and the intricate canal system provided a convenient transportation network for the capital's inhabitants.

Afterward her escort, a handsome, young Californian assigned to the embassy's military staff, had accompanied her to the infamous Patapong district. Here an entire square block of the city was filled with nothing but nude bars and massage parlors. Though they hadn't visited one of these dens of iniquity, they had eaten at a nearby restaurant known for its fresh seafood. The Thai cuisine was superb, and Miriam had eaten her fill of spicy shrimp, scallops, and lobster.

She'd boarded the helicopter the following morning, shortly after dawn. Doing her best to accustom herself to the constant chopping whine of the Huey's rotor blades, Miriam now anxiously awaited the conclusion of the long journey that had started out three days ago in Fort Detrick, Maryland.

Knowing full well that her ultimate destination was less than a half-hour distant, she grabbed her restraining harness when the Huey's cabin began to shake violently. Outside, the midmorning sky remained clear, and Miriam wondered if they were having some sort of engine problem. Her fears were alleviated with the approach of the helicopter's systems operator, Lieutenant Charlie Kirdyo.

"Don't worry, Doctor. It's only a little turbulence. It will pass shortly."

Lieutenant Kirdyo's prediction soon came to pass;

the shaking stopped as abruptly as it had started. Miriam caught the Thai airman's kind glance.

"How much longer until we're there?" she asked.

Kirdyo peered out the open hatchway and pointed toward a tall mountainous peak just visible on the northeastern horizon.

"That's Phu Bia, the highest mountain in Laos. We'll be setting you down at its base, at the village of Ban Son on the mountain's southern flank in another ten minutes or so."

Like Miriam, Kirdyo was dressed in a dark green flight suit and helmet. The only noticeable difference in his attire was the .45-caliber pistol he had strapped to his hip. The mustached airman had a calm, easygoing manner. He spoke perfect English, and had a face that reminded the toxicologist of a Thai version of the actor Stacey Keach.

"Have you landed at Ban Son before, Lieutenant?" she queried.

"I'm afraid not, Doctor. That's Pathet Lao country."

Miriam peered out the hatchway and absorbed this curt response. Back at the embassy in Bangkok, she had been briefed on the current activities of the Pathet Lao. This militant Marxist organization had been fighting to control Laos for decades. Responsible for the deaths of untold thousands of innocent civilians, the Pathet Lao were notorious for their violent, unconventional methods of political persuasion.

As Miriam looked out to the slopes of the distant, nine-thousand-foot peak that had called her halfway around the world, she pondered the deadly epidemic that awaited her below. The initial reports, though vague, told of a mysterious disease, of unknown origin, that was ravaging the countryside. Hardest hit were the inhabitants of Ban Son, where dozens of men, women, and children had already succumbed to a fatal sickness that had no known treatment. As a toxicologist, Miriam Kromer was to root out the source of this deadly epidemic and eliminate it, so that it would kill no more. This urgent, all-important task would be far from an easy one, and she could only pray that her extensive training would prove sufficient in the difficult days to come.

The high-pitched whine of the Huey's rotors changed pitch as the helicopter began losing altitude. Less than a thousand feet of airspace now separated them from the rolling terrain below.

As they passed over a narrow river valley, Miriam spotted a dozen or so figures emerging from the tree line. On the back of each of these shabbily dressed individuals was a large wicker basket, and they all seemed to be following a footpath that led up into the surrounding hills.

It was Lieutenant Kirdyo who identified them. "Those are Hmong tribespeople, most likely from the village of Ban Tian Ca."

"What's that they're carrying in those baskets?" asked Miriam.

"It's raw opium poppy," answered Kirdyo matter-of-factly. "Welcome to the Golden Triangle, Doctor!"

It had only just turned nine A.M., and already a wave of humid, oppressive heat blanketed the village of Ban Son. The naked bodies of the handful of children who ran down the rut-filled, muddy thoroughfare serving as the town's main street were long ago drenched in sweat. Even the scrawny dogs they played with were affected by the warmth, which sapped the very volume of the occasional feeble yelp one let out.

From the shaded interior of a large, wall-less open-air clinic, Father David Goss watched the playing children with envy, for a few blessed seconds escaping the death and suffering that had been his constant companions for more days than he could remember.

He did his best to wipe off his wire-rimmed glasses and pat dry his forehead with a soaked handkerchief. On this scorching morning, he felt every one of his fifty-three years and then some. Weariness weighed down his limbs and clouded his thoughts.

Earlier, for a terrifying, lonely moment, he had lost sight of his purpose here. This crisis of faith had been very real. Fighting the temptation to give up and abandon his healing mission, he implored the One Father to give him the strength to carry on. It was through prayer that he eventually retapped the spiritual light needed to reaffirm his faith.

Shamed by his moment of weakness, he had set out on his morning's rounds with a renewed determination to share this healing light with his patients. For even if he couldn't cure the sickness that consumed their fever-racked bodies, at least he could prepare their souls for the heavenly realm that lay beyond.

With a heavy sigh, Goss took a last fond look at the lively children before returning to his morning duties. Each of the makeshift clinic's twenty-four cots were occupied. His patients ranged from mere infants to wizened elders. All displayed similar symptoms, and each would share the same fate.

Though death had yet to visit them on this particular morning, Goss felt its cold presence hovering closeby. With such a morbid thought in mind, he joined his young Laotian nurse, Mei, who was in the midst of her rounds.

Like the true angel of mercy that she was, Mei stood before a cot holding a sunken-cheeked, emaciated oldtimer. Bloody spittle ran down the patient's chin, and he appeared to have fallen asleep with his eyes wide

21

open. As she reached out to feel for a pulse, Goss signaled her not to bother.

"Forget it, Mei," he advised. "His time of earthly suffering is over."

Goss closed the old man's eyelids, made the sign of the cross over his wrinkled forehead, and covered the fresh corpse with a white sheet.

"I feel so powerless," Mei declared, her voice quivering with emotion.

The priest's response was interrupted by a low-pitched, monotonous chant, emanating from the opposite aisle. There, beside a cot holding a white-haired woman, stood a bald-headed, middle-aged Laotian in an orange robe. It was from this wide-eyed individual's lips that the chant came.

Both Goss and Mei watched as the man began stroking the old woman's body with a long, white feather. Next a censer of incense was ignited, and a pencil-thin stream of pungent smoke was waved over the prone patient's head. The chant intensified.

"So, the shaman has returned. Shall I get him to leave?" Mei calmly asked.

Goss shook his head. "Why bother, Mei? He'll only return in an hour or so. And besides, who's to say that his methods are no sounder than our own."

The distinctive clatter of a helicopter could be heard, and the priest expectantly looked up to the tin ceiling.

"It appears that our long-anticipated visitors have finally arrived. Now we can only pray that they can come up with some sort of answer to this madness."

The priest turned and somberly led the way outside. Mei accompanied him, and they both followed the excited villagers heading to the broad clearing at Ban Son's southern outskirts. The ragtag group arrived at its destination just as the helicopter landed. The wash

22

of the still-spinning rotors kicked up a blinding whirlwind of choking dust, and they protected their eyes as best they could.

The dust settled only when the engine was turned off and the rotors spun to a halt. Father Goss wiped off the clouded lenses of his glasses and then looked on as a soldier emerged from the helicopter's hatchway. This alert, mustached figure carried an M-16 rifle. After a hasty scan of the clearing, he beckoned toward the Huey and another individual climbed out of the cabin. The priest could clearly see from this one's shapely build that she was female. This was affirmed when she removed her flight helmet and shook free a long mane of thick red hair. She carried a black medical bag, and Goss eagerly stepped forward to initiate the introductions.

"Welcome to Ban Son. I'm Father David Goss, the head of the local clinic, and this is my nurse, Mei."

"Pleased to meet you. I'm Dr. Miriam Kromer."

As they traded handshakes, the priest hastily sized up his visitor. She was certainly younger than he had expected. She had soft blue eyes and natural good looks that required a minimum of makeup. He liked the way she directly returned his appraising stare and got right down to business.

"Father Goss, I read your initial report with great concern and interest. Are the symptoms you detailed still prevailing?"

Goss nodded. "That they are, Doctor. And so is the death rate. If this disease isn't checked soon, we could lose the entire village by the onslaught of the rainy season."

Kromer responded while studying the collection of locals huddled behind the priest. "The symptoms that your report mentioned — headache, vomiting, high fever, and internal bleeding — could be characteristic of a fungal infection. Perhaps a natural-growing myco-toxin has entered the food chain here."

"That possibility has crossed my mind," said Goss. "But I'm far from an expert in such matters."

Kromer's glance returned to the priest. "Well, hopefully I can help. My doctorate's in toxicology."

"May I ask what hospital you're affiliated with, Doctor?" asked Goss.

"Of course you can, Father. I'm currently working for the Armed Forces Intelligence Center at Fort Detrick, Maryland."

This revelation caused the priest to flinch with abhorrence. "I never dreamed my report would reach the military."

Surprised by this reaction, Kromer did her best to be as honest as possible. "You have nothing to fear from me, Father. I'm only here to help."

The buzzing, mechanical drone of a small plane sounded in the distance, and all eyes went to the blue heavens. It was Lieutenant Kirdyo who pointed out a lone propeller-driven aircraft lazily approaching from the east.

Dr. Kromer identified this single-engine plane as a Piper Cub. It certainly looked innocent enough. Yet with its continued approach, the local villagers turned and ran back to town as if the devil himself were on their tails.

"What's gotten into them?" asked the puzzled toxicologist.

It was Mei who answered. "They're afraid of *chimi,* the yellow rain that is said to often follow such overflights. Many of the Hmong feel that this is the substance responsible for the plague that has struck this village."

Kromer's eyes opened wide with interest. "Do you happen to have any samples of this *chimi?*"

The priest reacted with instant disgust. "So that's what you've come for. I should have guessed your real motive. You don't believe this so-called yellow rain is real, that it's a man-made toxin being utilized to kill innocent men, women, and children?"

"Father Goss, that is only one of the things I'm here to determine," Kromer answered directly.

"Then let's get on with it," said the priest with a heavy sigh. "Though I begged for medicine and some decent equipment, all they send me is another spy. There was a yellow rain reported as early as yesterday, beside a stream only a few kilometers from this spot. I'm certain there is plenty of evidence left to keep you and your friends back in the Pentagon busy for months to come."

Kromer sensed the hurt and disappointment in his tone, yet readily accepted the priest's offer to escort her to the site. After relaying her intentions to the helicopter's flight crew, she followed Father Goss down a narrow earthen track that led away from the village. Included in this group was Lieutenant Kirdyo, who brought up the rear with a two-way radio and his trusty M-16 in hand.

The trail led down a steep hillside. As the sun continued to rise high in the clear sky, the heat intensified. Her flight suit already stained with perspiration, Kromer tied a bandana around her forehead to keep the sweat out of her eyes.

The priest seemed oblivious to the torrid temperature and kept up a blistering pace. As they continued their rapid descent, thickening bands of vegetation signaled that they were entering a river valley. Though the humidity persisted, the tall palm trees that now lined both sides of the trail helped block the incessant sunshine.

The exotic cries of jungle creatures filled the air with

song, while the constant crash of swiftly flowing water echoed in the distance.

Dr. Miriam Kromer subconsciously absorbed these alien sounds, yet found her thoughts pondering a vastly different matter. What was the reason for the priest's disgust upon hearing of her military affiliation and interest in the yellow rain? And why was he so reluctant to admit that the Hmong could be the victims of a deliberate biological attack? Perhaps he didn't think man was capable of such a dastardly thing. Kromer knew otherwise, and looked forward to gaining his trust so that she could present her case at a later date.

The crash of flowing water intensified, and as they rounded a broad bend, they were forced to halt at the spot where the trail crossed a shallow stream. Father Goss pointed to the thick vegetation hugging the other side.

"The yellow rain was said to have fallen over there, on the opposite bank."

Kromer reached into her pack and removed three gauze face masks. She distributed them with the briefest of explanations.

"I think it best if each one of us wear one of these."

Lieutenant Kirdyo watched the toxicologist don her mask and carefully copied her procedure. The priest seemed somewhat reluctant as he halfheartedly put on his own mask and then led the way across the stream.

It didn't take long for Kromer to discover a dark green palm frond covered with tiny yellow spots. Under the watchful eye of the priest, she utilized tweezers and scissors to cut off several samples, which she sealed in a plastic bag. The surrounding vegetation was similarly spotted, and as Dr. Kromer proceeded to gather more samples, Lieutenant Kirdyo's two-way radio activated with a burst of static. This alien electronic noise was replaced by a deep amplified voice that Kromer identified as belonging to Captain Samrong, the Huey's pilot.

"Lieutenant Kirdyo, it's imperative that you and Dr. Kromer return to Ban Son immediately. We have just received an order to return to Bangkok with all due haste."

Before Kirdyo could respond to this directive, the toxicologist took the radio out of his hands and spoke into its transmitter. "Captain Samrong, I'm afraid you don't understand. I have much work to do out here. I've not completed it."

The captain's amplified voice responded firmly. "No, Doctor, I'm afraid it's you who doesn't understand. This order directing you to return to Bangkok comes from your very own ambassador."

Not about to question such a supreme authority, Kromer tempered her defiance. "Very well, Captain. We're on our way back."

She handed the radio back to Kirdyo and bent over to take one more leaf sample before stowing her gear and following her escorts back to the path. As she was crossing the stream, a loud buzzing noise caught her attention. She looked up and spotted several massive hives built into the branches of the overhanging trees. At that very moment, a huge swarm of bees passed overhead and she found that she was virtually showered with tiny yellow droppings. A wide grin turned the corners of her mouth as she ripped off her mask and addressed her two companions.

"I believe it's safe to remove your masks, gentlemen. And by the way, I think I've just solved the mystery of the so-called yellow rain. It's nothing but bee defecation!"

As she pointed to the nearby hives, Lieutenant Kirdyo questioned, "Could such a thing be responsible for the sickness at Ban Son?"

"No, Lieutenant," replied Kromer. "It's not the yellow rain that's responsible. Most likely it's a natural fungal infection exacerbated by cholera, malaria, and the Hmong's chronic malnourishment. We just have to see about sending plenty of medicine and food up here, and getting Father Goss some additional medical help as well."

The priest appeared completely astounded as he looked up to the heavens and spoke out joyously. "Glory be! So there is a compassionate God up there after all!"

Three

It was one P.M. by the time the Huey carrying Dr. Miriam Kromer arrived in Bangkok. She immediately transferred to an awaiting Lockheed C-141 StarLifter, for a two-and-a-half-hour flight to Clark Air Base in the Philippines. Yet another change of aircraft took place there. This plane was her current means of transport, a prop-driven, C-2A Greyhound.

They had been flying due north for almost four hours now, had long ago passed over Taiwan, and were currently somewhere over the East China Sea.

It was a moonless, pitch-black night. From the co-pilot's seat, the toxicologist stared out into the inky blackness, dressed in the same dark green flight suit and helmet she had donned that morning back in Thailand. In her lap was a notebook holding the report that she had just completed, concerning her morning's findings on the southern slopes of Phu Bia.

To the constant drone of the Greyhound's dual turboprops, she mentally recreated that moment when she'd determined the real source of the so-called yellow rain. Bee defecation had sent her on a wild-goose chase halfway around the world.

Yet even with the proof she had, she knew that several of her associates back at Fort Detrick would stubbornly stick to their belief that the Pathet Lao were waging biological warfare. She would do her best to counter these claims and, of course, to fulfill the promises she had made to Father Goss.

The audible pitch of the airplane's engines abruptly changed, and Kromer felt an alien pressure on her eardrums. She looked to her left and watched as the pilot pushed down on the steering yoke and inched the dual throttles forward. Assuming that they would be landing shortly, Kromer restlessly stirred.

"You never did say which airport we were bound for," she remarked.

"I was just waiting for you to ask, Doc," answered the Greyhound's pilot, as she scanned the myriad of glowing digital instruments displayed before her. "If you'll look down there on the northern horizon, I believe you'll be able to see the field's landing lights."

"I don't see anything but a wall of black," observed Kromer, who was peering out the cockpit window. "Shouldn't there be some city lights showing down there?"

"Not in the middle of the East China Sea, Doc," returned the grinning pilot, whose helmet was stenciled Lt. Jan "Big Mamma" Grodsky.

Kromer absorbed this unexpected response and assumed that she knew what the pilot was referring to upon spotting a postage stamp-sized, rectangularly shaped series of glowing lights far in the distance.

"Do you mean to say that we're going to be landing on an aircraft carrier?" she asked.

"That's affirmative, Doc. I take it you're a carrier virgin."

"A what?" returned the toxicologist.

The pilot answered while readdressing the throttle. "A carrier virgin is someone who's never landed at sea before."

"That's me, all right," said Kromer, whose stomach tightened at the mere thought of such a thing.

"Well, there's no need to get your blood pressure up, Doc. Just sit back, relax, and enjoy the ride. If you'd like, just flip that switch on your right arm rest and you can listen to our landing instructions."

Kromer activated the switch, and took in a series of curt, static-free directives from the carrier's tower. Most of these instructions made little sense to her. They seemed to be in some sort of code, and were delivered by a smooth, male voice with a relaxed tone to it.

A carrier landing was definitely something she hadn't anticipated, and there could be no hiding her nervousness. The mere thought of hurtling out of the black sky, with no sense of altitude or distance, toward a floating target that seemed incredibly small and insignificant, was terrifying. Her pulse quickened, and a thick band of sweat gathered on her forehead.

The lights of the carrier approached more quickly than she had expected, as the voice of the ship's landing signal's officer broke from her headphones.

"You're lookin' good, Big Mamma. Ride the ball and keep on comin'."

The cabin shook violently as an intense wind gust triggered a sickening loss of altitude. Lieutenant Grodsky expertly adjusted the throttle, and the Greyhound's turboprops whined in response.

"I've got the orange," calmly remarked the pilot.

"So I see, darlin'," returned the LSO's satiny

voice. "Keep it clean, dearest. . . . Right up!"

This roller-coaster ride at two-hundred knots continued without pause, and as the flight deck rapidly approached, Kromer fought to control her rising nausea. They appeared to be traveling much too fast. Yet the voice of the LSO was strangely reassuring.

"Grab the deck, Big Mamma. You're just about home!"

Seconds later, the Greyhound slammed down onto the deck with a gut-wrenching bang. Even with the restraining harness pulled tight around her, Kromer found herself roughly jolted forward as the aircraft's tail hook grabbed the second deck cable and screeched to an abrupt halt.

"That's a hell of a way to make a living, Lieutenant," managed Kromer between grateful breaths of relief.

"It's all just a day's pay for me, Doc," replied the pilot. "Anytime you're ready for a lift home, just give me a call. There're no frequent flier miles, but we certainly aim to please."

"I'll remember that," said Kromer, who couldn't begin to imagine what a carrier take-off would be like.

With shaky legs, the toxicologist exited the C-2A on-board delivery aircraft and followed a Marine corporal into the ship's immense, box-shaped island. They climbed downward, deep into the bowels of the carrier. After circumventing a virtual maze of ladders and passageways, Kromer found herself entering a doorway marked with a familiar red cross and labeled Infirmary.

"Ah, you must be Dr. Kromer." The greeting was made by the alert black orderly who had been waiting for her beside the reception desk. "You're expected in the physician's lounge. If you'll just follow me."

The orderly led her past a spacious, spotlessly clean clinic. Several patients were waiting there, including the recent victim of a nasty burn to his right forearm. Adjoining the clinic was a brightly lit surgical theater. Several gowned individuals were prepping for an operation, and Kromer marveled that their equipment equaled that of the most modern land-based hospital.

At the end of the tiled corridor was a closed door guarded by an armed Marine sentry. With Kromer's approach, the Marine saluted, then smartly pivoted to knock on the door and open it. Kromer left her escort behind at this point and entered a large, cheerfully decorated room smelling of freshly brewed coffee. Similar to that of any major hospital, the lounge sported an assortment of comfortable furniture and a fully stocked buffet table.

There was no one else present, except for the two khaki-suited officers seated at one of the tables, sipping coffee and sorting through a stack of photographs. Both of them stood upon her entrance. It was the tallest of these men, a dignified, crew-cut gentleman with a square jaw and piercing, steel-gray eyes, who initiated the introductions.

"Welcome aboard the *Enterprise*, Dr. Kromer. I'm Captain Webster. And this is my senior medical officer, Commander Philip Jackman."

"That's Phil to you, Doctor," offered the slightly built commander. "Now how about helping yourself to some food and drink. I understand you put in your fair share of miles getting here."

Though Kromer had not eaten since lunch, her fatigue and the alien roll of the ship kept her appetite to a minimum. "Some black coffee would sure be appreciated," she said, fighting back the urge to yawn.

"You've got it," returned the likable commander.

While he went over to pour her a cup, Kromer's glance settled on the photographs visible on the table. Captain Webster was quick to note her interest.

"Go ahead and have a look if you'd like. And please, have a seat."

Kromer sat down at the table and picked up the stack of eight-by-ten-inch, black and white photographs. The first of these showed six naked male corpses, laid out on the bare concrete floor of what appeared to be a makeshift morgue. Each of the victims were middle-aged Orientals. A close-up displayed a series of circular black lesions, one to three centimeters in diameter, dotting the face and neck of one of the bodies. The other photographed corpses showed similar marks, and Kromer thoughtfully vented her curiosity.

"When were these photographs taken?"

"About two hours ago," answered the captain. "They were snapped in the gymnasium of Okinawa's Naha upper school. That's where this morgue has been set up."

Kromer responded while the carrier's senior medical officer arrived with her coffee. "When I was initially briefed in Bangkok this morning, I had no idea that this epidemic had gotten so out of hand."

"I'm afraid this is only the tip of the iceberg," said Commander Jackman as he heavily seated himself opposite the toxicologist. "Altogether, there have been twenty-seven other fatalities, all displaying similar manifestations. The hospitals in Naha are cur-

rently packed with hundreds of scared patients showing all the preliminary symptoms, which initially
mimic a severe viral infection. If the disease continues on its present course and we remain unable to
treat it, the casualties could reach catastrophic proportions—and we could be faced with one of the
worst epidemics of this century."

"Any idea as to what we're up against here, Doctor?" asked Captain Webster.

Kromer studied a close-up of the circular, black lesions. "It could be plague, or even anthrax for that
matter. To find out for certain, I need a fully
equipped toxicology laboratory and plenty of tissue
samples."

The carrier's commanding officer consented without a moment's hesitation. "As of this moment, the
ship's lab is at your disposal. I'm certain you'll find
its facilities more than adequate. As for those samples, since we're currently off the northern coast of
Okinawa, we could have you in Naha to collect them
yourself within the hour."

The telephone began ringing. Webster reached out
for the handset located beside his armrest and spoke
into the transmitter. "Captain, here . . . I hear you,
Red. I'm on my way."

Webster appeared momentarily lost in thought as
he hung up the handset and stood. "I'll be in the
CIC if you need me, Phil. And Dr. Kromer, if there's
anything I can do for you, just holler."

Without further explanation, he turned and exited. Upon his departure, the atmosphere inside the
lounge seemed to lighten. Commander Jackman
took a long drink from his mug and caught his
guest's tired gaze.

"By the way, I'd like to personally welcome you

35

aboard the *Enterprise*. Command speaks most highly of you. We're very fortunate to have you on our team."

"I just hope I won't let you down, Commander," said Kromer as she gratefully sipped her coffee.

"Hey, that's Phil to you," shot back the personable medical officer. "I wish there was time for you to get some shut-eye, but men, women, and children are dying from this epidemic as we speak. So I'd better see about getting you immediate transport to Naha. And we'll have to get you fitted into a biohazard containment suit."

Miriam Kromer nodded in consent and diverted her gaze back to the top photograph. The black lesions displayed were the sole visible clues to the mysterious, deadly disease whose diagnosis, treatment, and eventual elimination was now her number one priority.

Captain Steven Webster strode into Combat Information Center on the *Enterprise* like he owned the place. This large, equipment-packed compartment was the nerve center of the ship. It was here that the voluminous data gathered by the carrier task force's various defensive sensors was integrated, the objective being to protect the *Enterprise* from attack.

A pair of elevated command chairs was placed in the center of the CIC. Seated in one, before an immense, digitally lit perspex screen, was Commander Samuel "Red" Rayburn, the *Enterprise*'s executive officer. Though he had gone prematurely bald soon after graduating from the Naval Academy, the XO had a full, rust-colored mustache that he kept impeccably groomed. Thus the source of his nickname.

Red had flown a Grumman A-6 Intruder during Viet Nam, and had over 3,000 flight hours and 600 carrier-arrested landings to his name. Always one who got right down to the guts of a matter, Red spoke up as Captain Webster climbed into the vacant seat beside him. "It was a Seahawk off the *Bunker Hill* that first tagged the bogey with dipping sonar a little over ten minutes ago."

Webster absorbed this curt report while studying the navigational chart displayed on the large, clear plastic screen that hung before them. In a matter of seconds, the captain was able to determine the exact location of the *Enterprise,* along with the assorted frigates, destroyers, cruisers, and support vessels comprising the carrier battle group. Webster paid particular attention to a single flashing red star located on the extreme northern sector of the chart. This was the last known position of their so-called bogey.

"Where's the *Hawkbill?*" he questioned.

"At last report, they were patrolling due west of us," answered the XO.

Webster diverted his eyes from the screen and directly met the serious gaze of his second in command.

"Red, if we indeed have an unfriendly submarine out there attempting to penetrate this task force, we're going to have to rely on Slaughter and his crew to convince her that she has no business here."

"I hear you loud and clear, Skipper," returned the XO as he rolled the clipped end of his mustache. "I'll convey the word to the *Hawkbill* at once."

Commander Chris Slaughter and his XO, Lieutenant Commander Benjamin Kram, initiated their bi-weekly inspection of their current command in the *Hawkbill*'s aft engine spaces. Though not the most modern attack sub in the fleet, the USS *Hawkbill* was a potent underwater platform, capable of holding its own against any adversary. Over two hundred and ninety feet long and displacing well over four thousand tons, the *Hawkbill* was fitted with an upgraded BQQ-5 sonar suite, a newly installed BQR-23 towed array, and a sophisticated fire-control system. Four torpedo tubes angled out beneath the fin, each capable of launching a variety of weapons, including the Mk48 dual-purpose torpedo and the Harpoon anti-ship missile. One hundred and seven officers and enlisted men made up the crew, many of them having just been born when this sub was originally launched from the San Francisco Naval Shipyard back in the early seventies.

The air was heavy with the wax-like scent of warm polythylene as the boat's two senior officers headed forward after completing their inspection of that portion of the sub fondly known as *Hawkbill* Power and Light. A single S5W pressurized water-cooled nuclear reactor was located here. This was the heart of the Sturgeon-class vessel's propulsion system. The heat produced by this device drove a pair of geared steam turbines that powered a single propeller shaft capable of producing a forward speed of well over thirty knots.

Quite satisfied with the performance of the engine-room staff, Chris Slaughter led the way through a thick, steel hatchway. At six feet, two inches, the *Hawkbill*'s thirty-seven-year-old captain took extra care not to bump his head as he stepped into the passageway that would take them directly into the galley.

Tall for a submariner, Slaughter nonetheless circumnavigated the cramped spaces of his command with a minimum of bumps and bruises.

The XO barely had to duck his head as he climbed through the hatch and sealed it behind him. Benjamin Kram was a good four inches shorter than Slaughter. A native of Redondo Beach, California, the blond-headed XO curiously sniffed the air of the passageway and lightly commented.

"Smells like we're finally getting some real steaks for chow, Skipper."

"I concur," said Slaughter as he proceeded forward. "I must admit it will be a welcome relief after a solid week of turkey stew, turkey chow mein, and turkey patties."

"Chief Mallot tried to explain low cholesterol and the health benefits—of turkey"—Kram remained close on his skipper's heels—"but unfortunately, he didn't get through to the crew. Why for a while there, when he served that turkey loaf last Sunday, I thought we might have a mutiny on our hands."

"That would sure be one for the papers," reflected the captain. "I can see the headlines now. Chowhound mutineers take over sub. Demand junk food."

There were wide grins on the officers' faces as they entered the rather spacious compartment reserved for enlisted men's meals. A handful of sailors were present, eating at tables covered with red checkered cloths. A rerun of last season's final Dodger-Mets game played from an elevated video monitor. Slaughter eagerly looked up to check its progress.

"Fernando better start throwing some strikes," urged Seaman First Class Ray Morales in between bites of steak. "Otherwise, this game's history."

Slaughter noted the portly pitcher's poor mechanics as he delivered one ball after the other, then voiced his own opinion. "Tommy better pull him now. It looks to me like Fernando's really struggling."

"Struggling ain't the word for it. He's dying out there," said Morales, who looked over to see where this comment originated. Genuine surprise painted the Hispanic's face upon viewing the *Hawkbill's* commanding officer. He instantly sat up straight.

"I'm sorry, Captain," he uneasily added.

"At ease, sailor," returned Slaughter, who watched as the Dodger pitcher proceeded to walk in the tying run. "And you're right, Mr. Morales. He is dying out there."

Morales responded, a bit more relaxed now. "You should know, Captain. After all, pitching was your specialty back at the Academy. Scuttlebutt has it you turned down an offer by the Giants."

"Actually, it was the Cardinals," corrected Slaughter. "And who knows if I would have made it out of spring training. The way I look at it, Uncle Sam offered me a lot better job security."

A heavyset, crew-cut man wearing a stained apron walked out of the food preparation area. One look at the newly arrived pair of officers caused this individual's youthful face to light up, and he readjusted his wire rims and spoke out warmly.

"Good evening, Captain Slaughter, Lieutenant Commander Kram. Don't tell me it's inspection time already."

"That it is, Mr. Mallot," returned Slaughter, who had seen enough of the baseball game. "Why don't you start out by giving us tonight's menu?"

Petty Officer First Class Howard Mallot readily complied with this request. "In honor of payday

40

we're serving New York strip steaks, onion rings, corn on the cob, garlic toast, cole slaw, and hot peach cobbler à la mode for dessert."

"That lineup sounds like a real tasty winner," said Slaughter. "Looks like the crew won't be voicing any complaints about the chow selection tonight."

"About that special low-fat diet I tried out on the men last week," the sensitive head chef put in, "I still think it makes sound health sense in the long run."

"We're not doubting your intentions, Chief," observed the XO. "It's just that the crew was ready for some diversity. Turkey is still turkey, no matter how you disguise it."

A sailor walked by with a plate of fresh chow, and Mallot carefully surveyed the man's food.

"Damn," said Mallot to no one in particular. "Those rings still look overcooked."

"Could it be that new oil you're cooking in, Chief?" offered the XO.

"You mean the canola oil, sir?" returned Mallot. "No, that's not the cause. I'm afraid we've got us a bad thermostat on the deep fryer. The last couple of temperature checks showed a slight deviance from normal. Yet from the looks of those rings, I'd say that the oil is hotter than I suspected."

"Sounds to me like it's time to replace that thermostat," suggested Slaughter, as a seaman assigned to the radio room entered the galley and handed him a folded message. After thoroughly reading this communiqué, he handed it to his XO. Benjamin Kram hurriedly skimmed the dispatch, while Slaughter readdressed the *Hawkbill*'s head cook.

"Mr. Mallot, you'd better have your men complete the meal preparations at once. And be prepared to indefinitely delay normal serving hours."

41

Fully aware that this most likely meant the *Hawkbill* was being called into action, Mallot nodded in compliance. "Aye, aye, Captain."

With this, Slaughter turned for the forward hatchway, with his tight-lipped XO close behind him. They wasted no time heading directly to the control room. This compartment was lit by a muted red light to protect the crew's night vision. In this space, the size of a one-car garage, was situated a wide variety of manned consoles that could influence the sub's speed, depth, course, and fighting abilities.

Waiting for the two senior officers beside the periscope well was the boat's navigator and current officer of the deck, Lieutenant Rich Laycob. A product of the Naval ROTC program, Laycob had served on the *Hawkbill* for over a year now. Known as a practical joker, the navigator was all business as Chris Slaughter and Benjamin Kram joined him at the conn to determine the sub's current operational status.

"Mr. Laycob," the captain said in a subdued tone, "we've just received a flash dispatch from the *Enterprise,* ordering us to investigate a suspected breach in the task force's northeastern security perimeter by an unidentified submerged contact. Here are the exact coordinates where this penetration supposedly took place. The XO will take the conn, while you plot us an intercept. If there's indeed a hostile submarine out there, I want to tag it long before it knows we're on to them."

"You've got it, Captain," answered the navigator as he took the dispatch and hurried over to the nearby chart table.

"Bring us around slowly to course zero-three-zero, Ben. And take us down to four hundred feet," instructed Slaughter. "I'll be over at sonar if you need me."

"Shall I sound battle stations?" asked the XO.

The captain shook his head. "Let's hold off awhile, Ben. At least until we've got the first real hint of a positive contact. For all we know, that Seahawk may have merely chanced upon an unwary whale."

As the *Hawkbill* silently turned on its new course, Slaughter crossed the control room and approached a large console manned by three individuals. Each seated man wore headphones, and had his attention focused on the bank of glowing cathode-ray screens and digital readouts he was assigned to monitor. It was to the sailor situated at the far right position that the captain was drawn. This was Senior Sonar Technician James Echoles, or Jaffers as he was known to the crew.

At the moment, the big, black enlisted man was one of a trio of sailors acting as the sub's eyes and ears. By the utilization of both passive and active means, it was up to these three to determine the presence of other vessels, both submerged and on the surface, and any other physical obstacle that could endanger the *Hawkbill*.

At present, only the passive mode of observation was being used. This was the most stealthy means of detection available to them. It primarily relied on a series of strategically placed hydrophones, positioned around the boat's hull. These ultrasensitive listening devices relayed a cacophony of both artificial and natural sounds into the sonar console for interpretation and analysis by the technicians.

As the senior sonarman on duty, Jaffers was the one Slaughter was relying on to convey the first concrete evidence of another submarine's presence. He had demonstrated his incredibly sensitive hearing ability on many past occasions. Yet when this quality was combined with a probing intellect, an unyielding determination to succeed, and an almost uncanny power of intuition, what resulted was one of the best sonar techs in the entire US Navy. Considering himself fortunate to have such a talented sailor in his crew, Slaughter gently touched the sonarman on the shoulder.

"Evening, Jaffers. What have you got out there?"

The senior sonarman looked up from his console as if he was breaking from a trance.

"Hello, Captain," he replied with a grin. "You caught me trackin' the *Enterprise*."

"How would you like the chance to go after some real game?" Slaughter offered with a wink.

Jaffers was quick to take the bait. "I've been prayin' for somethin' excitin' to come along and shorten the time left for chow. I hear Mallot's gone and broke out the prime sirloin steaks—and I don't mean turkey."

"As far as I'm concerned, you can have steak every day for the rest of this patrol. All you have to do is tag a submerged contact that's supposedly been shadowing the task force from the extreme northeastern security quadrant."

"Is it Ivan?" asked the senior sonarman.

"The Airdale who got the initial drop on them couldn't get a definite. Hell, we still don't even know if it's another submarine or not."

"Well, you certainly came to the right place to find out the answer to that question, Captain. Just get us within range, and leave the rest to me."

"I was counting on that, Jaffers. Lieutenant Lay-

44

cob is plotting the intercept. We'll be going in nice and quiet, with a passive search mode only."

"That's the way I like to do my huntin', Captain. Can we deploy the towed array?"

"I don't see why not," answered Slaughter, as he looked at his wristwatch. "I'll check with navigation and get you details on our approach. Meanwhile, you can brief your men on our new objective."

"I'll get on it at once, sir," said Jaffers, who appeared anxious to get down to some serious work.

Satisfied that the sonar team could meet this challenge, Slaughter proceeded over to the chart table, where he joined the navigator. Rich Laycob was in the midst of formulating a plan of attack, that would take the *Hawkbill* immediately beneath the *Enterprise* task force. Effectively masked by the variety of sound signatures being produced by these ships as they continued sailing north, the *Hawkbill* would then creep off to the northeast, deploy the towed sonar array, and sweep the area where the Seahawk helicopter had made the initial contact.

Slaughter had no objection to this plan, and quickly went about implementing it. An hour and a half later, it produced the desired results, when senior sonarman James Echoles picked up the distant signature of an unidentified submerged contact, following the task force on the extreme eastern boundary of its security perimeter. It was at this point that battle stations was sounded, and the *Hawkbill* cautiously moved in to further investigate.

Back in the crew's mess, this call to alert sent those sailors in the midst of a meal scurrying to their action stations. This included Howard Mallot and his staff, whose job it was to secure the galley for possible combat.

A pair of sailors were tasked to clear off the dirty plates and batten down the dining room. This left Mallot and a single seaman stationed in the galley.

Because of the captain's forewarning, Mallot had long ago completed the bulk of the food preparation. There were only a couple of steaks cooking on the grill as he switched off the flame and cut the power to the deep fryer. To keep the hot oil from sloshing around, he closed the lid of the fryer and then turned his attention to stowing away any loose items. Noise was a submariner's worst enemy; a can or pot striking the deck had to be avoided at all costs.

Mallot was in the process of sealing shut the china bin when the *Hawkbill* lurched forward in a sudden burst of speed. This was followed by a tight port turn that sent the portly chef crashing into the side of the sink to his right. As he struggled to regain his balance, he noted with some degree of satisfaction that all of the various kitchen implements stored around him had so far remained in place.

"*Hawkbill*'s sure going some place in a hurry," observed Mallot, who was forced to hold onto the edge of the sink when the bow suddenly angled sharply downward.

The young seaman who had been assisting him failed to find a handhold, and smacked into the forward bulkhead with his shoulder.

"Are you okay, lad?" asked Mallot, his tone full of concern.

"I believe so, Chief," replied the seaman, as he tightly held onto a strip of elevated coaming. "What in the world's happening out there?"

The deck canted hard to the left, with the down angle on the bow now a good thirty degrees.

"My guess is we're playing cat and mouse with another submarine," offered Mallot. "The captain warned me earlier that this might be coming down."

It was as the *Hawkbill* turned hard on its right side that Mallot's attention was diverted by the sickening scent of smoke. He sniffed the air curiously while hastily scanning the narrow compartment. His startled gaze finally halted on a gathering plume of black smoke emanating from the direction of the deep fryer.

"Holy shit!" he exclaimed. "The damn thermostat must have failed. Inform the conn while I hit the extinguisher!"

Fire was one of the most terrifying events that a submariner could experience. Because of the restricted confines, if flame didn't get them, toxic fumes would. Well aware of this fact, Mallot reached out to activate the range-guard extinguisher system. After burning his hand on the switch, he was forced to abandon the galley when a choking column of thick smoke completely filled the food-preparation area.

He was gasping for breath as he stumbled out into the mess, but was immediately aware of the voice blasting from the boat's intercom.

"Fire in the galley!" it reported tensely.

A piercing electronic alarm followed, and Mallot struggled to put on an oxygen mask. He allowed himself three deep breaths to clear out his lungs before forcefully speaking into the mask's throat mike.

"This is Chief Mallot. I'm in charge in the crew's mess. Pressurize the middle-level fire hose!"

One of his alert co-workers, who also wore a mask, handed him this hose, which had a thin, arm-length nozzle. He turned toward the galley, then charged into its smoke-filled entranceway.

"Come on, men!" he bravely yelled. "Let's work that hose in here!"

Throughout the *Hawkbill*, the fire alarm brought dread. Especially in the control room. Chris Slaughter had been bent over the chart table when word of the emergency reached them. After putting on his oxygen mask, he rushed over to the periscope well, all the while ordering the OOD to break off pursuit of the other submarine.

"Take us up to sixty-five feet. Emergency ascent!" he firmly ordered.

Only one thing mattered now, and that was getting the boat to the surface as quickly as possible. But first they had to attain periscope depth, so he could make certain there was no surface traffic topside.

It seemed to take the *Hawkbill* an eternity to climb out of the cold, black depths. His palms stinging from his hard grip on the steel handrail he'd grabbed to keep from falling backward, Slaughter contemplated a worst-case scenario. Envisioning toxic black fumes filling the boat with agonizing death, he looked out to the digital depth gauge and silently willed the sub upward.

At eighty feet the steepness of their climb noticeably lessened. By the time they had passed the seventy-foot level, Slaughter had already raised the main scope. No sooner did the lens break the sea's surface than he initiated a lightning-quick, 360-degree scan. A blessed expanse of vacant black sea greeted him, and he immediately gave the order to surface.

Slaughter was in the process of backing away from the periscope well when a portly newcomer wearing a portable oxygen mask and a smoke-stained, water-soaked uniform, rushed into the control room.

"Captain, Petty Officer Mallot reporting, sir. There's heavy smoke in the forward compartment, mid level. But the fire is out. We had to use the range-guard system and two pressurized hoses to extinguish it. There are no injured personnel, and the damage appears to be limited to the deep fat-fryer thermostat."

Slaughter's relief was instantaneous. "Thank God that's the extent of it. Let's ventilate the boat, and then see what we can do about relocating that bogey we were chasing when this whole damn thing came down."

"C-Captain Slaughter, sir," stuttered Mallot nervously. "For what it's worth, I take personal blame for this entire incident. I should have replaced that damn thermostat the moment I suspected it of malfunctioning."

"Relax, Mr. Mallot," instructed Slaughter. "If there's anyone to blame, it's the manufacturer who's guilty of selling the Navy faulty equipment. You were only doing your best. Besides, if we had stuck to your turkey diet, none of this would have even happened!"

Four

Approximately halfway between Okinawa and the Japanese mainland lay tiny Takara Island. Of volcanic origin, Takara rose from the sea some one million years ago, making it a relatively young landmass in terms of earth time. Seven and a half miles long and three miles wide, Takara was for the most part comprised of desolate, mountainous terrain. Only its southern shore was populated. The majority of this island's inhabitants lived and worked around a horseshoe-shaped bay, that had direct access to the sea beyond.

Takara was first settled by a small group of Japanese fishermen from Kyushu, back in the mid-sixteen hundreds. Because of its inhospitable terrain, this was the extent of its development until the early days of World War II, when the Japanese Navy established an observation post on the island. It was to this facility that a teenage ensign by the name of Yukio Ishii was dispatched in the closing days of the war. Ishii's primary responsibility had been to monitor the passage of allied air and sea traffic in the vicinity, but when the threatened invasion of the mainland failed to materialize and the atomic bomb sealed Japan's fate, Ishii had returned to Tokyo as one of the vanquished.

Just as post-World War II Japan saw the demise of one segment of the population—the militarists—it presented an unprecedented opportunity to many others. Ishii was one of those who took advantage of this situation, and he directly participated in the rebirth of his homeland. Still in his late teens, with his hopes and ideals intact, he enrolled in college and graduated seven years later, with degrees in both biochemistry and medicine.

Having a talent for both basic research and business, Ishii's first entrepreneurial venture was the marketing of kelp in the treatment of iodine deficiency. Success in selling this product led him to develop a line of pharmaceuticals, each of which was derived from an organism that had its home in the sea.

As additional capital began pouring in, he turned his genius in another direction—developing a way to extract a variety of minerals from the seafloor itself. This boosted his company, Ishii Industries, to one of the fifty largest private businesses in all of Japan. To grow even farther, all it needed was a suitable base of operations. Ishii eventually found this base on Takara Island.

Now a decade had passed since he'd astounded his competitors by announcing the relocation of his entire business to this relatively isolated isle. An extended lease secured from the government gave him complete stewardship of Takara until well into the next century. With an eye to future expansion, he'd built a multimillion yen industrial facility on the shores of Takara Bay. This ultramodern complex included a city capable of sustaining over a thousand occupants with all the comforts of the mainland.

Like an ancient feudal lord, Ishii was responsible for all aspects of his employees' well-being. He stressed old-fashioned family values, tempered by the simple tenets of his unique version of Zen Buddhism. This resulted in a loyal, contented workforce, who enjoyed excellent pay, a liberal vacation policy, and the security of having a job for life.

Forty-eight years had passed since Yukio Ishii had first set foot on his island domain. At the ripe old age of sixty-six, he now knew no other home.

One of his favorite places for reflecting on his vast accomplishments, and putting them into perspective, was a spacious, elevated plateau he had discovered as a mere teenager. This five-hundred-foot ridge rose from the sea on the southeastern edge of Takara Bay. It afforded a spectacular view of both bay and the industrial/city complex that hugged its northern shore.

The dream-filled days of Ishii's youth had long since passed. Yet he still took every available opportunity to climb up onto the plateau and gaze out at the sparkling blue waters of Takara Bay. This was exactly what he was doing on a gloriously warm, early spring afternoon, when the mere thought of being cooped up in an office all day filled him with dread. Exercise, fresh air, and meditation were the tonics that kept him from surrendering to the relentless call of the advancing years.

Except for the gray that colored his shoulder-length hair and thick, Fu Manchu-style moustache, Ishii could easily pass for a much younger man. Dressed as he was in a loose-fitting white robe and billowing pants, he appeared the perfect example of physical fitness. His small, wiry frame was compact and toned with muscle, while his posture was erect and had an almost noble bearing to it.

With an intense, hawk-like movement, he angled his piercing, sea green gaze on the distant shoreline. Here, beside the bay's main pier, two submarines were docked. Like lethal predators, their matching black, V-shaped hulls glistening in the sunlight, the *Katana* and the *Bokken* were being attended to by a scurrying crowd of deckhands. Both of the Romeo-class vessels were fully operational, and were already playing an all-important role in the great drama that was presently unfolding.

Thrilled by the mere thought of the great victory that would soon be achieved, Ishii sensed another's presence behind him. He turned and readily identified the middle-aged newcomer who wore a loose-fitting outfit identical to his own, and a long, bamboo sword swinging at his side.

"Ah, it's you Satsugai," greeted Ishii warmly. "I was just admiring your command down below."

"I'm sorry I'm late, Sensei," replied Captain Satsugai Okura with a humble bow. "My final inspection of the *Katana* took longer than I had anticipated."

"Were any unexpected problems encountered?" questioned Ishii, his voice filled with concern.

"It's nothing that can't be remedied before our next scheduled sailing date, Sensei."

Ishii's relief was most apparent. "That's certainly good to hear, Satsugai. Now, enough of this talk of daily duty. An afternoon as glorious as this one deserves to be solely dedicated to the mastery of the

Way. Shall we proceed, my friend?"

Without waiting for a reply, Ishii bent down and picked up a bamboo sword, identical to the one Okura carried. Then, with a light step, he joined the *Katana*'s commanding officer at the center of the dirt-filled clearing. The two men faced each other, bowed, and adopted an opening attitude, with sandaled feet as far apart as the width of their shoulders, knees slightly bent, and both hands on the hilts of their swords.

It was Okura who initiated the attack when he raised his sword upward, then slashed down toward his opponent's left shoulder. In response, Ishii swung his sword up in a semicircle, blocking the blow with the side of his bamboo blade. There was the loud crack of wood on wood, and Okura continued his offensive by thrusting forward toward Ishii's chest. With the agility of a cat, the gray-haired elder dodged this blow, countering it with an upward sweep of his blade. Okura leaped aside, missing a blow to his crotch by the merest of inches.

A few seconds passed, the swordsmen silently appraising one another, before Okura once more went on the offensive. This precipitated a lightning-quick series of blows that ended with Ishii delivering what would in actual combat be a killing blow to the top of Okura's head.

Okura appeared to be slightly out of breath as he lowered his sword and bowed.

"Forgive me, Sensei," he softly muttered. "It appears that my thoughts are elsewhere this afternoon."

"Distraction can't be permitted for one who

seeks mastery of the Way," instructed Ishii. "Remember, if in his mind the warrior doesn't forget one thing, that being death, he'll never find himself caught short."

Okura appeared dejected as he lowered his eyes and replied. "Too often lately I find myself unable to focus my thoughts clearly."

"When this happens, Satsugai, listen to the sounds of wind and water. Maintain a calm surface and a fighting spirit within, and you shall become at one with the Way."

While absorbing this piece of advice, Okura walked heavily over to the edge of the plateau and stared down to the bay. Ishii was quick to join him.

"You can't hide your heart from me, old friend," said the elder as he followed the direction of Okura's glance. "I know your thoughts are still with the *Katana*."

"How very right you are, Sensei. Failure can never be excused."

"Nonsense, Satsugai. Not even the Ninja have control of the elementals."

Okura looked up and caught Ishii's eye. "My strike team should have anticipated that sudden wind change. After all, their training was my direct responsibility. Thus their failure is also my own."

This provoked an emotional response. "And who's to say that we failed, Satsugai? Though it's true our primary objective wasn't accomplished, this proved to be a most effective field test. Now all that remains is for us to return to Okinawa and finish the assignment."

"Then the operation is continuing as planned,

Sensei?" asked the surprised mariner.

"Why of course it is, my friend," answered Ishii. "Why shouldn't it? The enemies of Nippon remain in place on our holy soil even as we speak. We have taken a blood oath to remove these barbarians from our midst once and for all—and to return our island nation back to the guidance of our divine Emperor."

There was a renewed urgency to Okura's tone as he responded to this. "Sensei, please let me take the *Katana* back to Okinawa, so that my crew can show their worth to this greatest of all causes."

"Patience, my friend," advised Ishii with a grin. "I was expecting such a request from you, and must regretfully turn you down. Captain Sato and the *Bokken* are ready to sail with the tide. So take this time to fast and find yourself in meditation. And before the next new moon rises, the *Katana* will sail into battle once more, this time straight into the mouth of Tokyo Bay!"

The first colors of dawn were just painting the eastern horizon, when the SH-3H Sea King helicopter carrying Dr. Miriam Kromer returned to the USS *Enterprise*. The exhausted toxicologist had worked through the night, the majority of her time spent at Naha General Hospital, Okinawa's primary health care facility.

Ever thankful that a helicopter had been provided for the hour flight to and from Okinawa, Kromer left the familiar confines of the Sikorsky Sea King. She certainly wasn't looking forward to another carrier landing on a fixed-wing aircraft, and she didn't even want to think about a catapult assisted take-off.

Commander Philip Jackman was waiting for her on the windswept deck. The good-natured medical officer was full of questions as he escorted her below decks.

"How did it go, Doctor? Is it really as bad as the reports indicate?"

Kromer breathlessly answered, while following him through a twisting series of passageways and ladders. "It's a nightmare come true in every sense of the word. Naha General is an absolute madhouse. Every available bed is filled, and the emergency room has over a hundred-patient backlog on new admissions."

"And the death count?" asked Jackman as he led his guest into the carrier's infirmary.

"When I left, there were forty-seven confirmed fatalities at Naha alone. There could easily be three times that number elsewhere, with many more to come."

This sobering account stunned the medical officer, and he halted beside his own clinic's vacant admissions' desk.

"Then you still don't know what the disease is— or how to treat it?" he somberly questioned.

Miriam Kromer looked him right in the eye and replied. "Just give me that lab time you promised, and hopefully I'll be able to answer that question, Commander."

"I had my staff prepare the ship's pathology laboratory for your exclusive use. If there's anything you need that you can't find, just ask for it and it's yours."

Kromer fought back a yawn. "For starters, how about a microscope and a thermos of black coffee?"

The medical officer pointed toward a closed doorway on the right side of the corridor. "I believe that can be arranged, Doctor. One half of your request is waiting for you behind that door. I'll meet you there with the coffee."

As she expected, the laboratory was more than adaquate for her needs. Her primary job was to analyze several tissue samples she'd brought back from Naha. To do this, she prepared a slide and inserted it into an electron microscope. By the time Philip Jackman arrived with her coffee and a platter of sandwiches, Kromer had completed her initial scan. There was a look of thoughtful relief on her face as she sat up and beckoned the medical officer to join her.

"I'll trade you a peek for a mug of coffee, Commander," offered Kromer.

"You've got yourself a deal, Doctor," replied Jackman, handing over the requested mug and bending to peer into the microscope. "By the way, what am I looking at?" he added.

"That slide contains pleural fluid, drawn from a victim's lungs," answered Kromer between sips of her drink. "Do you see those tiny boxcar-shaped organisms at the slide's center?"

"Yeah, I see 'em," replied Jackman.

"Well, they happen to prove that the disease we're up against is none other than anthrax. Now, how do I go about informing the health authorities back on Okinawa of this fact?"

This matter-of-fact revelation was excitedly received by the carrier's senior medical officer. He rushed over to the telephone, and within seconds, Kromer was on the line with the head of Okinawa's public health department.

To combat this deadly disease, she ordered that the sick be dosed with massive intravenous injections of penicillin G. Kromer also advised strict isolation, and she said that mass immunizations should begin as soon as vaccine could be rushed from the Michigan Department of Health.

"To think all of this is being caused by contact with a diseased animal," observed Jackman as the toxicologist hung up the phone and returned to her coffee.

"I beg to differ with you, Commander," countered Kromer. "If an infected animal had been the cause, the anthrax toxin would have attacked its human victims either thru the skin or the gastrointestinal tract. Yet in the majority of patients I examined the spores had gathered exclusively in the lymph nodes and lungs, indicating that the anthrax was inhaled."

"But if that's the case, where did it originate?"

To answer this question, Kromer pulled out the map of Naha that the public health authorities had given her. Dozens of red X's were drawn along the city's northern outskirts.

"Those red marks show the locations of the victims' residences," she explained. "Note how close they are, collectively, to the security boundary of Kadena Air Force base."

"And what's that supposed to mean?" quizzed the puzzled naval officer.

Kromer's response was firm and deadly serious.

"Commander, in the entire recorded history of medicine, never before has society faced a sudden outbreak of inhalation anthrax like we're seeing today. There's only one way this amount of toxin arrived here, and that was by man, either deliberately or by accident."

Her companion's expression went from confusion to sudden enlightenment. "Dr. Kromer, there's a newcomer aboard the *Enterprise* I'd like you to share this with. He's Vice Admiral Henry Walker, the Director of Naval Intelligence."

The Flag Quarters of the USS *Enterprise* looked like an exclusive men's club complete with wood-paneled walls, plush red carpet, and French provincial furniture. Vice Admiral Henry Walker fit these dignified surroundings perfectly. His neat white hair and movie-star good looks were more befitting for a bank president than an intelligence officer. This was especially apparent as he sat behind the FQ's sole desk and carefully studied the map that the only civilian in the room had just handed him.

Seated before Walker in identical high-back leather chairs were Captain Steven Webster, Commander Philip Jackman, and Dr. Miriam Kromer. Each of them looked on expectantly as the handsome flag officer completed his examination of the map and then looked up to address the red-haired individual who had just brought it to him.

"Your conclusions are most convincing, and I must say extremely frightening, Doctor. How do you advise that we proceed?"

Kromer liked his direct manner, yet she responded cautiously. "I think our first step should be to query the Air Force and see if they're responsible for the release."

"And if they're not?" continued Walker.

Though she certainly couldn't prove it, the toxicologist voiced her belief. "Then we've got a third party on our hands, one that thinks nothing of releasing a deadly toxin that could wipe out an entire city."

Ever the skeptic, Captain Webster broke in at this point. "Oh, come on, Doctor. I guess next you'll be telling us these biological terrorists could be headed for Tokyo—or even the US mainland."

Walker quickly interceded. "Go easy on her, Steven. Because your offhanded remark might not be so far off as you think."

With a deliberate slowness, the admiral stood and forcefully continued. "What I'm about to tell you is to be held in the strictest confidence. Three days ago, on the night before the first anthrax victim was discovered, a Japanese patrol boat made radar contact with an unidentified surface vessel off Kadena's southern security perimeter. This contact mysteriously disappeared, and the possibility is good that it could have been a submarine. On the very next morning, the body of a young Air Force sentry was found floating off this same beach. A preliminary autopsy indicated that the airman died of a broken neck some twelve hours before his corpse was discovered.

"Yet what really scares the dickens out of me, now that we've had the benefit of Dr. Kromer's report, is a log entry from the SAC air traffic-control tower at Kadena. It shows that at 8:03 P.M., a little

61

more than an hour after the Japanese patrol boat first made radar contact with the supposed bogey, all air traffic bound to and taking off from Kadena had to be rerouted, when the winds unexpectedly shifted from south to north."

"My God, they were after our base!" exclaimed the carrier's senior medical officer.

"Who was?" asked Steven Webster.

It was Miriam Kromer who dared to reply. "That's irrelevant, Captain. Because the one thing you can be certain of is that if they're able, they'll be back to finish the deed."

"And we're going to be out there, just praying that those cold-hearted bastards have the balls to give it another try!" added Henry Walker, his eyes wide with excitement.

Five

In the mid-nineteen-fifties the Soviet Navy introduced a new line of diesel-powered, medium-range attack subs that were to be designated by NATO as the Romeo class. Designed to protect the USSR from the threat of Western carrier and amphibious forces, the Romeos were fitted with an assortment of advanced offensive sensors. These included the new Fenik passive sonar array that was placed within a bulged casing set into the upper portion of the sub's V-shaped bow.

A pair of Type 37D diesel engines and two electric motors powered a set of twin propellers housed within individual circular guards located forward of the horizontal hydroplanes and a single rudder. Such a propulsion system was capable of sustaining a sixteen-knot surface speed, and of making fourteen knots submerged.

The interior of a Romeo was characterized by a single usable deck, with the batteries stored below. Six twenty-one-inch torpedo tubes could be found in its bow, and two in the stern. The primary weapon fired from these tubes was the primitive but effective M-57 anti-ship torpedo.

Twenty of the Romeos were constructed at the

Gorky Shipyards before the Soviet navy underwent a drastic change of strategic policy. Long-range cruise missiles delivered by a new generation of submarines, surface warships, and aircraft, would now be the weapons of choice for defending Soviet waters. This resulted in the immediate termination of the Romeo program, as it no longer fit into the navy's new war plans.

A number of the already completed subs were transferred to other navies—those of Egypt, Bulgaria, Algeria, and Syria. It was also decided to share the plans of the Romeo-class sub, and the technological skills needed to build them, with the People's Republic of China. Between 1960 and 1982, eighty-four units were completed at the Wuzhang, Guanzhou, Jiangnan, and Huludao shipyards. Several of these vessels were subsequently made available for export. It was in this manner that Ishii Industries purchased a pair of Chinese-made Romeos for use by the company's undersea mining subsidiary.

One would have to look very close to tell these two vessels apart. Two-hundred and fifty-four feet in length, with a submerged displacement of 1,700 tons, the *Bokken* and the *Katana* had individual complements of fifty-six crew members each. As was the case on any ship of size, the morale of her sailors was directly influenced by the personality of their commanding officer.

When Captain Hiroaki Sato was initially given command of the *Bokken*, he wasted no time implanting his personal style of leadership on his crew. A retired, twenty-year veteran of the Japanese Maritime Self-Defense Force, Sato prided himself as a strict, no-nonsense disciplinarian. As far as he was concerned, the *Bokken* was but an extension of his own being. While at sea, any jokes, horseplay, or small talk would not be tolerated. He viewed any such behavior as a wasteful diversion of his crew's focus. He had learned long ago that the operation of a submarine was a dangerous, deadly serious business, requiring iron discipline and a shared spirit of seamanship.

Much to his delight, his current employer allowed him to shape his crew's mental outlook with a unique series of Zen-like meditation exercises: hours of intensive prayer and study combined with a simple vegetarian diet, to promote a stringent martial philosophy, similar to that of the legendary Ninja. So successful was this program, Dr. Ishii ordered him to share it with his associate, Captain Satsugai Okura, the CO of the *Katana*.

Sato had first met Okura over two decades ago, while both were cadets at Eta Jima, Japan's naval academy. Several years later, they both sailed together on an Oyashio-class vessel, the first indigenously designed submarine in the postwar Japanese fleet. Eventually each man got his own command, and then they were reunited at Ishii Industries some twenty years later.

As was the case in their early student days, the competitive spirit was still strong between them. Though they both shared the same political goals, Sato had to admit that he wasn't all that disappointed upon receiving news of Okura's latest failure. For now the *Bokken* had been called upon to rectify the *Katana*'s shortcoming.

Anxious to prove his crew's superiority, Sato hurriedly left the hushed confines of the *Bokken*'s control room. A narrow passageway, lined with snaking electrical cables and shining tubes of stainless steel pipe, led him to the forward torpedo room. It had been fifteen hours since they had left the protective confines of Takara Bay. The majority of this southerly transit had taken place submerged, at snorkel depth.

As he entered the sub's forward-most compartment, he found it dominated by a large steel pallet on which the torpedo reloads were stored. Standing in front of this structure, beside the ladder leading up to the emergency hatch, were men dressed completely in black. Only the whites of their eyes showed through their masks as they bowed in silent greeting.

Sato returned this gesture and, as always, found himself invigorated to be in this group's presence. The mysterious teachings of the ancient Ninjitsu had always fascinated Sato. And here were five men who had selflessly devoted an entire lifetime to hard work and tireless discipline so that they could call themselves Ninja. Sato was thus extra careful to address them in a subdued, respectful tone.

"We will be at our destination shortly. You have trained all your lives for this moment. Now is the time to become at one with the Way. Flow with the rhythm of the elementals. And above all, be patient. We must not fail like the others!"

Doing his best to emphasize this last point, Sato added. "The *Bokken* will be waiting for you once you have delivered the death wind. Then we'll be off for Kyushu, to strike the US naval installation at Sasebo. For the glory of the Emperor, let us restore the values that the Westerners have stripped from our people's souls. As our glorious ancestors decreed in the not-so-distant past, revere the Emperor, and expel the barbarians!"

66

No sooner were these rousing words out of his mouth than the boat's intercom chimed twice. Knowing full well what this signal meant, Sato faced his silent audience and excused himself with a bow.

Back in the control room, his XO, Lieutenant Kenji Miyazawa, was waiting for him beside the chart table.

"We should be directly off Naha Point, Captain," informed the XO.

"Now we shall see how competent your navigational skills are, Lieutenant Miyazawa," replied Sato as he led his XO over to the periscope well.

"Up scope!" ordered the *Bokken*'s captain.

It was Miyazawa who depressed the lever that sent the scope hissing up from its storage well. Sato peered into the eyepiece and initiated a hasty 360-degree scan. With the night sea slapping up against the scope's lens, he spotted the blinking red strobe of a channel buoy barely a hundred yards distant. Most satisfied with this sighting, Sato backed away from the eyepiece and beckoned his XO to have a look.

"So, your time spent at the American sub school was not wasted after all," observed the captain. He then watched as Miyazawa bent over the scope and carefully adjusted its focus.

Halfway through his sweep of the horizon, the XO halted his scan. "Captain, I think you'd better take a look at this," he suggested worriedly.

Quick to replace him at the scope, Sato was forced to readjust the focus. Once this was accomplished, he closed in on the flashing red light of the channel marker, when much to his horror, the black night suddenly became like day. Unexpectedly illuminated by the powerful spotlight of a hovering helicopter, the sea filled with a pair of patrol boats and a sleek frigate.

"Down scope! Emergency descent!" he forcefully ordered.

This directive was closely followed by the shrill voice of the *Bokken*'s sonar operator. "Captain, sonar reports a variety of surface traffic topside! Bearing two-two-zero and rapidly closing."

As the hull of the *Bokken* began angling sharply downward, the loud, hollow ping of an active sonar search sounded inside the control room. The XO was among those whose eyes instinctively went to the compartment's ceiling, as if to search out the source of this terrifying racket.

"They must have been just sitting up there waiting for us!" he frantically observed.

Sato sensed the fear that undercut his second in command's tone, and reacted firmly. "Get a hold of yourself, Lieutenant! This is no time to panic. The *Bokken* is still the fox, and it's we who have the advantage."

"Something has just entered the water directly above us, Captain!" cried out the sonar operator.

This news provoked an instant response from Sato. "Rig for depth-charge attack!"

This command had barely been voiced when the compartment filled with a deafening blast. Seconds later, a massive shock wave smacked into the sub's hull. Tossed violently to and fro by this agitated wall of water, those not restrained by safety harnesses were thrown down to the control room deck, as was a lot of loose equipment. The sub's captain ended up flat on his back beside the periscope well. As a geyser of water sprayed from a ruptured ceiling valve, Sato struggled to stand.

"Someone get me a wrench!" he loudly ordered.

The lights flickered and dimmed as a young seaman fought his way over to a bulkhead-mounted tool box. From it, the frightened sailor removed a wrench, which he proceeded to hand over to the captain. Bruised and soaked, Sato attacked the ruptured valve with this tool, and the flow of water abated.

Not taking the time to celebrate, Sato turned toward the helm. "Quartermaster, get me a damage control report! Planesman, how does she respond?"

The seated, harness-secured sailor responsible for steering the *Bokken* answered while hastily scanning the numerous dials and gauges mounted before him. "Sluggishly, sir. Yet I still show forward speed and hydraulic pressure remains constant."

This was followed by the deep voice of the quartermaster. "I've got numerous reports of minor leaks and injuries throughout the boat, sir. Yet the hull is intact and the engine room remains on-line."

"So this old fox still has some life left in her," reflected Sato with a satisfied grin. "Helm, bring us around hard to course three-three-zero, and make your depth eighty feet."

"Aye, aye, sir," replied the planesman.

The angle of the deck canted sharply to the left, and the assorted equipment jarred loose by the exploding depth charge slid toward the port bulkhead. Doing his best to avoid this debris, the XO returned to the chart table.

"Captain, are you aware that the chart shows numerous reefs in the channel due north of us?" he questioned.

"That's exactly why that route offers us our only salvation," replied Sato. "If there's an opening in this trap, that's where we'll find it."

The *Bokken*'s commanding officer appeared calm

69

and collected as the angle of the deck leveled out. His composure held even when another depth charge exploded. This blast and the ensuing shock wave were far less violent than the previous ones, and the *Bokken* rode them out with ease.

"So, they've lost us already," said Sato, who turned toward his XO and added. "Empty your mind of all doubt and fear. Surrender your flow to the one void. And the Way shall lead you homeward like a long-lost pilgrim. Lieutenant Miyazawa, have you already forgotten that—"

These words were cut short by a gut-wrenching concussion, as the *Bokken* slammed into a submerged reef. Of an even greater intensity than the initial depth-charge attack, this forceful impact once more sent the crew crashing to the deck. The overhead lights completely failed, while dozens of valves burst open, engulfing the compartment in an icy shower of seawater.

It took several frantic minutes for the stunned XO to regain his footing and locate an emergency battle lantern. This dim red light illuminated a scene of utter devastation. Numerous dead bodies lay in the gathering water, including that of Captain Hiroaki Sato.

"Helm, blow emergency ballast and get us topside at once!" ordered Miyazawa, who readily assumed the responsibility of command.

Only the continued roar of spraying water met this frantic directive, and the XO staggered over to the diving console to carry out this order himself. The extreme angle on the bow indicated that the *Bokken* was in the midst of a steep, uncontrolled dive, and it took a supreme effort on the XO's part just to remain upright.

Miyazawa passed the unconscious helmsman and noted that the shattered depth gauge showed them rapidly approaching the sub's crush threshold. Doing his best to control the rising panic that left him increasingly chilled and breathless, he fought his way to the console that regulated *Bokken's* trim. With shaking hand, he reached out and pulled down the elongated red and white striped lever beside the trim indicator. In response, a roaring blast of venting ballast filled the control room with blessed sound. And the last thing the XO was aware of, before dropping to the deck in a state of shock-induced unconsciousness, was that the direction of the depth gauge had miraculously reversed itself.

"This little baby is what our ambush off Okinawa netted," said Vice Admiral Henry Walker as he pointed toward the screen, on which a slide of a surfaced submarine was projected.

From the darkened confines of the *Enterprise's* Flag Quarters, Captain Steven Webster and Dr. Miriam Kromer listened intently as the distinguished Director of Naval Intelligence added, "She's called the *Bokken*. Translated from Japanese that's the bamboo sword used in the martial art of kendo. The *Bokken* is one of two vessels of this class purchased from the People's Republic of China by Ishii Industries, for the proposed purpose of mining undersea mineral deposits."

Walker addressed the remote-control unit that he held in his hand, and the screen filled with a map of the Ryukyu Islands. He then utilized a pointer to highlight a tiny island in this chain, located approximately halfway between Okinawa and the Japanese island of Kyushu.

"Both the *Bokken* and her sister ship, the *Katana*, whose name refers to yet another type of martial-arts sword, are based here, on Takara Island. This is the home of Ishii Industries."

A slide showing an immense bayside industrial complex replaced the map, and Walker continued.

"Ishii Industries is a private, multibillion yen company specializing in the manufacture of ocean-synthesized pharmaceuticals. Other subsidiaries are supposedly involved in the extraction of various minerals from the seabed, as well as the use of ocean-harvested organisms in the treatment of diseases such as cancer."

Next, the screen filled with the photograph of a white-haired Oriental gentleman immaculately attired in a stylish business suit. This elder's intense green stare and full Fu Manchu mustache gave him a menacing appearance. Walker proceeded to reveal his identity.

"This is Dr. Yukio Ishii, the firm's founder and current CEO. Though he is a private man, our file on him is thick. Ishii is the reputed leader of the Black Dragon Society, a right wing organization, whose aim is to restore a strong, militaristic Japan, free from all foreign influence."

Yet another slide showed Ishii decked out in a white martial-arts costume, a slender sword held high overhead.

"Ishii is also a self-avowed samurai and the holder of a fifth dan in kendo," revealed Walker. "He has published several volumes of Zen poetry—and a fascinating history of the Ninja."

As the screen filled with an overhead view of Ishii Industries and the adjoining bay, Walker's tone intensified. "Our analysis of the contents of several sealed tanks discovered on the *Bokken* proved them to contain active anthrax spores. These spores are believed to have originated in a clandestine biological warfare laboratory located somewhere in this complex. I have been ordered to destroy this lab at once. We've already dismissed a surgical airstrike or a cruise-missile attack as being too risky. Hundreds of civilians work at this complex, and we'd like to limit the damage to the BW lab if humanly possible."

"Why not utilize a submarine to penetrate the bay, and then land a SEAL team?" suggested Steven Webster.

Walker slyly grinned, and used the remote control unit to return to the slide of the surfaced submarine.

"My thoughts exactly, Captain," concurred Walker. "Yet because of the likely presence of hydrophones and CAPTOR mines in those confined waters, what do you think about using the enemy's very own submarine to accomplish this task? The *Bokken*'s radio transmitter was completely destroyed when they hit that reef, and as far as Ishii knows, the boat is still operational."

"Is the *Bokken* seaworthy?" Dr. Kromer asked.

Walker met the toxicologist's intense glance and confidently replied. "Even as we speak, we've got her in drydock, pounding out the dents. So far, we've found nothing that can't be repaired in the time allotted. Since her hold was filled with enough supplies for a two-week deployment, and contingency plans were found for a strike at our naval installation at Sasebo, I'd say they're not expected back for a good ten days yet."

"May I ask who's going to drive her?" questioned Webster, ever the skeptic.

Walker addressed his reply directly to the carrier's commanding officer. "I've decided to pull selected crew members off the USS *Hawkbill*. They'll be asked to volunteer, and then be temporarily placed out of active service."

"But they're nukes," returned Webster. "What do they know about running a diesel-electric submarine sporting technology that was outdated before they were even born?"

Once again, Henry Walker's distinguished face was distorted by a sly grin. "Good point, Captain. And to get our boys acclimatized, I'll be calling in some very special naval consultants, who happen to know this particular class of submarine from stem to stern. If we're living right, perhaps we can even convince them to go along for the ride."

Still not satisfied, Webster probed further. "And if they manage to get the sub into that bay in one piece, how are our SEALs ever going to find the right lab? That place looks like a maze."

Before responding to this query, Admiral Walker took a long look at the redheaded civilian seated beside the *Enterprise*'s CO.

"Dr. Kromer, I was hoping we could tap your unique expertise one more time. Could you find that lab if it indeed exists?"

The toxicologist answered after only a moment's hesitation. "Such a facility would demand specialized venting equipment and biohazard level-Four work spaces. It shouldn't be too difficult to locate."

"Good," replied Walker with a furtive wink. "Then you won't mind going along, and showing our boys just where their explosives will do the most damage."

74

Six

The winds blew in from the Gulf of Mexico in warm, humid gusts. Bill Brown pointed the blunt bow of his twenty-foot sloop to the north, and watched as the mainsail was extended by the stiff breeze. He was reaching, or sailing with the wind abeam, and in response, his Falmouth Cutter plunged through the sparkling blue waters of Sarasota Bay at a crisp fifteen knots.

Only after he was completely satisfied with the trim of the jib and the staysail did Brown reach out for the thermos and refill his mug with black coffee. He leaned back against the plastic-covered cushions that lined the boat's square stern, and listened as the spirited sounds of *Victory at Sea* projected from the cabin. Richard Rodger's superb soundtrack was one of his very favorite recordings, and Brown correctly identified the haunting piece currently playing as "The Song of the High Seas."

With this tune as a fitting accompaniment, the sixty-seven-year-old, retired US Navy veteran sipped his piping-hot coffee. Dreamily, he looked to his right, where the Gothic outlines of the Ringling Mansion could be seen on the nearby shore. Built in the 1920's by John Ringling of circus fame, the mansion was now open to the public. On its spacious, palm tree-lined grounds was an art and circus museum, and an exact replica of England's Globe Theatre.

Brown used to be a frequent visitor to the theater and the art museum. That was back in the days when his wife Mary was still alive. A true lover of the arts, Mary had dragged him to many a play and art-show opening. He had genuinely enjoyed these events, which abruptly ceased when cancer took his companion of forty years away from him.

With Mary's passing eight months ago, yet another chapter in Brown's life ended. Before that a thirty-year naval career had come to a close; as had a decade spent working at the Electric Boat division of General Dynamics.

He was all alone now, with no family to speak of save for a single son who had followed in his father's footsteps, having just been made XO of a 688-class, nuclear-powered attack sub. Since the majority of his close friendships dated from his early Navy days and these men were now scattered throughout the country, Brown filled the void created when his wife died by focusing his energies on his sailboat.

He'd purchased the craft three years ago, naming it *Arcturus*, for the giant, first-magnitude fixed star in the constellation Boötes. He'd done this before retiring from Electric Boat and before their move to Longboat Key, Florida.

Mary had been an avid sailor, and together they'd turned the boat into a second home. Designed and built for cruising, *Arcturus* was relatively small at twenty feet, though its wide beam created a remarkable amount of space below. Two quarter berths doubled as seats for the dinette. When not in use, the table slid aft under the cockpit. There was a gimbaled kerosene stove to port and a chart table and ice box opposite. The starboard quarter berth was also the seat for the navigation station, with a hanging locker, double bunk, and head forward. The trim was mahogany, the deck fittings bronze, with a skylight just aft of the mast, over the main cabin.

Arcturus was a joy to sail in open waters, and for the first couple of years they'd spent many an enjoyable hour exploring the scenic coast of Florida. Their longest trip together had been around the Straits of Florida to Nassau. They had been in the process of planning a cruise into the Caribbean Sea when Mary had first fallen ill. She'd passed away six months later, never again to set foot on the *Arcturus*.

A sea gull cried out harshly overhead, and Bill Brown glanced upward into the cloudless, powdery blue sky. The warm sun felt good on his ruggedly handsome face and firm, bare chest. He finished off his coffee and picked up a battered corncob pipe, which he packed with tobacco and lit with a well-used Zippo lighter. The familiar, rich scent of rum-soaked burley met his nostrils, and Brown returned his line of sight to the sea before him.

He followed a leaping pod of dolphins past a channel marker and turned *Arcturus* into the wind as a Boeing 727 roared overhead, having just taken off from the nearby Sarasota-Bradenton airport. The sail momentarily luffed, and Brown began tacking on a zigzag course to the west. Longboat Key now lay before him. This was where his bayside condo was located, directly overlooking the pier where *Arcturus* was docked.

In another week, he planned to sail into the open waters of the Gulf and turn south for the Fort Jefferson National Monument on the Dry Tortugas. Afterward, he would stop off at Key West and spend several days on Big Pine Key as the guest of Pete Frystak, a retired Navy buddy who ran a small resort there. The cruise would encompass some five hundred miles and would take several weeks to complete.

This voyage was to be his first extended sail without Mary. The pain of her untimely loss had hurt him deeply, and for an entire month after her burial, he'd visited her gravesite daily.

At first he'd resisted the urgings of his son to leave Longboat, if only for a couple of days. It proved to be time itself that eventually healed the great wound caused by Mary's death. Gradually he'd readjusted his lifestyle, finding new purpose within the cramped confines of his sailboat.

Ever thankful for this unlikely savior, Brown found himself looking forward to the long voyage he would soon be undertaking. Confident that *Arcturus* could meet any challenge the sea might have in store, he redirected his attention back to his present course. He was halfway across the bay, tacking to windward, with his destination, Longboat Key, clearly visible on the western horizon. The warm wind hit him full in the face, and he did his best to keep his sails from luffing.

With *Victory at Sea* still blaring from the tape player, he shifted the well-chewed bit of his pipe from one corner of his mouth to the other. The channel remained free of other surface traffic, and Brown figured he could be safely home in time for lunch.

It was as he reached out for his thermos to refill his mug, that a bright orange and white Coast Guard helicopter swooped low overhead. Brown looked on with surprise as this vehicle turned and initiated yet another low-level pass, this time halting in midair and hovering directly above him. The deep clatter of the chopper's spinning rotors rose to an almost deafening intensity as a helmeted figure emerged from the open hatchway, megaphone in hand.

"Commander Bill Brown?" cried out an amplified female voice.

Brown waved in recognition and ducked into the forward cabin. Seconds later, he returned with his own megaphone.

"How can I help you?" he questioned.

"Commander," replied the helmeted ensign, "we've got an emergency call for you. Do you have a telephone on board?"

"I'm afraid not," returned the retired veteran. "May I ask who's on the line?"

"It's Vice Admiral Henry Walker, sir."

This revelation caused Brown to mutter to himself. "What in hell does ole' Henry want, the date of the *Cubera*'s next reunion?"

"Commander Brown," added the voice from above. "If you'll just follow us to dry land, we'll patch you through via the chopper's comm line."

His curiosity now fully aroused, Brown beckoned that he understood and watched as the helicopter turned to the east and sped off toward the distant shoreline. Since he had been headed in the opposite direction, he was forced to engage the rudder, and all too soon the *Arcturus* was running with the gusting wind at its back.

He made landfall at the Ringling Mansion pier. The young Coast Guard ensign was waiting for him there. After helping him secure the *Arcturus*, she led him on foot to the helicopter that had landed in the broad clearing beside the mansion.

The pilot offered Brown the private use of his cockpit and showed him how to operate the chin-mounted radio transmitter. After putting on a pair of headphones, Brown sat down in the deserted cockpit and listened as a burst of static was replaced by a familiar, scratchy male voice.

"Hello, Bill. Are you there?"

"I'm here all right, Henry," replied Brown.

"Good," said the Director of Naval Intelligence. "I hope this call out of the blue hasn't inconvenienced you any."

"Actually, you caught me in the midst of a sail."

"So I understand, Bill. Please bear with me, and I'll have you back on that beautiful bay of yours before you know it."

"Are you calling from Washington?" asked Brown.

"Believe it or not, I'm speaking to you from the FQ of the USS *Enterprise*, off the coast of Okinawa on the East China Sea. I know it's been much too long since we last talked, but I've got a problem out here that I could sure use your help solving."

"I'm flattered, Henry. Since I retired and Mary passed away, I've got nothing but spare time on my hands. So how can I be of assistance?"

Walker got right to the point. "How would you like an all-expense-paid trip to Okinawa?"

Momentarily caught off guard by this offer, Brown hesitated a second before responding. "I don't suppose it would help for me to ask what this is all about."

"All I can tell you, Bill, is that it indirectly involves a little incident that we shared in the Barents Sea back in 'fifty-eight."

This cryptic remark hit home, and Brown anxiously sat forward. "I hear you, Henry. When do you need me?"

"There's a MAC flight leaving Homestead tonight at twenty-one hundred hours your time. Can you make it?"

Brown looked at his watch and saw that he had just over nine hours to pack and complete the short flight south to Homestead Air Force Base.

"I'm on my way, Henry," he said without a second

thought.

"God bless you, Bill. I knew I could count on you. Now there's only one more thing. Are you still in touch with Pete Frystak?"

"As a matter of fact, I talked to Pete just yesterday," answered Brown. "I was planning to sail down to Big Pine Key and visit him and Kathy sometime next week."

"I'm sorry to disrupt your plans," replied Henry Walker. "But there just happens to be an extra seat on that MAC flight with Pete's name on it. Is he available?"

"You know Pete, Henry. He never did like the idea of retiring from the Navy in the first place. And besides, he could use a break from that resort of his before the season starts up again. If you'd like, I'll give him a call and ask him along myself."

"I'd appreciate that. I'm sorry I can't tell you more, but that will have to wait until you get out here. Until then, take care of yourself and have a safe flight."

With this, the line went dead and Bill Brown removed his headphones and thoughtfully gazed out the cockpit window. In the near distance, the billowing jib of the docked *Arcturus* caught his eye, and he took a second to contemplate the strange conversation he had just concluded.

His relationship with Henry Walker went back almost thirty-five years. Back in 1958 Walker had been assigned to the USS *Cubera* as Brown's XO. In the years that followed, they'd become close friends, with Walker eventually going on to his own command and much more. His attainment of flag rank was a great achievement. Brown's respect for Walker ran deep, and there was no doubt in the retired veteran's mind that something extremely serious had prompted his old friend's unusual request. Anxious to find out what this great mystery was all about, Brown got on with the task of contacting Pete Frystak, yet another shipmate from the past, and passing on Henry Walker's invitation.

Pete and Kathy Frystak had purchased the Blue Conch five years ago, upon Pete's retirement from the US Navy. For the close-knit couple, the place was a dream come true. They had fallen in love with the Florida Keys when Pete had been assigned to the Key West Naval Station. Twenty-five years later, they had scrimped and saved to get enough cash for a substantial down payment on a three-acre resort property put up for sale by its elderly proprietor.

The place was situated on Big Pine Key, halfway between Marathon and Key West. It occupied an elongated strip of white sand beach overlooking the sparkling blue waters of the Atlantic Ocean. A dozen gabled-roofed cottages were interspersed amongst the palm trees. Each had two bedrooms, two baths, a full kitchen, and a screened-in porch that offered an unobstructed view of the sea.

Originally built half a century ago, the Blue Conch resort had ridden out many a tropical storm and its fair share of full-fledged hurricanes. As was the case with any beachfront property, the elements had taken their toll on the resort's man-made structures. Over the years, a conscientious maintenance program had kept each of the cottages habitable. Yet, as it was with a classic car, it took a lot of effort on the Frystaks' part to keep the property properly maintained.

While Kathy concentrated on supervising the housekeeping staff and running the office, her husband was in charge of all repairs. Pete's current project was to put a new tile roof on each cottage. He'd initiated this major renovation with the assistance of his two full-time Cuban maintenance men.

As the last of the winter season's guests packed up and returned to their homes in the north, Pete and his crew went to work on the first of the roofs. The old tiles were removed, along with the thick felt underneath. When it was determined that the plywood sheathing was warped and buckled, Pete decided to remove it also and start from scratch.

A truckload of four-by-eight foot plywood panels was brought in from Miami. Pete made certain they were dry and well seasoned, so they wouldn't warp due to the Key's everchanging weather conditions. This sheathing was then nailed directly to the rafters.

The fifty-eight-year-old retired veteran worked right alongside his crew. He had never been afraid of hard physical labor, and instead thought of it as mere exercise. As a result, his stomach was still firm and his muscles were tight, like those of a man half his age.

Once the sheathing was in place, a new layer of felt was installed. This water-resistant, thirty-pound membrane was made from wood fibers and recycled paper that had been saturated with asphalt oil. The flat, orange roofing tiles were then laid atop it and nailed directly into the plywood sheathing. Though expensive, such an outer covering was fireproof and extremely durable. Barring a direct hit by a hurricane, it would last half a century.

The three men had just finished installing their first roof. Proud of this accomplishment, they tackled the next cottage like old pros, and had the job done in half the time the first one had taken. If the weather cooperated, Pete hoped to finish the entire project in four more weeks. This would allow the resort to be fully operational by the time the first families began arriving for the summer.

As was his habit, Pete was up at the crack of dawn. He began his morning with a three-mile jog on the beach. The sky was clear, and it promised to be another perfect day for working outdoors. He returned home to shave and shower, then joined his wife on the porch for a breakfast of grapefruit, prunes, cereal, a bran muffin, and coffee.

His crew had already taken off in the truck for Miami, to pick up some supplies, so Pete went to work on the third roof alone. Since they had already removed the old sheathing, he spent the rest of the morning installing new sheets of plywood on the rafters. He did so with the help of a well-used claw hammer and two-inch common nails, which he drove into the vertical edges of each panel six-inches apart.

The sun climbed high into a cloudless blue sky, and Pete's bare chest was all too soon covered with sweat. Kathy had applied sun block to his face and exposed back, and instead of burning, his skin was tanned a deep bronze. He only stopped to take an occasional sip from his water bottle and renew his supply of nails. It was during one of these brief breaks that he spotted Kathy approaching from the direction of their cottage. Supposing she was on her way to announce lunch, he took a second to wipe his forehead with the back of his arm.

"I don't suppose you've come over here to lend me a hand," the retired submariner called from the angled side of the gabled roof.

Kathy looked up, shading her eyes from the harsh sunlight. "I'm afraid not, Pete. Bill Brown's on the phone for you. He says it's urgent."

The veteran's tone turned serious. "You don't say. Is the skipper feeling all right?"

"He sounds okay to me, Pete."

"I hope he hasn't gotten cold feet and is going to

cancel his visit," said Pete as he began climbing down off the roof. "He needs to get out of Longboat, to get back into the swing of things."

"That's easy enough for you to say," offered Kathy, who held the ladder while her husband returned to terra firma. "Considering that Mary's been gone less than nine months now, I'd say he's doing remarkably well."

Pete unhooked his tool belt and wiped his compact torso dry with a terry-cloth towel. "You don't know the skipper like I do, Kath. He needs to quit feeling sorry for himself and return to the real world. And the only way he's going to do that is by being around other people and getting his mind off his loss."

"I still think we shouldn't rush things, Pete. When he's ready, we'll be right here, waiting for him."

Pete responded while leading the way back to their cottage. "Sometimes a guy needs a little push from his friends to get back on track, and that's just what I plan to give him. Hell, the skipper always took the time to give me plenty of good advice when we sailed together on the *Cubera*. Now it's time for me to return the favor."

Kathy could only shrug her shoulders as her headstrong husband continued on to the screened-in porch attached to the back side of their cottage. A telephone lay on the redwood picnic table there, and while Pete picked up the receiver, she went indoors to get him a glass of lemonade. From the kitchen, a screened window looked directly onto the porch, so her husband's conversation was clearly audible.

"I understand, Skipper. Listen, if you're in, so am I. Kath is just going to have to learn to accept it . . . I read you loud and clear, Skipper. See you tonight at Homestead at eighteen-hundred hours."

She looked on as her husband hung up the handset

and thoughtfully redirected his gaze to the nearby ocean. Completely forgetting the lemonade, she charged out onto the porch.

"May I ask just what it is I'm going to have to learn to accept, Pete?"

There was a distant, serious look in her husband's eyes as he turned his gaze away from the sea.

"Honey, I'd love to share it with you. But all I can say is the skipper needs me for a week or so. So can you help me throw some things together? Because the way things look, we'll be leaving for Japan — tonight."

Chief Stanley Roth's final assignment for the US Navy was as an instructor at the Basic Enlisted Man's Submarine School at New London, Connecticut. Thirty-five years ago, at the tender age of twenty-two, Roth had attended this very same institution. A long, rewarding career had followed, most of which he'd spent beneath the seas as a submariner.

As Roth faced retirement, this last duty station was a fitting place for him to put his life into some sort of perspective. He had never found the time to marry or start a family, preferring instead to dedicate himself totally to his duty. In many ways by not having children, he'd been able to escape the rapid advancing of the years. He still saw himself as a young man, filled with vision, energy, and purpose. Yet this illusion collapsed the day the Navy announced his forced retirement and sent him to New London to count the days left until he would be a civilian again.

Though he would have liked to spend this time at sea, Roth made the best of a situation he had no control over. The way he looked at it, this would be his last chance to share some of the knowledge he'd gathered during his thirty-plus years on submarines with a whole new generation of undersea warriors.

Returning to New London was like traveling back in time. As he entered the hallowed corridors of Bledsoe Hall, he was met by the same engraved placard that had greeted him over three decades ago. It read, Through These Doors Pass the Finest Submariners in the World. Yet proof of the passing of time was quick in coming, as Roth caught his reflection in a nearby mirror. There could be no denying the slight paunch that showed on his five-foot, seven-inch frame, or the conspicuous bald spot that graced his skull. These were especially evident when he saw the bright-eyed enlisted men swarming down the hallways on the way to classes. Feeling every one of his fifty-seven years and then some, Stanley sucked in his gut and continued on to the simulator room, where his first class of the day would be held.

A dozen young students dressed in blue dungarees waited for him beside a full-scale mock-up of a submarine's control room. Chief Roth wasted no time in getting down to business.

"Good morning, gentlemen. What you're looking at here is a ship's control and diving trainer. Today I'm going to use it to teach you how to pilot a submarine. If you'll do me the honor of following me onto the platform, we'll get started."

Roth led the way up onto the simulator. He pointed toward the forward bulkhead, where two seats intended for the helmsmen were located.

"Robnick, you take the inboard chair. Reed, you've got outboard."

As the two students took their positions, Roth added. "Okay, gentlemen. Buckle up."

With the rest of the class gathered tightly behind him, Roth continued. "The basic scenario goes like this. You've got a three-hundred-sixty-foot long, multimillion dollar submarine in your hands. I'm going to take on the roles of both OOD and diving officer, and I'll crank up a flank bell. I want you to reach and maintain periscope depth. Are you with me?"

The two nervous students gave a tentative nod, and Roth instructed them to grab the hydraulically powered, partial steering wheels positioned in front of them. They did so, and immediately the deck of the trainer angled sharply upward.

"Easy does it, gentlemen," advised the veteran. "You're putting too much angle on those planes. Don't forget that we're haulin' ass thru the water at well over thirty knots. Minimize the use of those planes, and it will be a hell of a lot easier to maintain the trim angle. Limit your rise and dive to five degrees, and you'll be able to catch the bubble and lock it in."

As soon as the young sailors applied this advice and gained control of the simulator, Roth called out loudly, "Flooding in the torpedo room!"

A piercing, electronic alarm followed, and the chief assumed the roles of both diving officer and the officer of the deck. "Officer of the deck, we can't maintain ordered depth. Recommend emergency surface."

"Diving officer, emergency surface the ship!"

"Full rise, stern and fairwater planes!"

The helmsmen yanked back on their steering columns and the trainer once more angled sharply upward. The rest of the class had to hold on to each other to keep from falling backward, as the simulated sound of venting ballast blasted from a pair of elevated speakers.

"Surface! Surface!" ordered Roth, who resumed the role of diving officer. "Watch that trim angle. Get it down . . . Get it down . . . That's it. Now we're going to breach, so brace yourselves. And don't forget the flooding going on in the torpedo room — we still don't know the status of it. Now she's going to pop out of the water and drop back in."

The trainer violently shook, and as it dipped abruptly downward, Roth made a cutting motion across his throat signaling that the exercise was over.

"This is exactly how it's going to happen on the boat, gentlemen. I can't emphasize enough how important this training is to your success as submariners. Unlike a surface vessel, we can't call the Coast Guard or throw out life rafts when a casualty comes down. When you're a thousand feet under, the only thing that's going to save you is the capability of the crew. That's why we spend a major part of our budget on your training. And believe me when I tell you these big bucks are going to pay off. Because if a crisis situation ever develops down there, you could be the one who's going to jump in and save your ship. So with that said, let's move on to the damage-control wet trainer."

The group of students appeared genuinely moved by Roth's passionate outburst as they followed him into an adjoining room. The floor here was cut by a twisting series of steel ladders that led to a lower level. This pipe-lined confined space was designed to be a scale mock-up of a portion of a submarine's engine room.

"What you're lookin' at here is the infamous damage-control wet trainer. I'm going to put you down there at the start of a casualty, and then turn on the water to simulate flooding. Take your time, do a good job, and remember that safety is our number one priority. Now do it, gentlemen!"

The students proceeded to climb down into the trainer with all the gusto of a group of condemned criminals. Stanley Roth remembered well his own first experience in this simulator, and he couldn't help but grin as he ducked through a nearby hatchway and sealed himself inside the control room. Waiting for him there, seated in front of a computer console, was yet another veteran instructor, Chief Ezra Burke.

"How are you doing, Ezra?" greeted Roth. "Are we ready to rock 'n' roll?"

Chief Burke flashed him a thumbs-up. "I'm ready when you are, Stanley. How do you want to start them out?"

"Let's begin with the port and starboard lube oil, to get them in the spirit of things. Then we'll hit them with the collision alarm and open up the ceiling gaskets."

Chief Burke addressed his keyboard and fed this request into the computer. Meanwhile, Roth walked over to the large, double-paned picture window and gazed down at his class. They looked worried and nervous, but the mood below turned to near panic when water began pouring into the compartment with the force of a high-pressure fire hose.

"Flooding in the engine room!" cried the group's senior petty officer.

They scrambled for the tools that were laid out on a nearby table. At the same time their leader attempted to direct them to the various valves from which the water was pouring.

"Here we go," reflected Roth as he continued watching from the observation window.

The water was well over the trainees' ankles by the time the first student reached one of the wildly spraying valves and vainly struggled to stem the onrush with a wrench. As it turned out, two other sailors had been ordered to contain this very same leak, and they merely stood in the gathering water, watching their co-worker attack the ruptured valve.

"So much for team work," muttered Roth as he reached for the intercom and spoke forcefully into its microphone. "You've got two men down there who aren't doing a damn thing! Scene leader, redirect them, and do it on the double. That water level's going nowhere but up!"

Down in the trainer, the soaked senior petty officer turned to carry out this directive. Unfortunately, as he pivoted he slipped on the wet deck and went sprawling, ending up flat on his back.

Roth shook his head and covered the microphone with his hand as he disgustedly addressed Chief Burke. "All right, Ezra, shut it down. I'd better get down there and convey the wrath of God."

Roth unsealed the hatch and climbed down to the floor below. As he poked his head inside the trainer, the sounds of coughing and dripping water met his ears.

"Gentlemen, get over here!" he instructed.

The students somberly gathered before him. Each of them was thoroughly soaked, and Roth laid into their leader with a vengeance.

"Petty Officer Robnick, you're supposed to be the man in charge. You had a serious flooding casualty here. You can't just assign men to fight that without a follow-up. Two of your guys were just standing there for the last two minutes, picking their damn noses, while seven-hundred gallons of water a minute poured into this trainer. If you see that somebody's not getting the job done, get some replacements in there."

The soaked leader of the group looked close to tears as he nodded in response to this advice, and Roth softened his tone as he continued.

"It's obvious to all of you now that a submariner has only one real enemy, and that's the sea. So when I go back upstairs and hit you with the next casualty, I want you to attack it like you were fighting a war for your lives. Can you handle it, Mr. Robnick?"

The group's senior petty officer cleared his throat and spoke out. "I'll try my best, sir."

"That's all I'm asking," replied Roth as he pivoted and returned to the control room.

Chief Burke was waiting for him at the computer console, a sealed envelope in hand.

"This just arrived for you, Stanley. It's marked urgent."

Roth quickly tore open the envelope and read its contents.

"Well, I'll be," he muttered. "You're never going to believe this, Ezra, but I've just received new orders from COMSUBPAC. I'm being reassigned to Okinawa of all places. Now what do you make of that?"

"It's obvious that the US Navy isn't going to let go of one of its best," replied the grinning assistant instructor. "But before you run off to pack, how do you want to handle those potential bubbleheads down in the trainer?"

Having momentarily forgotten about his class, Stanley Roth walked over to the observation window.

"In honor of my respite, hit 'em with the flange," ordered Roth.

"One ruptured flange it is," repeated Ezra Burke, who efficiently readdressed his computer keyboard.

Seconds later, the trainer filled with a deafening roar as 700 gallons of wildly spraying water per minute poured out of a single pipe fitting at the center of the compartment. Several of the students were immediately knocked to the deck by the force of this unexpected spate. That gained the full attention of their shocked associates.

"Now that's flooding," observed Stanley Roth. "Welcome to the submarine force, gentlemen!"

Seven

The wardroom of the USS *Hawkbill* had a multitude of uses. It served the sub's officers as both an eating and recreational space, and it provided a large table at which study and work could be undertaken. It was this latter activity that brought together Commander Chris Slaughter, Lieutenant Commander Benjamin Kram, and the sub's senior sonar technician, James "Jaffers" Echoles. A tense, serious atmosphere prevailed as the trio sat around the wardroom table, intently listening to the muted, throbbing sounds being projected from the speakers of a portable cassette player.

"That's the best I've got," offered Jaffers, who reached forward to turn the tape machine's volume knob to maximum amplification. "We picked this up on the lateral array seconds before *Hawkbill* initiated its pursuit. The source has got to be battery powered. Nothing else could be so quiet."

"Impossible," countered the XO. "We chased them for a good quarter of an hour at flank speed. And when we were forced to break off because of our galley fire, the bogey still had a couple of knots on us. No diesel-electric boat afloat has that kind of speed."

"Perhaps we're dealing with some kind of newfangled, air-independent propulsion system," offered

Slaughter. "They could be running a closed-cycle diesel, or maybe even a Stirling."

"I think it's fuel cells," Jaffers declared. "That would account not only for the bogey's lack of signature but for its great speed and prolonged submerged endurance."

The sonar technician rewound the tape. As he hit the play button once again, Benjamin Kram queried, "Do you think this is something new that Ivan's trying out on us?"

"It could very well be," replied Slaughter. "Even with the so-called end of the Cold War, the Soviets are still putting out more new classes of submarines than we are."

Jaffers was quick to interject. "Unless Ivan has figured out some radical new way to muffle a nuclear reactor, I still say it's powered by fuel cells. And there's only one country that's advanced enough to put such technology to work. I'll put my money on a modified Japanese Yuushio, specially configured to give it that extra get up and go."

"If that's the case, why hasn't the Japanese Maritime Self-Defense Force shared knowledge of such a unique vessel with us? Aren't we supposed to be allies?" asked Kram.

The captain shook his head. "Not when it comes to new technologies with potential commercial applications, Ben. If Jaffers is correct, the first we'll officially see of it is, along with everyone else, on the open market."

A moment of thoughtful silence followed as the distant, alien, pulsating noise of the escaping underwater bogey continued to play from the tape machine. With its conclusion, Jaffers hit the stop button and voiced his opinion.

"It sure would be a feather in *Hawkbill*'s cap if we

could be the first to expose such a novel submarine for the whole world to see."

"If they dare cross our path again, we'll grab that feather, Jaffers," said Slaughter. "Because this time we'll be ready for them."

The senior sonar operator was in the process of rewinding the tape, when Chief Mallot entered the wardroom. Ever since the fire, the portly chef's perpetual smile was noticeably absent. Still blaming himself for the entire incident, Mallot was all business as he handed Chris Slaughter a folded message.

"Captain, I was in the radio room delivering some hot joe, when this arrived for you."

Slaughter carefully read the dispatch, and then handed it to his XO.

"What's for chow, Chief?" asked Jaffers as he pocketed the cassette tape. "I'm starved."

"We're serving ham steak, baked beans, cranberries, and corn," Mallot answered.

Surprisingly enough, it proved to be the captain who responded to this. "Sounds good, Mr. Mallot. But you'd better set a few extra places at the table. Because as it looks now, *Hawkbill* is going to be welcoming some unscheduled guests shortly."

The cabin of an airborne MC-130 Combat Talon transport was a cold, noisy, inhospitable place. With a bare minimum of creature comforts, this aircraft was used for a variety of deep-penetration special operations missions. Its advanced avionics and onboard radar allowed its crew to locate extremely small drop zones and to drop the payload over unfamiliar territory with a great degree of accuracy.

Nighttime parachute drops over water were particularly challenging. In such instances, any number of complex factors could come into play, many of them capable of causing disastrous results.

The four members of SEAL Team Three had learned long ago to put fear out of their minds. Besides, on this particular evening, they had more important things to ponder, such as the long-cherished leave that they had just been forced to cut short. Less than seven hours ago, they'd gotten this new call to duty as they were beginning a tour of the exotic fleshpots that lay outside the main gate of the Subic Bay naval station. Much to their disbelief, they'd found themselves herded into a van by a group of burly Marines, and then whisked off to nearby Clark Air Base. It was there that the MC-130 had been waiting for them.

It was rapidly approaching seven P.M., and the tasteless MREs (Meals Ready to Eat) that they had been served for dinner hadn't lightened their moods any. They had been in the air now for over five and a half hours. Because their course had been almost due north, this put them somewhere over the East China Sea.

As usual, the team's orders were sketchy at best. They had been merely instructed to initiate a prearranged parachute drop into the black sea below. Further orders would await them. With the hope that this mission was only another readiness exercise dreamed up by some idiot in the Pentagon, and that they'd be able to get back to their leave as soon as it was completed, the members of SEAL Team Three did their best to make themselves comfortable.

The cabin was illuminated by a dim red light, to protect their night vision. With nothing better to do than try to get some shuteye before their jump, the SEALs were stretched out on a hard bench that extended the length of the cabin.

During their gruelling fifteen-week indoctrination program in Coronado, California, each man had received a nickname that had stuck with them ever since. Cajun was the team's point man. Born and raised in the swamp country outside of Lake Charles, Louisiana, Cajun was a crack shot and an expert tracker. Lean and mean, he was a former linebacker at Tulane, where he'd gained notoriety after smashing an opposing quarterback's spine during a sack. He'd joined the Navy soon afterward, and the way he saw it, now he was breaking necks for the government and getting paid for it.

Old Dog was from neighboring Hereford, Texas, where he'd grown up on a cattle ranch. It was always said that if Bigfoot had a human equivalent, Old Dog would be it. Though a little lacking in the brains department, this six-foot, five-inch, muscular hunk of a Texan thrived on pain, and liked to inflict it too.

Warlock came from the other end of the spectrum. Seemingly frail and mild-mannered, he hailed from Nashua, New Hampshire. By the time he was twenty, he'd already graduated MIT with honors. Yet instead of immediately going on for his doctorate, he decided to take a couple of years off and see what the "real" world was all about. He had always liked boats and electronics, so he joined the Navy. It was at the Navy's amphibious base on Coronado Island, California, that he blossomed into full manhood as a SEAL, learning fifty ways to kill a man, and that was just with his bare hands.

Traveler was the stud of the group. This smooth-talking lady's man from the Show-Me state sported wavy blond hair and clear blue eyes that drew women like honey did flies. A born mimic and a natural comedian, Traveler had a deadly serious side to his personality. And when the chips were down, he was the guy that the team turned to.

Watching the slumbering SEALs from the console located beside the rear hatchway to the MC-130, was the

97

airplane's jumpmaster. She was just noting that she could actually hear the snores of the commando known as Old Dog over the roaring whine of the four Allison turboprops when word arrived from the cockpit that they were nearing the jump site. She immediately awakened Traveler, and looked on as the strikingly handsome SEAL passed on the word to his teammates.

There was a bare minimum of conversation as the members of SEAL Team Three groggily returned to full consciousness and prepared their equipment. In addition to parachute and black wetsuit, each man was decked out in full combat gear. This included a Model 22 Type 0.9mm silenced pistol, especially developed for the SEALs by Smith and Wesson. Constructed completely of steel to prevent rust in the salt-water environment, this pistol had its own nickname—Hush Puppy, in reference to its role as a guard-dog killer.

A bright yellow light, positioned above the rear hatch began blinking, and the jumpmaster pointed toward it and spoke out as loudly as she could.

"You'll be jumping in two more minutes. Please line up beside the hatch in order of deployment."

Cajun was the first in line, along with the heavy pack containing their deflated rubber raft. Old Dog and Warlock followed, with Traveler bringing up the rear.

"Are you sure you don't want to change your mind and come along with us, honey?" Traveler asked the jumpmaster. "There's plenty of room for five in our raft."

The jumpmaster shook her head and grinned. "No thanks, sailor. I get seasick, even in the bathtub!"

The yellow light was replaced by a blinking green one, and the jumpmaster spoke to the rest of the team while addressing the instruments on her console.

"We've got a go for deployment at eighteen thousand

98

feet. Please hold onto the static line while the hatch opens."

As instructed, the SEALs reached up and grabbed the sturdy, woven steel cable that extended the length of the cabin. Because of their present altitude, which was the highest one at which a jump could be made without oxygen, they planned a two-minute free fall before opening their square, ram-air inflated chutes manually.

The whine of the Combat Talon's turboprops increased to an almost deafening intensity as the hatch slowly opened. A gust of chilling night wind swept inside, while outside a curtain of pitch blackness hauntingly beckoned.

"We're just about there," advised the jumpmaster, who had to practically scream out to be heard. "Have a safe jump, and I hope to see all of you again real soon."

The light turned a solid green, and she forcefully added. "Go for it!"

Cajun kicked out the life raft, whose chute would be triggered automatically by barometric pressure, and then leaped out of the hatch himself. Old Dog and Warlock followed close behind, with Traveler taking a second to flash the jumpmaster a teasing wink before joining his associates.

The first thing Traveler was aware of as he attained a stable spread position with a strong back arch was the sudden silence. Because of the pitch-black night sky, he had little sense of acceleration except for the force of the strong wind blowing up from below.

It took him ten seconds to attain his terminal velocity of approximately 120 miles per hour. Balanced precariously now on a huge ball of air that allowed him to escape the conscious pull of gravity, Traveler did his best to relax and pull his hands and feet in closer to his body. Though he could easily go into a spin, backloop, or barrel roll at this point, he kept himself as level as possible to prevent an unnecessary collision with one of his blackness-veiled teammates.

Quick glances at his chest-mounted altimeter and stop watch showed that he still had over a minute of free fall to go. This was fine with Traveler, who enjoyed sky diving whether it took place during the day or night. Free fall was especially thrilling. The mere thought of plummeting through the air at 174 feet per second cleared his mind and gave him a high more powerful than drugs or alcohol, one almost as intense as sex.

He had made his first jump back in Missouri, at the age of sixteen. His instructor was a former Army Ranger, who'd made him complete a dozen static line jumps before allowing him his first short free fall. Less than a month later, Traveler had progressed to a thirty-second delay, and could even do a variety of midair hand, foot, leg, and body turns.

Parachuting was one of the primary reasons he'd joined the Navy and volunteered for the SEAL program. The SEALs equipment was the best made, and he especially enjoyed jumping with one of the square, ram-air inflated canopies that allowed for pinpoint accuracy and an incredibly gentle landing.

A loud, pulsating tone began emanating from the audible altimeter he wore strapped to his chest. This was all the warning he needed to check his stopwatch and then count off ten seconds before pulling the rip cord.

Traveler looked up expectantly when his chute finally deployed. The darkness limited his vision, yet he instantly knew that something was not right. For some reason or other, his canopy had failed to properly inflate. He vigorously shook the risers, and when the chute still didn't clear, he had no choice but to cut away the main chute and open the reserve.

It took him eleven more long seconds to activate the calipers and cut away the twisted main canopy. By this time, the audible altimeter was emitting a nerve-racking constant tone, which indicated that he was well under 2,500 feet, and would all too soon run out of open sky.

Traveler never had the time to panic. Instead he focused his concentration on yanking free the reserve chute and making absolutely certain that it deployed properly.

The opening shock of the inflating canopy bounced him upward like a puppet on a string. He looked up, and the blossoming chute greeted him like a long-lost lover. Only then did he check his altimeter and note that all of this had taken place a mere 1,200 feet above sea level.

While Traveler began carefully freeing himself from his harness to prepare for splashdown, his three teammates were already swimming for the flashing white strobe that indicated the position of their raft. Cajun was the first to reach it. As he began the time-consuming task of cutting free the raft's parachute harness, Warlock arrived and triggered the vessel's compressed air-inflation device. Both SEALs were in the process of climbing into the now-inflated raft when Old Dog made his presence known with a loud splash and a fit of steady coughing.

"Hey, Old Dog, quit swallowin' up all the ocean and leave some water for the fish!" Cajun suggested as he positioned himself in the raft's bow.

As Warlock climbed aboard, Old Dog made his appearance beside the raft in a frothing white wake of agitated seawater.

"Shut up and give me a hand," he managed to get out between gasps of air.

It took the combined efforts of both Cajun and Warlock to get their hefty associate out of the water.

"Where the hell is Traveler?" Cajun asked as he returned to the bow.

"I hope he didn't stop to make a play for that jumpmaster," remarked Warlock. "If he was only a few seconds late leaving that plane, he could be miles from here."

"I'm just prayin' he's not shark meat," said Old Dog, who was propped up against the side of the raft amidships. "That blue-eyed bastard still owes me fifty bucks."

Several tense minutes followed as they vainly scanned the surrounding waters for any sign of their teammate. The sea itself was calm, with only an occasional gentle swell slapping up against the side of the raft. The air temperature was in the midseventies, while a myriad of stars shone forth from the crystal clear heavens.

From his position in the stern beside the flashing strobe, Warlock did his best to stand so he could increase his line of sight.

"Cajun, would you check the pack and see if there's a whistle in there?" the MIT grad asked. "Sound will travel a hell of a lot farther than this light will."

"Will do, Warlock," replied Cajun as he bent over to rummage through the supply pack. Seconds later, he pulled out what appeared to be a large revolver. "It's no whistle, but will a flare gun do?"

"Hold it, you guys," interrupted Old Dog. "I think I hear somethin'."

A barely audible splashing sound emanated from the distance, and Warlock spoke out firmly. "Pop out a flare, Cajun!"

Cajun pointed the revolver overhead, pulled the trigger, and a blindingly bright orange ball shot up into the heavens.

"Hey, Traveler, over here!" shouted Old Dog, in a booming, deep voice that could have waked the dead.

But it was Cajun who spotted the lone figure swimming toward them with a smooth Australian crawl.

"Hey Traveler, where ya' been?" shouted Old Dog.

Traveler reached the raft and calmly lifted himself onto the gunwales saying, "Thanks, ladies, for not starting the party without me."

Old Dog lifted him the rest of the way out of the water as though he were merely a wet rag. Meanwhile, after replacing the flare gun, Cajun pulled a long coil of rubber-coated wire out of the supply pack. He curiously examined a sealed, fist-sized plastic box that was attached to one end of it.

"What do you make of this gizmo, Warlock?" he asked.

Warlock seemed genuinely interested in the device and reached over to take it out of Cajun's hands.

"Well, I'll be," he muttered as he studied it more closely.

He activated a switch on the side of the box, and it began transmitting a piercingly loud, high-pitched beeping sound. Without a second thought, he then tossed the box overboard, being extra careful to tie the loose end of the coil onto the side of the raft.

"What's it for, Warlock?" quizzed Cajun.

"Maybe it's to keep the sharks away," offered Old Dog.

Traveler grinned. "Knowing the Navy, it's probably designed to draw the sharks right to us."

"It's not sharks it's calling," said Warlock, "but fish of a much more lethal nature. You see, this is the latest bait for catching submarines."

A pained expression crossed Old Dog's face as he figured out the nature of their next mode of transportation. "Shit, so that's what this whole thing's about. I should have known they weren't going to drop us off in the middle of nowhere just for our health. Pigboats make me nervous. After all, us Texans like wide open spaces."

"Well you certainly got plenty of that, partner," shot

103

back Traveler. "Right up in that skull of yours."

"Fuck you, Trav!" cursed Old Dog. "I should have left you in the drink and let Jaws finish you."

"But you didn't, did you?" returned Traveler. "That fifty I owe you is the greatest life-insurance policy a guy could ever have."

"Hey, over there!" interrupted Cajun. "I think we've got us a bite!"

The team followed the direction of Cajun's finger and watched in amazement as a periscope broke the water's surface, less than ten yards from their bow. Its appearance was accompanied by a frothing white swath of bubbling ballast as the USS *Hawkbill* rose up from the depths like a monstrous behemoth.

"Now don't forget to mind your manners, ladies," Traveler advised facetiously. "We're about to mix with the real US Navy!"

Eight

The view from the passenger seat of the jeep was a breathtaking one. For the past half-hour, Dr. Miriam Kromer had been content to sit back and soak in the magnificence of Okinawa's rugged northern mountains. Her distinguished chauffer, Vice Admiral Henry Walker, was a safe, courteous driver, who handled the twisting, narrow roadway like an expert.

They had left Naha just as dawn was breaking and had headed due north. Once they'd passed Kadena Air Base, the traffic was at a minimum, and for the most part, they'd had the whole road to themselves.

"That peak up ahead is Yonaha mountain," instructed the Director of Naval Intelligence, as he downshifted the jeep to assist it in rounding a steep curve. "At one thousand six hundred and fifty feet, it's the island's highest elevation."

Dr. Kromer spotted this rounded peak through the thick forest of pine trees that hugged the road. "I never realized Okinawa was so hilly," she lightly commented. "I thought it would be much more tropical, filled with nothing but jungle and rice fields."

"Only about twenty out of every one hundred acres of land here are suitable for crops," replied Walker. "And as for those rice fields, until America constructed a series of dams in these hills after World War II, the principal crops here were sweet potatoes, sugar cane, and garden vegetables."

Kromer absorbed this information while the jeep began to make its way up a steep incline. The vehicle momentarily coughed and sputtered, and it took Henry Walker several tries to find the proper gear for climbing.

"I'm afraid my driving's a little rusty," apologized the silver-haired flag officer.

"You're doing just fine," returned the toxicologist. "I must admit, it sure is a welcome change of pace to be traveling by car. I've had my fill of helicopters, carriers, and airplanes."

The jeep reached the top of the rise and Walker shifted into third gear to begin a long stretch of fairly flat, windy roadway.

"I want to thank you again for agreeing to join our team, Dr. Kromer. This is certainly above and beyond the call of duty on your part."

The redhead looked to her left and smiled. "To tell you the truth, Admiral, next to working in the lab, I enjoy being out in the field. Office work stifles me."

"Tell me about it, Doc," replied Walker with an introspective grin. "I've sailed nothing but a desk for too many years now. And by the way, I had a chance to read up on you a bit. I believe I know your father. Is he the Dr. Charles Kromer who was chief of staff at Bethesda Naval Hospital back in the seventies?"

Kromer nodded. "That's him, all right. Dad officially retired five years ago, though he still sees patients three days a week at a Washington, D.C., low-income clinic."

"Well he did a hell of a fine job at Bethesda, and I'm certain he'd be very proud of his daughter right now if he knew what you were taking on."

This sincere compliment hit home, and Kromer was momentarily lost in thought before replying.

"It was because of my father's involvement with

106

treating Viet Nam veterans exposed to Agent Orange, that I became interested in my current line of work. He was one of the first to speak out on the dangers of biological and chemical warfare, and I know this operation to destroy the anthrax lab would gain his full support."

The jeep entered a broad, steeply banked curve that opened up to a short stretch of narrow asphalt pavement. A closed, chain-link security fence blocked the road here, and Walker was forced to hit the brakes and shift the jeep into neutral. No sooner did the vehicle come to a complete halt than a fully armed Marine wearing camouflaged fatigues materialized out of the woods and approached them.

"Good morning," the sentry said in a no-nonsense tone. "May I see your ID's?"

Both of the jeep's passengers handed over the heavy plastic identification cards that had been issued to them back in Naha. The Marine studiously scrutinized the stamp-sized photograph that graced each one before handing them back and saluting.

"Welcome to Alpha Base, Admiral Walker, Dr. Kromer. We've been expecting you. Please drive carefully, and don't forget to keep your headlights on bright."

With this enigmatic greeting, the sentry stepped aside and hit a remote-control switch that caused the gate to swing open.

Henry Walker put the jeep into gear, and as they began moving forward once again, his passenger noticed that the roadway they were now following stretched barely twenty yards before abruptly ending at the solid rock face of a mountain. Walker showed no signs of braking, and Miriam Kromer was quick to voice her concern.

"Uh, Admiral, I think you're about to run out of pavement up ahead."

Strangely enough, this observation generated only a

sly smile as Walker continued driving straight toward the wall of rock. As it turned out, Miriam Kromer was spared further distress when that portion of the mountain situated directly in front of the road began rolling upward and a tunnel was exposed. The jeep drove right into this abyss that was lit by an occasional overhead lamp.

"You're just full of surprises, aren't you, Admiral?" Miriam managed to say between relieved breaths.

"Just wait," returned Walker eagerly. "You haven't seen anything yet."

The dimly lit tunnel was obviously conveying them deep into the mountain's core, and Henry Walker's words echoed in the dark void.

"This facility was originally designed by the Japanese for use during World War II. The war was over before it was fully operational, and that's when we took it over."

A series of flickering lights beckoned invitingly up ahead, and all too soon the narrow tunnel opened up into a huge, brightly lit cavern that had been literally hollowed out of the mountain's base. The road sloped downward here, and Walker momentarily stopped the jeep so that his passenger could take in the amazing vista before her.

It proved to be the blindingly bright sparks of a welder's torch that drew Miriam's glance to the cavern's floor. Here an immense dry dock was situated, a 250-foot-long, silver-skinned submarine perched securely inside it. Dozens of metal workers wearing hard hats were gathered around this vessel's v-shaped hull, on which the visible damage was mainly confined to the bow.

As she caught sight of the adjoining two-sided pier, and the channel of water that disappeared into yet another dark tunnel, the toxicologist struggled to find the words to express herself.

"So this is Alpha Base. Why it's simply amazing!"

"We're extremely fortunate that this facility was available," replied Henry Walker. "Security in this operation is a number one consideration, and by staffing Alpha with US Navy personnel exclusively, we can, hopefully, keep the lid on our little secret."

He carefully put the jeep into gear and slowly drove them down to the floor of the cavern. Here they parked, exited the vehicle, and began making their way on foot to the dry dock.

"Is this facility used often?" Miriam asked. She couldn't seem to take her eyes off the approaching submarine.

Walker was quick with an answer. "Would you believe that this is a first. Alpha is what we call a Doomsday facility. It's designed to be utilized by our submarines for refit and repair in the event of a global nuclear war."

As they began climbing up the gangway that led to the sub, two gray-haired civilians could be seen standing on its exposed sail. One of them let out a piercing whistle, while the other shouted out in warm greeting.

"Good morning, Henry. What took you so long?"

The Director of Naval Intelligence stopped dead in his tracks, looked up at the source of this query, and answered while shaking his head in astonishment. "Bill Brown, Pete Frystak, why you old water rats! I wasn't expecting you until later this afternoon."

"And here I thought they called you director of intelligence," Brown responded with a teasing wink. "See you in the wardroom, Henry."

The two civilians disappeared off the sail, and Walker explained who they were while escorting Dr. Kromer toward the sub's forward hatch.

"I served with Bill Brown back in nineteen fifty-eight, when I was his executive officer aboard the USS *Cubera*. He's a hell of a guy, and almost as good a submariner as Pete Frystak, who was our weapons officer. Pete could fix everything aboard that pigboat but a broken heart."

A grease-covered sailor emerged from the deck hatch that they were about to transit, and Henry Walker took a moment to address him.

"How does she look down there, Chief?"

The mustached petty officer replied while utilizing a handkerchief to wipe grease off his forehead. "I'm afraid it's not a pretty sight, Admiral, especially in the forward torpedo room."

"In your opinion, will we be able to meet our repair schedule?" added Walker.

"Just keep the manpower and supplies flowing and we'll certainly give it our best shot, sir," returned the petty officer directly.

"I hear you, Chief," replied Walker. "Thanks for your time."

They traded salutes, and as the chief went on with his business, Henry Walker looked over to readdress his redheaded guest.

"Have you ever been inside a submarine before, Doc?"

"Does Disneyland count?" asked Kromer in all seriousness.

"Well, no matter," returned Walker. "Just follow me and take your time. It's a bit tight at first, but you'll get used to it eventually."

The heavy scent of machine oil flavored the air as Kromer began to make her way down a steep ladder. The hatch was barely wide enough to accommodate her shoulders, and it was with great relief that she finally dropped down onto the deck below. This put her in a cramped passageway, and it proved to be her alert escort who alleviated her fear of more such descents.

"This submarine is a Romeo-class vessel. It was origi-

110

nally designed by the Soviet Navy. It has only one usable interior deck, with the batteries stored below. So you can relax. This is the extent of our climb."

Walker pointed down the forward passageway, where the intense spark of a welder's torch glowed in the distance.

"That's the way to the bow torpedo tubes. We're going to proceed the other way which is aft, past the control room and into the living spaces."

They began transitting a pipe-lined passageway that was amazingly narrow, and Kromer vented her curiosity. "Admiral, if this submarine is of Soviet design, then how do you know her layout so well."

"Good question, Doc," said Walker without breaking stride. "You see, I toured one in New London once before. And the guy who piloted that particular Romeo to the beautiful shores of Connecticut is waiting for us just up ahead."

Not certain what he was talking about, Kromer followed him into the largest compartment yet encountered. There was an amazing amount of machinery packed into this relatively small space. The low ceiling was covered with valves and snaking pipes, while the bulkheads were lined with a variety of old-fashioned, bulky consoles, with not a single computer keyboard or digital readout in evidence.

"It's a bit outdated, but this is the control room," the vice admiral informed her. "This compartment is the nerve center of the boat."

He pointed toward the forward bulkhead, where two leather-upholstered, deck-mounted chairs with seat belts attached to them faced a pair of airplanelike steering wheels and a wall of dials and gauges with Japanese labels.

"That's where the planesmen sit," he added. "By controlling the hydroplanes and the rudder, they can turn the sub and determine its depth."

Walker next referred her to an adjoining console that had dozens of small toggle switches and red and green glass bulbs on it.

"And that's the diving console, Doc. It doesn't take much imagination to figure out why we used to call it the Christmas tree. By flicking those switches, the diving officer can influence the buoyancy of the sub and cause it to dive by venting off the air entrapped in the boat's ballast tanks. As these tanks fill with seawater, the boat loses its positive buoyancy and sinks beneath the surface."

"And if you want to surface?" questioned Kromer.

"Then the procedure is reversed, and the vent valves are shut, while compressed air is released into the tanks, expelling the seawater and sending the boat topside once more."

"Is this same system used in today's US submarines?" asked the toxicologist, who was amazed with how simple it all sounded.

Walker answered while guiding her past the control room's other consoles as they continued heading aft.

"The basic principle is similar, but the equipment in our nuke boats is several generations more advanced than what you're seeing around you. In fact, that diving console back there doesn't look much different than the one I learned to operate back in the nineteen fifties."

He quickly pointed out the stations belonging to radar, sonar, and fire control, and showed her where the periscope was stored. They ducked through another hatch, and entered a passageway lined with several curtained compartments. Kromer didn't want to miss a thing, and she pushed aside one of the curtains and peeked inside. A cramped stateroom, about the size of her closet back home, met her eyes. Completely filling it was a narrow, three-tiered bunk, with the mattresses barely a foot apart from each other.

"How in the world do you turn over?" quizzed the puzzled scientist.

"You don't," answered Walker, who also peeked around the curtain.

"It sure doesn't look very comfortable," continued Kromer.

"And this is officer's country, Doc. Wait until you see where the enlisted men bunk. Compared to their quarters, this is the lap of luxury."

Kromer looked glum as she joined Walker back in the passageway. Quick to pick up on her sudden mood change, the senior officer did his best to lighten her spirits.

"You're not having second thoughts, are you, Doc? Believe me, you have nothing to worry about. This old rust bucket's guaranteed to have a private cabin for the captain's use, and that's where we plan to stow you. Hey, cheer up. I smell fresh coffee perking!"

Another hatch led them to the wardroom. This compact, wood-lined compartment was dominated by an elongated table, where the two gray-haired civilians they had seen outside were seated, contentedly drinking coffee.

"I should have known we'd find you guys hogging the joe," greeted Walker.

Bill Brown stood and warmly embraced the flag officer.

"Damn, but it's good to see you again, Henry. What's it been, three years now since I've seen that ugly mug of yours?"

Walker attempted some quick mental arithmetic before responding. "Has it really been that long, Bill?"

"It certainly has, Henry," Brown replied. "That's when you did us the honor of attending the last annual *Cubera* reunion. Of course, I see you've had a little change of rank and job description since then. We're all damn proud of you, Henry."

"I'll second that, Admiral," said Pete Frystak as he stood and offered the flag officer a hearty handshake.

"Why, thank you, Pete," returned Walker. "You're certainly looking as fit as ever. The resort business appears to have been good to you."

"It's a lot of work, but Kath and I love it down there in the Keys."

"And how is your lovely bride?" asked Walker.

Pete Frystak shrugged his shoulders. "What can I say? Kath's as headstrong and stubborn as ever. Yet after thirty-five years of marriage, I still wake up every morning knowing I'm the luckiest guy in the world to have her by my side."

A fond grin turned the corners of Walker's mouth. "I'll never forget the day you two were hitched. You know, I can't say I've been to a wedding on a submarine since."

Suddenly remembering his own guest, Walker turned to beckon forth Miriam Kromer.

"I'm sorry, Doc. Let me do the honor of introducing Bill Brown and Pete Frystak, two of the finest sailors I've ever had the privilege of serving with. Gentlemen, this is Dr. Miriam Kromer."

They traded handshakes, and Kromer instantly liked this group of handsome, silver-haired veterans. They reminded her of her father and of his warm-hearted friends on the hospital staff back in Washington, D.C.

"Gee, Henry," deadpanned Bill Brown. "I didn't realize we were going to have to take a physical for this job."

"I'm not a physician, Mr. Brown," she said. "I'm a toxicologist, based at Ft. Detrick, Maryland."

"A what?" quizzed Pete Frystak.

Henry Walker was quick to intercede at this point. "We'll be explaining all that during this afternoon's briefing, once everyone has arrived. And speaking of the devil, how in the hell did you guys beat us here?"

"That MAC flight you put us on out of Homestead was able to leave earlier than originally scheduled," explained Bill Brown. "Headwinds were at a minimum, and here we are."

"I'm still thanking my lucky stars that both of you were available," said Henry Walker. "By the way, what do you think of Alpha Base?"

"It's absolutely incredible," Pete Frystak responded. "Why I've never seen anything quite like it before."

"At least now I finally know where all of our tax dollars are disappearing to," added Bill Brown.

"As I was explaining to the doc here," said Walker. "Most of this facility was completed at the expense of the Japanese. It was scheduled to come on-line in the fall of nineteen forty-five, and by that time it was ours."

A young sailor entered the wardroom, carrying a large thermos and two mugs.

"I've got some more hot coffee here," he said uneasily. "I'm afraid the galley is for the most part still inoperable, though I could throw together some cold sandwiches if you'd like."

"The coffee will do for now, sailor." Henry Walker beckoned his associates to sit down.

As the orderly exited, Walker filled the two mugs and handed one to the toxicologist. He took a sip before continuing.

"Have you gotten a chance to see much of this Romeo yet, Bill?"

Brown looked up from his mug and answered. "We were just finishing up a preliminary walk-through when you two arrived."

Walker intently searched his old shipmate's eyes. "What do you think, Bill, can we sail her again?"

Brown's serious gaze didn't flinch. "I don't see why

115

not. Though a lot depends on the condition of her diesels and batteries."

"Too bad we don't have the expert services of Stanley Roth," said Pete Frystak. "He'd be able to size up the state of that engine room soon enough."

Henry Walker couldn't help but smile. "What would you say if I told you that Master Chief Stanley Roth was on his way to Alpha Base from New London, Connecticut, even as we speak?"

"That's wonderful news," observed Bill Brown. "Stanley knows the engine room of a Romeo better than any American alive today. He'll get this pigboat up and running if he has to complete a full overhaul all by himself."

"That's all well and fine, Skipper," interrupted Pete Frystak. "But speaking as your former weapons officer, this boat's going nowhere until that forward torpedo room is squared away. There's still a hell of a lot of work up there before that compartment's shipshape."

"I understand that, Pete," returned Brown. "Yet overall, for a Soviet-designed submarine built for export by the People's Republic of China, I'd say she doesn't look all that bad. Especially after that little collision she was involved in. What did she hit anyway?"

Henry Walker took a long sip of coffee and scanned the faces of his audience while he replied. "This little lady tangled with a reef off the coast of Kadena Air Force Base and lost. Over two-thirds of her fifty-man crew died from injuries sustained as a result of the initial collision. Most of them suffocated to death, when chlorine gas was released out of the battery well."

"You never did say who she belongs to, or what they were doing off Kadena," astutely observed Bill Brown.

Walker once more took a moment to study the faces of his audience before responding. "I was going to cover all of that during this afternoon's briefing, once the entire team has arrived. But here it is in a nutshell. This vessel's name is *Bokken*. It belongs to Ishii Industries, a privately owned conglomerate based on Takara Island in the Ryukyu chain. We have gathered solid evidence which proves that the *Bokken* was being utilized to smuggle deadly biological toxins into Kadena, with the purpose of releasing them into the air downwind of the SAC base. We have further proof that this attack was not to be an isolated one, but that a subsequent biological release would take place at our naval facility at Sasebo in a week's time."

"I hate to show my ignorance once again," interrupted Pete Frystak, "but what exactly is a biological toxin?"

Walker looked over at Miriam Kromer, who expertly answered this question.

"Put simply," she explained, "it's a disease, that in this instance has been made in a laboratory for the express purpose of killing human beings."

"And I suppose this lab just happens to be on Takara Island," continued Bill Brown. "And that the *Bokken* will have something to do with removing it from the face of the earth."

Walker solemnly nodded that the veteran was correct and went on to add, "In a week's time, I hope to use the *Bokken* to penetrate the bay on which this lab is situated and then land a SEAL team to destroy it. Dr. Kromer has graciously consented to accompany the SEALs and ensure that their explosives eliminate the entire installation."

"Wouldn't it be a lot easier to use one of our own subs for this purpose?" asked Pete Frystak.

Henry Walker took a sip of coffee and then answered the retired weapons officer. "That's been seriously considered, Pete. And I wish we could. Unfortunately, the bay we've been tasked to penetrate is filled with hydrophones and CAPTOR mines. As you may very well know, the CAPTOR is one of the new SMART weapons that are programmed to allow friendly vessels to pass without harm, but they explode beneath those that don't belong. They do so by analyzing the sound signature of the approaching ship.

"Since the *Bokken* is homeported in this same bay, and because the bastards at Ishii Industries still don't know we have her, we should have a clean shot coming in. Though going out could be another story."

Bill Brown had one more concern to voice. "And just who do you plan to get from today's nuclear Navy to drive the *Bokken*, Henry? You know as well as I that we lost our last qualified diesel-electric crew back in the fall of nineteen ninety, when they retired the *Blueback*."

The Director of Naval Intelligence sat forward and got right to the point. "I'm pulling fifty of the brightest submariners in the entire US Navy off the USS *Hawkbill*, a Sturgeon-class attack sub that has been operating in the vicinity. In fact, they should be arriving here any minute now, along with that team of SEALs. I'm relying on you to teach these youngsters all you know about the Romeo-class — and the operation of a diesel-electric."

Henry Walker stood for added emphasis. "I know it's not going to be an easy job for any of you. The crew of the *Hawkbill* comes from a new, improved navy. They're nukes, weaned on computers and other new-fangled high-tech gear, that wasn't even on the drawing boards when we were their age.

"Yet I can assure you, you'll never meet a more intelligent, receptive, inquisitive bunch of sailors as those lads. And they're going to be relying on you to teach them the intricacies of this boat, and more importantly, how to operate a submarine the old-fashioned way, with sweat, brains, and guts!"

Nine

Captain Satsugai Okura was not only a veteran submariner, but an accomplished pilot as well. He'd learned to fly at the Eta Jima Naval Academy as a junior ensign. His instructor had said he was a natural, and he'd been considering a career in aviation when he went to sea in a submarine for the first time. From that moment on, however, there was no doubt in his mind that the life of an undersea warrior was for him.

One of the benefits of his current job was that his employer allowed him to command a submarine and fly the company plane whenever time allowed. And what an amazing, historic aircraft this was!

Dr. Ishii, who was also an avid flyer, had purchased the Model-21 Zero fighter shortly after the war's conclusion. It had been built by Mitsubishi in 1943, and was in mint condition. The twenty-three-foot-long, all metal, low-wing monoplane had a clean, smooth exterior, and weighed less than 5,500 pounds. Captain Okura knew very well that it was this incredibly light weight, combined with a powerful fourteen-cylinder, 950-horsepower Nakajima Sakae engine, that had made the Zero the most agile of all World War II fighter planes.

Okura's current flight had begun when he'd taken off from the Takara Island airfield shortly after breakfast. This was not to be just an ordinary pleasure flight, and he'd turned the Zero on a southerly heading at an altitude of 15,000 feet. It took him a little less than an hour to complete the two-hundred-and-ten-mile flight to Okinawa.

A storm front had recently moved through the area, and Okura was forced to descend to 5,000 feet to get below the cloud deck. The air at that altitude was a bit unstable, yet the legendary fighter handled like a dream as Okura passed over the rugged northern portion of the island, and continued on toward its major population centers that lay farther south.

Back in 1944, over a thousand Japanese Zeros had flown over this same island, in the greatest kamikaze attack of all time. Twenty-six American ships were lost during this engagement, with another one hundred and sixty-four seriously damaged.

Okura wondered what it would have been like to participate in such an endeavor. The kamikaze, or divine wind, embodied all that was noble and brave. To put one's life on the line for the sake of the Emperor was the ultimate test of loyalty, and Okura was invigorated by the mere thought of thousands of brave young pilots diving to their deaths, in defense of Imperial Nippon.

Except for the fact that his plane carried no armaments and had its wing and fuselage insignia covered, Okura's Zero could very easily have participated in this same attack. Yet almost half a century had passed since the divine winds last blew. During this span of time, Japan had been forced to accept a humiliating, unconditional surrender, and to face the indignity of a long, Western occupation. Such a thought sickened Okura, who wondered what the thousands of brave kamikaze pilots would think of this horrifying outcome.

But Dr. Ishii's Black Dragon Society existed to make certain they hadn't died in vain. Its ultimate goal was the removal of the foreign occupiers from Japan's holy soil and the reascension of the Emperor to his rightful place as supreme leader of the Japanese people.

Proud to be a part of this movement, Okura made certain to steer well clear of Kadena Air Base. To escape the American radar screens, he put the Zero into a steep dive, and followed a lush green valley at near treetop level all the way to the outskirts of Naha.

The capital city was his ultimate goal, and he gained a couple of hundred feet of altitude at this point before circling it. It was now time for the next portion of his flight plan to begin, so Okura slid back the plexiglass canopy and readied his camera.

A chill blast of air entered the open cockpit, only to be countered by the fleece-lined, leather bomber jacket and soft helmet that he wore. Okura smiled upon sighting a large white ship docked in the distance. With this goal in mind, he turned the Zero toward Naha harbor and reached down to snap on the camera's telephoto lens.

Dr. Yukio Ishii spent his morning working in one of the seven Biohazard Level Four laboratories that occupied a separate building at his Takara facility. This lab was specially designed so that any substance handled in it could not be accidentally released into the outside environment. A large shatter-proof, triple-paned window looked out onto a well-lit, white-tiled corridor, along which the other labs were situated. Every possible precaution had been taken to insure the safety of Ishii and his staff in this portion of the complex, including a variety of highly enforced sanitary procedures, an extremely powerful ventilation system, dozens of ceiling-mounted emergency shower heads, and the required wearing of a self-sustaining biohazard-containment suit. Made of a lightweight, puncture-proof plastic compound, this head-to-toe suit was similar to those worn by the astronauts. It included a fully enclosed helmet, and was ventilated by means of an oxygen tether.

Dr. Ishii was decked out in such an outfit as he diligently worked on setting up an all-important experiment designed to determine the potency of the latest batch of anthrax toxin. His assistant was Yoko Noguchi, the newest member of his staff. Attaining the services of this talented twenty-six-year-old toxicologist had been something of a coup for Ishii. After graduating number one in her class at Tokyo University, she could have chosen to work for any number of prestigious institutions. Much to Ishii's delight, she'd chosen his, arriving on Takara only three days ago.

A glass cage holding a large rat had been set up in the center of the lab. Several plastic ventilation tubes connected it to an adjoining air compressor. It was immediately beside this compact device that Ishii and his assistant were huddled.

"Prepare for strain introduction, Miss Noguchi," Ishii advised somewhat impatiently. "I'm anxious to see if this new preparation process is an effective one."

Yoko Noguchi carefully picked up a partially filled test tube with a gloved hand and poured its clear contents into the mouth of the glass beaker that was mounted on top of the compressor. Her hand was trembling slightly as she opened the valve positioned beside the beaker and watched the liquid disappear into the machinery below.

"Good," said Ishii, whose own gloved hand went to the compressor's power switch. Before turning it on, he added. "This minute sample has been diluted in such a way that only a tiny fraction of the anthrax will be inhaled. Yet because of our new process, it should be just as powerful as our old method, which required increased amounts of the actual toxin to be utilized. Now we shall see if it works as well in practice as in theory."

Ishii switched on the power switch, and the compressor activated with a muted hum. All eyes went to the glass cage, where the rat curiously sniffed the current of just introduced, tainted air. After a single breath, the rodent's lungs suddenly seemed to freeze. The bulging-eyed creature vainly attempted one more frantic inhalation before being caught in a fit of violent shaking. A second later, it was dead.

A satisfied grin turned up the corners of Ishii's mustached mouth as he caught the serious glance of his research assistant.

"So, Miss Noguchi. It appears that science has triumphed one more time."

"That it has," replied the soft-spoken toxicologist. "Please excuse my boldness, sir. But may I ask why such an enhanced strain is needed? Surely nature's very own strain of anthrax can kill just as effectively."

Ishii answered cautiously. "As explained during your initial orientation, an all-purpose vaccine for diseases such as anthrax must be tested against the most virulent form of the organism in existence before it can be deemed a success."

"But surely we would never encounter such a genet-

123

ically mutated strain in the outside world," countered the young scientist.

"Can you honestly say that with all certainty, Miss Noguchi?" replied Ishii.

A steady thumping noise diverted his attention to the display window that fronted the lab. Knocking on the triple-paned glass was a man decked out in a leather bomber jacket. Ishii was quick to identify him as Satsugai Okura. The veteran mariner held a large envelope in his free hand, and his expression told Ishii that he had important news.

"Excuse me, Miss Noguchi," Ishii said with a polite bow. "But it appears that I'm needed elsewhere at the moment. You may get on with the autopsy. And please, let's continue our discussion over tea later. Your views are most interesting, and since you are now a part of our family, I have many of my own ideas to share with you."

Ishii bowed again, before turning and exiting the lab by way of a sealed hatch in the side wall. This led him directly into an adjoining dressing room. Only after stripping off his containment suit and replacing it with a white martial-arts robe did he continue on through yet another sealed hatch and then into a nearby office, where Okura was waiting for him.

"Whatever is so urgent, Satsugai?" Ishii asked lightly. "We were just testing the latest batch of genetically altered anthrax toxin, and the initial results are most promising. This new strain appears to have three times the potency of the old one."

Okura found it difficult to hold back his excitement. "That's very good to hear, Sensei. But wait until you see the results of my just concluded aerial reconnaissance of Naha. It's everything that we hoped for and more!"

Okura opened the envelope he had been carrying and pulled out several large black and white photographs. Ishii led the way over to the room's sole desk, reached for his bifocals, and snapped on a halogen lamp. He then took the photos and began to examine them.

The first print showed an immense white ship with a bright red cross painted on its hull. It was tied to the pier of a crowded dock, and Okura was quick to identify it.

"That's the US Navy hospital ship, *Mercy.* It arrived sometime late last night. Note all the ambulances parked beside it."

Ishii went on to the next photo. It showed an aerial view of a solidly built, four-story brick building surrounded by a packed parking lot. Again it was Okura who provided the commentary.

"What you're looking at now is Naha General Hospital. Once more, note all the ambulances lined up in front of its entrance. Why it appears that every emergency vehicle on Okinawa is in use."

Ishii grunted and examined the print that followed. This was a street scene, taken from an altitude of barely a thousand feet. The narrow, twisting thoroughfare was conspicuously empty, except for a group of individuals dressed in what appeared to be hooded, biological-containment suits complete with oxygen tanks on their backs.

"This shot was taken as close as I dared fly to the entrance of the SAC base. It should be noted that all of the streets in this area were similarly vacant, while on those closer to the heart of Naha, it was business as usual."

Ishii heavily responded. "So Satsugai, it indeed appears as if Captain Sato and the crew of the *Bokken* have succeeded with the first half of their mission."

"Sensei," returned Okura guardedly, "strangely enough, my monitoring of Kadena's main radio station made no mention of our attack."

"What's so strange about that, Satsugai?" replied Ishii as he handed back the photos. "This isn't the kind of tragedy that the proud US military likes made public. You watch, there will be absolutely no mention of this costly incident in their newspapers either. Yet once the scientists at Kadena complete their tests and realize the extent of the contamination present, the Air Force will make up some lame excuse to permanently close the facility. And that will be it for SAC's presence on Okinawa. Now, if only things go this well at Sasebo."

"Hopefully, my overflight of the American Navy base there eight days from now will show similar results," said Okura.

Ishii grinned and shook his head to the contrary. "I'm afraid that's one surveillance flight you won't be making, my friend. You see, I've decided to move up our schedule. One week from tonight, the *Katana* will set sail for Tokyo Bay. Then you will hit the Americans a lethal blow with our latest batch of toxin, eliminating their Yokosuka naval facility and the ring of air and army bases that encircle the capital city. And at long last, Nippon will be free from foreign military occupation!"

Ten

It took Stanley Roth the better part of twenty-four hours to make it to Alpha Base. As it turned out, the most trying part of this long trip was the relatively short drive up from Kadena. It took place in a driving rainstorm, and the narrow, winding road up Okinawa's northern spine was particularly treacherous.

In his entire thirty-four-year naval career, the balding, pot-bellied master chief had never dreamed that a facility like the one he was currently entering had ever existed. The side of a mountain that opened up to reveal the top-secret military facilities within belonged in the world of fiction, not reality. Or so he thought, until the van that had conveyed him from Kadena drove into the dark tunnel and continued on deep into the mountain's interior.

Stanley certainly wasn't prepared for the scene that awaited him when they reached the mountain's hollowed-out core. So astounded was he by it, he had his driver halt a moment at an overlook so he could take in the incredible scope of it all.

At the floor of the immense, brightly lit cavern that now lay before him was a channel of water, leading to a dual-sided pier. Floating on one side of this structure was what appeared to be a Sturgeon-class nuclear-powered attack sub, the majority of its sleek hull still underwater. And beside that, in dry dock, was the familiar profile of yet another submarine. Because this vessel was out of the water, its hull was completely visible. Some fifty feet shorter than that of the warship beside it, this vessel left no doubt in Roth's mind about its class.

"Holy Mother Mary," muttered Stanley as the reality of it all began to sink in. He finally knew why he had been called these thousands of miles to the other side of the world.

His mind was awash in memories as they continued down to the pier, and when he left the van, he wasn't all that surprised to spot three silver-haired figures emerging from the Sturgeon-class sub's aft hatchway, followed by a younger officer in khakis. It was apparent that they hadn't seen Stanley as yet, and the newcomer grinned in anticipation of the reunion that would all too soon be taking place.

He tried to act as nonchalant as possible as he slung his seabag over his shoulder and made his way up the nuclear sub's forward gangway. An alert seaman carrying a combat shotgun checked his name off a list of authorized personnel, and Stanley silently continued aft, toward the group of ex-shipmates he still hoped to take by surprise. Their backs were toward him, and he could actually hear part of their conversation.

"That was a hell of a fine tour, Commander Slaughter," said the velvety voice of Vice Admiral Henry Walker, who'd been Stanley's first XO thirty-five years ago aboard the USS *Cubera*.

"I'll second that," added Pete Frystak, the *Cu-*

bera's ex-weapons officer and for many years Stanley's closest friend.

"And I'm going to take you up on that raincheck for a ride in this little lady, Commander," said a deep voice that could only belong to Bill Brown, the *Cubera*'s skipper and one of the finest men Stanley had ever served under.

Relishing this special moment, Stanley stepped forward as his ex-skipper continued.

"I wonder if your men realize what they're about to get involved in, Commander. The difference between this ship and the Romeo is like day and night."

"I'm sure it's nothin' they can't handle, Skipper," intervened Stanley Roth, who had already sized up the situation and now made the best of his surprise appearance. "I guess we're just going to have to teach them the basics all over again — reintroduce them to the world before computers. I sure hope they don't mind getting their hands dirty."

"Stanley!" exclaimed Pete Frystak as he stepped forward to hug his old buddy.

"I guess we can all breathe easier. Master Chief Roth is — at long last — here," commented Henry Walker with a wide smile. "Now tell me, Roth, who spilled the beans to you about this mission?"

Before answering him, Stanley traded a warm handshake with Bill Brown.

"To tell you the truth, Admiral, it didn't take an officer's commission to figure out what the hell was goin' on here the moment I laid my eyes on this incredible place." Stanley winked. "But it really became obvious when the three of you climbed out of that hatch. I take it that it's nineteen fifty-eight played all over again?"

"You've just about got it right, Stanley," returned Henry Walker, who was noticeably relieved. "For a minute there, I thought that we might have had a slipup in security."

Suddenly remembering their host, Walker looked toward the middled-aged officer in their midst and added. "Commander Slaughter, I'd like you to meet Master Chief Stanley Roth. We're going to be relying on Mr. Roth here to size up the conditions inside our Romeo's engine room and then teach your men the ins and outs of running those Chinese diesels."

"Ah, so she's a Chink," reflected Stanley as he turned his glance back toward the dry dock. "How soon do you plan to get her under way?"

The white-hot spark of a welder's torch flew up from the *Bokken's* still dented, V-shaped bow, as Henry Walker tentatively answered. "How does a week sound to you?"

Stanley's eyes opened wide in astonishment. "A week you say? Just because you're an Admiral doesn't entitle you to ask for miracles, Henry."

Walker's tone softened. "I'm not asking for a miracle, Stanley. Just do me a favor and look over that engine room real good. Whatever you need to get it back in shape, just ask for it and it's yours. And to give you a hand, you've got a group of Commander Slaughter's best and brightest at your service."

"I don't suppose you're going to share with me exactly where it is you're in such a hurry to get to—and why it's got to be on this particular Romeo," questioned Roth.

"You'll be getting a full briefing as soon as you're settled in," promised Henry Walker. "Though I can tell you right now that the voyage we've got in mind should only last fourteen hours each way at the most."

"That sounds a bit more reasonable," replied the portly master chief, who looked at his ex-shipmates and added, "Did Henry talk you two old salts back onto the company payroll for this one?"

"Let's just say that both Pete and myself have decided to volunteer our services as consultants," said Bill Brown diplomatically. "While you're doing your thing in the engine room, we'll be passing on our wisdom to the lads who will be operating the rest of the boat."

"Who knows, perhaps if we behave, Henry might even allow us to go along for the ride," offered a grinning Pete Frystak.

"Things must have gotten awfully dull at that resort of yours, Frystak," teased Roth. "Does Kathy know what you're considering?"

The veteran weapons officer grimaced. "You've got that three-week winter's stay on Big Pine Key you've always wanted in exchange for keeping your trap shut, Stanley."

"That's a deal!" Roth sealed the agreement with a handshake.

"You know," Stanley reflected. "This might not be such bad duty after all. So before I go and get sentimental, I'd better have me a look at those diesels."

"I'll expect that preliminary report from you tonight at eighteen hundred hours," instructed Henry Walker.

"Not only does he want miracles, he's a slave driver as well," playfully muttered the pot-bellied Master Chief as he turned to make his way over to the dry-docked Romeo.

"See you shortly, Stan," said Pete Frystak, who remained alongside Henry Walker, Bill Brown, and Chris Slaughter at the aft hatchway.

"Stanley seems as fiesty as ever," observed Brown.

"The years sure haven't changed him much," Frystak reflected.

"We're lucky to have him aboard," said Walker. "If anyone can pick apart the *Bokken*'s engine room and make it tick, it will be Stanley."

"But can he pass along his knowledge to my men?" asked Slaughter. "When we're out at sea a week from now, they're the ones who are going to have to do the majority of the work in that engine room."

"Relax, Commander," advised Henry Walker. "Chief Roth's last assignment was as senior instructor at the Basic Enlisted Submarine School in New London. The way I hear it, he got his boys so motivated they practically jumped all over themselves to volunteer for duty inside the wet trainer."

"I always said, next to his technical knowledge, Stanley's best quality was his ability to work with other people," said Pete Frystak. "He's the ideal man for this job."

"I've certainly got full confidence in him," added Bill Brown. "I remember those days on the *Cubera*. If Stanley couldn't fix something, you could consider it permanently broken."

The *Hawkbill*'s captain appeared distracted as he looked at his watch and queried, "What's the schedule for the rest of the afternoon?"

Walker momentarily eyed Brown before answering. "After your men get settled aboard the *Bokken*,

I thought they'd take a general tour of the boat. We'll exclude the forward torpedo room, where most of the yard work is being done. Pete, would you mind organizing this tour?"

"Not at all, Henry," replied Frystak.

"Afterward," continued Walker. "I'd like to break down the group into smaller segments and begin concentrating on specialized duties such as diving the boat, operating its sonar, radio, and weapons systems. Even though the distance from Alpha Base to Takara Island is only two hundred miles, I want every aspect of the *Bokken* mastered by sailing time, which remains one week from today."

"My navigator, Lieutenant Laycob, is fluent in Japanese," interrupted Chris Slaughter. "He'll be able to translate the technical gauges and console labels into English."

Henry Walker seemed most pleased with this news. "Excellent, Commander. Get him on it at once. The only way we're going to succeed is by making this a team effort. So please, don't be afraid to share your thoughts and ideas."

This prompted an instant response from Bill Brown. "I think we're going to need a detailed work schedule to gauge the men's daily progress. We should also have a department-by-department list of individual personnel, with a qualification test of some sort to be given before we sail."

"Admiral, do you have any idea how long we'll be at sea?" questioned Chris Slaughter.

"If all goes as planned, three days at most," returned Walker.

"Then, with your permission, I'll have my galley staff transfer over enough foodstuffs to last us at least ten days," suggested the *Hawkbill's* CO.

Walker nodded. "That will be fine, Commander."

"I'd sure like to see some charts of Takara Island and that bay we'll be penetrating," Pete Frystak said.

"We should have something stored below in *Hawkbill's* chart bin," Slaughter responded. "Do you want to have a look?"

Before answering, Frystak instinctively looked to his ex-CO to get permission.

"Go ahead, Pete," said Bill Brown. "There'll be a meeting with the refit people on the *Bokken* at fifteen-thirty. Then I'd like to pull together all the department heads and formulate that training schedule."

"Aye, aye, Skipper. I'll be there." Frystak followed Chris Slaughter back down into the *Hawkbill's* hatch.

This left Henry Walker and Bill Brown alone on deck. A moment of thoughtful silence passed as they both gazed out at the dry-docked Romeo-class submarine.

"We're certainly going to have our work cut out for us," reflected Brown.

"That we will, Bill. But together we've faced some pretty dicey situations and met them head on."

Walker established eye contact with his former commanding officer before continuing. "I realize it's asking an awful lot to want you to just put your life on hold and fly out here."

"Nonsense, Henry. In a way, it's good to be needed, to have a real purpose again. Ever since Mary passed on, all I've had is time and plenty of it. If it wasn't for my sailboat, I don't know what I'd do to keep my sanity. And the *Arcturus* will be waiting for me back in Longboat when this thing's completed."

"Mary was certainly a great gal," said Walker with a sigh. "I'll never forget that surprise luau she threw for your fortieth birthday. Brother, were we socking down the rum that night! And when you put on that grass skirt and began to hula, I thought I was going to bust my gut laughing."

Bill Brown couldn't help but grin at this memory. Yet his happiness soon faded to melancholy. "I miss Mary so damn much, sometimes I think I can't get through another day without her," he admitted, his voice filled with emotion. "My god, Henry, we shared over two-thirds of our lives, though I spent most of that time at sea. I seemed to be perpetually leaving her on some dock with tears in her eyes. But not once did I hear a peep of complaint from her."

"Mary had a special way with the wives of the crew," Henry Walker recalled. "When we were at sea, she always gave a helping hand to the families that needed one. Don't forget, it was Mary who drove my Monica to the hospital when our first child was born. And I can't count the number of times she was over at our house with that blessed tool kit of hers — whenever the plumbing backed up or the fridge gave up the ghost."

"She did enjoy working with those tools." Brown's heavy mood was beginning to lighten. "Do you know, once I even overheard her discussing the proper way to replace a frayed electrical cord with Stanley Roth, during a dependent's cruise aboard the *Cubera?*"

Henry Walker smiled. "She was one in a million, Bill. And you should thank the good Lord for allowing both of you the time you had together. But life moves on. And I'm sure Mary would want you to put her passing behind you. As you very well know, life is too short to waste in mourning what will never be again. Just be thankful for the memories you have, and in that way Mary will never really be that far away from any of us."

A group of young sailors dressed in civvies and carrying seabags emerged onto the *Hawkbill*'s foredeck and began exiting the sub by way of the gangplank. Bill Brown's thoughts changed focus as he noted that these individuals were headed straight for the dry dock.

"So there goes the first of them, Henry. I pray to God they can pull this thing off."

"With you, Pete, and Stanley around, how can we fail?" joked the grinning Director of Naval Intelligence.

"We won't let you down, Henry. Though I hope I can say as much for that toxicologist you introduced us to during the briefing. Assigning her to a SEAL team is like throwing her to the dogs."

Walker's handsome face broke out in a full grin, and he shook his head. "From what I've seen of the good doctor, she's more than capable of taking care of herself. Don't let her frail frame fool you. Dr. Miriam Kromer's a tough one. And in this instance, I'm afraid it's the men of SEAL Team Three who are going to have their hands full."

A narrow, earthen footpath had led them up into the thickly forested slopes of the mountain whose hollowed-out core was the site of Alpha Base.

Miriam Kromer was glad to escape the stuffy confines of the cavern and join the SEALs in what was supposed to be "a mere stretching of the legs."

From the moment they'd left the fenced-in security perimeter, the SEALs had set a blistering pace. This hike was well into its second hour, and it took a total effort on the toxicologist's part to keep up with her four muscular escorts, who had the added handicap of carrying fifty-pound backpacks.

Miriam had always prided herself on her excellent physical state. She swam, rode a bike, and jogged regularly. Twice a week, she even attended aerobics classes. Since she always enjoyed a good hike in the woods, she saw no reason why she couldn't keep up with the SEALs, who'd remained cold and distant ever since Admiral Walker had introduced them to her. It was obvious that it had not been their idea to ask her to join them on this mission, and now they were trying to intimidate her by displaying their physical prowess. If at all possible, Miriam was not going to give them the satisfaction of breaking her.

Their present course took them alongside a dried-out creek bed, its banks lined with lofty pines. The wiry, wavy-haired SEAL nicknamed Cajun led the way, as he had from the start. Second in line, some twenty yards behind, was the serious-faced giant known as Old Dog. Close on the Texan's heels was Warlock. He was the brains of the outfit, and Miriam felt very comfortable with the MIT graduate around. Unfortunately, she couldn't say the same for the blond-haired Romeo who had been incessantly dogging her for the last quarter of an hour. She had met her fair share of guys like Traveler in the past. Blessed with abundant good looks and motivated by

137

overactive hormones, such men were determined to make every female they met fall in love with them. Miriam certainly had no intention of falling for such a heartbreaker, yet no matter how hard she tried to increase her stride to escape his pesterings, the persistent commando was right at her side.

"Just yell, honey, if it's too much for you," advised Traveler as they crossed the creek bed and began climbing up a scrub-filled embankment.

"I'm fine," replied Miriam between breaths. "But I'm glad I usually run at least ten miles a week."

"That's great, hon," returned Traveler with a self-satisfied smirk. "But we do at least that much every morning, and that's before breakfast!"

A series of steep switchbacks led them out of the valley and farther up into the forested slopes. The rain that had accompanied them for the first hour of the hike had dissipated, but the humidity remained, and with the temperature hovering in the mid-eighties, Miriam's fatigues were soon drenched in sweat.

The steeply sloping gradient of the path did not let up, and she could feel the effects of this climb in her thighs and the backs of her legs. She was thirsty, hungry, and out of breath, but determined not to falter.

Trying her best to focus her concentration solely on her leaden stride, she looked up in astonishment as Traveler proceeded to sprint the rest of the way up the incline with apparent ease. True to form, he was waiting for her at the top of the switchback, with a Cheshire-cat grin lighting up his sweat-free face.

"Not bad, hon," he calmly observed, while scrutinizing her body with all the intensity of an anatomy student. "Hey, are you married?"

Barely stopping to catch her breath, Miriam did her best to ignore this irrelevant query, and hurriedly continued up the next switchback. Traveler was not to be denied, and rushed back to her side.

"I take that as a no," he said as he matched her stride step for step. "Then tell me, hon, are you at least shacked up with anyone?"

Again Miriam increased her pace to escape this pest. And once more the persistent SEAL caught up and addressed her.

"Well, another no. Would you like to be shacked up then? I'll tell you, hon, a body like yours shouldn't be wasted."

This comment proved to be the proverbial straw that broke the camel's back, and Miriam halted and vented her anger while looking the commando right in the eye.

"Look, buster, I don't know what your problem is, but could you please give me some space. And quit calling me honey!"

Warlock was sipping from his canteen when he overheard this outburst. He quickly sized up the situation, and backtracked to intervene.

"Come on, Trav. Give the lady a break!" he firmly warned. "She's a special VIP guest, not one of your barfly girl friends."

Traveler calmly replied, "Keep your shirt on, Warlock. I was just testing the waters a bit. There's no harm in that I hope. You guys have no sense of humor." Shaking his head in mock disgust, he added, "See you later, Doc," making a special effort to emphasize this last word.

Traveler continued on up the trail, leaving Warlock behind to defend his honor.

"Don't mind Traveler. He's really quite harmless."

"That type usually is," said Kromer, who had no trouble at all matching Warlock's steady pace.

They reached the top of the switchback, and she gratefully found that this was the extent of their upward climb. The path leveled out now, and they followed it through a forest of stunted oaks.

"How are you doing, Doc?" asked Warlock, his tone showing true concern. "Are we pushing you too hard?"

"I'll survive," said Kromer. "Though I'll certainly sleep well tonight."

Several minutes of contemplative silence followed as they continued on through the oak grove. Strange-sounding birds with deep fluid voices called from the twisted branches that gently swayed in response to a soft breeze.

"You know, I'm impressed that an outsider like yourself has volunteered to tag along with us," Warlock said softly. "But you know, I'm beginning to wonder if your presence is really that necessary."

"Admiral Walker seems to think that it is," snapped the toxicologist.

Warlock sensed her frustration, but pushed on regardless. "I'm not about to go second-guessing an admiral, Doc. But couldn't you just draw us a detailed picture of what that BW lab looks like. It would sure save a lot of wear and tear on your part."

"I wish it were that simple," replied Kromer. "But from what I understand, the building complex you'll be entering has a number of different industries based under one roof. I've worked at several different biological warfare labs, and know precisely what to look for. It could take you days to find the lab."

Warlock's response to this was simple. "Not if we take down the whole damn place it won't."

The path led them past a massive wall of rock that had several large caves cut into it. Much of the rock face was chipped and blackened, and it was Warlock who explained the significance of this damage.

"See those tunnels, Doc. The Japs hid in them when our invasion force landed here to take the island back in nineteen forty-five. That blackened area—those are scorch marks caused by the flame-throwers that eventually burned those bastards out."

"I understand there was quite a battle to take this island," said Kromer.

"One hundred and twenty thousand soldiers never lived to return home," Warlock declared bluntly.

As they passed the last of the caves, the footpath began to gradually slope downward. They rounded a sharp bend in the trail, and entered a wide, tree-lined valley. The air seemed cooler there, and the gusting wind carried the hypnotic, throbbing cries of forest creatures.

They had long ago lost sight of the rest of the team, but Warlock seemed content to amble on at a moderate, relaxing pace. This was fine with Miriam, whose feet were beginning to hurt from the new combat boots she was wearing.

The distant crash of cascading water first signaled the obstacle that soon blocked their route. It was in a clearing beside this rain-swollen stream that the other SEALs were waiting.

Old Dog had removed his pack and was propped up against a fallen tree trunk digging into an MRE. Cajun and Traveler were also in the process of lightening their loads as the two stragglers arrived.

"I don't suppose there's a convenient bridge nearby?" Warlock's gaze was fixed on the swiftly moving waters of the stream.

"If ya'll don't want to get wet, I could scout upstream, around that bend yonder," offered Cajun.

"Do it," instructed Warlock. "But don't waste any time tracking possums. We've got at least another five miles to go, and I want to get back while the chow's still hot."

Cajun tied a brown bandana around his forehead, then silently disappeared into the surrounding woods. Miriam followed Warlock's lead, and sat down against the tree trunk beside Old Dog. She was genuinely surprised when Traveler approached and humbly addressed her.

"I meant no disrespect back there, Doc. It's just that we haven't had leave in over a month. And you are quite an interesting and attractive lady."

"Apology accepted," replied Kromer sincerely.

Traveler seemed almost likable as he continued. "You know, I don't ever remember bringing an outsider along on one of our ops. I sure hope it doesn't get hairy."

"It makes no sense to me," said Old Dog, who talked while chewing on a mouthful of dehydrated peaches. "No offense, ma'am, but they had no business assignin' you to us like they did. We're a fine-honed fightin' team that eats together, sleeps together, and, when necessary, kills together. You'll only end up gettin' in the way."

The shrill blast of a whistle sounded in the near distance, and Warlock anxiously stood.

"Sounds like our resident coon hunter has found something. Mount 'em up, ladies!"

They found Cajun a quarter of a mile upstream, beside a fallen tree trunk that conveniently crossed the raging waters.

"It ain't the Lake Pontchartrain causeway, but it will get us across just the same," said the bayou-born point man.

Warlock seemed to be in a hurry as he beckoned them forward. "Let's go for it, ladies."

With the grace of a tightrope walker, Cajun crossed over, with Traveler following close behind. As Miriam prepared to give it a try, Warlock expressed his concern.

"Can you handle it, Doc?"

The toxicologist flashed him a thumbs-up. "No problem. Back in school, I used to compete in gymnastics, and after taking on a balance beam, this should be a snap."

"As you most likely know, the trick is to concentrate on a point straight ahead and not to look down," advised Warlock. He noted that Old Dog didn't seem to be in any hurry to follow in his teammate's footsteps.

"What's the matter, big guy? You look a little pale."

Old Dog responded, though his glance remained locked on the swiftly moving waters. "It's nothin' but some bad peaches, Warlock. You guys go ahead, and I'll bring up the rear."

With Warlock's assistance, Miriam climbed up onto the fallen-log bridge and began crossing over. She was careful to walk in as straight a line as possible, with her arms extended for balance. Two-thirds of the way across, she encountered a slippery section of loose bark, and for a fraction of a second, she lost her balance. Fortunately, her forward momentum carried her past this obstacle and into the arms of Traveler.

Warlock crossed without incident, and this left only Old Dog on the opposite bank.

"Come on, big guy. Time's a-wasting!" shouted Warlock, as he joined the others on the sandy shoreline.

Old Dog waved and tentatively climbed up onto the fallen trunk. Miriam could tell that he was going to have problems the moment he took his first cautious step forward. His big body was too tense, and his huge combat boots were practically as wide as the walkable surface of the log.

Two times he lost his balance and almost fell into the roaring stream. But he managed to stay upright, and Miriam actually thought he might make it all the way across until he hit the slippery part of the log. This time his frantic efforts to remain standing were in vain, and he tumbled off the trunk to land headfirst in a relatively shallow portion of the stream only a few yards from where his shocked teammates stood.

Without a second's hesitation, Miriam jumped off the bank to assist him. Oblivious to the icy current that incessantly pulled at her, numbing her legs, she fought her way over to the fallen commando, whose head remained under water. She needed all of her strength to turn him over, and was greeted by a fit of coughing as Old Dog snapped back into consciousness and attempted to clear his lungs of the water he had swallowed.

By this time, the other SEALs had arrived, and with their help, the big Texan was able to sit up and

144

eventually to stand. The water barely covered his shins, and he appeared more embarrassed than anything else as he looked his redheaded savior in the eye and voiced his gratitude.

"Thanks, Doc. As far as I'm concerned, it's not so bad havin' you around after all. I guess this means welcome to the team!"

Eleven

Bill Brown snapped awake from a sound sleep and, for a confusing moment, forgot where he was. As an amplified pa announcement blared in the distance he reoriented himself. Groggily, he reached up and switched on the small overhead reading light that was mounted on the bulkhead above his head. This illuminated the cramped stateroom that the *Hawkbill*'s XO had so graciously surrendered for his use during the refitting.

Before sitting up, the veteran took a moment to allow his thoughts to clear. The long flight from Florida had exhausted him, yet he had been too excited to sleep until he'd gotten a look at Alpha Base. The spirited reunion with his ex-shipmates, his walk through of the *Bokken*, and Henry Walker's fascinating briefing, at which time he'd met the other participants in the mission, had followed.

It had been Pete Frystak who had finally suggested that they try to get some shuteye. Brown had resisted at first, but had soon found himself yawning and struggling to keep his eyes open. The *Hawkbill*'s alert XO, noting his fatigued condition, had practically begged Brown to take his stateroom and get some rest.

A quick check of his watch showed Bill that he had been out a good four hours. This was much longer than he had planned to sleep, and he stiffly sat up, intending to get on with the work that lay before them.

Brown hadn't slept on a submarine for well over twenty years. The tight spaces, the sounds, the rich scent of machine oil that permeated the air sure hadn't changed, and he made his way over to the washbasin, with only his aching joints as evidence of the years' passing.

He felt much better after brushing his teeth and shaving. He even had something of an appetite as he pulled on his well-worn khaki trousers, tucked in his faded denim workshirt, and without bothering to put on socks, slipped into a pair of comfortable rubber-soled boat shoes. Only after he'd pocketed his corncob pipe, tobacco pouch, and lighter did he continue on to the nearby wardroom.

Seated there, sipping on a glass of milk, was a young officer who seemed to be totally immersed in the large chart spread out on the table before him. Before Brown could introduce himself, a portly, crew-cut newcomer wearing a stained apron entered the wardroom from the opposite hatchway. He carried a platter of sandwich fixings, which he placed on the table before walking over to personally greet Bill.

"Ah, you must be Commander Brown. It's an honor to make your acquaintance, sir. I'm Petty Officer First Class Howard Mallot, the chief cook and bottle washer around here."

This introduction caught the attention of the seated officer, who looked up as Mallot continued.

"I understand from Vice Admiral Walker that you

used to be his CO back in the days of the diesel-electrics. Perhaps you knew my father, Chief Bomar Mallot. He was the head of the galley aboard the *Pickerel.*"

"The *Pickerel* was a fine submarine, Mr. Mallot." Brown couldn't help but eye the platter of food. "I toured her several times, though I don't believe I ever met your father."

Howard Mallot wasn't the type who missed much, and he was aware that the white-haired veteran had missed dinner.

"Please help yourself to some chow, Commander. I brought out some freshly sliced turkey, whole wheat bread, low-fat swiss cheese, and a variety of condiments."

"Don't mind if I do, Chief," said Bill Brown. "I'm famished!"

"How about some coffee?" asked Mallot.

Brown answered while bending over to prepare a sandwich. "By all means, Chief. I take it black and Navy strong."

As Mallot left to fulfill this request, Brown sat down beside the wardroom's other occupant.

"Good evening, sir," said the young officer softly. "I'm Lieutenant Rich Laycob, the *Hawkbill's* navigator."

"Pleased to meet you, Lieutenant," replied Brown, before taking a bite of his turkey sandwich.

The sub's chief cook returned with a couple of mugs and a thermos of steaming coffee, and Bill Brown made certain to pass on his compliments.

"This turkey's excellent, Mr. Mallot."

"Thank-you, sir. Too bad you missed all the trimmings that went with it at dinner."

Brown poured himself some coffee and responded. "To tell you the truth, I was so beat I didn't even know I missed a meal, until now."

"Well, there's more if you're still hungry," said Mallot, who addressed his next remarks to both seated figures. "You know, I just returned from a tour of that Chinese-made pigboat, and whoever designed that galley sure didn't give much thought to the cooks. There's hardly any workspace, and the equipment is positively ancient."

"Did she have any food left on board?" asked Rich Laycob.

"The only item in the pantry that wasn't spoiled was rice, and plenty of it," answered Mallot. "I counted ten fifty-pound sacks."

"I seriously doubt if even our hungriest chowhounds would go through that much during this mission," observed the navigator.

Mallot nodded in agreement. "Captain Slaughter wants me to take along only what we need for this cruise. Even with this trip's short duration, it's still going to be a challenge. So I plan a full dress rehearsal meal in three more days."

"What's on the menu?" questioned Brown as he polished off the rest of his sandwich.

Mallot smiled. "I've decided this cruise should have a Japanese theme."

"Just count me out when it comes to the sushi," said Brown, who looked up as the *Hawkbill*'s commanding officer strode into the wardroom.

Chris Slaughter addressed his initial remarks to the chef. "Chief, it looks like the gang over on the *Bokken* could use some more mid-rats. Can you handle it?"

"I'll get on it at once, sir," returned Mallot, who made it a point to readdress the veteran subman before leaving. "See you later, Commander Brown."

Mallot exited, and Slaughter poured himself some coffee and remained standing.

"Sounds like you've got quite a cook there," said Bill Brown between sips from his own mug.

"He's one of the best in the fleet." Slaughter patted his stomach. "In fact, his food's so good the only battle this crew's been involved in is the battle of the bulge."

"If this bay we're being sent to is as tight as it appears, then I'm afraid that's going to change real quick, Captain," countered the somber-faced navigator. "I've been going over these charts, and there certainly doesn't seem to be much room in there for us to work in."

With mugs in hand, Bill Brown and Chris Slaughter gathered around the seated navigator, who pointed to the mushroom-shaped bay visible on the topmost chart and continued.

"The inlet itself is less than a quarter-mile wide. The channel there appears deep enough, though that's where the first hydrophones will be positioned."

"And the CAPTORS?" quizzed Slaughter.

Rich Laycob pointed to the bay's center. "The mines will probably be moored here, in a half-moon pattern designed to protect the inner shoreline."

Bill Brown used the scarred stem of his pipe to highlight the inlet, and he casually expressed his opinion. "I wouldn't be surprised to find some mines blocking the entrance to the bay itself, along with a few other surprises like an old-fashioned sub net."

"I don't know about the sub net," said Slaughter. "But as long as the *Bokken's* signature is locked within the mine-field's computerized memory, I don't feel the CAPTORs are our main concern. That is delivering the SEAL team safely. Lieutenant Laycob, how would you handle the drop-off?"

The navigator took his time answering. "Because of the limited depth of the bay, our best bet is to drop them off just after dusk, approximately five hundred yards offshore. That will give them at least ten hours of darkness to row to land, do their dirty work, and return to the drop-off point for pickup."

Once more Bill Brown utilized the stem of his pipe as a pointer. "It looks like there's a river running into the eastern part of the bay. Encountering that fresh water could play havoc with our trim and cause an unnecessary breach. So how about using the western portion as our drop-off point? Besides, the beach there appears to have cover extending all the way down to the waterline."

"Looks good to me," said Slaughter. "If this chart's accurate, the SEALs should only have a hike of a mile or so before they reach the first security perimeter. Meanwhile, we're going to be experiencing the hardest part of this whole operation, which will be waiting for the SEALs to return."

"Time does have a strange way of slowing down in those situations," observed Bill Brown. "But I'm sure we'll have our hands full. Don't forget, those hydrophones are going to pick us up the moment we penetrate that inlet. They're going to have a hell of a time figuring out where we disappeared to and why we never made it to the pier."

"That's why it's imperative that those SEALs get in and out of there in the shortest amount of time possible," added Slaughter.

Bill Brown sat back and looked up at Slaughter. "Having Dr. Kromer along should help."

The *Hawkbill*'s CO returned his glance. "That woman sure is something special to volunteer for an operation such as this one."

"Scuttlebutt has it that Henry Walker conned her into it," said Brown.

Slaughter grinned slyly. "It seems that the admiral didn't do a bad job enlisting your services either."

This remark caused a broad smile to light up the veteran's tanned face. He took a long sip of coffee before voicing himself.

"Even when Henry was my diving officer on the *Cubera*, he had an irresistible way of asking for something. It was as if he took it for granted that his request would be met, and he only posed the question as a mere formality."

"Earlier today, when the admiral explained this mission's command structure, he asked you if it was okay to have me as the sole CO of the *Bokken*. Was this one of those questions that he already had the answer to?" questioned Slaughter.

"Hell, yes!" replied Bill Brown. "I wouldn't have it any other way, and Henry damn well knows it. And besides, I'm getting too old to assume full responsibility for a complex operation like this one. I'm going along merely as a consultant, to oversee operations and to provide input only when I deem it necessary to the successful completion of this mission."

"As far as I'm concerned, Commander Brown," said Slaughter, "you'll still be the senior officer aboard."

"That's all well and fine, my friend," replied the veteran submariner. "But don't forget that as of today, in the eyes of the world, you're officially a civilian. So why not start out by calling me Bill?"

"Bill, it is," repeated Slaughter, who liked the honest chemistry that was developing between them.

Brown felt likewise and, after polishing off his coffee, turned his attention back to the top chart.

"In all likelihood, it's going to be hell to pay to get out of that bay with our feet dry. But we'll face that problem as it comes. Right now, we've got to focus on getting that commando team safely ashore, so they can blow that biological warfare lab to kingdom come. Because the one thing you can bet the farm on is that the maniac responsible for all this isn't going to stop with just Kadena and Sasebo. Yokosuka and our Tokyo bases will be next. And then it will be on to Guam, Honolulu, and, before you know it, the US mainland itself!"

Dr. Yukio Ishii pulled up to the entrance of the dormitory at nine A.M. sharp. He'd no sooner put the solar-powered golf cart into neutral, than the front door to the building swung open, and Yoko Noguchi emerged into the sunlight and headed straight down the brick walkway that led to the road.

This was the first time he had seen the young scientist without her laboratory garb on, and he was most impressed with the naturalness of her beauty. She had a schoolgirl innocence, that was emphasized by her short bangs, big dark eyes, and knee-length, white silk skirt. Ishii waved in greeting, but did not bother to get out of the cart as she continued down the walkway toward him.

"Climb in," he instructed as she reached the road.

She scooted into the cart beside him, and Ishii added. "What an absolutely gorgeous morning it is

153

for me to give you that tour I promised. I hope you slept well, Miss Noguchi."

"I'm afraid it was another late night at the lab, sir," Yoko replied while Ishii put the cart into gear and started driving them forward.

Ishii looked concerned. "Any problems?"

"Nothing serious. I just lost track of the time while initiating some aerosol experiments."

"It appears that destiny has brought you to the right place to lose track of time, my dear," returned Ishii. "Except instead of misplacing hours, I lose entire years to my work!"

Ishii turned the cart onto an asphalt roadway that led them away from the massive industrial complex beside which the dormitory was located. A series of scrub-filled foothills stretched before them now. They appeared to be unoccupied except for dozens of tall, wildly spinning windmills. These structures were of the most modern construction, complete with pivoting, airplane-style propellers that efficiently caught the wind no matter which direction it was blowing from.

"This is our little wind farm," observed Ishii proudly. "When I first came to Takara, I noticed that the constantly blowing trade winds were funneled through this valley. These windmills are responsible for a fifth of the electricity we use here."

He turned onto a road that ran parallel to the foothills, and Yoko spotted a series of massive electrical pylons and accompanying cables. These stretched all the way into the surrounding mountains.

"What other power sources do you rely on?" she asked.

Ishii was anticipating such a question and eagerly

answered it. "Solar energy provides us with another fifth of our total power requirement, while the rest is produced by hydroelectrical means. In this way we can keep our import of costly, pollution-causing fossil fuels to a bare minimum."

"That's most impressive, sir," observed the young scientist, whose curiosity was still not satisfied. "May I ask though where this hydroelectrical power source originates? I didn't think Takara Island had any major rivers."

"It doesn't," returned Ishii, who liked her probing intellect. "We have developed a way to tap the very energy that courses through the seas. Much as we did with these windmills, we have strategically placed several specially designed turbines in the waters off Takara's northern coast. A strong, constant current cuts the Ryukyu chain here, and it's this surge that spins our turbines and provides the power that satisfies the majority of our energy requirements."

"Ingenious," reflected Yoko, who was equally impressed with what she next viewed.

What appeared to be over a dozen, large, rectangularly shaped ponds were cut into the floor of the valley. As they passed by the first of these miniature lakes, several individuals could be seen patrolling the gently sloping shoreline, with wide, pole-mounted nets in hand.

Not bothering to wait for the question he knew would soon be voiced, Ishii continued his role as tour guide.

"This is a portion of our aqua-farm, Miss Noguchi. In these ponds we raise such delectables as prawns, lobsters, oysters, and catfish. Sizable growths of kelp and seaweed are also grown here. We

155

have cordoned off portions of the adjoining sea in order to raise species that need more space to feed — salmon, tuna, and even shark, whose flesh I find particularly satisfying."

"So this is where that delicious lobster I had for dinner two nights ago came from," said Yoko.

"I'm glad you enjoyed it. Our lobster crop this year was excellent, and we have already begun exporting a sizable number to the mainland."

Ishii made this comment while steering the cart onto a dirt road that led back toward the bay. The bulk of the industrial complex could be seen to the left, while a double-wide, chain-link security fence stretched along the right side of the road, a thick forest of trees beyond it.

From Yoko's vantage point, a freighter docked at the facilities main pier could be seen. Several trucks were lined up beside this ship, which was unloading its cargo by means of a conveyor belt.

"It appears that the folks in mineral extraction will be busy tonight," said Ishii as he guided the cart onto the concrete pavement that followed the bay back to the complex. "That ship's hold is filled with hundreds of tons of newly excavated nodules, picked off the floor of the Pacific at a depth of some ten thousand feet. Our preliminary analysis shows it to be rich in manganese."

"My father always said that the greatest mineral treasures of all lay untouched on the bottom of the sea," said Yoko.

Ishii was quick to respond to this comment. "I understand from your personnel dossier that your father was a geologist. Too bad he didn't live long enough to see the day when his prophetic observation would come true."

"There's so much here that my father would have been fascinated with." Yoko turned to face her silver-haired escort. "When I first considered applying to work here, one of my father's ex-colleagues mentioned that your wife was one of the first female geologists to graduate from Tokyo University."

"That was many, many years ago, my dear," reflected Ishii dreamily.

"Is your wife still alive?" Yoko asked, as innocently as possible.

Ishii's tone turned bitter. "My wife was one of the thousands of unfortunate souls burned to death when the American atomic bomb fell on Nagasaki on August 9, 1945."

A moment of constrained silence followed as the cart passed by the main pier. Yoko saw that two other vessels, a submarine and a sleek patrol boat, were also docked here. She was surprised when Ishii failed to turn left onto the road that would have taken them back to the laboratory. Instead they continued on beside the sparkling waters of the bay.

A gull cried out harshly overhead, and Yoko looked up into a clear blue sky. Now that they were closer to the water, the air temperature had dropped several degrees, and she was thankful for the light sweater she'd decided to wear. Deciding against asking any more personal questions, she sat back to enjoy the tour that was turning out to be much more extensive than she had expected.

Some sort of park was visible up ahead. Ishii slowed down the cart as they approached this immaculately manicured field of grass on which a dozen youngsters were doing kendo exercises. An eagle-eyed instructor led the children, orchestrating the movements of their bamboo swords with his out-

157

stretched hand.

"Are you familiar with the way of the sword, my dear?" asked Ishii.

"As a child, I used to have my own bokken," replied Yoko. "But now my favorite martial-art is judo."

Ishii continued, while slowing the cart to a virtual crawl. "Perhaps when you get completely settled in, you'll join me in the gymnasium on Saturday mornings, when a few of us get together to practice. As you may very well know, there's much more to the ancient sport of kendo than merely striking two swords together."

"I'd enjoy that," said Yoko, who really wasn't certain what he was referring to.

On the far side of the practice field was an airstrip, complete with a small tower and a quonset hut. Ishii remained silent until the cart was parked beside the closed doors of the metal hangar, then spoke out in a cool, composed voice.

"Several days ago, you asked me why it was necessary for us to develop a new, deadlier strain of anthrax toxin. I'd like to take this opportunity to inform you that Ishii Industries has taken this step not only to formulate a proper vaccine, but also to investigate the theoretical use of such toxins in the future defense of the Japanese mainland."

This off-the-wall remark caught Yoko by complete surprise, and she hesitated a moment before responding. "Do you have a Ministry of Defense grant to initiate such experiments?" she questioned.

Ishii laughed. "The Ministry of Defense, that's a misnomer if I ever heard one! No, Miss Noguchi, we have taken this initiative on our own."

"But the government?" countered the young scientist. "How can you even think of proceeding with such a dangerous experiment without their support and approval?"

Ishii remained cool, and in complete control. "It's evident that you're young and innocent, my dear. But the idealistic days of childhood and university life are over. It's my duty to welcome you to the world as it really is. In all honesty, what do you know about this government you speak of? Just because it's there, do you allow it to take control of your destiny as if it were some omnipotent force unable to err?"

Having no answer to this, Yoko could only wait for her new employer to continue.

"I hate to be the one to disillusion you, my dear, but the current government of Japan is nothing but a weak, corrupt lackey of our military occupiers, the United States of America. To prove this point, one only has to look at our current national energy policy. This shortsighted program relies almost exclusively on oil from the Persian Gulf to run the country's industrial machine. Yet what happens when this source is interrupted, as it was in the winter of nineteen ninety? Faced with a potential loss of over eighty percent of our petroleum reserves, Japan was forced—against its will—to practically write out a blank check to the US treasury. And did our government learn from this costly mistake and change its policy, focus its attention on alternative power sources such as those that run this island? On the contrary. Because the weak-willed fools who run our nation are still afraid of any innovation that could upset their precious status quo or anger our old friend, Uncle Sam.

"It was no different in the days that preceded

159

World War II, my dear. At that time our energy-starved nation faced a similar dilemma. Yet instead of dealing directly with the problem and finding alternatives, the government did nothing. It was this inaction that allowed the militants to assume power. And from then on, Japan's doom was sealed."

"But we are a democracy now," dared Yoko. "Our government is but a reflection of the will of the people. And if they're not satisfied, they'll vote out the incumbents and elect new officials who will carry out their desires."

"That would be so if our citizens had the vision to know what was really in their best interests," returned Ishii. "Unfortunately, most of them can't see beyond their next bowl of rice."

The elder sighed and beckoned Yoko to follow him on foot.

"Come, my dear. Enough of this rather heavy talk. Now I want to show you the one material object that's closer to this old man's heart than anything else on the face of this planet."

Yoko was amazed at how quickly Ishii changed the direction of their conversation. It was almost as if he'd planned this outing just to test her political preferences. Fascinated by his own peculiar beliefs, she followed him over to the closed doors of the hangar.

"In my mind, nothing symbolizes the true inventive soul of the Japanese people like the aircraft that awaits us inside," said Ishii as he swung back one of the massive doors and walked inside to activate the lights.

The fluorescent tubes snapped on overhead, illuminating a single, light gray airplane with bright red rising-sun decals on its wings and both sides of its fuselage. A yellow stripe encircled the aft part of the freshly painted metal fuselage, another stripe brightened the base of the vertical stabilizer. Only when Ishii went on to explain this aircraft's history, did Yoko realize how incredibly preserved it was.

"My dear, this is my pride and joy, a Type 0, Model-21 fighter escort, originally built by Mitsubishi in nineteen forty-three. She's one of ten thousand five hundred eighty of such aircraft designed for Japan by the master aeronautical engineer Jiro Horikoshi."

They reached the Zero's side, and Yoko carefully touched the smooth, flush-riveted fuselage as her host continued.

"Sadly enough, today only a handful of such aircraft remain in existence. As a pilot, I can personally attest to her marvelous handling qualities. Designed around lightness, simplicity, and ease of maintenance, the Zero could out maneuver any plane the enemy had, even the highly vaunted English Spitfire."

"She's certainly a good-looking piece of machinery," Yoko commented.

"She's much more than that, my dear," replied Ishii with rising emotion. "The Zero was built with a minimum of government interference. Aircraft such as this are poignant reminders that one must not neglect to consider the private sector when it comes to the defense of our ancestral homeland.

"Much like Jiro Horikoshi, I want to make a contribution to the security of Japan. As we get to know each other better, you'll see that my vision is a relatively simple one. All that I really desire is a country free from foreign occupation. Under the divine leadership of our holy Emperor, we will expand

161

our sphere of influence to include our rightful colonies in Southeast Asia, China, Korea, and Indonesia. Only then can we truly flourish and successfully compete with such economic giants as the rapidly emerging European Economic Community."

"In all honesty, I don't think today's Japan is doing that badly," said Yoko. "If you ask me, your plan for the future hints at the reawakening of militarism, but that's something the people won't stand for."

"The people," repeated Ishii with disgust. "What do they know of the realities of geopolitical power? But that's irrelevant at the moment," he added in a softer tone. "You are a member of our family now. And all I ask of you is to keep an open mind. Attend our lecture, exercise, and meditation sessions, and don't be afraid to express your own opinions when challenged. In other words, dare to grow with us in consciousness, my dear, and the Way will lead you homeward like a long-lost pilgrim."

"No one ever accused me of having a closed mind before," said Yoko.

"I didn't think so," replied the grinning elder. "You're much too intelligent for that. You are also a welcome breath of fresh air around here. I'm relying on you to give me a better understanding of the modern generation that comprises mainstream Japan, so never be afraid to speak your mind around me. And in such a manner we can continue to learn from each other, and to become fuller individuals as we do."

Ishii projected an almost fatherly warmth as he beckoned toward the open doors of the hangar and added. "I don't know about you, but all this talking and fresh air has done wonders for my appetite.

Please do me the honor of joining me for brunch in my private dining room, and perhaps you'll share with me what it's like to be a university student in modern-day Japan."

"I'd enjoy that," responded Yoko, allowing the elder to gently take her by the arm and guide her out into the welcoming sunlight.

Twelve

Pete Frystak was simply amazed at how quickly he readjusted to the life of a submariner. It was almost as if he had never retired at all, but had merely been on extended leave during these last couple of years of civilian life. The familiar sights, smells, and sounds of the boats had never left his blood after all. And he'd never realized how much he'd missed them until fate had called him back into service for this mission.

But he was concerned about his wife. There had been no hiding the hurt in Kathy's expression as he'd hurriedly packed his seabag and arranged transport to Homestead. Fortunately, their faithful, hardworking staff would help her run the resort while he was gone, and the Cuban maintenance men would proceed with the roofing project. If all turned out as planned, he'd be back in Big Pine Key in less than two weeks, none the worse for wear and full of pleasant memories.

Unable even to drop Kathy a postcard to let her know he was okay, Pete was currently moving into his new quarters aboard the *Bokken*. For the first couple of nights after arriving at Alpha Base, he had bunked in the relatively luxurious confines of the

USS *Hawkbill*. Yet now that their sailing date was rapidly approaching, it was time to live exclusively aboard the vessel that would soon be taking them into harm's way.

He had been assigned space in the Romeo-class sub's forward officer's quarters. Though this meant sharing a cramped area not much larger than his closet back home with five other sailors, he really didn't mind at all. Their cruise promised to be a short one, and anyway, most of his time would be spent on watch in the torpedo room.

The accommodations consisted of narrow, three-tiered bunks. The top ones appeared to be already occupied, so he gratefully eased himself onto a bottom bunk.

The mattress proved to be unusually firm, which was fine with Pete. At home, to get additional support, he slept with a board under his Serta.

A locker was located beneath the bunk, and Pete was in the process of filling it with the personal belongings he'd brought along when a man carrying a seabag entered the quarters.

"Excuse me, sir," the newcomer said politely, "but I guess we're bunkmates."

Pete turned and eyed a tall, lanky youngster at most twenty-one years of age. This fellow was dressed in gray sweats, and had the scarred remnants of teenage acne on his beardless chin. The veteran instantly sensed his shyness, and did his best to make the lad feel right at home.

"Pete Frystak's the name. But please, call me Pete."

The young man still seemed afraid to directly meet the veteran's gaze as he hesitantly responded. "I'm Ensign Adrian Avila — Adie for short."

Frystak flashed his warmest smile and, while exchanging a handshake, questioned him further. "What's your specialty on the *Hawkbill*, Adie?"

"I'm currently training to qualify as a weapons officer, sir," returned the young sailor.

"No kidding," said Frystak. "That was my specialty. So I guess we'll be working together on this tub. And hey, I'm serious about calling me Pete."

Ensign Avila finally found the nerve to make direct eye contact with him, and even managed a slight smile.

"Pete it is, sir," he firmly replied.

The veteran shook his head. "Now if I could just get you to drop that 'sir' crap, we'd really be cooking."

Frystak turned back to his unpacking and added. "Say, I hope you don't mind, but I took this bottom bunk. Though I don't plan to spend much time in the rack, when I do crash, my days of climbing for shuteye are over."

Ensign Avila picked the other bottom bunk, and wasted no time emptying his seabag.

"Where are you from, Adie?" asked Frystak while unloading his toiletries.

"I was born and raised in Plano, Texas."

"Plano, Texas," repeated Frystak. "I don't believe I've ever heard of the place."

"It's a northern suburb of Dallas with a population of over one hundred thousand," said Adie with evident pride.

"Well, I make my home in the Florida Keys," revealed Frystak. "Ever been to the Keys?"

Shaking his head that he hadn't, Ensign Avila furrowed his brow. "Isn't that where Ernest Hemingway lived?"

"That's the place, son. If you like to fish, boat, or just play in the sun, you've got to come down and visit us someday. My wife and I run a resort down there. It's nothing fancy, but it sure beats the hell out of living in a big city or fighting the snow and ice up north."

"Back at college, I did a paper on Hemingway," said the shy Texan, who was slowly coming out of his shell. "He was sure some kind of guy."

"That he was," returned Frystak. "Do you have a favorite Hemingway book?"

Adie thought a moment before answering. "I guess it's *The Old Man and the Sea.* One of my dreams is to go marlin fishing one day."

"Then come on down to Big Pine Key," offered Frystak. "I can't guarantee you a marlin, but I believe we could scare up a sailfish or two."

This remark served to totally break the ice, and Ensign Avila's face broke out into an expectant grin. "Do you mean it, Pete?"

"Why of course I do. You just give us a call in advance, and we'll see what we can do about making a conch out of you."

"A what?" quizzed the Texan.

Frystak smiled. "A conch is a native of the Florida Keys. It's also a local variety of mollusk. I'm sure you've seen the large, pink and white shells they live in."

"Do you mean the type you can blow in like a trumpet, and put up to your ear to hear the sea?" asked Adie.

"That's the one," said the veteran, who concluded his unpacking by removing his Bible and placing it on the stateroom's small, fold-down desk.

"I see you read the Good Book," observed Adie.

"We don't see many of those on the *Hawkbill*."

"That's too bad," replied Frystak. "Wait until you get chased around by a tin can and get some depth-charges dumped on you. That never fails to bring a crew religion."

"Were you in World War II, Pete?" asked the young Texan.

"Hey, I'm not that ancient! Though I did manage to see a little underwater action off the coast of Korea and later Viet Nam."

This revelation gained Adie's complete attention. "I didn't realize subs were involved in those conflicts."

Once more, the top-secret nature of Pete Frystak's past assignments kept him from sharing his exploits, and he cryptically responded. "You'd be surprised, son. But I guess that's why they call it the silent service."

In an adjoining passageway, Master Chief Stanley Roth was in the midst of a thorough inspection of the *Bokken*, to assess its operational readiness. He started off in the forward torpedo room, where the around-the-clock efforts by the yard crew were finally starting to show results. The gouges and dents to the outer bow had been repaired, and now the internal structural damage was being corrected.

Roth noted, with some degree of satisfaction, that the replacement batteries had arrived from the States. He didn't envy the men whose job it was to crawl into the dark, cramped recesses beneath the main deck and install them.

Of course, his prime concern was the sub's engine room. His initial series of inspections found the machinery in this compartment in sad need of an overhaul. As he continued to work his way aft to check on his men's progress there, he could only pray that the young "nukes" from the *Hawkbill* were able to make some sort of sense out of the engine room's various components. These had originated in such diverse places as China, the Soviet Union, Albania, and Poland. Because regardless of Henry Walker's plan, the *Bokken* wasn't going anywhere until Stanley was completely satisfied that the diesels were in proper working order.

His route aft took him through the control room. Several of the *Hawkbill's* sailors were gathered there, in the process of settling into their new positions, and Stanley took a moment to visit with them.

He was surprised to spot a somewhat familiar figure attempting to squeeze his six-foot, three-inch, two-hundred-pound bulk into one of the two, tiny upholstered leather chairs set before the helm. His curiosity aroused, Stanley went over to greet the man.

"Are you going to fit, sailor?" he lightly questioned.

The brown-haired youngster answered while doing his best not to hit his knees up against the partial steering column that was mounted into the deck before him. "I'll make it, sir. Though it's going to be tight."

"Did you recently attend basic sub school?" asked Stanley, as he vainly attempted to place the helmsman's face.

"Not within the last two years," the youth replied.

"That's funny," said Stanley. "I could have sworn I just had you in one of my classes there."

A sudden look of enlightenment lit the sailor's

169

green eyes. "I'll bet it was my kid brother, Clark."

"Seaman Foard!" exclaimed Stanley, who finally remembered the name. "And if I remember correctly, your family is from Kansas City."

The youngster smiled fondly. "You've got it, Chief. My name's Bill."

They exchanged a hearty handshake and the helmsman added, "I guess Clark has grown some since I last saw him. How's he doing in school?"

"He's turning into a first-rate bubblehead," said Stanley. "Though, like yourself, he was having a bit of a problem squeezing himself into the tight spaces of our trainers. I take it you help drive the *Hawkbill*."

"That's correct, Chief," returned Foard as he gripped the hydraulically powered steering wheel and vainly attempted to pull it backward. It budged only after a strained effort on his part.

"I hope the helm isn't always this stiff," observed Foard. "It's like driving a car without power steering."

"You hit the nail right on the head," returned Stanley. "The *Hawkbill*'s like driving a souped-up Corvette, while this boat handles more like a nineteen fifty-six Chevy truck. It'll take some time to get used to, but you'll get the feel of it soon enough. Just track me down in the engine room if you've got any problems you can't solve. And don't be shy, like that kid brother of yours."

Leaving him with a playful wink, Stanley next stopped at the adjoining diving console. Here Chief "Mac" McKenzie, the *Hawkbill*'s grizzled COB (Chief of the Boat), was trying to make some sort of sense out of the lines of red and green lights situated beside row after row of plastic-tipped toggle switches. Mac and Stanley had already met, and Stanley was grateful for the COB's fifteen years of submarine experience.

"Hello, Mac. Ever see anything like this before?"

"Yeah, in a friggin' museum!" answered the disgruntled COB. "This is sure one for the books, Roth. If these red lights belong to the hull-opening indicators, how can I read them under conditions of night adaptation, when this compartment will be lit only in red?"

"I guess that's why we switched to indicators shaped as circles and dashes on our newer subs," said Stanley.

"Well, that sure as hell's not going to do me much good," returned the crew-cut chief, whose arms were intricately tattooed.

"Mac, with your years of experience, you'll figure out a way to read them."

The COB's response was ominous. "You'd better hope so, Roth. Otherwise this cruise is going in one direction only, and that's straight down!"

Stanley could only shrug his shoulders, and as he turned to continue aft, he nearly stumbled over the pair of legs extending from beneath the hooded radar console.

"Find anything interesting in there, sailor?" asked Stanley.

"As a matter of fact, I have," returned a muffled voice.

Seconds later, Seaman First Class Ray Morales scooted out from beneath the console, holding an old-fashioned transistor tube in his hand.

"I haven't seen one of these since I picked apart my grandfather's hi-fi set," Morales reflected. "Why, I'd bet there's not a single microchip on this entire vessel."

"You're probably correct, sailor," agreed Stanley, who took the tube and briefly examined it before handing it back.

"Chief, do you really think this radar unit can cut it?" questioned Morales.

"I don't know why not," Stanley replied. "Those tubes may be a bit outdated, but they'll get the job done all the same. Just remember to give this unit some time to warm up, and it will work just as good as your radar back on *Hawkbill*."

"No offense, Chief, but I'll believe that when I see it with my own eyes," said Morales, who despondently shook his head and then returned to his inspection.

In a way, Stanley couldn't blame the young radar technician for his skepticism. He was expected to put his trust in a piece of equipment that was already an antique.

The same went for the other members of the crew. These highly trained youngsters were being asked to take a step backward in time, to a technological level at which microprocessors and computer keyboards didn't exist. Such an abrupt change, by its very nature, would be confusing, and Stanley only wished that the crew could have more time to adjust to this radically new environment.

The differences in technology were especially apparent at the next console he visited. Seated before a confusing collection of dials and gauges, with a set of bulky, old-fashioned headphones over his ears, was the *Hawkbill*'s senior sonar technician. Stanley had yet to meet this individual, though he had heard a bit about Petty Officer First Class James "Jaffers" Echoles from his shipmates.

Jaffers, as he preferred to be called, had worked his way up through the enlisted ranks and, if scuttlebutt was to be believed, would soon be offered a commission of his own. The sailors Stanley had spoken to had praised Jaffers as an industrious, hardworking individual who thought nothing of sitting through a double-duty shift if his unique talents were needed.

Stanley had great respect for those sailors who had mastered the arcane art of sonar. Having been a prospective sonarman himself in his early Navy days, he was well aware of the complexities of this all-important job.

The briefest, inconsequential sound—one the untrained observer would pass right by—often meant the difference between living and dying in the competitive, complex world of undersea warfare. Intuition also helped, as well as an uncompromising attention to detail, and a disciplined, well-focused attention span. Because he lacked the patience to sit before a console for hours at a time, concentrating on unraveling the sounds of the sea, Stanley had decided not to specialize in sonar. Yet he respected those gifted sailors who made this demanding job an art form.

At the moment, Jaffers seemed to be having some problems getting his headphones to properly fit. Taking extra care not to take the big, black petty officer by surprise, Stanley got his attention with a wave of his hand.

"Can I help you with those, sailor?" asked the veteran, as he ambled up to the edge of the console.

Jaffers removed his headphones while responding. "I'm afraid these Chink headphones are hopeless."

"They certainly look like something from the dinosaur age," returned Stanley. Then he introduced himself. "Mr. Echoles, I'm Chief Roth. Though my domain on this cruise is the engine room, I'm familiar with most of this pigboat's systems, and I'd be happy to give you a hand if you ever need help."

Jaffers seemed surprised by this. "No kidding, Chief. Do you mean to say there's actually someone still alive who knows how to operate this old-timer?"

"Watch it, Mr. Echoles," returned Stanley playfully. "Or I'll take back that offer to help. By the way, is it okay if I call you Jaffers?"

"Please do, Chief," said the senior sonar technician as he fiddled with the dials of his console. "I see that my notoriety has preceded me."

"That's usually the way it is with the best and brightest," said Stanley. "Scuttlebutt also has it that you own a race horse."

"You wouldn't happen to be a sporting man, would you, Chief Roth?" asked Jaffers.

Stanley winked. "I've been known to put down a few two-dollar combinations in my time, son."

"I thought that might be the case," replied Jaffers, who instantly liked where Roth was coming from. "Actually, I only own a piece of a horse, along with my father and uncle. She's a spirited three-year-old filly that we picked up in Arlington on a two-thousand-dollar claim. We're going to clean up this coming summer down at Fairmont Park."

"That's in Illinois, isn't it?" said Stanley. "Why there?"

"That's home for me, Chief. Why I grew up so close to the track, I could hear the starting bell from my crapper!"

Stanley laughed and knew he'd have no trouble at all getting along with this colorful individual.

"Say, Jaffers, what do you know about the Fenik passive array set you'll be monitoring here?"

Jaffer's tone turned serious. "Only what we learned back in sub school, and that wasn't much, since the Feniks have been pretty well obsolete for the last three decades."

"I realize it's far from the BQS-6 you're used to operating, Jaffers. But this is all we have to work with. If you'd like, I'd be willing to give you a hand getting the feel of it. Back in nineteen fifty-eight, I manned this same station aboard an abandoned Soviet Romeo. I found the array itself extremely reliable, though its range and sensitivity were rather limited."

"I'd appreciate the help, Chief," replied Jaffers, whose attention went back to the bulky headphones that lay in his lap. "Now if I could only do something with this uncomfortable contraption. Say Chief, do you think it would be all right for me to bring over my set from the *Hawkbill?* All I'd have to do to make it compatible is patch in a new socket adaptor."

Stanley saw nothing wrong with this idea and responded accordingly. "By all means, son, go ahead and give it a try. And I'm certain that you'll find your superiors wide open to any other suggestions that will make your job any easier."

The potbellied veteran looked at his watch and added. "Please excuse me while I go and check out the action in this tub's engine room. I left instructions for a couple of your shipmates to begin an overhaul of our Chink diesels, and Lord only knows what kind of trouble they've managed to get themselves into in the meantime."

"I hear you, Chief," returned Jaffers. "But please

go easy on them. They're nukes, and aren't used to getting their hands dirty."

Stanley flashed him a salute and continued aft, down the narrow passageway that led through the crew's mess and into the engine room. It was as he was passing by the galley that a captivating aroma caught his attention. A bespectacled, heavyset man, wearing a stained apron stood beside the galley's open grill, in the process of overseeing the source of this tempting scent. Stanley couldn't help but take a closer look.

"Looks good and smells even better," he remarked as he peeked over the cook's shoulder and spotted a variety of sizzling strips of meat and cut-up vegetables. "But exactly what is it?"

"I call it Howard's turkey teriyaki," answered the proud chef as he looked over to see who he was addressing. "You must be another of Admiral Walker's friends," he correctly assumed.

"Chief Stanley Roth at your service. Now I don't suppose you'd be giving out any free samples?"

Without a second's hesitation, Mallot scooped a portion of the teriyaki onto a plate, and handed it to Stanley along with a fork. The veteran readily tasted a biteful, and a look of pure bliss lit up his face.

"Why it's absolutely marvelous!" he said.

"The secret's in the marinade," offered Mallot. "It's a combination of canola oil, light soy sauce, brown sugar, garlic, and grated gingerroot. If I was at home, I'd also throw in some sherry."

Stanley polished off the rest of his sample and shook his head admiringly. "Son, you certainly know how to cook a mean teriyaki."

"Thanks, Chief." Mallot took this compliment in stride. "Just you wait until I get used to cooking in

176

this closet. Then I'm going to prepare some real Jap delicacies."

"If it's anything like that sample I just tasted, I'll certainly be looking forward to chow time on this rust bucket. Incidentally, whom do I have the honor of addressing."

The potbellied chef wiped his hand on his apron and offered it in greeting. "I'm Petty Officer Howard Mallot, Chief. And you're welcome in 'Howard's Kitchen' anytime, day or night!"

"You're on," said Stanley, as he placed his empty plate in the tiny sink and somewhat reluctantly turned to get on with his duty.

A short transit down a pipe-lined passageway led him directly into the engine room. Here he found three of his machinists gathered around one of the compartment's two 2,000-horsepower diesel engines. The men seemed totally absorbed in an examination of the exhaust manifold, and Stanley got right down to business.

"How did that oil pressure test go, gentlemen?"

The *Hawkbill's* senior machinist, Petty Officer First Class Bob Marchetto, answered somewhat tentatively. "The pressure reading seems a bit low, Chief. We ran the engine until it attained operating temperature, then shut it off and installed the pressure gauge in a port of the main oil gallery. We started her up again and checked the pressure twice more, once at idle and once at maximum governor speed. And in each instance, the reading was below the specs you gave us."

"And your diagnosis?" tested Stanley.

The brawny senior machinist answered while thoughtfully stroking his beard-stubbled jaw. "It could be a worn oil pump, or perhaps the pump's pressure-relief valve is stuck in an open position. Then there's always the possibility that the engine bearings are worn."

Stanley seemed pleased with this response. "I'm impressed, Mr. Marchetto. But there's one possibility you overlooked. Before we go tearing out the oil pump or needlessly replacing those bearings, how about first checking the oil itself. Perhaps all we've got here is the use of an improper oil weight with too low of a viscosity."

Stanley led them over to the oil reservoir. He removed the cover plate and, with the assistance of a small flashlight, peered inside to check the contents.

"Holy Mother Mary!" he exclaimed in astonishment. "Just look at that sludge down there! This place was a breakdown just waiting to happen."

Each of the three machinists had a look as Stanley continued. "As I always tell my people, don't neglect that oil. It's the life's blood of an engine, and if not changed regularly will cost you in the long run each and every time."

Satisfied that he had made his point, the veteran got on with the task of readdressing this problem. "Mr. Marchetto, you may have the invaluable assistance of Seaman Tabor here to find a way to drain that reservoir. And while you're at it, pull the oil filter. Odds are it's just as dirty. Seaman Orlovick, you come with me."

Stanley led the way aft. The sailor he'd picked to accompany him was a short, wiry, intense young man with a no-nonsense attitude. He had been a reactor specialist on the *Hawkbill.*

"What do you think of your new duty, son?" Stanley asked.

Orlovick thought a moment before replying. "It

sure is different than the *Hawkbill*."

"I imagine so," returned the veteran as he climbed down onto the catwalk that separated the two engines. "Ever repair a bubbler before?"

"A what?" quizzed the youngster.

Stanley was expecting just such a response and answered directly. "A bubbler is a prototype masking device, that was incorporated into vessels of this class to decoy the opposition's torpedoes. It does so by encompassing the sub's hull in a wall of bubbles. I've seen it at work on an experimental basis and can personally attest to its effectiveness."

"If that's the case, why don't our submarines utilize such a device?" the alert machinist asked.

"We tried it out on the Barbel class," informed Stanley. "Yet the advent of the submarine-launched decoy made it obsolete. Of course, the bubbler's less than fifty percent success rate didn't hurt its demise either."

As they passed by the spot where the twin propeller shafts entered the reduction gears, a sailor could be seen sitting on the deck and frantically sorting through a tool locker. Spotting him, Stanley stopped dead in his tracks.

"Miller, didn't I tell you over two hours ago to begin repacking those shafts?" questioned the perplexed veteran.

Seaman Miller looked up and nervously cleared his throat. "Uh, Chief . . . I was just checking for a schematic."

"A what?" said Stanley in utter disbelief.

"An instructional manual of some sort, sir," timidly replied the freckle-faced sailor.

"I know what a schematic is, you knucklehead!" burst out Stanley. "But what I don't understand is

179

why you're wasting your time searching for one that's most probably written in bird tracks."

Stanley pointed to his head and firmly added. "The only manual we've got on this pigboat is right up here. So start using it, or we'll never leave this damned underground garage!"

The young, red-faced sailor still appeared to be flustered, so Stanley softened his tone. "Look, son, I'm not getting personal with you. It's just that it's going to take some very special smarts to get this sub running smoothly. And since none of us is all that familiar with this Chink hardware, we're going to have to improvise and learn as we go. Remember, an engine is still just an engine, whether it's made in Detroit or Peking. And as one of Uncle Sam's best, you're trained to meet any challenge, including this one. So get in there and open up that shaft coupling, and before you know it, you'll be drawing me that schematic."

This did the trick. Seaman Miller showed a bit more confidence as he stood up and replied. "I'm sorry for the delay, Chief. I'll get on it at once."

"That's the spirit," said the veteran, as he pivoted to make his way aft.

Well aware of the youngster who followed behind him, Stanley directed his eyes upward and vented his frustration with a quick, barely whispered prayer. "Lord, just give me the patience to get through this one last mission, and I swear you'll never hear from me again!"

Thirteen

The sky had been pitch black when the Sikorsky Sea King helicopter dropped them into the water approximately two miles off Okinawa's northern shoreline. Even in a full wet suit, the shock of plunging feet-first into the cold sea brought Dr. Miriam Kromer to full alert. Her great fatigue instantly was displaced by a surge of adrenaline as she fought to keep her head above the white cap-topped waves. Beside her, the members of SEAL Team Three quickly went to work inflating their raft, and soon all of them were in this black, rubber vessel, paddling vigorously toward the shore.

They traveled in that direction for over an hour, and the toxicologist was all but oblivious to the first faint colors of dawn painting the eastern horizon. As always, the SEALs were setting a blistering pace, and it took a total effort on her part to keep up with them. The palm of her hand stung where it made contact with the paddle's wooden handle, and her back and neck were almost numb with pain. Though one part of her wanted to just give up, to abandon this ridiculous challenge, an inner voice urged her to push on even harder. So far, the latter preference had won out, though how much longer it would she couldn't really say.

She supposed she had something to prove, not only to the SEALs but to herself. Throughout her life, Miriam had thrived on challenge. In her school days, her competitive spirit had been expressed both in the classroom and on the playground. She never got a grade lower than an *A*. And she captained the gymnastics, field hockey, and softball teams.

College was no different. If anything, the additional competition only made her work harder. Because of her father's influence, she had chosen her field before she began her freshman year, and she had faltered only once, because of a young man she was dating. Actually, this fellow had been her first and, so far, her only love. He was handsome, bright, and incredibly persuasive, and because of him, Miriam almost gave up a career in toxicology to join him as family physician.

Uninvited, Miriam had been drawn to his off-campus apartment one icy December evening. She'd entered through the back door, which he always kept unlocked, and had immediately smelled the rich sandalwood incense burning inside. Jim Morrison and the Doors blared forth from the stereo as she quietly sneaked into the bedroom to surprise him. As it turned out, that night the surprise was on her.

Miriam had caught him making love to a big-busted, Oriental nurse who doubled as a student teacher. She had never felt real pain until that moment, and had run from the apartment, tears cascading down her cheeks. She'd cried herself to sleep, then had awakened several hours later to come to a startling conclusion. She would never again put herself in such a vulnerable position. She would never feel such pain again.

From that night on, she applied herself to her studies with a new ferocity. With her competitive spirit reawakened, she eventually graduated number one in her class, then had the good fortune to be accepted in the Armed Forces' graduate studies program at Ft. Detrick, Maryland.

As far as Miriam was concerned, there was no more intellectually stimulating opportunity on earth. With the entire world as her laboratory, she was on a life and death quest, her goal to identify, control, and eliminate some of the most deadly natural substances known to man. The proliferation of biological weapons only made her job that much more challenging. And this was especially the case now that genetically altered toxins were beginning to make their nightmarish ways into the world's arsenals.

No stranger to commitment, she considered her current assignment the perfect opportunity to demonstrate that. The mysterious Dr. Ishii was challenging her to make a stand, to become personally involved in ridding the earth of the scourge he would inflict on untold millions. The SEALs were pushing Miriam to the very edge of her physical endurance. If she was worthy, she would pass this test and be in on the completion of the mission. Unable to contemplate failure, she did her best to ignore her pain-racked body as she dipped the paddle in, at the limit of her arm's extension, and swept it backward with a powerful push.

"I think I saw some surf breakin' up yonder," observed Cajun from the raft's rounded bow. "I bet that's the beach."

Old Dog voiced his concern from a position immediately behind their point man. "What if it's a reef?"

"Then we throw you overboard, big guy, and float over it," remarked Traveler, who was paddling opposite the Texan.

"Breath easy, Old Dog," said Warlock from his seat in the stern beside Miriam. "If Cajun saw breaking surf, then that can only mean the beach is close-by. Because before they dropped us in the drink, I got a chance to study the bathymetrics of this approach. And unless we got pushed off course by a hell of an unexpected current, the nearest reef is miles from these parts."

"There it is again!" exclaimed Cajun, who pointed toward a frothing line of white surf, several hundred yards in front of them.

Miriam Kromer only had one thing on her mind. "When can we stop paddling?"

"Now's as good a time as any, Doc," said Warlock, and he lifted up his own paddle. "That goes for the rest of you misfits as well. No use wasting energy when we can let the tide do the work for us."

There was a collective sigh of relief as the team quit paddling. The only female in their midst was especially appreciative of this respite, and she sat back and gratefully stretched out her aching arms.

"In a couple of days, we'll be making this trip for real, two hundred miles north of here," said Warlock. "The only differences being a submarine will drop us off and our reception committee on land will be far from friendly. That's why it's imperative we make a clean entry on the beach."

"Hey, Doc, ever go surfing?" interrupted Traveler.

"I'm afraid I haven't," answered Miriam.

"Well, that's going to change real quick," added Traveler, who began stowing away the loose equipment at his feet.

The other SEALs followed his example, paying extra attention to the waterproof sacks holding their weapons. They completed this task just as the crashing of surf echoed clearly in the near distance. The raft surged forward as if in the firm grasp of a submerged hand. Miriam could see the surf line now, as well as the bare outline of a distant beach. She expectantly sat forward, and regripped her paddle when Warlock called out firmly.

"Mount 'em up, ladies! The more forward speed we have going into this, the easier it's going to be to catch that curl."

All of the SEALs began forcefully clawing at the water with their paddles, Miriam spiritedly stroking as well. The pounding of the breakers intensified, and she could actually feel their deafening rumble in the back of her dry throat. Her pulse quickened as the raft bobbed upward on the back of an advancing wave. And there was a sickening sensation in the pit of her stomach as they abruptly dropped downward into a deep trough, only to be lifted upward once again.

The team's paddling now attained almost frantic proportions, and in response, the raft shot forward in an incredible burst of wave-induced speed. Never before had Miriam experienced the raw force of a fully formed, twenty-foot-high wave. They *were* surfing now, the raft and its occupants tightly tucked into the wave's well-developed curl.

"Ya-hoo!" cried Cajun, as he leaned forward, his

right hand held high over his head as if he were a cowboy on a bucking bronco.

Behind him, Old Dog appeared tense, while Traveler was taking it all in stride, still calmly chewing away on a toothpick that had materialized shortly after they'd first hit the water.

Much like a child on a roller coaster, Miriam was caught between fear and total exhilaration. Warlock seemed equally enthused, yet he called out a warning when the curl began closing in on them overhead.

"We're gonna' lose it! Hold on!"

As soon as these words were out, the sea came crashing down in an icy torrent. For a frightening second, Miriam thought they had capsized and that she was trapped underwater. But then the upright raft popped out of the agitated wall of water that had just fallen on them. Spread out before them now was a wide, sandy beach, whose palm trees were just being illuminated by the first rays of dawn.

Cajun leaped into the shallow water, followed closely by Traveler and Old Dog. As they struggled to guide the now-lightened raft up onto the beach, Traveler provided encouragement.

"Come on, ladies, pull! I've got a hot date with the platter of ham 'n' eggs waiting for me somewhere up there!"

Bill Brown and Henry Walker watched the SEALs hit the beach from the cover of a nearby sand dune. As the first rays of the sun broke over the horizon, they were able to see the commando team gather on the sand without the aid of the thermal-imaging binoculars they'd brought along.

186

"That must have been one hell of a ride in," remarked Bill Brown as he put on his aviator-style, wire-rimmed sunglasses. "Is the surf always this rough up here?"

"This sea condition is highly unusual," replied the Director of Naval Intelligence. "There's a low-pressure system passing to the west, and that's what's generating these monster waves. The normal size of the surf here is a good half what we're seeing this morning."

"Well, if they can handle these conditions, they should have no trouble at all taking on the protected waters of Takara Bay," said Brown.

The commandoes were in the process of dragging their raft up onto the gently sloping sand as Henry Walker pulled a large, black plastic police whistle out of his pocket. "Shall we see how the good doctor is getting along?" he asked.

"I almost forgot she wasn't a regular member of the SEAL team." Brown's gaze was locked on the five, wet-suited figures pulling the raft up onto the beach.

Walker stood, put the whistle to his lips, and blew three distinct, high-pitched blasts. He also waved his arms overhead, and the commandoes soon spotted him.

Bill Brown also rose. After brushing the sand from his khakis, he followed his ex-shipmate down toward the water line. With each advancing step, the pounding of the surf intensified, until the very sand seemed to tremble as a result of the sea's fury. The white-haired veteran had a new respect for the commando team's seamanship. Up close, the breaking surf could rival the giant waves that smashed onto

187

Oahu's northern shore.

"Good morning, gentlemen." The devilishly handsome SEAL known as Traveler smiled. "Surf's up. Where're your boards?"

Henry Walker had to scream to be heard. "That was a wonderful approach. Anyone care to try it again?"

"I'm game if the Doc here is willing," replied Traveler.

This prompted an instant response from the serious-faced toxicologist. "Thanks, but no thanks. I've already had my adrenaline rush for the morning."

"I was just teasing, Dr. Kromer," returned Walker. "All of you did a hell of a fine job this morning, and the least I can do is offer you a lift back to Alpha Base."

The SEALs readily accepted, and as they made their way up the road where the van was parked, Bill Brown fell in beside Miriam Kromer.

"Was that ride as scary as it looked?" asked the veteran.

"At least when we hit the surf I didn't have to paddle." Miriam gingerly rubbed the callused skin of her left palm. "Though I do believe I left my stomach on the crest of one of those waves."

Brown couldn't help but feel sorry for the attractive redhead who reminded him of his wife. Both women had that highly competitive spirit. It had often gotten his Mary into difficult situations. He remembered when she'd volunteered to work in a Red Cross blood drive and had ended up chairman of the entire chapter.

"How are the SEALs treating you?" probed Brown.

Miriam replied softly so as not to be overheard. "Amazingly enough, pretty good, considering that I'm the first outsider that's ever been allowed to accompany them on one of their operations."

"They do seem like a pretty tight bunch," said Brown. "But I guess that's part of the territory."

Even though Miriam barely knew the man who walked beside her, she liked his genuineness and his soft-spoken manner. "They're an incredible bunch of characters. To tell you the truth, when I first met them I didn't like them at all, and I'm sure the feeling was mutual. But we put up with each other for Admiral Walker's sake, and slowly but surely they began to open up to me."

"Respect is the first bridge to trust and acceptance," offered Brown. "And it has to be earned, which speaks well of you, Doc."

Not one to take a compliment lightly, Miriam blushed. "I hope I've truly earned their respect," she reflected. "Lord knows they've got mine. Though each one of them has his idiosyncrasies, it's somewhat comforting to know they'll be around in a life-or-death situation. In a way it's almost like hanging out with your brothers. They might give you the business now and then, but they'll always be around to protect you from the neighborhood bully."

As they climbed up a sea grape-covered sand dune, she added, "They'll be taking me out on the rifle range this afternoon, and then there's going to be a little introductory hand-to-hand combat session. How's your work on the *Bokken* going?"

Brown held back his response until they had climbed up onto the dirt trail that would lead them directly to the van. "So far, so good. The repairs to the bow are just about completed. And the young submariners picked to run her are well on their way to familiarizing themselves with the boat's unique operational systems."

"Is it true that you'll be accompanying us?" Miriam asked hopefully.

Brown readily answered. "How could I resist Admiral Walker's gracious invitation? And two ex-shipmates of mine wouldn't miss this cruise for the world. If I don't go along, who's going to be there to keep them out of trouble?"

Miriam was relieved to hear this news, and she couldn't help but laugh as Traveler's voice rang out ahead of them, as he spotted the parked van.

"All right, ladies! Ham 'n' eggs here we come!"

This same dawn found Dr. Yukio Ishii seated on his favorite plateau, overlooking Takara Bay. A storm had just passed over the island, and as it moved off to the west, the rain-washed morning sky stretched overhead in a clear, powdery blue expanse. The air itself was sweet with the promise of spring, and the elder felt at one with the bright pink cherry blossoms that were just beginning to break through on the grounds below.

When he'd left for his pilgrimage four days ago, the buds of these same trees had been tightly sealed. With their opening, a great secret was symbolically revealed, and Ishii was aware of the very essence of time.

Even without his presence, the world went on. This was most obvious as he peered down at the sprawling industrial complex just stirring to life on

190

this glorious new day.

Looking like so many ants from this lofty vantage point, his employees traversed the narrow streets, obediently heading off to work to fill another day's rice bowl. Yet how many of these pitiful creatures really understood their rightful place in the grand scheme of things? To the majority of them, this was but a job, a way to pass time, that most precious gift of all.

Of course, a treasured handful of his associates had successfully lifted the veil of consciousness and now understood their place in the Way. During his brief absence, these were the souls he most missed communing with. But the call to cleanse himself had been a strong one. And though there was still much work to be done to insure his dream's success, Ishii had left the everyday world of man, to walk the wild, unpopulated hills of his island home.

For four lonely days, he'd seen not another soul. With only an occasional mouthful of cool spring water to give him subsistence, he'd surrendered his body and soul to the great nature spirits that haunted Takara's hills and valleys.

He'd found shelter in a quiet grotto that lay near the island's eastern shore. Here a crude plywood lean-to protected him from the wind and the rain. Ishii carried no spare clothing. He had only the white robe on his back. The only time he spoke was to mutter his prayers, except when he addressed a stray dog that had befriended him along the way before abruptly running off to chase a rabbit.

The basic simplicity of this primal lifestyle clarified the elder's inner vision. And now he was prepared for the great victory it had taken him a virtual lifetime to achieve.

Ishii found it strange that the only person he really wished he could have brought along to share his many insights was Yoko Noguchi. On the day before he'd left on his unannounced retreat, he had spent the better part of a morning with this delightful young woman, giving her a tour of the grounds.

Unlike many of his employees, she had a probing intellect, and wasn't afraid to speak her mind. There could be no doubting her potential talent as a scientist, though her political beliefs left a lot to be desired. Like many young adults, Yoko had a naive trust in Japan's current government. As if this so-called democracy had any real concern for the cherished will of the people!

There came a time in every society's development when the people needed to realize that a pure democracy was not the best way to be governed. The average citizen was too self-centered, too concerned with minor, everyday wants and desires to be an effective leader. Rather than be wasted on such persons, political power was best kept in the hands of an elite, those whose vision went beyond the mundane.

Ishii had living proof that such a system worked, here on Takara. And if he could convince Yoko Noguchi of this fact, he'd have a powerful new ally who could be a conduit to an entire generation that desperately needed spiritual awakening.

Yoko's generation and the ones that would follow were the real future of Japan. Above all, they had to be cleansed of the corrupt western cultural influences that blinded them to the richness of their heritage. Like a malignant cancer, the evils generated by rock and roll, drugs, and petty consumerism had to be removed before the contamination was irreversible. Ishii could only help them make the first all-important cut. Then it would be up to leaders such as Yoko Noguchi to continue the revolution, by showing her contemporaries that the true path to self-fufillment lay in not imitating Western values. It could be found instead in the shrines of their ancestors.

Stimulated by this lofty thought, Ishii foresaw a day in the not so distant future when Japan would be reborn in spirit. And like a cherry blossom opening to the first call of spring, the land of the Rising Sun would flourish as it had in centuries past, before the coming of the barbarian.

The sound of heavy footsteps broke behind him, and Ishii didn't have to turn around to identify their source. Called thusly back to the everyday world of man, the elder summoned forth a voice that was hoarse from disuse.

"So, you have not missed our appointed practice time, Satsugai."

"Sensei, we have been very worried about you," replied the concerned submariner. "No one has seen you for four entire days."

Ishii held back his response as he stood upright and bowed deeply toward the rising sun. Only then did he turn to face Okura, who was dressed in a white robe similar to his own.

"There was no reason to worry, my friend. It's good for the soul to break free from the world of man now and then, and to lose itself in nature. I hope that you used this time wisely to establish your own oneness with the Way."

"That I have, Sensei. I have found my peace of mind through fasting and prayer."

"Then let us see the results," replied Ishii, who bent over and removed two samurai swords from the lacquered box placed beside his prayer rug.

These weapons had orange tassels hanging from their hilts, which were composed of diamond-shaped, mother-of-pearl inlay. The razor-sharp steel of the blade itself had a smoky, wavy pattern to it, the result of a special tempering process known as sambon sugi.

"I hope you don't mind if we forsake the bokken and utilize the katana on this glorious dawn," remarked the elder. "These swords are said to have been among those used by the great samurai Saigo Takamori and his followers. It's hard to believe that over a century has passed since those one hundred brave warriors raised their swords against the Western-influenced fools in the Meiji government, those who had the effrontery to outlaw the samurai way of life. Though the government rifles ripped our samurai brethren to shreds, their spirits have lived on, to guide our souls and to return Nippon to the path of righteousness."

Ishii then handed one of the swords to Okura, and took a second to tie a white hachimaki around his forehead. This particular samurai headband had a bright red rising sun dyed in its center, and emblazoned in black ink on its sides were the words Shichisho Hokoku (serve the nation for seven lives).

"Remember, Satsugai," added Ishii, "if in his mind the warrior doesn't forget one thing, that being death, he'll never find himself caught short."

Both men faced each other at the center of the

clearing, bowed and then adopted an opening attitude, with knees slightly bent and both hands on the hilts of their swords. Ishii appeared content to let his younger opponent make the first move, and Okura all too soon obliged him.

With a quick fluid motion, the submariner slashed down at Ishii's neck. Without shifting his feet, Ishii needed only a minimal movement of his katana to counter this powerful blow. Not to be denied, Okura yanked his sword aside, and raised it high over his head, seemingly taunting the elder to strike out at his exposed body. Ishii took the bait and lunged forward, yet not before Okura was able to cut downward and block this blow.

Ishii loudly grunted and pulled his katana free. His eyes gleamed with determination, and he wasted no time in once again taking the offensive. They exchanged a lightning-quick series of blows that filled the air with the raw, metallic clash of steel upon steel.

Ishii was in the process of cutting downward toward his opponent's head when Okura alertly ducked, just as the fatal blow was about to hit home. From this crouching position, he proceeded to sweep his sword upward, catching the hilt of Ishii's sword in the process, and separating it from the startled elder's grasp.

As the sword clattered to the ground, Okura took a step backward and bowed. Ishii returned this gesture, appearing pleasantly surprised by the bout's outcome.

"So, it appears that the master is now the student," observed Ishii. "I have waited many dawns for this momentous day to come, my friend. At long

195

last you are at one with the Way, and now not even death will interfere with your divine mission."

He beckoned Okura to join him at the overlook. After stashing their swords in the lacquered box, both men stood on the rocky lip of the plateau and gazed out at the glimmering waters of the bay.

The sun had long since broken over the horizon, and was quickly rising in the blue sky. It promised to be a warm day. Even the circling gulls seemed to be celebrating the arrival of spring by calling out to each other in constant streams of animated bird chatter.

It was the shrill blast of a ship's whistle that diverted the attention of Ishii and Okura to the pier. A small trawler had just cast off its lines, and as it turned for the sea, it passed yet another docked vessel, whose gray, v-shaped hull was for the most part submerged.

"How are things aboard the *Katana?*" questioned the elder, whose gaze remained locked on the sleek submarine he had just asked about.

"All is going as planned, Sensei," answered this vessel's captain. "Our latest refit was completed with a minimum of difficulties. The only system currently not on-line is our passive sonar array. Several critical components of the Fenik unit were found to be functioning improperly. We're awaiting replacements, which are to be flown in from the manufacturer."

"Do you foresee any delay in carrying out your scheduled mission, Satsugai?"

Okura's response was firm. "The *Katana* will be ready to put to sea as planned, Sensei. Even if the sonar components fail to arrive in time, the array can still be operated using the old parts."

196

Ishii's relief was most apparent. "That's all I wanted to hear, my friend. I have waited too long for this momentous day to have it delayed by a mere mechanical problem.

"This only goes to show how important it is for us to replace our current fleet of submarines with more advanced vessels of our own design. Though both the *Katana* and the *Bokken* have served us well, they are rapidly approaching obsolescence, and will all too soon need to be retired."

"Sensei," remarked Okura guardedly. "Recently we had an unexpected visitor aboard the *Katana*. An employee by the name of Yoko Noguchi was interested in a tour of the boat."

The mere mention of the young scientist's name caused a warm grin to raise the corners of Ishii's mustached mouth, and he casually questioned. "And did you give her this tour?"

"Why of course, Sensei. She was most adamant, and said that you had already approved this request. I hope that I did the right thing."

"You need not be concerned, Satsugai. Miss Noguchi is a valued new member of our family. So tell me, how did she enjoy the *Katana?*"

Okura hesitated a moment before answering this question. "If I remember correctly, she appeared to be a bit claustrophobic, and wasn't all that at ease, especially in the tighter spaces. She asked the usual questions, though she was particularly interested in our range, speed, storage capacity, and maximum submerged endurance. She was also curious as to the whereabouts of the *Bokken*."

"And how did you answer her?" asked Ishii, who had yet to give Yoko the clearance needed for access to this particular piece of sensitive information.

"Since she was not on the Class-A security list, I gave her the standard reply, Sensei. As far as she knows, the *Bokken* is presently at an undisclosed location, probing the seabed for mineral deposits."

"Excellent, Satsugai. Hopefully, once she proves herself loyal, we can reveal the true manner in which we are utilizing our submarine fleet."

Most satisfied that Okura had handled this situation properly, Ishii added, "Now how about joining me in the commissary for some breakfast? I don't know about you, old friend, but after fasting for four days, I'm positively famished!"

Fourteen

It was shortly after noon when the penstocks were opened, and the sea came flooding into the drydock where the *Bokken* was berthed. The crew spent some anxious moments before learning whether or not the repairs to the bow had been successful. Things were especially tense in the forward torpedo room, where Pete Frystak and his men closely monitored the compartment for any leakage. And all breathed a long sigh of relief, when word came down that they were safely afloat, for the torpedo room remained as dry as the day it was originally constructed.

It was a very happy retired weapons officer who escorted a group of yard workers up onto the deck of the now floating submarine. Close at his side was his bunkmate and invaluable assistant, Ensign Adie Avila.

"Well, there goes the last of 'em," remarked Pete Frystak as the gang of metal workers exited the *Bokken* via its aft gangway. "The torpedo room is all ours now. Shall we see what they left us?"

Adie nodded and turned for the forward access trunk that would take them straight down into this compartment. The young Texan took his time transiting the trunk's narrow steel ladder. It was primarily designed for emergency egress, which made descents awkward at best.

Only when he was firmly on the deck below did Adie peer up the trunk to address his associate. "Careful with those last couple of rungs, Pete. They're treacherous!"

Much to the startled sailor's surprise, Pete Frystak proceeded to smoothly slide down the sides of the ladder like a fireman did with a pole. As he plopped down onto the deck, he issued his shocked shipmate an all-knowing wink and said matter-of-factly, "A guy can learn a lot hanging around these pigboats for the better part of three decades, Adie. So wipe that surprised look off your face, and let's get to work making room for those fish we'll be taking on shortly."

On the opposite end of the *Bokken,* Stanley Roth was in the midst of a surprise inspection of the engine room. Now that they were afloat, sailing time was quickly approaching, which meant that the diesels had to be completely operational. There could be no going back for spare parts or more instruction once the boat's CO gave the order to cast off lines. This would be especially real to them once they entered enemy waters, and the veteran submariner wanted to be absolutely certain they had done all the vital preparatory work beforehand.

His first stop was at the oil reservoir. He really didn't know what to expect as he used a screw driver to remove the cover plate, then switched on a flashlight and peered inside. The golden sheen of fresh oil met his eyes, and he couldn't help but be gratified.

"Well, I'll be," he muttered. "My arteries should be so clean."

Yet another pleasant surprise awaited him beside the reduction gears, where Seaman Miller was well into repacking the shaft coupling. Assisting him with this time-consuming task was Senior Machinist Bob Marchetto.

"That's the way to keep at it, Miller," Roth praised. "Now if your assistant there gives me a good report on those diagnostic tests, my day will really be made."

As usual, Bob Marchetto was all business as he looked up and replied, "You hit the nail right on the head, Chief. Once we drained and replaced the oil and put in a new filter, she passed the oil pressure test with no trouble at all. We also got positive results with the intake-manifold vacuum reading, and the cylinder-compression leakage and balance tests."

"If you weren't so damned ugly I'd kiss you, Marchetto," joked Stanley. "Because next to this rust bucket floating like it is, that's the best news I've heard today. Now, I don't suppose that Orlovick has had any success with that bubbler?"

"Last I saw, he was still at it," reported Marchetto, who seemed impatient to get back to the job at hand.

"Keep up the good work, men," said Stanley as he turned aft to check on the status of the prototype masking device.

Expecting to find the unit stripped down and in dozens of pieces, he was surprised to find the machinery almost entirely intact. Seaman Orlovick was working on the fuse box positioned beside the compressor, and Stanley wondered if he had even bothered to remove the outer casing of the machine and examine the components inside. Hoping that this wasn't the case, Stanley nonetheless greeted him somewhat soberly.

"I thought I asked you to pull apart this unit and make it tick again, Orlovick. It looks to me like you didn't even start yet."

"On the contrary, Chief," returned the serious-faced reactor specialist. "I've already stripped it down, cleaned its interior parts, and put it back together. And if you just give me a second to replace this fuse, I'll let you know if my efforts were a success or not."

Embarrassed by his misjudgment, Stanley lightened the tone of his reply. "Take all the time you need, Orlovick. Can I help you?"

Not bothering to respond to this, the young sailor redirected his attention to the fuse box. It took him less than a minute to complete the installation and then reach up for the starter switch.

"Shall I, Chief?" he questioned.

"By all means, give it a try," directed Stanley.

Orlovick hit the switch, and the unit remained unceremoniously silent. He tried it again, and when it still didn't start he turned to address Stanley, his face etched with both disappointment and puzzlement.

"I don't understand, Chief. It's only a dressed-up compressor, and I know I put it back together properly. It's got to work."

"Easy does it, son," said Stanley, who sensed Orlovick's frustration. "Sometimes when you're dealing with older equipment, especially of various origins, it takes some special techniques to get it going. Let's see if I can give you a hand with this sucker."

The grinning veteran literally did just that. He stepped up to the unit and forcefully slapped the starter box with the side of his palm. Almost instantly, the compressor activated with a high-pitched whine.

"Looks like we've got one bubbler masking device ready for action," said Stanley. "Now let's just pray that we won't need to use it."

Making his own tour of inspection in the still somewhat unfamiliar confines of the *Bokken*'s control room was Lieutenant Commander Benjamin Kram. The blond-haired XO of the *Hawkbill* would be the OOD for the majority of their upcoming voyage, and he wanted to get as comfortable with his new surroundings as possible.

Kram had gone on record as opposing the use of the Romeo-class sub from the very beginning. In his mind, it would be better to use the *Hawkbill* and take their chances on penetrating Takara Bay in a craft that they were experienced at operating.

He had voiced his concerns to his CO, and Chris Slaughter had promised to share them with Admiral Walker. Yet the Director of Naval Intelligence had apparently already made up his mind; he'd felt the added risks involved in sailing the captured sub were worth taking. And now that the bulk of the repairs to the *Bokken* had been successfully completed and the three veterans had shared their expertise, this decision was evidently unchangeable.

With no alternative but to make the best of the situation, Benjamin Kram had reluctantly accepted his new duty. His career goal had been to get command of one of the new SSN-21 Seawolf-class nuclear-attack submarines that were just putting to sea. He had hoped the *Hawkbill* would be a stepping stone to such an advanced vessel, but he'd suddenly found himself going in the opposite direction. One only had to set eyes on the antiquated equipment that currently surrounded him to realize this fact.

Touring the *Bokken's* control room was like stepping back in time to the 1950's. With not a single computer keyboard in evidence, all of the operational input had to be done on old-fashioned, tube-powered consoles that were obsolete four decades ago. Valves had to be turned by hand, and as Chief McKenzie, their COB so aptly put it, the diving console was like something out of a museum.

Surprisingly enough, the crew was accepting this unique assignment with a minimum of gripes and complaints. Kram really hadn't known what their reaction would be as the reality of this operation sank in, but it turned out that most of the crew looked at this new duty as a challenge. Therefore, morale was high, which made the chances for a successful outcome that much better.

The crew's esprit de corps was evident as Kram passed by the helm. The dials, instruments, and gauges mounted into the bulkhead had been labeled in Japanese, but with the navigator's invaluable help, the labels had been translated into English. Assisting Lieutenant Laycob with this relabeling effort was the helmsman. Bill Foard took advantage of his height, and was able to reach even the topmost gauge without having to resort to a ladder.

Beside the helm, Chief McKenzie was in the

process of simulating a dive. With amazing swiftness, Mac's fingers flew across the dozens of red and green toggle switches mounted before him. Back on the *Hawkbill,* this same process could be accomplished by the mere push of a button. It had taken the grizzled COB many hours of intense study and practice to get accustomed to a diving console that differed little from those on World War II-era submarines.

Ray Morales had put just as much effort into learning the equipment of the adjoining radar station. The hard-working young technician had already completed stripping down the unit and, after giving it a thorough cleaning, had reassembled it down to the last vacuum tube. As always, Morales took pride in his work, and now as the XO watched he polished the upper glass plate of the radar screen until it shone like a mirror.

"Lieutenant Commander Kram," said a nearby voice. "What do you make of this?"

The XO looked to his left and discovered that the source of this question was seated at sonar. Jaffers was one of his favorite shipmates, and Kram proceeded over to his console. The senior sonar technician immediately handed him a set of lightweight headphones.

"I was working on isolating the port hydrophones mounted directly beneath the sail," continued Jaffers in all seriousness, "and that's when I first came across it. I don't believe I've ever heard a signature quite like it before."

Curious as to what Jaffers was referring to, the XO put on the headphones. A loud, resonant snoring sound met his ears, and it didn't take Kram long to figure out what was going on.

"You say that this hydrophone is mounted directly beneath the sail, Jaffers?" said Kram, who found it hard to keep a straight face.

Jaffers also found it hard to remain serious as he replied. "That it is, sir."

"Well then, Jaffers," responded the grinning XO, "maybe we should tape it, and leave it to the yard foreman to figure out which one of his workers was napping on government time. Man, that guy's really cutting Z's something fierce!"

Both men burst out laughing at this point, and only quieted when the sub's acting quartermaster approached them.

"Lieutenant Commander Kram," he soberly said, "Captain Slaughter requests your presence in the wardroom, sir."

"Very well, sailor," returned the XO, who excused the bearer of this message and removed the headphones.

"This is one unidentified contact we're definitely not going to have to worry about, Jaffers," added Kram, who fondly patted the sonarman on the back and then turned to the aft hatchway.

When he'd last left the captain, Slaughter had been immersed in a study of their mission's navigational charts. Kram had already sketched out a projected route, and he supposed the captain had some changes he wanted implemented.

The XO knew he was fortunate to have Chris Slaughter as his commanding officer. The two men had a tight, trusting relationship. Perfectly happy to let his XO have a fair share of responsibility, Slaughter delegated power whenever possible. Unlike some commanding officers, who wanted to dominate those that served under them.

This equal sharing of responsibility had permeated the crew, who saw themselves as a closely knit team. A baseball player in his Academy days, Chris Slaughter had certainly learned the value of teamwork. His current success as a CO was proof that the lessons he'd learned on the ball field could be applied to running a submarine.

Proud to be a part of this crew, Benjamin Kram continued down the passageway that led to the wardroom. As he approached the aft hatchway, an appetizing scent met his nostrils. Suddenly aware that he hadn't eaten a bite since having a light breakfast, Kram stepped through the hatch and laid his eyes on the virtual feast Chief Mallot was in the process of serving the captain.

"Ah, there you are, Ben," greeted Slaughter. "Please join me."

The XO readily accepted, taking a seat at the wardroom table immediately beside the captain.

"I hope you brought your appetite along," Slaughter added.

Kram gazed at the collection of food-filled platters. Mallot was quick to identify each dish.

"Here it is, gentlemen, the first hot meal cooked exclusively in this galley. In honor of our new home, I cooked up a batch of tempura-battered shrimp, my already infamous turkey teriyaki, miso soup, steamed veggies, green tea, and all the fried rice you can eat. Ken Pei!"

"It looks wonderful, Mr. Mallot," said Chris Slaughter. "But where's the silverware?"

A devilish gleam came to Mallot's eyes as he

reached into the pocket of his apron and pulled out two pairs of chopsticks.

"You can't eat an authentic Japanese meal with a knife and fork," he instructed as he handed out the wooden utensils.

Neither one of the officers protested, though it took some practice on their part to perfect their techniques. Of the two diners, Slaughter proved to be the most adept with chopsticks, while his XO dropped more food back onto his plate than he was able to get into his mouth. Nevertheless, Benjamin Kram's face lit up in delight when he bit into one of the juicy fried shrimp.

"You've got a real winner with this tempura, Chief," he observed between bites. "The rest of the crew is going to love it."

"I hope you're not planning on making them use chopsticks," said Slaughter as he washed down a bite of teriyaki with some piping hot tea. "Half of them might starve to death."

Mallot chuckled. "Don't worry, Captain. I'll make certain to transfer over enough silverware from the *Hawkbill* to take care of any of our boys without a sense of adventure."

"Sense of adventure, hell!" exclaimed the XO, who impotently looked on as a slice of turkey fell onto his lap. "These damn things take coordination plus."

"Don't be afraid to use that thumb," instructed Slaughter. "That's the secret to these things."

The captain went on to provide a hasty demonstration that Kram did his best to imitate. It took several more misplaced bites before the XO's patience was rewarded and he dared take on his rice.

"There's plenty more if you'd like it," offered Mallot. "Otherwise, I'll be back with some fresh green tea ice cream."

Mallot left the two officers alone to finish their meals. They did so with a minimum of conversation. After completing his fill, Slaughter pushed away his plate and watched as his subordinate tackled the rest of his rice.

"You've got it now, Ben. By the time this operation's over, you'll be eating peanuts with those things."

"How did you ever become such an expert with chopsticks, Skipper?" asked Kram as he reached out to refill their teacups.

"During my junior year at the Academy, we had a Japanese exchange student from the Eta Jima Academy bunking in our dormitory. His name was Osami Nagano. He was shy, but a good kid who adored baseball. I invited him to a couple of games, and he reciprocated by taking me to his favorite Japanese restaurants in the area. Believe it or not, I'd never even laid my eyes on a pair of chopsticks until then, and Osami demonstrated commendable patience in teaching me the basics."

"Where's he now?" asked Kram, who was content to sit back and sip his tea.

"The last I heard, Osami was in line to take command of one of Japan's newest Yuushio-class submarines. That's the Seawolf of the Japanese Maritime Self-Defense Force."

"If he only knew what we were about to get involved in . . ." reflected the XO.

Slaughter sat forward and lowered his voice. "From what I gather from Admiral Walker, it's highly unlikely anyone in the Japanese military will ever learn of this operation, even if there's a successful outcome. It's just taking place too close to their home waters."

"I hear you, Skipper. And I imagine that if the tables were turned, the Japanese would be equally as secretive. Allowing a maniac to run loose in their backyard wouldn't be good for their world image, and they'd quietly eliminate Ishii. Maybe even by sending in your old friend Osami in his Yuushio."

"Unfortunately, we've managed to pull the dirty duty once more," remarked Slaughter, whose glance met that of his XO. "By the way, Ben. I looked over the route you picked and can find no fault in it whatsoever. By passing Yokoate Island on the west, we've got an almost straight line into Takara. That makes it a trip of some one hundred and sixty-five miles from Alpha Base. If the engine room gang can give us a submerged, snorkel depth speed of at least twelve knots, we should be able to get there in the better part of fourteen hours."

"That's not soon enough as far as I'm concerned, Skipper. I still wish that we were sailing aboard *Hawkbill*."

Slaughter's intense glance narrowed. "You might feel that way now, Ben. But wait until we pass through that inlet and enter Takara Bay. I'm sure going to be breathing a lot easier knowing that our signature is preprogrammed as a friendly inside of any CAPTOR mines we might be meeting up with. No, Ben, I believe in this instance, Admiral Walker made the right decision. And now we're just going to have to be the ones to live or die with it."

* * *

Henry Walker and Bill Brown left the modular trailer that served as Alpha Base's headquarters building and slowly made their way back toward the pier. This rectangular concrete structure extended into a black channel of water, and currently had a submarine floating on each side of it. The nuclear-powered *Hawkbill* was clearly the larger of these vessels, its streamlined hull stretching a good fifty feet longer than that of the *Bokken*.

Only a token workforce was visible on the Romeo-class submarine's deck. Conspicuously absent were the pounding of the metal workers' hammers and the blindingly bright glow of their acetylene torches. The hollowed-out cavern instead echoed with the high-pitched whine of a forklift at work. It was positioned at the tail end of a large flatbed truck parked beside the *Bokken*'s stern. Pete Frystak and a young sailor could be seen examining the contents of the first of six elongated cases the forklift had pulled off the truck's bed. Knowing full well what the ex-weapons officer was looking at, Bill Brown nevertheless commented.

"I wonder what could be in that crate? Ole Pete's examining it like it was the Holy Grail."

"Let's take a look," said Henry Walker, and he led the way over to the kneeling veteran.

Frystak's eyes were wide with wonder as he looked up from his examination of the shiny green torpedo that lay inside the case. "I know I shouldn't even bother asking, but where in the world did you ever find this fish, Henry? Why it's a brand-new Soviet M-57 anti-ship torpedo!"

The grinning Director of Naval Intelligence answered in his usual cryptic manner. "You'd be surprised what you can find for sale today on the international arms market, Pete."

"Well, wherever they came from, it's sure nice having them," replied Frystak gratefully. "Even though these fish are almost as obsolete as the sub we'll be loading them into, it sure beats going to sea without any punch."

"Too bad we couldn't update the *Bokken*'s fire-control system so we could take along some wire-guided Mk 48's," added Bill Brown.

"There are a lot of operational systems I would have liked to update," returned Henry Walker. "But we're very fortunate just to be able to get the *Bokken* on her way in the time allotted. How does that forward torpedo room look, Pete?"

"I was just beginning a comprehensive inspection of it, when I was informed of this delivery," answered Frystak. "The yard work appears to be first rate, and as long as those welds hold, we should be just fine."

Henry Walker seemed pleased with this report and responded accordingly. "We can all be proud of that yard crew. They did the impossible and still gave us time to spare."

"Are you going to need any help onloading these fish, Pete?" asked Bill Brown.

"Lieutenant Commander Kram is taking care of that, Skipper," said Frystak.

"Well, just holler if you need a hand," offered Brown.

"And don't forget that final briefing in the *Bokken*'s wardroom at eighteen-hundred hours," Walker reminded.

"I won't, Henry," replied Frystak. He went over to

supervise the removal of the next crate, as his two ex-shipmates turned to continue on down the pier.

Bill Brown was momentarily lost in thought as he spotted several yard workers gathered behind the *Bokken*'s sail, loading a collection of loose repair gear into a trio of wheelbarrows. Henry Walker also noticed this group and commented.

"Once that bunch completes the final cleanup, she'll be all yours, Bill."

"I certainly agree that the yard had done a damn fine job," said Brown.

Walker grunted. "Just be around to tell me that after you complete your first test dive."

"You mean our first and only." Brown halted beside the *Bokken*'s gangway. "I hate to bring this up again, but are you absolutely firm on getting us out of here in twelve more hours? It sure would be nice to spend a full day at sea, testing out those systems first."

"I realize that, Bill. But it's imperative that you arrive at Takara at approximately the same time the *Bokken* was originally expected. And as far as we can tell, that's dusk tomorrow evening. You're just going to have to do all your tests while on the way to the island."

"That's asking an awful lot of this young crew, Henry. Just when they'll begin to get the feel of the boat, we'll be leading them into harm's way."

Walker's response was tinged with frustration. "There's nothing I can do about that, Bill. I'm relying on you, Pete, and Stanley to get them through. I just wish I could go along with you. But as it looks now, I'll be off for the *Enterprise* right after our final briefing."

Brown sensed the tenseness of his reply and lightened his own tone. "Henry, you've done a hell of a fine job clearing away all the red tape and putting this whole thing together."

"I couldn't have done it without your able assistance, Commander Brown. Now just do me one big favor: bring everyone back home safely, including yourself. And I promise you I'll never miss another reunion again."

Bill Brown's face broke into a smile. "Admiral Walker, you just made yourself a deal!"

Fifteen

Yoko Noguchi's day off had been eagerly anticipated. For the past six days, her work schedule had been a hectic one, with exhausting twelve-hour shifts not uncommon. She had planned to spend the day doing her laundry and catching up with the minor personal chores she had neglected, until the message arrived ordering her back to the laboratory. Her first impulse had been to ignore it. She deserved a day of rest, but to prove her loyalty, she didn't dare not respond to this unexpected call to duty.

She made the most of her walk over to the lab building. Spring was in the air, and the blossoming cherry trees that lined the sidewalk were proof that it had arrived. This would have been a perfect day to take a hike into the surrounding mountains, and Yoko somewhat reluctantly took a last fond look at the powdery blue sky before proceeding indoors.

She was met by an unusual flurry of activity. It appeared that she had not been the only one called in, for the tiled corridor was crowded with scurrying lab technicians. All of the Biohazard Level Four laboratories were occupied, including the one that had been reserved for her personal use.

Yoko's dour-faced superior was waiting for her at

his desk. Well into middle age, he had a personality as flat as his sense of humor, and the only thing he seemed to live for was his work. Barely lifting his eyes from the computer's monitor screen, he ordered her to get to work at once on a greatly expanded batch of the new, genetically altered anthrax toxin. The amount he wanted produced was over a thousand times greater than the earlier lot, and Yoko was dying to ask what need they could possibly have for it. Somehow she managed to summon the self-control to hold her tongue, and after meekly nodding in acquiescence, she was surprised when her superior conveyed yet another directive. Once the toxin had been prepared, she was to oversee its loading into an unspecified number of specially designed, portable, aerosol cannisters, and was to inform him the second this process was completed.

Yoko's pulse quickened as she silently made her way over to the dressing room. It was obvious that such an enormous amount of anthrax could have only one use. Her thoughts returned to her extended conversation with Dr. Yukio Ishii. He had mentioned his sincere interest in biological warfare, and there could be no ignoring the direction of his political beliefs.

And there was her recent tour of one of the submarines to consider. When she had initially joined the company, she'd been told that Ishii Industries had two such vessels, identical to each other. Both submarines were supposed to be involved in the firm's undersea mining ventures and Yoko had kept this in mind as she'd made her tour of the *Katana*. Strangely enough, she'd found it lacked a bottom-scanning sonar unit. Such equipment would be absolutely vital for locating submerged mineral deposits.

And the *Katana* had not been outfitted with a single articulated manipulator arm or an ROV (Remotely Operated Vehicle). This meant there would be no way to obtain a mineral sample, except at minimal depth where a diver could safely operate.

And the *Katana* had been taking on a variety of stores while docked. This most likely meant that she would be joining her sister ship at sea. Such a vessel would be the perfect clandestine-delivery system for the anthrax-tainted cannisters Yoko had just been ordered to fill. Since the effective shelf life of this toxin could be measured in mere days, she knew the time to act was now.

Doing her best to move as inconspicuously as possible, she quietly slipped back out of the lab building. The warm spring air greeted her like an old friend, and she knew that she would be able to get in today's hike in the mountains after all.

On that very same morning, in the cool, calm waters approximately one hundred and sixty-five miles due south of Takara Island, a surfaced submarine pointed its V-shaped bow northward. The rugged mountains of Okinawa's northern shoreline lay well astern of this vessel, and the narrow tunnel from which it had emerged had long since sealed itself.

Three men were crowded into the navigational control station set atop the sub's open sail. Each one utilized binoculars to intently scan the waters immediately before them.

"It drops off quickly now," observed Bill Brown, his white hair fluttering in the crisp sea breeze. "We should be clear to dive soon."

More concerned with any surface contacts that

might inadvertently be made in these waters, Chris Slaughter queried the seaman who stood to his left. "How's it look, Mr. Morales?"

Ray Morales answered without bothering to lower his binoculars. "The sea's all ours, Captain."

As soon as these words were spoken, the bridge intercom barked with a burst of static. This was followed by a firm, amplified voice.

"Captain, Dr. Kromer requests permission to join you topside."

Slaughter bent over and spoke into the intercom. "Send her up."

A good thirty seconds later, Miriam Kromer climbed out of the access trunk cut into the floor of the sail, her long, red hair tied back in a ponytail. She inhaled a deep lungful of fresh sea air, then looked up to scan the partly cloudy sky.

"It's a gorgeous morning for a cruise, gentlemen," she gratefully observed.

A moderate-sized swell struck them abeam, and as the *Bokken* rocked from side to side, the toxicologist was forced to hurriedly reach for the bulkhead to steady herself.

"That it is, Doc," replied Bill Brown, whose own balance did not falter. "Have you got your sea legs yet?"

Kromer shook her head that she hadn't. "I took some Dramamine earlier just to be on the safe side. And now I'm glad I did. For such a calm-looking sea, it sure feels rough."

"Don't forget that you're sailing on a vessel without a stabilizing keel," explained Bill Brown. "The ride should smooth out once we submerge."

Once again Kromer was forced to steady herself when a swell rocked the *Bokken* and she was amazed to find her three associates totally unaffected by this unsteady motion.

"And when will that be?" she impatiently questioned.

Chris Slaughter seemed to ignore this query as he spoke into the intercom. "Conn, this is bridge. What's the sounding?"

"We're just approaching the fifty-fathom curve, Captain," replied an amplified voice.

Again Slaughter addressed his remarks into the intercom. "Conn, increase speed to two-thirds. Come right ten degrees, to course zero-two-five."

"Zero-two-five it is at two-third speed, Captain," repeated the Conn.

With a minimum of fanfare, Slaughter backed away from the intercom speaker and almost casually remarked, "Doc, Bill, you'd better get below."

"Then we'll be submerging now?" asked Kromer.

"That's affirmative, Doc," said Slaughter with a bit more emotion. "It's showtime!"

The toxicologist took a last fond look at the morning sky before meeting the kind gaze of Bill Brown.

"Now's when it gets interesting," said Brown with a wink.

Kromer tried hard to relax, yet her heart was pumping wildly as she began climbing back down into the access trunk. The familiar confines of the control room soon surrounded her. And just as Bill Brown completed his own descent, the compartment filled with the forceful, amplified voice of Chris Slaughter.

"Clear the bridge! Dive! Dive!"

This was followed by two raucous blasts of the diving alarm. Miriam Kromer was barely aware of

Bill Brown's hand on her arm as he guided her over to the diving console. Here the *Hawkbill*'s blond-haired XO had assumed the role of diving officer. He stood alongside McKenzie, who, as chief of the watch, would activate the console's buttons and toggle switches.

"Shut the induction, Mac," instructed Benjamin Kram.

Mac flipped one of the switches and waited until it flashed red before reporting. "Straight board, sir."

"Inform Mr. Roth to shut down diesels and to close exhaust and air-intake valves," ordered Kram.

This order was relayed to the engine room, and only after word arrived that it had been successfully carried out did the XO add. "Switch over to electric motors."

"Hatch secured!" declared a voice from behind.

This prompted an immediate response from Benjamin Kram. "Bleed air into the boat!"

The control room suddenly filled with a loud whistling roar, and Miriam Kromer's hands shot up to her ears as an alien pressure began pressing on her eardrums. Quick to note both her concern and discomfort was Bill Brown.

"Don't worry, Doc. That pressure you feel is being intentionally pumped into the sub to confirm that she's watertight. This way we know if we have a hatch or air-induction valve stuck open before we go under."

"Pressure's holding!" reported one of the crew.

"Open vents!" ordered the XO.

As Chief McKenzie's hands flew across a row of toggle switches that turned from red to green, the distant noise of rushing air could be heard. Chris Slaughter had worked his way over to the diving console by this time and calmly took over.

"I've got the dive, Ben. Three degrees down bubble, Mr. Foard. Put your stern planes on full dive."

The big helmsman pushed his steering column all the way forward and held it there, and the deck began tilting down by the bow. In the background, the faraway hiss of rushing air continued to sound, along with the muted throb of the *Bokken*'s twin, battery-powered propellers.

Miriam Kromer had to hold onto the back of the diving officer's stool to keep from falling forward. There was a certain tension in the air and on the faces of the men who stood beside her.

"Make your depth sixty-five feet, Mr. Foard," ordered Chris Slaughter.

"Sixty-five feet it is, Captain. I show eight knots, on course zero-two-five true." returned the helmsman, whose eyes never left the instruments that were mounted on the bulkhead before him.

Ever so slowly, Foard began pulling back on his steering column, and in response, the *Bokken* began leveling out.

"The conn's yours, Ben. Good job everyone," said Slaughter in a tone of almost casual indifference.

The captain's coolness didn't temper the brief flurry of excited chatter that filled the compartment as the rest of the men vented their anxieties.

The toxicologist appeared puzzled as she scanned the relieved faces of these celebrants, then turned to Bill Brown for an explanation. "Is that it? Are we submerged?"

"That's it, Doc," answered the grinning veteran, who continued on with an almost dramatic flair. "Be it known to all good sailors of the seven seas, that on this date, Dr. Miriam Kromer was totally submerged beneath the waters of the East China Sea. In consequence of such dunking and her initiation into the mysteries of the deep, she is hereby designated an honorary submariner. Be it therefore proclaimed that she is a true and loyal daughter of the wearers of the dolphins."

Back in the *Bokken's* engine room, there was no outburst of relieved voices as the sub plunged into the cold, dark depths. Instead, the machinists were anxiously gathered beside the compartment's forward bulkhead, doing their best to stem the watery flow from a wildly spraying, ruptured ceiling valve.

"Shouldn't we inform the captain of this break?" questioned one of the younger sailors, who was totally soaked from head to soggy foot.

Heedless of his own soaking, Stanley Roth answered while doing his best to attack the valve with a wrench. "You call this a break, son? Why, it's only a small fracture. No need to bother the captain. We'll handle it ourselves."

Much to the veteran's dismay, his grip on the valve unexpectedly slipped, and a virtual torrent of water knocked him to the slippery deck on his rear. Quick to replace him with their tools were Senior Machinist Bob Marchetto and Seaman Orlovick. Ignoring the spraying water, they efficiently cut off the overhead flow by turning off the valves located on each side of the break. As the leak slowed to a virtual drip, they collectively gazed down at their fallen coworker, expressions of pride and satisfaction painting their faces.

"What in the hell are you grease monkeys gawking at?" shouted Stanley. "Find me a dry towel. And get some mops in here and clean up this mess before one of you goofballs slips and breaks his goddamn neck!"

A scene of a much calmer nature was unfolding in the sub's forward torpedo room. Not long after the diving alarm rang out and the *Bokken's* bow angled down beneath the sea's surface, Pete Frystak initiated a comprehensive inspection of the compartment's six torpedo tubes. He did so with the assistance of Ensign Adie Avila, who currently had his head and upper torso tucked inside the tight confines of tube number six. Frystak waited close-by, and appeared genuinely concerned as his young assistant pulled himself out of the twenty-one-inch tube.

"How's she look, Adie?" questioned the veteran.

Adie answered while switching off his flashlight. "As far as I can tell, it's bone dry in there, Pete."

The veteran's relief was most noticeable. "That's great news, son. We can give those yard workers back at Alpha Base an *A* plus for quality control. Except for that small leak in the outer seal of number two, they're as good as new."

"I don't suppose the captain is going to let us take a test shot," remarked Adie.

Frystak looked the young sailor right in the eyes and answered him. "That's the way it appears, Adie. Which means we're going to have to do it right the first time or spend all of eternity trying to figure out where the hell we went wrong."

"Do you think it will actually come to firing a torpedo?" quizzed the neophyte torpedoman.

Pete Frystak replied as he walked over to the

223

nearby weapons pallet and carefully patted one of the shiny green, M-57 anti-ship torpedoes on its blunt nose. "That's what these fish are here for. And that's why they took us along."

The torpedo pallet filled the majority of the compartment's interior space. It had mattresses spread out on its top, and was currently home for the members of Seal Team Three.

"Okay, ladies, get set for the sixty-second drill," said Traveler, who was one of the four commandoes currently sprawled out there.

Pete Frystak and his assistant had to stand on the steel edge of the pallet's lower frame in order to see what the SEALs were up to. Apparently they had just field-stripped their weapons, and as Traveler spotted the two onlookers, he casually addressed them.

"Greetings, gents. Ever see a sixty-second drill before?"

"I don't believe we have," replied Pete Frystak, who was amazed at the amount of hardware spread out on the mattress before him. "That looks to be quite an arsenal," he added. "What are you outfitted with?"

Traveler was the first to answer. "I've got one of the new improved, gas-operated M-16A2 assault rifles. It's got a thirty-round clip that spews out 5.56mm rounds to an effective range of about five hundred and fifty yards."

"The parts spread out before me belong to a 5.56mm Colt Commando," offered Warlock. "This baby's got a shorter barrel than the M-16, and because of the reduced muzzle velocity, is designed for use at closer ranges."

"That's certainly not the case with this honey,"

said Cajun, as he lovingly stroked the loose polygon-bored black barrel of his weapon. "This here's a Heckler and Koch PSGl sniper rifle. I've shot a lot of weapons in my time, but this one takes the cake. Any target within eight hundred yards you can consider eliminated. She fires a 7.62mm cartridge, that's carried in a twenty-round magazine, and is topped by a state-of-the-art Hensoldt six by forty-two scope with LED-enhanced manual reticle. Boy oh boy, could I have some fun with this little lady down in the swamps."

"None of that fancy stuff for me," observed Old Dog. "I'll stick with my good ole' M-16A2, that's got the added punch of a breech-loaded, pump action M203 40mm grenade launcher. She might not have the range of Cajun's H&K, but she can sure kick ass with a variety of antipersonnel, armor-piercing, buckshot, and riot-control rounds."

Pete Frystak couldn't help but be impressed. "I sure wouldn't want to tangle with you guys in a dark alley. Now what's this sixty-second drill all about?"

Traveler replied while handing the veteran a palm-sized, digital stopwatch. "At your discretion, just give us the word and hit the top button. We'll take it from there."

Frystak briefly looked over at Adie before returning his gaze to the SEALs. "Go for it!" he shouted as he activated the watch's digital counter with a single push of his right index finger.

There was the immediate clash of metal upon metal as the SEALs began reassembling their weapons. They did so with incredible swiftness, demonstrating an amazing degree of dexterity along the way. In a matter of seconds, the dozens of disjointed parts that had been spread out before them began to take on a more familiar shape, as the commandoes expertly snapped them together.

The first one to complete the assembly of his rifle was Warlock, who clipped in the last piece of his Colt Commando in an astonishing forty-three seconds. Traveler's M-16A2 assault rifle was completed five seconds later, with Old Dog snapping on the grenade launcher of his fully assembled M-16 three seconds later. The uniquely shaped, long-barreled sniper rifle was proving to be the greatest challenge. Yet Cajun took it all in stride, and coolly nodded toward their timekeeper as the last piece snapped into place.

Pete Frystak hit the timer button and held up the digital stopwatch for all to see.

"Now I see why you call it the sixty-second drill," observed the veteran, who shook his head in amazement at realizing that it had taken them exactly one minute to complete the exercise.

As he returned the watch to Traveler, the good-looking commando offhandedly remarked, "I've been on a lot of pigboats in my time, but this one is the strangest of all. Even the torpedoes look weird."

"That's because they were designed and produced by the Soviets," replied Frystak.

"And you're going to be able to shoot the suckers?" countered Traveler.

"You'd better hope so, mister," returned the veteran. "Especially if we've got an unfriendly reception committee waiting for us in Takara Bay."

"Hey, Pops, is the scuttlebutt really true about you old-timers snatchin' one of these Romeos right out of Ivan's hands back in the fifties?" asked Cajun.

Before answering this question, Frystak agilely lifted himself up onto the pallet. Here he directly faced the SEALs, sitting cross-legged on one of the mattresses.

"The incident you're referring took place in nineteen-fifty-eight. I was the weapons officer aboard the USS *Cubera*, a post-World War II GUPPY-2-class diesel-electric attack sub that was the nuke of its day. Bill Brown was the skipper, Henry Walker our XO, and Stanley Roth was the senior machinist."

Adie Avila remained perched on the pallet's edge, and joined the SEALs as a rapt audience while the veteran continued.

"It was summer in the Arctic, and we were patrolling the Barents Sea, at the very edge of the pack ice, when we first spotted her. Assuming we'd caught Ivan napping, the skipper ordered us in to take a closer look. I was OOD at the time, and was on the periscope, just waiting for the Russians to pull the plug and dive. Yet as we continued to close in, I caught sight of a wisp of smoke rising from the bridge and knew they were in trouble. Yet never in my wildest dreams did I realize the extent of their difficulties. For a boarding party found evidence of an intense fire and the sub had been totally abandoned. Needless to say, we didn't waste any time securing a line and towing her back to Norway."

"Why didn't the Reds scuttle her before they abandoned ship?" interrupted Warlock.

"We were asking ourselves the same question," answered Frystak, "when the refit yard at Tromsö provided the answer. In their haste to leave the burning sub, the Russians failed to fully engage the vessel's scuttle cocks. As the crew drifted off in their life rafts, they apparently never knew of their shortcoming. And as far as we know, the Soviet Navy still believes Romeo 201 to be on the icy bottom of the Barents Sea."

At this point, Traveler broke in. "It sure sounds like Ivan gave us a hell of a gift. What did we ever do with it?"

Frystak sat forward, and his eyes lit up with enthusiasm. "From Norway, Romeo 201 was transferred to Holy Loch, Scotland. Here we oversaw a complete refit of the sub, a job that entailed even more work than we put into the *Bokken*. Once 201 was seaworthy again, we sailed her to New London, where the brass had a field day studying what was then considered to be an example of state-of-the-art Soviet undersea technology."

"That's quite a sea tale, Pops," observed Cajun. "Thanks for sharin' it with us."

"Not at all, gentlemen," returned Frystak. He intently scanned the faces of his audience as he added, "Besides, if things work out on this mission, in thirty more years you'll have an even more amazing story to tell."

For Miriam Kromer the dive was almost anticlimactic. She hadn't anticipated it to go so quickly and smoothly. Except for the moderate tilt of the deck and the pressure on her ears during the initial descent, they could still be cruising on the surface for all she knew. This was especially so now that they had leveled out and reached snorkel depth.

She was extremely proud of the crew. They had done a wonderful job. There had been some concern that the *Bokken*'s unfamiliar equipment would be unmanageable, but Miriam certainly didn't see any evidence of this during her time in the control room.

If anything, the men gathered there went about their work in an efficient, calm, and professional manner.

Of course, much of the credit went to the men who'd trained them. They were fortunate to have the services of the three veterans. Together with a select group of officers brought over from the *Hawkbill*, these men had carried out an intensive training program that had so far resulted in an almost faultless voyage. Miriam could only pray that this would remain the case during the rest of the cruise.

Soon after they had attained periscope depth, she excused herself from the control room and began to make her way aft. She suddenly felt exhausted, her fatigue no doubt brought on by the excitement-packed morning, and she just wanted to rest in her bunk for a few minutes. She had no trouble finding her quarters. Gratefully she removed her athletic shoes and lay down on the firm, single mattress.

Now that they had reached snorkel depth, the diesels could be switched back on, and she clearly heard the steady throbbing hum of the dual engines. The air smelled of machine oil, a scent that had bothered her at first, though she was finally getting accustomed to it. When she'd mentioned her initial aversion to this scent to Bill Brown, the personable veteran had related a story concerning his wife. It seemed she couldn't stand the smell of machine oil either. Since it permeated his uniforms and skin, one of the first things she did whenever he returned from a cruise was to send him to the shower. Then she thoroughly washed his clothes in the strongest possible detergent.

One of the luxuries that Miriam really missed was a good hot soak in a real bathtub. Her last bath had been taken while she was staying at the US ambassador's residence in Bangkok. This seemed like a lifetime ago, though in reality it was only a little over a week since she had spent the night in Thailand. So much had happened to her since then, that she had trouble keeping up with the flow of time. Not only did she have no idea of the correct date, in her current environment she didn't even know if it was day or night.

Her week spent with the SEALs had gone by in a virtual flash. Each day, there had been another physical challenge to meet. And her nights had passed too quickly, tending to sore muscles and doing her best to catch up on sleep.

When Admiral Walker had called them in for their final briefing yesterday evening, she had hardly believed that the actual operation was about to begin. Reality had sunk in only after the distinguished Director of Naval Intelligence had said his goodbyes and returned to the USS *Enterprise* just before the team boarded the *Bokken*.

Now that they were under way, Miriam was ready for whatever fate had in store for her. It was too late to back out, and besides, she was actually looking forward, in a perverse way, to experiencing the thrill of real combat.

As she lay back on her pillow, the distinctive sounds and scents of the submarine all around her, she closed her eyes and issued a silent prayer for protection. Then she fell instantly into a deep, dreamless slumber.

She awoke ninety minutes later, aroused by the tempting aroma of freshly baked cookies. Her first impression was that this pleasing, familiar scent was but the byproduct of a dream. Yet when it persisted, she knew otherwise.

She arose from the cot and crossed over to her quarters' fold-down sink. Much like a train's pullman car, the toilet, or head as it is known on a submarine, was located beneath this small metal fixture. These were the only private facilities on the entire vessel, and she was ever thankful that the captain had surrendered his quarters for her exclusive use. She freshened up and, with a terry-cloth towel still draped around her neck, walked out into the passageway that led directly into the nearby wardroom. Much as she'd expected, it was in this simulated wood-paneled compartment that she found the cookies whose scent had awakened her.

Seated at the elongated table, a pile of charts and a heaping platter of chocolate chip cookies before them, were Captain Chris Slaughter and his navigator, Lieutenant Rich Laycob. The boat's portly chef looked disappointed as he stood beside them, and with Miriam's entrance his face lit up.

"Now I bet the Doc here will try one of my cookies," said Howard Mallot, who picked up the platter and held it out toward her.

Miriam needed no more prompting. She was a true chocolate chip cookie connoisseur, and on a scale from one to ten, the still-warm sample she bit into rated right at the top. It was moist, not too sweet, and filled with chunks of rich dark chocolate and crispy chopped-up pecans.

"Chief Mallot, these are absolutely delicious!" raved the toxicologist. "You must share the recipe."

Mallot readily did so. "The secret's in using half white sugar and half brown. Then I mix some vanilla with the eggs and stir in pure oat bran flour, salt, and baking soda, along with plenty of chocolate chips and chopped nuts. The oven's got to be precisely at three hundred and seventy-five degrees, and if you cook them a second over ten minutes, you'll blow the whole thing. If you'd like, I'll scratch down the complete recipe and leave it in your cabin."

"Please do," said Kromer, who took another cookie and sat down at the wardroom table.

While Mallot left to brew some fresh coffee, Chris Slaughter politely addressed the cookie-munching newcomer. "I hope your quarters are sufficient, Doctor."

"Actually, they're quite comfortable," she replied. "It's nice to get a moment's privacy around here. Thanks again for giving them up."

"Not at all," said Slaughter. "With a mission of this short duration, I wouldn't have used them much anyway."

"How do you like working with the SEALs, Doc?" asked the navigator.

Kromer answered as honestly as possible. "It was tough breaking the ice at first. But now that we're getting to know each other, things are going just fine."

"I guess working with a SEAL team wasn't part of the job description when you signed on at Fort Detrick," observed Slaughter.

Kromer carefully replied. "My position as an intelligence specialist has required that I become involved with some pretty strange assignments, but nothing quite like this one."

Slaughter rolled up the chart that had been spread out before him, then turned his full attention on the toxicologist. "I never realized we had that much of a problem with the proliferation of biological weapons."

"You'd be surprised, Captain," countered Kromer.

"They don't call them the poor man's atomic bomb for nothing. Almost every country on this planet currently has some sort of BW program. Besides being relatively cheap to create and disperse, biological weapons have quite a successful track record."

"I thought this was all high-tech stuff," offered Rich Laycob.

Kromer shook her head to the contrary. "Think again, Lieutenant. Among the earliest users of biologicals were the ancient Greeks and Romans, who used to foul their enemy's wells with diseased animal corpses. In thirteen-forty-six A.D., the Tartars hurled their plague victims over the walls of the besieged Black Sea port city of Caffa. When the inhabitants subsequently fled, they helped spread the plague throughout Europe. BW even made it to the pristine shores of the New World, when the British handed out smallpox-tainted blankets to the American Indians, resulting in the deaths of untold thousands."

"I recently read about an island off Scotland that's still off limits because of a World War II biological weapons test," remarked Slaughter.

"You're referring to Gruinard Island," responded the well-read toxicologist. "Interestingly enough, that experiment involved anthrax, and proved that its spores can survive in the soil for over fifty years."

Chris Slaughter appeared amazed by this revelation, and worriedly voiced himself. "It sounds like we'd have all hell to pay if such a toxin was released on the Japanese or US mainlands."

Kromer nodded in agreement. "Just look at the death toll we've already encountered on Okinawa, then multiply it by tens of thousands, and you can start to get an idea of what would happen if a major population center was attacked in such a manner."

It was at this point in the conversation that Bill Brown entered the wardroom. The white-haired veteran looked tired and pale. Even his voice lacked its usual vibrance as he addressed Chris Slaughter.

"I've just completed a walk-through of the boat and can report that all systems are fully operational. Other than the usual handful of minor leaks, our watertight integrity shows no signs of compromise."

"That's good news, Bill," returned Slaughter. "How are the men holding up?"

"As far as I can tell, morale remains excellent," answered Brown, somewhat lackadaisically.

Chris Slaughter sensed the old-timer's weariness and directly confronted him with it. "Bill, you look beat. Why don't you hit the rack for a couple of hours?"

"I'll be all right, Chris," countered the veteran. "It's nothing a strong mug of joe won't cure."

Slaughter remained unconvinced. "No, Bill, I'm serious. You've done more than your fair share of work around here, and I'm going to need you fully rested once we reach Takara."

Brown looked at the young officer in protest, yet found himself with little strength left to argue. "I guess I have been pushing a bit."

"You're more than welcome to use my quarters," offered Miriam.

"Thanks, Doc, but that won't be necessary," said Brown as he stifled a yawn. "I'm bunking with Lieutenant Commander Kram, and since he's got his hands full in the control room, I've got my peace and quiet."

He was all set to leave, when he turned to say one more thing, "Now don't forget to awaken me if the least bit of difficulty arises."

Slaughter couldn't help but grin. "That's a promise. Now get!"

Bill Brown showed every one of his sixty-seven years as he nodded and slumped off to his stateroom.

"There goes one hell of a fine sailor," observed Slaughter fondly. "Now I know why Admiral Walker speaks so highly of him."

"You should have seen him helping me chart our course," added Rich Laycob. "He worked with me for three hours straight, and the old guy seemed guilty just to take the time out to go to the head. At his age, I don't know how he can do it."

"At sixty-seven, he's certainly not ready to be put out to pasture," offered Miriam Kromer. "He's got plenty of productive years left in him. Commander Brown has just got to be reminded now and then that he's not a spring chicken anymore. My own father's no different. Though he's officially retired, he still sees his fair share of patients. And every once in a while, he bites off more than he can chew; then he's got to be coerced to ease up."

"I understand that the commander's associate in our torpedo room is no different," said Laycob. "The guys say he never lets up."

"They're a special breed all right," reflected Slaughter. "And we can thank our lucky stars they were willing to accompany us. Because when the going gets tough, it sure will be nice to have the benefit of their years of experience."

Slaughter looked at his watch and added, "Now, how about joining me forward and getting on with that navigational check, Lieutenant?"

"Yes, sir," snapped Laycob as he gathered his charts and stood.

Chris Slaughter also rose, but before leaving, he looked down at Miriam Kromer. "Enjoy those cookies, Doc. At least you've got the SEALs to help you work them off your waistline."

"I admire your willpower, Captain," replied the toxicologist, who was reaching for another cookie as he made this comment. "You know, these things are addictive."

Chris Slaughter patted his stomach and smiled. "Tell me about it, Doc," he added as he turned to the forward hatchway.

Sixteen

Morning found Dr. Yukio Ishii decked out in a white robe and billowing pants, briskly walking down the busy Takara pier toward the docked *Katana*. Only a few fluffy clouds dotted the blue sky, and it promised to be another clear, warm day. The previous evening had been a busy one, and though he was able to get little rest, he was hardly aware of any fatigue. After all, his lifetime goal was about to be achieved with the *Katana*'s sailing, and he was too excited now to sleep even if he wanted to.

As he approached the stern of the submarine, he passed by a truck that was in the process of being unloaded. He halted a moment to inspect this vehicle's cargo, packed in a number of open-sided, wooden-slat crates.

"Just a second, lad," said Ishii to one of the young dockworkers who had been stacking the crates on a two-wheeled handcart for transport to the submarine.

One look at the silver-haired elder from whose mouth this request emanated immediately caused the dockworker to stop working and bow deeply.

Oblivious to this show of respect, Ishii reached over and opened the top crate. Inside he found two dozen heads of lettuce. He noted with some degree of satisfaction that the green leaves didn't show any hint of wilting or spoilage, that the heads were firm and compact. He tore off a small piece and slowly chewed it, finding the lettuce succulent and fresh. Only then did he signal the laborer to carry on, while he continued on toward the *Katana*'s gangway.

Captain Okura could be seen in the sub's sail, and Ishii raised his voice in greeting. "Good morning, Satsugai. It seems that the Way is still smiling on you. Never before have I seen such a magnificent sunrise as today's."

Okura came over to the side of the sail to respond. "I just got through studying the latest meteorological forecast, Sensei. We should have smooth sailing all the way into Tokyo Bay."

"Surely that's another good omen," said Ishii. "Is all prepared for this evening's departure?"

Okura nodded. "As you can see, we're just taking on the last of the foodstuffs. All that remains to be loaded is our special cargo — and the brave team of ninja who will deliver it."

"I just came from the lab," Ishii informed him. "The aerosol canisters are being filled with fresh toxin, and they will be delivered here by noon. Though I can't say the same for our ninjitsu brethren. It seems that one of our lab workers is missing, and I sent them into the hills to search for her."

"Is it anyone I know?" asked the curious submariner.

"As a matter of fact, you do know her," Ishii replied. "She's Yoko Noguchi, the young scientist who recently toured your boat."

"Ah, that one." Okura sounded pensive. "I hope that she hasn't had an accident of some kind."

238

"We can't say for sure, Satsugai. All I can tell you is that she mysteriously disappeared from the toxicology lab shortly after being called in for a special work shift."

"The way you've been driving those poor lab workers, it's no wonder," said Okura. "I'll bet this was her day off."

"As a matter of fact, it was, Satsugai."

Okura had it all figured out now. "Check the trails beyond the wind farm. She's probably just trying to get a little fresh air. She'll be back soon enough."

But Ishii didn't agree. "Not that one, my friend. Like ourselves, she thrives on her work. Though she is new to us, and who really knows what's in the minds of the younger generation. Well, whatever be the case, let's just hope the ninja don't have to waste any more of their precious time locating her. Are their accommodations ready?"

"That they are, Sensei. The weapon's pallet has been removed to make room for them and their equipment. And because of this, we're carrying only six tube-loaded torpedoes. And even these, I don't anticipate having to utilize."

"A wise warrior is prepared for all contingencies," advised Ishii stoically.

The deep, throaty rumble of a diesel engine drew his attention to the other side of the pier, where a sleek patrol boat was about to pull up to the vacant slip located directly opposite the *Katana*. This formidable-looking vessel had a pair of two-inch deck guns mounted forward of the wheelhouse, and a dual rack of depth charges was positioned on its fantail. Its tall mast was bristling with aerials and radar dishes, along with several adjustable spotlights.

With a minimum of difficulty, the hundred-foot-long, attack craft reached the slip and cut its engines. While a group of sailors fastened its mooring lines, a bald-headed officer with a patch over his left eye emerged from the wheelhouse. Ishii returned this individual's crisp salute, then watched as he climbed down onto the main deck to the pier.

Ishii had a genuine fondness for this one-eyed naval man. Lieutenant Satoshi Tanaka had joined his organization five years ago, while in the midst of a somewhat tempestuous career in the Japanese Maritime Self-Defense Force. An avowed lover of rice wine and geisha girls, Tanaka had constantly been in trouble during his early cadet days. These vices almost had kept him from receiving a commission. And when he finally had gotten a ship of his own, it had been little more than a tugboat.

Tanaka had had to work extra hard to prove himself, and after ten years of tireless effort, he'd been given command of a Shirane-class destroyer. This had been a dream come true. The Shirane was a state-of-the-art warship. Over five hundred feet long, and displacing over 6,800 tons, it was powered by a pair of geared steam turbines that gave it a top speed of well over thirty knots. It had a complement of 350 men, carried three Sea King helicopters, and was equipped with a variable depth sonar and a variety of weapons systems, including two triple Mk32 torpedo tubes, a pair of Phalanx Gatling guns, a Sea Sparrow SAM launcher, two five-inch Mk42 guns, and an ASROC Mk16 launcher.

While the ship was in port in Sasebo, certain members of Tanaka's crew had crossed paths with some unruly US Marines. Tanaka had attempted to intercede on their behalf, and a violent brawl had ensued, during which the forty-seven-year-old naval officer had lost his eye. When one of his men later died as a result of this fight, Tanaka had been brought up on charges. Though the court of inquiry found him innocent, his prospects were now tainted. He lost command of the destroyer and once again found solace in sake. He was well on his way to self-destruction when Ishii learned of his plight and offered him work on Takara Island.

With Satoshi Tanaka's able assistance, Takara Bay had been outfitted with a top-rate defense system. And he'd overseen the purchase and subsequent refitting of the two Romeo-class submarines. His most current project had been the overhaul of the fast attack boat he had just docked. Altogether, Tanaka had proved to be an invaluable member of Ishii's family, one whose loyalty was beyond question.

"Good morning, Satoshi!" Ishii said as Tanaka strolled down the hastily arranged gangplank. "How did the refit go?"

Tanaka's hefty frame was outfitted in a starched white uniform bereft of any insignias, and his deeply tanned face broke out in a warm smile as he joined Ishii on the dock.

"Wonderfully, sir. You'll have to accompany us on a patrol soon and see for yourself. The new gas turbines give us an additional eight knots, and I can't wait to try out the towed, variable-depth sonar unit."

"I'd enjoy coming along on such a cruise," said Ishii as Tanaka spotted Satsugai Okura still perched on the *Katana*'s sail.

"Greetings, Captain!" Tanaka called in the direction of the sub. "So today's the big day."

"That it is, Satoshi," replied Okura from above.

"Just say the word and I'll join you." Tanaka was

241

quite serious.

"You're needed here, old friend," observed Okura. "Besides, you never were much of a submariner."

While both officers were still cadets, they had done trial time on a submarine, and Tanaka had experienced claustrophobia. Shortly afterward he had requested duty with the surface fleet.

"Well, the offer still stands, should you need me," the one-eyed mariner said.

"Why not join me on the *Katana,* Satoshi?" invited Ishii. "I believe we can find a suitable beverage on board to drink to Satsugai's safe return."

Tanaka's good eye twinkled. "Lead the way, sir. I never was one to say no to a send-off toast."

As they made their way to the *Katana*'s forward gangway, he added, "It's just too bad that Captain Sato hasn't returned yet. With him back, we could really have a proper send-off."

Ishii responded while beckoning him to lead the way up the ramp. "I'm not expecting the *Bokken* back for a good twenty-four hours. But I'll tell you what, when Sato returns, the party's on me, with a beautiful geisha for each one of us!"

Before Tanaka could react to this offer, the low rumble of an approaching diesel truck sounded behind them. Both men turned in the direction of this noise, and saw a large green pick-up truck with darkly tinted windows pull right up to the *Katana*'s gangplank. They were about to ignore it when a black-robed ninja with a sword hanging from his waist emerged from the driver's side.

Ishii was especially interested in this hooded individual, who walked crisply around the truck and yanked open its passenger door. The elder was somewhat surprised when Yoko Noguchi stepped out of the vehicle. The young scientist appeared disheveled, her face and clothes smudged with dirt. And strangely enough, her hands were tightly bound behind her back. Seeing this, Ishii immediately reversed his intended course and returned to the concrete pier.

"Whatever is the meaning of this?" he asked, his first concern was for Yoko's welfare.

The ninja faced the confused elder, bowed, and spoke out in a deep, raspy voice. "Sensei, Miss Noguchi was found on Katami ridge, with an unauthorized shortwave radio transmitter in her possession."

Astounded by this revelation, Ishii turned to meet the accused. "Is this true?" he queried.

Yoko nodded, ashamed that it was, and looked downward. This prompted a spirited response from the still unbelieving elder.

"But why would you do such a thing? You know this is a serious breach of your security pledge. Will you at least tell me who it was you were attempting to contact?"

Yoko remained silent, and it was the ninja who answered in her place. "Sensei, the frequency band of her transmitter was set on a channel reserved for the JMSDF (Japanese Maritime Self-Defense Force). Our homing equipment indicates that she was able to send a pair of brief broadcasts, the last of which occurred only seconds before we intercepted her."

Ishii's mood suddenly shifted from disappointment to rage. "And to think that I actually trusted you! Such treachery cannot be excused. At the very least I feel you owe me some kind of explanation, even if you are only a cowardly spy — a traitor on the payroll of the Western barbarians!"

The crestfallen scientist slowly lifted up her head

and bravely replied. "It's you, Doctor, who's the traitor. Your subterfuge threatens to undermine the democracy that has led Japan from the shame of unconditional surrender to a position of great economic power."

"So, it was for the sake of this precious democracy that you infiltrated my organization," observed the bitter elder. "And what may I ask did you hope to gain by this foolish act?"

"To stop you before untold thousands of innocent lives are lost as a result of your scheme to wrest power from the legitimate seat of government," Yoko blurted out. "You, Doctor, are just a throwback to the shortsighted militarists who led Japan into the disastrous war that brought our proud country to its knees. And if the last thing I ever do, helps bring you to justice, I'll go to my grave with my soul at rest."

"Justice?" cried Ishii with a wrathful laugh. "I'll show you justice, my dear. It will take you to the grave even sooner than you anticipated."

This said, the red-faced elder reached over and pulled the sword out of the ninja's scabbard.

"Satoshi!" he ordered. "Hold her in place from behind." To the ninja, he curtly added. "Prepare her to be beheaded."

The mere mention of this last word caused Yoko's eyes to widen in horror. And as the ninja roughly grabbed the hair on the top of her scalp and pulled her head forward until she was fully bent over at the waist, the full reality of her plight set in.

"And to think I had such great plans for you," whispered Ishii with an icy softness. "You were going to be my representative to the younger generations that will lead Nippon into the twenty-first century. The only trouble is, your soul has not yet progressed to the level of spiritual enlightenment needed to understand the true course of my ambitions. It's evident that the veils of samsara still blind you, and because of your distorted inner vision, you fell victim to the persuasive lies of the establishment. I pity you, Yoko Noguchi—so bright, so beautiful, with so much potential, yet lost to the true call of the Way."

Ishii halted at this point to draw in a series of deep breaths. Then, his hands firmly grasping the sword's hilt, he stood at Yoko's side and eyed the white skin of her exposed neck. Without another word spoken, he swung the katana overhead, then swiftly drove it downward.

The razor-sharp blade cut through skin and bone as if it were rice paper, and Yoko's detached head plopped down onto the concrete of the pier to lie in a crimson pool of blood. Satoshi Tanaka continued tightly holding her body from behind as he squeamishly watched blood continue to spurt from the cut arteries in the victim's open neck. He felt great relief when the ninja took the limp body from his trembling hands and he was able to step back and fight the urge to retch.

"Come, Satoshi," instructed Ishii in a calm tone. "Have you already forgotten about our send-off toast aboard the *Katana?*"

Amazed at how quickly the old-timer was able to adjust to this traumatic event, Satoshi Tanaka somehow managed to summon the self-control needed to voice a reply. "Of course I haven't, sir. It's just that I have never witnessed a beheading before."

"Then tell me, my friend, what did you think of it?" Ishii asked matter-of-factly.

Tanaka was momentarily distracted when the victim's blood-soaked head unexpectedly rolled over, and the young girl's eyes could be seen blindly staring up at them.

"It . . . cer-certainly was quick," stammered the shocked mariner.

Noting Tanaka's continued upset, Ishii walked over and gently took him by the arm and led him toward the submarine.

"What do you expect when you're judge, jury, and executioner all in one?" observed Ishii.

A concerned voice came from the direction of the *Katana*'s gangplank. "What was that all about, Sensei?" quizzed Satsugai Okura.

Ishii waited until he and Tanaka were well up the gangplank themselves before answering. "It seems that we had a rat in our midst, Satsugai."

"Has the security of the operation been compromised?" breathlessly asked the submariner.

"I seriously doubt it," returned Ishii. "I believe we eliminated the vermin before she could do us any real harm. However, I want to expedite the loading of the toxin. And I want the ninja on board and the *Katana* ready to sail at a moment's notice."

"I thought that one was asking too many questions for her own good," said Okura as he escorted them onto the sub's deck. "I guess I should never have allowed her to tour this vessel."

"Nonsense," replied Ishii. "We have nothing here to hide. And besides, the weak-willed fools she was reporting to are of little concern to us. They'll waste days in analysis and planning, and by the time they get the nerve to act, it will be too late."

As they prepared to climb down the forward access trunk, Ishii lightly added, "Now I hope you've got the sake warming, Captain. Satoshi here needs some fortification, and we must toast our success."

Chris Slaughter was taking his turn as OOD, when the excited voice of Ray Morales filled the control room.

"Radar shows land dead ahead, Captain!"

Slaughter rushed over to the radar station to see this sighting for himself.

"There it is, sir," said Morales, as he pointed to a jagged line visible beneath the glass display plate. "It's due north of us, at a range of about eighteen miles."

"Good work, Mr. Morales," replied Slaughter. "If the visibility topside cooperates, we should be able to eyeball it."

While crossing over to the periscope well, Slaughter addressed the acting quartermaster. "Inform Mr. Brown to join me here on the double."

"Aye, aye, sir," replied the quartermaster, a sound-powered telephone hanging from a harness around his neck.

Since they were already traveling at snorkel depth, no change was necessary for Slaughter to effectively deploy the periscope. But the eyepiece seemed to take forever to rise up, and he anxiously bent over and snapped down the dual grips as soon as they showed themselves.

A rubber coupling protected the eyepiece itself, and as Slaughter nuzzled up against it with his brow, the lens finally broke the water's surface. The first thing he viewed was the wave that slapped up against the lens. Then he saw an expanse of blue sky, and after initiating a quick 360-degree scan, he swung the scope to bearing zero-zero-zero. A slight adjustment in focus was necessary before the eyepiece filled with the green profile of a distant landmass.

"What's up, Chris?" a familiar voice asked.

"Have your first look at Takara Island, Bill," Slaughter offered as he backed away from the scope.

"You've got to be kidding me," countered the surprised veteran. "I thought that our ETA was a good hour away."

Slaughter grinned and pointed toward the eyepiece. "Look for yourself, Bill."

Brown did just that, and spent almost a full minute studying the view.

"Well, I'll be," he commented while readjusting the focus knob. "I can even make out the mountain range."

"That's it all right," concurred Slaughter. "The current gave us an unexpected boost, and Mr. Roth's miracle workers helped by keeping us at a steady thirteen knots."

Bill Brown stepped back from the eyepiece, then watched as the scope slid back into its storage well with a muted hiss.

"We might as well take this extra time to loiter off the inlet and initiate a complete recon of the inner bay," suggested Slaughter.

"That will sure make things easier for us come nightfall." Brown's evaluation was cut short by the agitated voice of their sonar operator.

"I've got an unidentified submerged contact, bearing one-two-zero, range unknown!"

Both Slaughter and Brown turned in time to see Jaffers anxiously hunched over the primitive dials and gauges of his console, all the while pressing his headphones up against his ears.

"Wait a minute, now it's gone!" observed the mystified senior sonar technician.

Without further delay, the sub's two senior officers crossed over to join him.

"Maybe it was just an anomaly of some sort," said Slaughter.

Jaffers shook his head to the contrary. "I don't know, Captain. But for a second there, I could have sworn something was sharing these waters with us. Lord, if I only had *Hawkbill*'s BQS-6."

"It could have been a whale sounding beneath the thermocline," offered Bill Brown.

"Or maybe another sub," added Slaughter. "Just stay on it, Jaffers. And don't be afraid to cry out the moment it shows itself again."

Vice Admiral Henry Walker sat in one of the two high-backed leather chairs that graced the captain's bridge of the USS *Enterprise*. From this elevated vantage point, he could see the nuclear-powered carrier's entire 252-foot-long deck. A shiny white F-14 Tomcat was in the midst of take-off at the forward port catapult. Yet not even the deafening roar of this aircraft's dual afterburners could distract Walker from the disturbing contents of the dispatch he had just read. It now lay half-folded in his lap.

"Damn!" he muttered to the khaki-clad officer sitting beside him. "It's confirmed, Steven. The Japanese Maritime Self-Defense Force is on to Ishii. I don't know how, but somebody tipped them off, and they're not wasting any time in getting a handle on the situation."

"How many ships are they sending in?" questioned Captain Steven Webster as he watched the just-launched Tomcat leap off the deck and gracefully soar upward to cruising altitude.

"So far, only one submarine," returned the worried Director of Naval Intelligence. "She's the *Nadashio,* one of their latest and most capable Yuushio class attack boats. It's under the command of Captain Osami Nagano, an Academy grad, of all things."

"And Captain Nagano's orders?" probed Steven Webster, who looked on as another F-14 maneuvered into its take-off position at the starboard catapult.

"To eliminate all Romeo-class submarines he encounters exiting Takara Bay," replied Walker with a heavy sigh.

This unforeseen development caused Webster to immediately cease scanning the flight deck. He met the concerned stare of Henry Walker.

"If we can't share knowledge of our operation with the Japanese navy, and there's no way to inform the *Bokken,* what can we do about it?" asked the perplexed surface officer.

Henry Walker held back his reply until the Tomcat completed its take-off. Only after the roar of the aircraft's afterburners had completely faded did he solemnly voice himself.

"For a start, we can pray that Bill Brown and his boys remain undetected. Then all we can do is pull in our planes and get this task force to head for Takara. At the very least, we can be within air range by tomorrow morning."

Seventeen

Chris Slaughter had always prided himself on being cool under fire. This was a trait he'd used to good advantage when he'd taken the mound in his baseball days. While others let the pressures of the moment distract their focus, Slaughter's concentration rarely faltered, even in the most dire situations. His coach at the Academy had always said he had ice water in his veins, and his teammates took this one step farther, giving him the nickname "Ice Man."

It had been Slaughter's father who'd helped develop the confidence and self-reliance that made such control possible. An Air Force Thud driver in Viet Nam, Slaughter's dad had survived the war with a chestful of medals—and a lot of horror stories about pilots who broke under pressure. Chris was but a teenager when he'd come home from the war, and his father had made it his business to spend as much time as possible with his impressionable son. They'd played ball, fished, and taken many an overnight camping trip together. And it was because of this closeness that Chris's father had been so instrumental in determining what type of man his only son would become.

Lately, Chris Slaughter had often found himself thinking of his father. This was especially the case now that his current command was about to go into harm's way. Though his dad hadn't lived to see him graduate from the Naval Academy or get his first commission, Chris constantly felt his presence. Under times of great stress, when a single bad decision could cost a man's life, he did his best to harken back to the advice his father had given him about the importance of making a choice and then sticking to it to the very end. It had been sound, for Slaughter had learned in Viet Nam that a commanding officer had to be unwavering to earn the confidence and loyalty of those who served beneath him. He must never appear hesitant in making a decision.

As Slaughter crossed the cramped control room of his present command, he made it a point to appear as calm and relaxed as possible. Yet in reality, this passive outward shell masked anxieties even more intense than those that had settled in the pit of his stomach on the eve of his pitching debut against the arch rival, Army. Coach had always said such anxiety was only natural—and sure enough, it had dissipated after his first pitch—and his father had admitted that before every combat mission he'd flown, he'd been a victim of this nervous tension that put doubts in the minds of lesser men.

So far, the cruise had gone remarkably well, and Chris couldn't help but derive confidence from this fact. His men had displayed an amazing ability to master the alien operational systems of the *Bokken*. It was almost as if they'd been trained on this outdated equipment. Yet a nagging doubt persisted. A baseball game or the seemingly endless exercises aboard the *Hawkbill* were vastly different from this mission. Lives and the honor of his country were at stake. Now was the time for him to summon the inner strength to lead his men.

"Bearing, mark!" broke the voice of Rich Laycob from the sub's periscope well.

The white-haired Bill Brown could be seen standing beside him, assisting with this latest navigational fix. Slaughter quietly joined them.

The navigator took a moment to fine-tune the scope's focus knob before backing away and noting the newcomer in their midst.

"Captain, I've got a solid fix on a beacon mounted on the tip of the inlet's eastern perimeter," he reported. "There also appears to be some sort of inhabited concrete structure close by."

Bill Brown took this opportunity to peer through the eyepiece himself, and offered his own thoughts. "I see it. Maybe it's the net keeper's hut."

Slaughter replaced the veteran at the scope and after completing a quick 360-degree scan, centered his line of sight on the promontory they would soon be passing. He spotted the flashing red navigational beacon and the adjoining hut. The lighting was poor, the sun having set over a half-hour ago, but Slaughter did his best to survey the fairly narrow channel of water that lay directly before them.

"I make the distance between us and the entrance to that inlet at about five thousand yards," observed Slaughter. "We should be well within the zone of their defensive sensors by now."

"If you've got a favorite prayer, now's the time to say it," offered Bill Brown.

Chris Slaughter folded up the scope's grips and sent it barreling back down into its storage well.

"Any sounds coming from that net, Jaffers?" he asked while turning in the direction of the sonar console.

The senior sonar technician had one of his headphones pressed tightly to his ear. He hesitated a moment before answering. "Negative, Captain. Do you want me to hit it again with active?"

"That won't be necessary," replied Slaughter. "Just call out the second you pick up the first hint that it's opening."

Jaffers held up his free hand and flashed an okay sign, and Slaughter quietly voiced his concerns to Bill Brown.

"This is a hell of a welcome for a vessel whose mere signature is supposed to unlock the front door to this place. Maybe there's some sort of recognition signal that we overlooked."

"Give them a couple more minutes, Chris," advised the veteran. "Those hydrophones of theirs should pick up all the recognition signals they need to open that sub net and signal the CAPTORS that we're a friendly."

"That's a big should, Bill," reflected Slaughter. "But I guess that's what this game is all about."

Brown nodded and calmly looked to his watch. Slaughter was very aware that the veteran exuded the leadership qualities his father had tried so hard to instill in him.

"Do you miss all this, Bill?" he whispered.

Brown smiled. "You'd better believe it, son. I

254

haven't felt this alive in years."

"Did you ever have trouble coping with fear when you were about to become involved in a dangerous operation?" questioned Slaughter directly.

Brown looked the young officer straight in the eye and replied. "To tell you the truth, Chris, I'm scared shitless right now. I guess the secret's not showing it."

"I hear you loud and clear, Commander," concurred Slaughter. "It seems that all my life I've been in positions where others look to me to be the brave one, and sometimes it's damn difficult to play the role."

"I don't trust a man who doesn't show fear, Chris. He's a fool, or he doesn't value human life. Command's a delicate balance of bravado and vulnerability. And from what I've seen, you've done a hell of a fine job mixing the two. There's no doubt in my mind that you've earned the respect of your men, which proves that whatever you're doing, you're doing it right."

"Coming from you, Bill, I take that as a real compliment," Slaughter replied. He felt a strong, personal bond developing between the two of them.

Brown felt likewise and added, "Returning to your earlier question, I guess what I really miss about all this, in addition to the adrenaline rush you experience whenever you put your life on the line, is working with fine young men like yourself. Old age and retirement can be awfully lonely, and I thank the good Lord for giving me this opportunity to serve alongside you and your brave crew."

"I'm the one who should be thankful, Bill," returned Chris Slaughter. "Because I've got a gut feeling it's going to be your presence here, and your two ex-shipmates', that's going to make the difference between this mission's success or its failure."

"Let's just pray it's the former," replied the grinning veteran. He then followed Slaughter over to the chart table.

Yano Sumiko was Takara Bay's net keeper. The Kyoto native had first come to the island in 1944 as a naval observer. Shortly thereafter, he'd been joined by a vibrant young ensign, Yukio Ishii, who had been sent to Takara on similar duties. Since Sumiko was several years older than Ishii, he took on the role of protective older brother, and watched as his new friend matured into full manhood.

With the war's conclusion, they returned to the mainland to get on with their lives. Unlike Ishii, Sumiko found nothing of real substance waiting for him back home. His young wife and child had been killed by an American bomb in the closing days of the conflict, and the rest of his small family had met similar fates. With no schooling or ambition to speak of, Sumiko aimlessly wandered the war-ravaged streets of Kyoto trying to find some purpose to his life. When six months had passed, and he still found himself wearing the tattered uniform he had arrived in, he decided to return to Takara, the only place where he'd felt real security. He remained on the island ever since, not once returning to the mainland.

For the next three decades, he lived the simple life of a fisherman. He never married again, and was content to spend his days eking a meager subsistence from the sea. He supplemented his seafood diet with the vegetables he grew himself from seed, and as the years progressed, he became an accomplished farmer. This was fortunate, for working the sea was no way for an old man to earn his living, and as his legs and eyesight weakened, he gave away his small boat and became permanently landlocked.

Soon afterward, Yukio Ishii returned to the island. Sumiko's wartime friend had grown into a great man with a fine mind and a large fortune. When he divulged his plans to make Takara his new base of operations, Sumiko was most pleased, and when Ishii offered him a permanent job, he accepted.

Sumiko was there the day Ishii broke ground for the base with a gilded shovel. He did his best to make himself helpful and earn his generous rice bowl, helping the many newcomers to Takara get settled. Thousands of construction workers were soon scrambling over the island, and Sumiko watched in amazement as an entire city emerged out of what was once nothing but volcanic rock.

Three years ago, he'd been assigned his current duties. As net keeper, Sumiko monitored the computerized console set up inside his cottage. At first, he'd feared he'd never be able to operate such a complex piece of machinery. But Ishii would not listen to his protests. He forced him to participate in a basic instructional course, and Sumiko soon found that the computer was not something to be

257

feared. Within a month, he was operating the sensor console on his own.

The job entailed very few hours of actual labor. Most of his efforts were of a supervisory nature, giving him plenty of time to work on his true love—his vegetable garden. Ishii graciously provided him free use of the cottage and the small patch of arable land that lay beside it.

Since it was early spring, Sumiko was working the soil to prepare it for planting. A mixture of sand, silt, and clay, in the past it had produced wonderful melons, cucumbers, and squash. And this year, Sumiko hoped to try some tomatoes.

Several hours ago, a truck belonging to the aqua-farm had dropped off a load of mulch that was derived from various sea plants. At once, Sumiko had gotten to work distributing this odoriferous substance throughout his plot. This job took longer than he had anticipated, and it looked as if he'd have to finish tomorrow. Regardless of this, he kept on working until the fading light made it impossible for him to see.

He was in the process of loading his tools into the wheelbarrow to return them to the storage shed when a loud, electronic alarm began buzzing in his hut. Since this alarm was directly tied in to the console he was assigned to monitor, Sumiko immediately returned to the cottage as quickly as his arthritic legs would carry him.

It was dark inside, so he turned on a lamp and then crossed over to the large table positioned by his futon bed. Without bothering to seat himself, he bent over and hit a single digit on the keyboard of the computer. Almost instantaneously, the monitor screen blinked alive.

SENSOR DETECTION—ZONE EIGHT

This message prompted him to once again address the keyboard, this time utilizing his two index fingers.

SIGNATURE I.D. SOURCE?

The computer took several seconds to respond to this request.

BOKKEN

Seeing this, Sumiko hesitated a moment. The *Bokken* wasn't expected back until sometime tomorrow afternoon. He wondered why he hadn't been informed of this schedule change. The submarine's commanding officer, Captain Hiroaki Sato, was a native of Kyoto and a good friend. Sato enjoyed farming almost as much as Sumiko did, and he had promised to help him with this year's planting. If all went well, perhaps he would have the services of the submariner's strong back in spreading the rest of the mulch.

Though operational protocol required him to inform Dr. Ishii's office of any early arrivals, Sumiko doubted that it was necessary in this instance. Most likely, Sato's crack crew had completed their assignment with time to spare. This would not be the first time they had done so, and that was a demonstration of his friend's competency. Hoping Sato would have a few days off before his next assignment, Sumiko once more addressed the keyboard.

DEACTIVATE DEFENSIVE SYSTEMS

Without a second's hesitation, the computer responded.

DEACTIVATED

The alarm quit ringing in the background, and Sumiko jotted down the exact time for his nightly report. This done, he went outside to retrieve his wheelbarrow, all the while visualizing the sleek undersea warship that would soon be passing beneath the narrow channel his small plot of land overlooked.

"I've got mechanical sounds dead ahead of us, Captain. Sounds like it's a sub net opening!"

Chris Slaughter listened to this excited report from his senior sonar technician and instantly felt relieved. The two officers who stood beside him around the chart table appeared similarly affected. Bill Brown had an almost boyish tone to his voice as he joyously commented, "We're in!"

The sub's navigator appeared equally enthused. "Nothing's going to stop us now!"

Slaughter looked down to the chart that lay before them, then pointed toward the route that was drawn in red grease pencil. It extended from the mouth of the channel they were presently transmitting into the western portion of Takara Bay.

"We should be passing the first mine field shortly," he soberly observed.

"The mere fact that they opened the net proves Henry Walker was right," said Bill Brown. "Those CAPTORS are going to offer us no threat whatsoever during this portion of our voyage."

Slaughter met the veteran's calm gaze. "We'll be at the drop-off point soon. Bill, would you mind heading forward and giving the SEALs my best?"

"Not at all, Chris," Brown responded. "For all

practical purposes, it's over up here, except for the waiting. I'll be happy to pass on the ball."

"I sure wouldn't want to be in their shoes right now," remarked Rich Laycob. "God only knows what's waiting for them on that island."

"Don't forget, we're not going to be having any cakewalk out here," Bill Brown said as he headed for the forward hatchway.

Just as Bill Brown was exiting the control room, Traveler was entering the forward torpedo room, with Miriam Kromer on his heels. The happy-go-lucky commando wasted no time spurring his teammates into action upon spotting them still sprawled out on top of the torpedo pallet.

"Okay, ladies, drop your cocks and grab your socks. We've got some war paint to put on, 'cause it's about time to rock 'n' roll!"

With a minimum of grumbling, the SEALs quickly dressed themselves, and soon all of them were attired in identical jungle-camouflaged fatigues. The toxicologist was similarly dressed, and had her long red hair neatly gathered on top of her head in a tight knot.

"Hey, Doc, how are you on puttin' on makeup?" asked Cajun as he tossed her two silver tubes of the sort oils used by artists were stored in.

Miriam removed the cap from one of these tubes, and indeed found it to be filled with a green, paint-like substance. It was Warlock who identified it for her.

"Don't worry, Doc. It's nothing but theatrical grease paint. The object's to cover all of your exposed skin with the same colors and general design that's printed on your fatigues. That way you'll blend into the natural environment of the island and offer as little a target as possible."

Warlock took the open tube from Miriam and squeezed out a large dab of black makeup, which he proceeded to smear beneath her eyes. With the assistance of a small mirror, Miriam painted her forehead green, and alternated this color with black until her whole face was covered in a swirling, reptilian pattern. By the time she'd completed coloring her hands and wrists, she had slipped into the Halloween spirit and watched with some amusement as Warlock helped Old Dog apply his makeup.

"You're lookin' good, Old Dog!" she said with a sarcastic wink. "Just a little mascara around those eyes and you'll be a real knockout."

The big commando wasn't at all amused by this comment and responded accordingly. "Up yours, Doc!"

Miriam noticed that Cajun had done a particularly good job with his camouflage effort. The Louisiana-bred SEAL's face, neck, and hands were expertly covered in bands of green, brown, and black. He had an olive green bandana tied around his forehead, and only the whites of his eyes showed beneath this strange, snake-like mask.

In contrast, Traveler had painted his face almost completely green, while Warlock had picked black as his primary color. All in all, the makeup only served to make them appear more intimidating.

The SEALs were in the process of gathering their weapons when Bill Brown entered the compartment and joined them beside the torpedo pallet. He looked each member of the team in the eye as he addressed them.

"Captain Slaughter sent me up here to convey his wishes for a safe return. We'll be in position shortly, and I want to see each one of you back here safe and sound once your mission on land is completed."

Brown's glance sought out the team's only female member, and he added, "How are you doing, Dr. Kromer?"

"Incredibly well," answered the toxicologist. "Considering I've felt worse butterflies before exams."

"Just wait till we hit the beach," interrupted Cajun. "That's when the reality of it all sets in."

"I wish I were physically able to go along with you," said Brown. "But these old bones made their last commando raid long ago. Good luck, kids. And hit that bastard with a charge with my name on it!"

While Brown was in the midst of this spirited send-off, Chris Slaughter was intently draped over the *Bokken*'s extended periscope. The control room around him was lit totally in red, and with his night vision intact, he could just make out a strip of deserted beach, some four hundred yards distant. A solid line of stately coconut palms veiled the surrounding jungle.

Slaughter forcefully voiced the orders. "All stop! Prepare to surface!"

As the submarine ceased its forward movement,

he added without diverting his glance from the eyepiece. "Quartermaster, inform the SEALs to prepare to deploy. Chief McKenzie, take us up to the surface, nice and easy. Then stand by to take us under the moment the team is clear."

The roar of venting ballast rumbled in the distance, and the bow of the *Bokken* angled slightly upward. With his hands tightly grasping the scope's twin grips, Slaughter initiated a quick 360-degree scan. Only after he was certain that the waters of the bay were clear of all surface traffic did he turn the lens back to the beach.

"Jaffers, any uninvited visitors in the vicinity?" he questioned.

His senior sonar technician was quick to answer. "Nothing but a bunch of shrimp, Captain. Sonar shows all clear."

"We've surfaced, Captain!" interrupted the boat's diving officer.

This revelation prompted an immediate response from Chris Slaughter. "Quartermaster, inform the SEALs that they're to deploy!"

With his line of sight still locked on the beach, Slaughter visualized the commando team as they hurriedly climbed out of the forward access trunk and assembled on the deck. Here they would open the deck-mounted capsule in which their raft was stored, and after throwing this inflated rubber vessel overboard, they'd load it with their equipment and then themselves.

Slaughter knew very well that this was a most critical moment. Both the *Bokken* and the SEAL team were extremely vulnerable on the surface. The commandoes had to get on their way as quickly as possible.

There was an alien tightness in his gut as he hastily initiated another 360-degree scan with the scope. Yet this time, when he turned his gaze back to the beach, the firm voice of the quartermaster called out behind him.

"The team is in the water, Captain."

The *Bokken*'s diving officer was quick to add. "Captain, the forward access trunk has been sealed. I show a green board."

"Take us under, Chief!" ordered Slaughter, his pulse quickening as the sound of onrushing ballast signaled that the dive into the protective depths had begun.

The upper deck was soon awash, and as the sail began to be covered with water, Chris Slaughter continued to expectantly gaze out the eyepiece. He carefully readjusted the scope's focus, and it was then that he sighted the team, vigorously paddling their raft toward the distant beach.

Eighteen

The waters of the bay were smooth and calm, and the team made excellent progress. Miriam Kromer did her best to contribute her share of muscle power. No stranger to the use of a paddle now, she met the SEALs blistering pace with a powerful, constant stroke. Just knowing their exposed position brought a new urgency to this effort, and she was oblivious to her aching back and arms.

Barely a word had been spoken since they'd left the submarine. This was fine with Miriam, who had her fair share of thoughts to keep her mind busy. Even though they were well into their mission now, the reality of it had yet to sink in. A commando raid of this type was something that belonged on a movie screen, or the pages of an adventure novel, not in an actual life. But here she was all the same, on a dangerous operation, with a group of men who did this kind of thing for a living.

Adding to the unreality of the moment was the mirrorlike stillness of the surrounding waters, the crystal-clearness of the star-filled heavens. The air was warm and humid, its scent tinged with the rich, salty smell of the sea. A gull cried out overhead, providing the lone accompaniment for the constant, muted sounds of paddles slicing into water.

The shoreline was quickly approaching. From her vantage point, Miriam could see the line of tall palms that ringed the narrow beach. The surf was barely existent. It was evident that they could not rely upon it to propel them onto the sand, so they utilized their paddles until the very last moment, when Cajun and Old Dog jumped overboard and guided the raft up onto the beach.

Silence prevailed as the others jumped out and helped drag the inflated craft out of the water. It was Cajun who signaled them to kneel in the sand while he scouted out a safe route into the underbrush situated some twenty yards distant. He was back in a matter of a few minutes, and together they lifted up the raft and carried it farther inland.

They hid it beneath a pile of palm fronds. Then, as Cajun returned to the beach to wipe out their tracks, the rest of the team removed the weapons from the waterproof equipment bags. They were fully armed by the time Cajun rejoined them.

Again without a word spoken, their point man led the way deeper into the underbrush, with Old Dog, Traveler, Kromer, and Warlock following at five-yard intervals. The toxicologist was somewhat surprised to find herself in a thick, semitropical forest, complete with strangely crying birds and humming insects. The overhead cover all but blotted out the starlight, and she found it difficult to see the narrow footpath that led them away from the bay.

It was good to be back on solid land again, even if the sights, smells, and sounds weren't all that familiar. The tight confines of the submarine had been an alien world to her. Its pitching deck and sickening diesel fumes were aggravated by the sub's cramped spaces and almost total lack of privacy. The men who took such vessels to sea were certainly a breed apart, and Miriam couldn't help but respect them.

It was as she was climbing over the rounded trunk of a fallen palm tree, that the loud, distinctive chirping of a cricket came from up ahead. Since the SEALs used a hand-held device to mimic this sound whenever they wanted to warn of danger, she momentarily halted to determine its legitimacy. Warlock soon caught up with her and, with his finger to his lips, cautiously led her farther down the path.

They met up with the rest of the group at a spot where the trail crossed a broad, sandy clearing. It was Cajun who used the tip of his knife to point out a barely visible, taut wire stretched out barely a half-inch from the ground and extending into the surrounding forest.

"It's a trip-wire, Doc," whispered Warlock. "Watch your step, and by all means, don't wander off the trail."

This warning hit home, and Miriam's pulse instinctively quickened. Finally, the first hint of fear was stirring deep inside of her. This was no mere exercise. The stakes were life or death.

She carefully stepped over the wire, and tried her best to put each foot down in the exact spot

Traveler had stepped in. It was a nerve-racking experience, knowing that the very next step could be a fatal one. During one of their training sessions, Warlock had demonstrated the techniques of mine warfare, and Miriam had seen her fill of deadly weapons that could easily blow off a foot or much worse.

She didn't have to go far until the distinctive manmade cry of the cricket once more called the team together. They took refuge behind a massive mound of cut brush, the glow of a bright spotlight readily visible through the trees ahead.

"I'll check it out," said Cajun, who wasted no time in disappearing into the underbrush.

The rest of the team crouched down to wait for his return.

"How are you feeling now, Doc?" asked Traveler as he handed her his canteen.

The toxicologist gratefully swallowed a mouthful of water before answering. "Cajun was right. All of a sudden, I'm scared stiff."

"Well, relax darlin'," advised Traveler as he took back his canteen and downed a sip himself. "Because as long as ole Trav is around, nobody's going to be messin' with you. And that, Doc, is a fact!"

Miriam had long ago made her peace with this well-meaning Lothario, and she found his words somewhat reassuring.

"God damn mosquitoes!" cursed Old Dog as he slapped one of the persistent insects from his neck.

Miriam was suddenly aware of a tickling sensation on her earlobe, and she brushed off the insect responsible for it in midbite. The standing water they had passed earlier provided a perfect breeding ground for these blood-sucking pests, Miriam reflected, wondering whether they carried malaria or not, the dreaded disease caused by a parasite transmitted by the female anopheles mosquito. This parasite enters the red blood cells, where it grows and eventually bursts, causing extreme anemia, followed by intense attacks of chills, fever, sweats, and great weakness. Though malaria could be controlled by simply destroying the mosquitoes' breeding places, the disease was still ranked as a major cause of death in the world's tropical areas, with some two million people dying from it each and every year.

As she slapped yet another mosquito off her forehead, Cajun silently emerged from the underbrush. Only the whites of his eyes showed as he breathlessly joined them.

"It's the western security perimeter, all right," he reported between gasps of air. "There's a real pretty barbed-wire fence, with video cameras coverin' all the angles. But I didn't see a single guard or, more important, any sign that they're usin' watch dogs."

"Can we cut our way through without being detected?" asked Old Dog.

Cajun was quick with his answer. "I don't think we have to go to all that trouble, big guy. If you ladies don't mind gettin' wet, there's some sort of sewer tunnel that empties out into a creek over yonder. As far as I can tell, it leads straight inside."

It was pitch black outside by the time Dr. Yukio Ishii and his two trusted senior naval officers climbed up the forward access trunk of the *Katana* and gathered on the sub's top deck. None the worse for wear after imbibing his fair share of sake, Lieutenant Satoshi Tanaka was his usual convivial self as he stretched his compact frame and looked up into the star-filled heavens.

"It's a beautiful evening for a cruise, Satsugai," he said to the *Katana*'s captain. "Too bad you won't be able to enjoy it from the surface."

Satsugai Okura grunted. "I'm quite happy to keep it that way, Satoshi. Besides, you were always the stargazer in our crowd."

"It is indeed a magnificent night," observed Ishii, who wondrously stared upward. "This is but another excellent portent of things to come."

A young sailor approached Okura and handed him a clipboard. Okura quickly read its contents before handing it back to the sailor and excusing him with a brusque salute.

"That was the final manifest," he revealed to his two associates. "As expected, the *Katana* will be ready to set sail with the tide change."

Ishii appeared particularly relieved at this news, but he was instantly distracted by the arrival of a single motorcycle on the adjoining pier. The driver of this vehicle was dressed all in black leather; even the flat dispatch case hanging around his neck was of that color and material. With a quick fluid motion, the man leaped off the motorcycle

271

and hurried up the *Katana*'s gangplank, not stopping until he reached Ishii's side.

"Excuse me, sir," the leather-clad messenger said, reaching into his case and pulling out an envelope. "I was told by the assistant director to deliver this to you at once."

Ishii quickly opened the sealed envelope and as he read its contents, a puzzled expression crossed his wrinkled face.

"This certainly is strange," he said thoughtfully. "But an hour ago, our esteemed net keeper allowed a submarine into the bay. And get this, Sumiko swears that it was the *Bokken!*"

"If that's the case, Captain Sato must have gotten lost somewhere between the bay's entrance and this pier," jested Okura. "Surely the senile old veteran read his computer screen improperly."

Satoshi Tanaka was quick to defend the net keeper's honor. "Yano Sumiko might be long in years, but he's still sharp as a tack. There can be absolutely no doubting his ability to operate the sensor grid."

"Then it's a glitch in the detection equipment that's responsible," offered Okura.

The one-eyed mariner shook his head to the contrary. "Highly unlikely, Satsugai. The entire system checked out perfectly during our recent inspection. And besides, there's been no hint of any operational difficulty."

"Who knows, perhaps the *Bokken* has indeed returned early," interrupted Ishii. "Since Sato helped design our hydrophone security system, maybe he's trying to test our alertness, and he's merely hiding

272

out there, waiting for us to detect him."

Tanaka wasn't about to buy this argument either. "That doesn't sound like the Hiroaki Sato I know. If the *Bokken* has returned early and is not tied up to this pier yet, then I fear she might have had an accident, that she might be stranded on the bottom of the bay."

"That, too, is a possibility," agreed Ishii, whose intense glance locked on the one-eyed veteran. "Satoshi, can that new towed sonar array you've been bragging about all afternoon locate the *Bokken* if such a tragedy has befallen them?"

"Most definitely, sir," snapped Tanaka.

"Then I want you to initiate a complete underwater scan of the bay at once," Ishii ordered. "And remember, haste is essential, for I dare not send the *Katana* to sea until this mystery is solved one way or the other."

Jaffers was in the midst of a sweep of the *Bokken*'s forward, port hydrophones, when a deep, low-pitched rumbling streamed in through his headphones. He needed only a couple of seconds to get an exact directional fix on this racket, whose source was easily discernible.

"Surface contact, Captain!" he firmly declared. "Bearing zero-two-five, maximum range. Sounds like a single-shaft patrol boat of some kind."

Chris Slaughter and Bill Brown stopped sipping coffee at the nearby chart table and came over to the sonar console as Jaffers excitedly added, "It's just gone active, sir!"

273

"There goes the easy way," said Bill Brown as he reached the senior sonar tech ian's side.

"I'd say it's time to creep ofı ⟍o deep water, gentlemen," offered Chris Slaughter. "Then we'll put her on the bottom, and pray they lose interest before the SEAL team signals for a pick up."

The team that Slaughter was concerned about had its own problems. For the past ten minutes, they had been crawling on hands and knees through a slimy, pitch-black sewer tunnel that was partially filled with runoff waste water. Not certain as to where this circuitous means of entry would deposit them, they pushed onward in the hope that this effort would not be for naught.

Miriam Kromer was particularly disgusted by this tunnel. It was barely wide enough to accommodate her shoulders, and she couldn't imagine how a giant like Old Dog was able to get through it.

As a child, she'd avoided tight, dark spaces whenever possible, and she now remembered why. When she was a seven-year-old, hiding under her bed, a box spring had collapsed on top of her, and the trauma produced by this horrifying event was ingrained in her to this very day.

Several times during the transit of the tunnel, Miriam feared that she wouldn't be able to continue. With her heart pounding wildly and her body thoroughly soaked in panic-induced sweat, she fought the urge to reverse her course. Most likely it was the SEAL who followed closely be-

274

hind her that kept Miriam from doing so. Somehow she summoned the fortitude to persevere, and felt great relief when the dimmest of flickering lights invitingly beckoned from the blackness up ahead. A cool draft of fresh air accompanied this sighting, and Miriam knew that her exhausting, emotional trial would soon be over.

Cajun had to remove the wire grate over the end of the tunnel before they could crawl out into the open. This put them in a foul-smelling, partially filled drainage pit. The brightly lit exterior walls of the industrial complex, less than one-hundred yards distant, could be clearly seen, and it was Traveler who pointed out their next hiding place—a collection of loose pipe at the very edge of the pit.

With Warlock's help, Miriam climbed up a small embankment and joined the team in hiding. Cautiously, she got her first good look at the collection of buildings they had been sent to penetrate. The complex was larger than she had anticipated, and a well-lit asphalt roadway extended along its perimeter. As a jeep carrying three armed guards sped down this thoroughfare, Miriam sighed heavily upon realizing the true extent of this mission's difficulty.

"There it is, ladies," observed Cajun somberly. "I'm officially open to suggestions."

Warlock was the first to respond. "I'd say the first thing we should do is find a shower and some dry clothes. Doc, do you have any idea what that slime we just crawled through was?"

"Around here, God only knows, Warlock," she answered.

It was Traveler who pointed out that two slightly built sentries were slowly approaching them on foot, having come from one of the buildings directly in front of them.

"I don't know about that shower," he whispered, "but I think I just spotted two fresh uniforms."

Miriam at first feared that their secrecy had been compromised, for the two sentries crossed the road and continued straight toward them. Yet the men's true motive became evident when they sat down on a nearby section of pipe for a cigarette break.

The toxicologist watched as Traveler looked at Cajun and made a cutting motion across his throat. Cajun nodded and joined him, dropping his pack and proceeding to close in on the two unsuspecting smokers. Like snakes, the two SEALs slithered in and around the sections of loose pipe, finally coming to a halt directly behind their quarry. Then, in unison, they sprang upward, yanked the guards backward, and cleanly broke their necks with a quick snapping motion. Minutes later the SEALs returned, the two fresh corpses in tow.

As the bodies were unceremoniously dumped on the ground before the rest of the team, Warlock coolly sized them up. "Old Dog, I'm afraid you're out of contention. Doc, since we need to get you into that complex to eyeball the lab, you get one of the uniforms. Trav, you get the other because this was your idea."

There was a lustful twinkle in Traveler's gaze as he eyed Kromer and began undressing.

"Come on, Doc," he whispered. "Time's a wastin'."

Somewhat reluctantly, she began unbuttoning her fatigues, while Warlock, Cajun, and Old Dog stripped the corpses of their khaki-colored uniforms. Miriam tried hard to forget about the unfortunate man whose clothing she was soon putting on. Just knowing that this was the attire he had died in made her extremely uncomfortable. The trousers were a bit baggy, and the shirt and jacket could have used some alteration, but as a whole, they really didn't fit that badly. As she hid her long red hair under the guard's cap and pulled the brim low over her forehead, Warlock handed her a handkerchief.

"You'd better get rid of that war paint, Doc," he suggested. "Right now, you look like something that just crawled out of the Black Lagoon."

Having completely forgotten about the camouflage makeup that covered her face, Miriam now did her best to remove it. Traveler did likewise, and after making some minor adjustments to the length of his new pants, he beckoned toward the nearby roadway.

"Are you ready, Doc?" he calmly asked.

Miriam found it hard to hide her anxiety as she nervously scanned the brightly lit industrial complex and then looked back to her teammates.

"I guess so," she managed, her tone unnaturally tense.

"Chill out, Doc," advised Warlock. "Take a couple of deep breaths and just act natural. And don't worry, you're in good hands."

"I'll say," added Traveler, who pulled down the brim of his cap and reached for Kromer's arm.

Fear weighed her down, as she hesitantly followed Traveler toward the roadway, though her cocksure escort appeared the picture of confidence, not in the least bit fazed by their precarious circumstances.

They had just reached the pavement when a jeep pulled out of a side street and headed straight for them. Sweat poured off Miriam's forehead, and she shuddered to think what would happen to them if they were captured. Traveler sensed her unease and did his best to calm her down.

"Jesus, Doc, relax. Right now you're wound up as tight as a virgin on her wedding night."

Only when the jeep passed them by without incident did she realize that their uniforms were an effective disguise, after all. She exhaled in relief, wiped her forehead dry with the back of her hand, and expressed herself.

"And to think I used to enjoy playing dress up!"

Traveler chuckled softly as he led them up the narrow street from which the jeep had just emerged. They passed by a block of windowless, four-story concrete buildings, then turned onto a wider thoroughfare with a busy supply depot on one corner. Several paneled trucks and vans were parked here, and on the loading dock were men in white coveralls and hard hats.

It was pure chance that guided Traveler's footsteps past a solidly built, two-story building with a conspicuous collection of ventilation pipes on its roof. One side of this structure had a massive, water-cooled air conditioner unit built into it, and Kromer halted to study it more closely.

"Traveler, I think that we just hit paydirt," she muttered as she studiously surveyed the familiar layout of the building's ventilation system. "This structure is almost an exact duplicate of the one housing our Biohazard Level Four laboratories back at Fort Detrick."

The SEAL followed her line of sight, and somewhat skeptically replied. "Let's have a closer look before we go and blow up the canteen by mistake."

An alleyway took them to the rear of the structure, where a small loading dock was situated. A number of sealed dumpsters were positioned here, and Traveler pushed Miriam behind one of these large bins when the dock's corrugated-steel doorway suddenly began rolling open. The toxicologist's fear was all but forgotten as she cautiously peeked around the bin and caught sight of a single figure dressed in a head-to-toe biohazard containment suit standing on the elevated dock. This prompted an instant response from her.

"This is the place, Traveler. I'm certain!"

The SEAL viewed the individual in the protective suit, who looked like an astronaut, and his skepticism quickly dissipated.

"Darlin'," he said. "That's all I wanted to hear. Come on, let's get back to the others."

Miriam readily complied with this request, and they quickly returned to the main thoroughfare and turned in the direction of the supply depot. It was as they spotted this brightly illuminated structure in the distance, that a pair of white-smocked technicians passed by on foot and greeted them in rapid Japanese. Both Miriam and Traveler could only bow in response to this apparent greeting, then continue on without breaking stride. During this brief confrontation, Miriam felt completely at ease and even remembered to keep the natural female sway of her hips to a minimum.

As they approached the supply depot, a white van could be seen parked at the curb, its engine running and no one inside. Such a convenient means of transportation could not be ignored, so Traveler carefully scouted the area for any signs of the vehicle's driver.

"I always say, why walk when you can ride. Hop in, Doc. From here on in, SEAL Team Three goes in style!"

With the assistance of the van, they were able to return to the site where they'd left the others in less than two minutes. Without a word spoken, Traveler jumped from the driver's seat and activated his hand-held recognition clicker. This was all the rest of the team had to hear to leave cover, hurriedly load their equipment into the van's rear compartment, and then jump in themselves.

"I'm afraid to ask, but where in the hell did you find the wheels?" questioned Warlock, as Traveler jammed the van into gear and sped back into the complex.

"Somebody up there must be on our side," Traveler answered, guiding the van down the side road that would take them to the main thoroughfare where the supply depot was located, "because it was just sitting at the curb waiting for us."

280

"And the lab?" continued Warlock.

This time it was Miriam who answered. "We found it. It's situated in a building that's almost an exact duplicate of a BW laboratory back at Fort Detrick."

"Way to go, Doc!" shouted Old Dog triumphantly.

"I'm sure gonna be happy when those charges are set and we get outta this place," said Cajun. "All these bright lights and concrete give me the willies."

"Well just hang in there a little longer, Cajun," advised Traveler as the van sped past the storage depot.

"What are we up against, Trav?" asked Warlock, ever pragmatic.

Traveler downshifted and then replied. "The building's a two-story, concrete structure with a loading dock in the rear and a water-cooled air-conditioning unit built into its western wall. It's got a shit-load of ventilation equipment on the roof, and it shouldn't take much to bring the whole thing down."

"Trav, you take Doc and set your charges inside that air conditioner," instructed Warlock. "I'll take the roof. Old Dog and Cajun can plant their explosives at the rear of the building and alongside the eastern wall. Do your best to place them where they'll do the most structural damage, and make certain to set those timers at maximum delay."

As the SEALs readied their equipment, Miriam Kromer's pulse quickened. Time seemed to have an almost dream-like quality to it as the van turned down the darkened alley that adjoined the suspected lab and Traveler turned off the ignition.

"Let's do it, SEALs!" ordered Warlock. A coil of rope ending in a razor-sharp grappling hook was draped over his shoulder.

The van's rear door was flung open and the commandoes sprang into action. Miriam only caught a brief glimpse of Warlock as he heaved the grappling hook upward and its sharpened claws firmly gripped the rim of the wooden siding that encircled the structure's flat roof. When he pulled the rope taut and began climbing up the side of the building, Miriam followed Traveler over to the massive air conditioner.

The SEALs were using plastic explosives. They looked much like white putty, had the same pliable, dough-like consistency. Miriam helped Traveler mold the explosives into long, sausage-shaped segments. He then proceeded to carefully place the charges at the base of the building, paying particular attention to the spot where the air conditioner was attached to the wall itself. Next he connected each individual segment with a fuse, which he subsequently attached to a master detonator that had a wind-up alarm clock on its face. The entire process took less than five minutes, but Traveler scrupulously rechecked his work before setting the timer and flashing Miriam a thumbs-up.

"We've got an hour to go until this entire block is nothing but dust. You did good, Doc. Now let's get you home safe and sound like the captain ordered."

This sounded fine to Miriam, who readily followed the handsome commando back to the van. Old Dog and Cajun were already waiting for them, and just as they all looked up to check on their missing teammate, Warlock came rappeling down the side of the wall. He landed hard, and after disconnecting his rope, headed straight for the van's cargo door, the others close behind.

Not a word was uttered as they sped back to the security perimeter. Here they reluctantly abandoned the van, and took off on foot for the sewer pipe that would convey them back into the surrounding forest.

As they climbed down the embankment and crossed the drainage pit, Miriam gathered her nerve in preparation for the next part of their escape route. She mentally visualized the raft that would be waiting at the other end of the pipe, and managed to get the courage to crawl down into the dank, dark tunnel.

Just knowing this was the only way to safety prompted her to focus solely on moving as fast as possible. They had completed the most difficult portion of their mission with an amazing degree of ease; surely she could survive this one last obstacle. Nonetheless, it seemed to take an eternity to complete their transit, and it was a very relieved Miriam Kromer who eventually crawled out of the pipe.

Without stopping to celebrate, the team continued on into the dense thicket of palms. Soon they were back on the footpath they had previously followed up from the beach, and Miriam made certain not to wander off its narrow confines. Once again it was Cajun who pointed out the trip-wire, and with his invaluable assistance, they were able to quickly locate the raft. This craft didn't seem heavy at all as they picked it up and sprinted for the nearby water.

Miriam needed no coaxing to put her back into her strokes, and because of the gentle surf, they were able to travel seaward with a minimum of difficulty. For once, the paddle felt good in her hand, and she reached forward and dug into the water without fear of straining her muscles.

They were a good four hundred yards from shore when Warlock deployed a miniature, battery-powered sonic emitter. This device was dipped overboard on a nylon rope, and its utilization prompted an immediate taunt from Traveler.

"Hey, Old Dog. Do subs still make you nervous?"

The big Texan answered without missing a single stroke of his paddle. "Not the one that gizmo's callin'. As far as I'm concerned, that pigboat's home sweet home!"

Nineteen

Dr. Yukio Ishii was not the type of man who liked to be kept waiting. That was especially true on this very special evening, when the *Katana* was scheduled to set sail on the voyage whose successful outcome would change the very direction of modern Japan. Patience was a trait Ishii greatly admired, and though the elder did his best to remain as calm as possible, he repeatedly paced the entire length of the pier while waiting for the report that seemed to be taking forever to arrive.

As he reached the end of the dock for the dozenth time, Ishii stared out at the V-shaped bow of the *Katana,* wondering if this whole search wasn't a colossal waste of time. It was surely within the realm of possibility that Yano Sumiko had indeed misread his computer monitor. Their net keeper was not getting any younger, and as he approached senility, all he really seemed to care for was that vegetable garden of his.

And then there was the chance that an equipment failure had prompted the phantom sound signature. As a scientist, Ishii knew that no system, no matter how well designed and maintained, was foolproof. This was especially true for one as complex as their hydrophone detection grid.

Seriously doubting that the *Bokken* had returned to port early and was disabled on the floor of the bay, Ishii looked up as a voice called out from the sub's sail.

"Sensei, I finally have some news for you!"

Ishii hurried down the pier and climbed onto the submarine's forward gangway. The *Katana*'s captain could be seen standing on the exposed sail, and as Ishii continued his approach, Okura said, "Satoshi has picked up some sort of sonic homing signal emanating from the western portion of the bay. He's currently moving in at flank speed to investigate."

"A sonic homing signal, you say?" repeated the puzzled elder. "Then perhaps Sato has really returned. I'll bet he's doing all of this just to test our alertness."

"That could very well be," returned Okura.

"Well, whatever is happening, we'll finally find the key to this time-consuming mystery. I imagine that your crew is anxious to put to sea, Satsugai."

Okura nodded. "They are, Sensei."

"Go below and preach patience," instructed Ishii. "You'll be off as soon as that one-eyed pirate of ours returns to escort you through the sub net."

Okura saluted and disappeared below, leaving Ishii alone on the *Katana*'s foredeck. Wishing that he had a pair of binoculars, the white-haired elder peered out over the black waters of the western portion of Takara Bay. Barely visible on the

286

horizon were the red and green running lights of Satoshi Tanaka's patrol boat. Even from such a great distance, the low rumble of this vessel's engines was just audible over the gentle cry of the gusting night wind.

Another individual was listening to this same rumbling sound from a vastly different vantage point. With the assistance of a pair of sensitive headphones, Jaffers was anxiously hunched over the sonar console, Chris Slaughter and Bill Brown standing close behind him.

"I've got increased revs on the patrol boat, Captain," revealed the senior sonar technician. "And they're headed our way!"

"Damn, they must have tagged the team's sonic emitter," said Brown.

"How far to the raft, Jaffers?" questioned Slaughter.

Jaffers readdressed his console before answering. "Less than a thousand yards and closing, sir."

"Can we get to them in time?" asked Bill Brown.

Chris Slaughter looked up and met the veteran's concerned glance. "It's going to be close, Bill. But for the sake of that SEAL team, we've got to give it our best. Otherwise, that patrol boat will rip them to shreds."

It was Cajun who first spotted the green and red running lights of the surface vessel approaching from the east. From a seated position on the raft's prow, he pointed out this unwelcome newcomer to his teammates.

"We've got company, ladies. Looks to me like it could be a patrol boat of some sort."

Old Dog momentarily stopped paddling and worriedly scanned the calm waters that surrounded them.

"Hey, Warlock, is that gizmo of yours even workin'?" he questioned. "I don't see any sign of da' sub."

Warlock replied while readjusting the line that held the sonic emitter. "Hang loose, big guy. These things take time."

"That's one commodity we don't have much of," returned Traveler, and he ceased paddling to check the position of the surface vessel Cajun had warned them about.

The running lights of this ship were clearly visible now. And since he could hear the throaty rumble of its diesels, Traveler had no alternative but to reach for his M-16.

Cajun also quit paddling, to ready his rifle. He snapped the scope cover off his Heckler and Koch, put the short, plastic stock up against his cheek. The starlight scope had limited see-in-the-dark capabilities, and as Cajun focused in on the intruder, he could just make out the large cannon mounted on this ship's foredeck.

"It's a patrol boat, all right, and it's haulin' ass straight for us," he calmly revealed.

"What can we do about it?" asked the only civilian in their midst.

288

Cajun answered, his eye still pressed up against the scope. "Doc, since there's no goin' back to shore, it looks like we'll just have to duke it out at sea. Our only chance is to hit them with as much lead as we can muster."

Warlock snapped a magazine into his Colt Commando and offered a brief game plan. "We've got another couple of minutes tops before we're within range. It will be to our advantage to let them get as close as possible before we open up."

Miriam didn't like the sound of this, so she suggested an alternative plan. "Maybe we can talk our way out of this."

Warlock looked at her in utter disbelief. "Doc, any second now those charges we set back on land will go bang. It's not going to take much imagination to figure out who's responsible, and having a nice chat is definitely not going to be on the bad guy's agenda."

The tension was growing, and Traveler intervened by handing the toxicologist a 9mm Smith and Wesson pistol.

"If it comes to a shooting war, just squeeze them off nice and smooth like we showed you back on Okinawa," he said as he snapped in a round and engaged the pistol's safety. "And remember, Doc, once those bullets start flying, your adrenaline will have you plenty pumped. So keep your cool and make sure your barrel is on target. And don't forget that as long as I'm around, you've got absolutely nothing to worry your pretty little red head about."

The growling roar of the patrol boat's engines

could be clearly heard now, and with the continued help of the scope, Cajun was even able to spot several figures standing beside its deck-mounted gun.

"I put them at about three hundred yards," estimated Warlock.

He had barely spoken these words when the roar of the diesels abruptly ceased. From the bridge of the patrol boat, a powerful spotlight was activated. The bright beam of this device cut through the blackness, and just as it was about to illuminate the raft, Cajun extinguished it with a single 7.62mm slug.

"Okay you ugly bunch of mother fuckers, let 'em have it!" cried Warlock.

This was all the SEALs needed to hear to let loose a deafening barrage of gunfire. Even Miriam Kromer joined in with her pistol, and soon the patrol boat's running lights were also put out.

"Old Dog, hit 'em with a grenade!" ordered Warlock.

The tall Texan was all set to launch one containing a high-explosive airburst, when the patrol boat's forward gun opened up and a large shell screamed overhead. All of the SEALs instinctively ducked. Yet this round went long, exploding in a geyser of water some twenty yards behind them.

Angered by this attack, Old Dog stood, pumped a grenade into his rifle's breech and, after aiming toward the patrol boat, depressed the separate trigger positioned in front of the modified M-16's magazine. There was a loud thumping sound, and seconds later a shower of searing-hot, razor-sharp fragments exploded directly above the target's bridge.

"Nice shootin', big guy!" exclaimed Cajun. "Next time hit 'em in the ammo locker, and this battle will be history."

Once more the patrol boat's forward gun fired. This round fell twenty yards short, and Warlock somberly explained what this meant.

"They've got the range now. Heaven help us on the next one."

Miriam Kromer had emptied her pistol's thirteen-round clip, and as she reached down to replace it, her hand was shaking so badly that Traveler had to snap the new clip in for her.

"I told you you'd be pumped, Doc," he whispered. "Now just breathe deeply and relax, and maybe you'll get lucky and take out that deck gunner."

A puff of white smoke from the patrol boat's bow indicated that another round was on its way. This one arrived with an earsplitting, piercing whistle, and exploded in the sea, less than five yards from the raft. A towering geyser of water shot up into the air and thoroughly soaked the team, who answered with a desperate barrage of gunfire.

"I don't like these odds, ladies," observed Traveler. "We need more firepower!"

"Gentlemen," interrupted Miriam in a tone tinged with hope. "There's something strange happening in the water on this side of the raft."

All eyes turned in that direction, to spot a

white swath of bubbling foam lightening the sea a mere ten yards away. It was Old Dog who identified this disturbance.

"It's da' sub!" he shouted.

"US Navy to the rescue!" added Traveler.

Warlock had more practical things on his mind. He put down his rifle and reached for his paddle.

"Come on, SEALs!" he joyously exhorted. "Paddle like you never did before!"

Satoshi Tanaka stood on the shattered bridge of the patrol boat that currently lay dead in the water. A corpsman worked on bandaging the bloody lacerations on his waist and thighs, while his second in command sprawled on the deck before him, half of his skull blown away.

Still having no idea of who was responsible for this unprovoked attack, the one-eyed mariner absently gazed at his ship's debris-strewn foredeck. With a gaff hook, a group of sailors had just retrieved the raft on which the mysterious attackers had first been spotted. It was empty, and as his men pulled it in for a comprehensive inspection, Tanaka listened to the worried young medic who was attending to him.

"There are still grenade fragments in your wound, sir. They require immediate hospital attention."

His thoughts far from any personal concerns, Tanaka firmly replied, "There's no time for such a luxury. I've got the spilled blood of our fellow shipmates to avenge."

Tanaka could see the sailor who had been inspecting the raft. Below on the foredeck, he pulled in a rope that had been attached to it. A small, compact device was tied to the end, and the sailor shouted up to the open bridge.

"Sir, I've found some sort of sonic homing device!"

Well aware that this was most likely the source of the signal that had originally called them to this portion of the bay, Tanaka tried hard to put the various pieces of the puzzle together. Seconds before the first shot had taken out their spotlight, the towed sonar array had picked up the signature of a rapidly approaching submarine. One of his men had actually sighted this vessel on the surface only minutes ago. It had apparently been called to this spot by the homing device, to pick up the intruders. Unfortunately the phantom sub had made good its descent before they could train their weapons on it. And with it, the men who had attacked them had disappeared.

Tanaka couldn't ignore the report that Yano Sumiko had relayed to them earlier. In this dispatch, the elderly net keeper had mentioned that he had allowed a submarine, which he presumed to be the *Bokken*, entrance into the bay. This had to be the same vessel they had just encountered, which meant only one thing. It was not the *Bokken* but another Romeo-class sub, belonging to the People's Republic of China, North Korea, or the USSR, that Sumiko had unknowingly allowed into Takara Bay.

Tanaka supposed these infiltrators had been

caught in the midst of an act of industrial espionage. That was why they had opened fire. And since they were now trapped in the bay, Tanaka saw only one course of action that could secure him revenge. With this in mind, he picked up the still-functioning intercom handset.

"Chief Agawa, I don't care what it takes, but I want that towed sonar array back on-line. We've got a phantom submarine to hunt down, and we're going to drop as many depth-charges as it takes to crack that vessel's hull wide open!"

Anticipating just such a reaction on the part of the patrol boat they had just confronted, Chris Slaughter ordered the *Bokken* down into the protective depths. With Bill Brown at his side, he anxiously stood behind the helmsman, tightly gripping a ceiling-mounted, steel handhold to counter the bow's steep down angle.

"That's right, Mr. Foard," said Slaughter softly. "Take us to the bottom, nice and easy."

The helmsman continued pushing forward on his control column, and as their angle of descent increased, several pieces of loose debris clattered up against the forward bulkhead. Those members of the crew not restrained by seat belts found it difficult to remain standing. Yet a newcomer in their midst demonstrated remarkable balance and agility as he entered the control room from the forward hatch. Pete Frystak appeared to be climbing up a steep incline as he joined the sub's two senior officers behind the helm.

"We've retrieved them all," reported the veteran weapons officer. "They're wet, cold, and exhausted, but otherwise they seem to be in excellent physical condition."

"That's wonderful news, Pete," replied Bill Brown. "With all that lead that was flying around topside, I'd say they're quite a lucky bunch."

Chris Slaughter spoke without taking his eyes off the depth gauge. "We had a little good fortune ourselves. If one of those rounds had hit the *Bokken*, we'd be headed down for a ten count and much more."

"What about the team's objective?" asked Brown.

Frystak directly met his ex-skipper's glance. "They succeeded in penetrating the complex, isolating the lab, and setting their charges. The first detonation should come any minute now."

A relieved smile turned the corners of Bill Brown's mouth. Yet before he could express himself, Jaffers called out from the nearby sonar console.

"The patrol boat is on the move again, Captain! Its current heading puts them smack on our tail."

"The bastard's following us to the deep water," said Slaughter disgustedly.

"Did you expect anything else?" returned Bill Brown. "After all, this is his turf."

"I wonder what ASW weapons they're carrying?" asked Frystak.

Chris Slaughter momentarily diverted his gaze to face the veteran. "I eyeballed a depth-charge rack on their fantail. I saw no evidence of any type of homing torpedo."

"We've just passed one-hundred feet," reported the tense helmsman. He had already begun pulling back on his control column.

Slaughter quickly turned his attention back to the depth gauge. "Level her out, Mr. Foard. If our bathymetric chart is accurate, we should be close to bottoming out, so brace yourselves, gentlemen."

Both Bill Brown and Pete Frystak reached up to grab an overhead support bar, just as the *Bokken* struck the sandy bottom of the bay with an abrupt jolt. The interior lights flickered, and as the shockwave faded, this proved to be the extent of the damage.

"Pass the word," ordered Slaughter firmly. "I want this boat buttoned down tight, and as quiet as a church. All personnel not on duty are to remain in their racks, with the galley closed until further ordered."

"If that patrol boat's got a towed sonar array, nothing short of a miracle is going to keep them off our back," commented Pete Frystak.

None of the sub's senior officers saw their sonar operator press the right receptor of his headphones up against his ear, as he hurriedly reached out to turn down the volume increase of the boat's hydrophones. But they did hear his warning.

"Something's just entered the water topside!" exclaimed Jaffers. "I think it could be—"

This sentence was cut short by a deafening, gut-wrenching blast that set the *Bokken* to reeling violently from side to side. Crew members and equipment went crashing to the deck, while the lights blinked off, on, and then off.

"Quartermaster, I need a damage report!" ordered Slaughter, who had been thrown to the deck beside the harness-secured helmsman. "And someone activate the emergency lighting system."

"I can't get to the light switch, Captain!" managed the fallen electrician's mate.

The lack of light enhanced their disorientation, and several frustrating and frightening minutes passed before the bright beam of a battle lantern cut through the murky darkness. It was Pete Frystak who held this battery-powered device. With calm, exacting precision, the veteran picked his way around the debris-strewn deck until he managed to locate the proper console and activate the emergency lights.

As a series of strategically placed, red lamps popped on, Chris Slaughter, Bill Brown, and several other crew members could be seen picking themselves up off the deck. No one appeared to be seriously injured, and as the officers scanned the control room for damage, yet another depth charge exploded close-by.

The violent concussion that accompanied this resounding blast shook the hull with the force of a major earthquake, and once more those crew members not held in place by restraints fell to the trembling deck. The emergency lighting system failed, and this time water sprayed from overhead.

The *Bokken*'s retired weapons officer was quick

297

to switch on the battle lantern, and as he struggled to get to his hands and knees, he angled the beam upward and spotted the broken water valve on the ceiling beside the periscope.

"I need some tools, pronto!" Pete Frystak loudly shouted.

He stood and fought his way across the slippery, angled deck. He was met at the periscope well by an alert sailor holding a variety of wrenches. Another sailor joined them, and together they worked at stemming the leak that already had them soaked in frigid seawater.

Meanwhile Chris Slaughter and Bill Brown once more picked themselves off the deck. Ignoring the fractured valve, they focused their attention on the quartermaster, who was readjusting the shoulder harness of his sound-powered telephone.

"What's that damage report, Chief?" quizzed Slaughter.

The quartermaster momentarily delayed his reply because his last call remained unanswered. "All stations report in but the engine room, sir. They show similar damage to our own, with no serious leaks or injuries."

"Why don't I go aft and check on Roth and his men?" volunteered Bill Brown.

"Do it, Bill," returned Slaughter. "But for God's sake be careful."

Bill Brown headed for the rear hatch, and as he passed by the periscope well, he noted with some degree of satisfaction that Pete Frystak and his two co-workers were making progress with their efforts.

"It's looking better, Pete," observed Brown, who was extra careful not to lose his footing in the gathering flood.

His ex-shipmate took a second to look up and slick back his soaked hair. "Thanks, Skipper. Do you mean you're not going to give us a hand?"

"You don't need this old man getting in your way," said Brown. "Besides, Stanley still hasn't reported in."

"He's probably just napping, Skipper. But if it's more serious than that, don't hesitate to give me a call."

"Will do, Pete." Brown stepped through the aft hatchway and cautiously made his way down a passageway lit only by dim, muted red light.

As he passed through a compartment where a group of enlisted men were berthed, he spotted a makeshift first-aid station where an overworked corpsman was attending to a variety of cuts, bumps, and bruises. The young, blond sailor who waited at the back of the line appeared extremely frightened and close to tears, so the veteran made it a point to stop beside him.

"Get a hold of yourself, sailor," he instructed in a firm tone. "What's your name and where are you from?"

The terrified young man shakily responded in a barely audible, high-pitched voice. "I'm Seaman Second Class Jed Potters, sir, from Tallahassee."

"I'm from Florida myself, son," returned Brown. "And we certainly wouldn't want the folks back in the Sunshine State to see you like this. You're a US Navy submariner, Mr. Potters. And

299

as such, you're one of the brightest and best this country has to offer. So show some guts and pride, son, and don't let a couple of measly depth charges scare you."

This hasty pep talk seemed to hit home, for Potters cleared his throat, inhaled deeply, and squared his shoulders.

"Yes, sir!" he responded, more clearly now. "I'll try my best, sir!"

"That's all I'm asking," said Brown as he nodded and then continued on his way aft.

He found the hatch that led directly into the engine room dogged shut. Before unsealing it, he took a fire axe and struck its flattened head up against the lower portion of the hatch. Only when it rang out hollow did he proceed to undog the hatch, confident that the compartment inside wasn't completely flooded.

Much to his dismay, the engine room's deck was covered by almost an inch of water. Stanley Roth and his men were gathered beneath the split pipe responsible for this flood, and Brown braved an icy soaking to join them.

"Do you need some help, Stanley?" he asked.

Roth answered while watching one of his machinists attempt to stem the flow by closing a valve on the far side of the break. "We'll get a handle on it, Skipper. It's just that some of these valves are so rusted, every time we go to close one, the damn things snap off."

A thunderous, booming explosion sounded, and Brown was forced to grasp the rail of the catwalk as yet another depth charge rattled the hull. The already muted light dimmed further, and Brown could barely see the valiant group of sailors who continued their fight against the onrushing sea.

"Hold on, Stan!" exclaimed Brown. "I'll get a battle lantern."

"Try the ledge beside the hatch, Skipper!" suggested the soaked master chief.

One of the battery-powered torches was indeed there, and Brown gratefully switched it on. As he returned to share its light with the struggling machinists, he heard Stanley Roth's question.

"Skipper, are we just going to sit here on the bottom until one of those ash cans gets lucky and blows a hole in us?"

Before Brown could respond to this, there was a loud screech of grinding metal and the water suddenly stopped flowing.

"I have a feeling that Commander Slaughter's patience is just about exhausted," answered Brown. "So if I were you, I'd have your boys pump this compartment dry and then stand by for action!"

Back in the *Bokken's* control room, Bill Brown's prediction was about to come true. Frustrated by being powerless to halt the nerve-racking series of depth-charge attacks, Chris Slaughter and Pete Frystak stood beside the sonar console, anxiously waiting as Jaffers completed the latest scan of conditions topside.

"They're coming around real slowly, Captain," said the sonarman somberly. "Sounds to me like

301

they've just put some sort of towed array in the water."

This revelation caused an anguished look to cross Slaughter's face, and he uncharacteristically cursed. "Damn! If they pin us down with active, we're goners. What I wouldn't give for just one of *Hawkbill's* wire guided Mk 48's right now."

Pete Frystak was quick to offer an alternative. "We're carrying a full load of fish. Why not use them?"

"Without a wire to guide them, we'd have to surface and put a torpedo right down that patrol boat's throat," countered Slaughter.

The veteran slyly grinned. "As a matter of fact, that's just what I had in mind. Back in fifty-seven, while patrolling the Formosa Straits to keep Mao's Taiwan invasion fleet contained, *Cubera* was pinned on the bottom by a Chinese frigate. Though the official word was that the Chink warship hit a mine and sank, I can tell you differently."

"And I suppose you were on board at the time," said Slaughter.

Frystak's eyes lit up. "Hell, Commander, not only was I on board, who do you think came up with the tactic that sunk them?"

Like any successful hunter, Satoshi Tanaka instinctively sensed it was time to move in for the kill. Oblivious to the pain caused by the shrapnel embedded in his lower torso, the one-eyed mariner staunchly stood at his post on the patrol boat's bullet-scarred bridge, scrupulously scanning the dark waters directly in front of them. Several minutes had passed since they had released the last depth-charge, and Satoshi was patiently awaiting his senior chief's appearance before beginning the next and hopefully final round.

Padded steps behind him signaled this individual's presence, and he turned and beckoned Yoshi Agawa to join him at the railing. Also a veteran of the Japanese Maritime Self-Defense Force, Yoshi was a hardworking, disciplined sailor whom Satoshi Tanaka had personally recruited. There could be no missing the dark lines of fatigue and worry that etched the weary chief's face as he stepped onto the bridge and conveyed the status update his CO had been awaiting.

"Sir, the array has been fully deployed and is ready to be activated."

"That's wonderful news, Yoshi," replied Tanaka, who added. "And the spotlights?"

Yoshi answered while pointing to the bow, where two sailors could be seen rigging a temporary lighting fixture. "They will be on-line momentarily, sir."

Tanaka was pleased with this report, and quickly expressed his reaction. "Surely our first round of depth charges damaged our prey and put fear in their hearts. Now we'll administer the killing blow. Activate the array and pipe it through the public address system, Yoshi. Together we'll listen to their death throes."

Yoshi Agawa obediently nodded and then addressed the keyboard positioned beside the helm.

303

Seconds later, a loud blast of scratchy static emanated from the bridge's elevated PA speakers. Agawa readdressed the keyboard to make an adjustment, and the static was replaced by a steady, throbbing hum.

"The hydrophones are picking up the sound of the submarine's battery-powered engines," observed Yoshi.

Tanaka expectantly rubbed his hands together. "Ah, so they finally got the nerve to get off the bottom, and they're trying to make a run for it. This only makes the hunt that much more exciting. Hit them with active, Yoshi. We'll get their exact position, and put them out of their misery once and for all."

Once more the senior chief typed a series of commands into the computer, and the speakers projected a single, distinctive ping. When a series of rapid pings followed, however, Agawa appeared confused and frantically returned to the keyboard.

"What is the matter, Yoshi?" questioned Tanaka, who was just as puzzled as his subordinate. "Suddenly you've gone as pale as a ghost."

"It can't be!" exclaimed Agawa in a tone of utter disbelief. "But we were just ranged by another boat's active sonar!"

At this moment the patrol boat's replacement spotlights snapped on. With his gaze now drawn in this direction, Satoshi Tanaka pondered his senior chief's ominous warning while looking out to the waters directly before them. And it was then he spotted the surfaced submarine, some fifty yards off their bow — and the white wakes of the four torpedoes streaking straight toward them.

Dr. Yukio Ishii was standing at the end of Takara pier, when he saw the patrol boat's spotlights activate. Satsugai Okura stood beside him, listening as his worried employer vented his anxiety.

"Good. Satoshi's most probably scanning the wreckage his depth charges created. Soon we'll know what this is all about, Satsugai."

"I still think that is a Russian sub, Sensei," offered Okura. "They're so desperate, they'll go to any length to get high-technology secrets."

Ishii held back his own opinion as he intently watched the vessel's progress. He could hear the throaty roaring of the boat's engines as its throttle was fully engaged, and he prepared himself for the inevitable blast of an exploding depth charge. But instead of a single massive detonation, there followed a quick succession of four individual blasts, these at a different pitch than the previous ones. At the same time, the patrol boat's lights were abruptly extinguished and a frothing geyser of debris-laced seawater shot up into the air at the precise spot where the patrol boat had just been positioned.

"My heavens! What has just happened out there?" questioned Ishii. He appeared genuinely confused by this entire sequence of events.

Okura was equally as dumbfounded, though as a veteran naval officer he knew very well this last blast could only signal the end of his old friend Satoshi Tanaka.

"I can't say for certain, Sensei," he shakily managed. "But it appears the patrol boat has just exploded. Perhaps they hit a mine, or maybe it was an engine malfunction."

Ishii was all set to argue otherwise, but an even louder series of blasts sounded from the direction of land. Surprised by this unexpected commotion, the stunned elder turned his head and looked on as a massive, mushroom-shaped cloud of smoke and flame shot high into the night sky directly over the main industrial complex. So bright were these flames, they clearly illuminated Ishii's horror-filled face as he struggled to find words to express his shock.

"The complex! The laboratory! My life's work! No, this cannot be!"

A siren began wailing in the distance, and a series of secondary explosions signaled that this conflagration was far from over.

"What should we do, Sensei?" asked Okura, spurred by the warrior's need to meet violence with violence. "Should I release the ninja, then use the *Katana* to hunt down the phantom submarine that's responsible for all of this?"

"Absolutely not!" shouted Ishii. "You must set sail at once, and get on with your original mission."

Okura dared to challenge this order. "But what about the ones who caused all this death and destruction, Sensei? Surely we can't just let them get away with such a horrific crime."

A renewed sense of purpose guided Ishii, and as the raging flames were reflected in his eyes, he responded, "I will handle tracking down these perpetrators. You have only one divine duty, and that is to guide the *Katana* safely into Tokyo Bay. Besides, once the *Katana* is safely through the net, all I have to do is rearm the mine field, and our so-called phantom submarine will be doomed. So get on with it, Satsugai, before all of our hard work and sacrifice is in vain!"

Twenty

Pete Frystak tried hard to maintain a poker face as he listened to the report that was being conveyed to him via the intercom handset mounted into the bulkhead beside the port-side torpedo tubes. His expectant audience included Adie Avila, Miriam Kromer, and the four SEALs. None of them took their eyes off the serious-faced veteran as he concluded his conversation and thoughtfully hung up the handset.

"Well, Pops, what's the verdict?" Traveler eagerly asked. "Did our torpedoes score or not?"

This was the question each of them had in mind, and Frystak responded to it coolly and collectedly.

"Ladies and gentlemen," he said with a minimum of emotion. "That was Commander Slaughter on the line. He informs me that we took out that patrol boat, and that a tremendous, land-based explosion was just monitored by our hydrophones. A subsequent periscope observation showed flames extending well over one hundred feet into the air above the very heart of Ishii Industries."

As the faces of his audience lit up with excitement, Frystak broke down and joined them in a boisterous celebration that included a spirited exchange of high fives.

"All right!" cried Cajun.

"Way to go SEALs!" shouted Old Dog.

Traveler appeared especially jubilant, and he shared his joy with Miriam Kromer.

"Hey, Doc. I told you there was nothin' to worry about. That lab is history!"

The toxicologist found it hard to believe what she was hearing was true. "Do you mean that's it? It's all over?"

"That's all she wrote, Doc," replied Warlock. "Now we just have to lay back and enjoy the cruise home."

As they continued with another round of high fives, Pete Frystak silently motioned for his assistant to join him beside the fire-control panel. Only when both of them had reached the relative isolation of this console, did Frystak speak out softly.

"I hate to spoil the party, Adie. But this patrol isn't over just yet. We've still got to get out of this bay, and Commander Slaughter wants us to reload all four bow tubes."

"But with that patrol boat snuffed, who are we going to shoot them at?" quizzed Avila.

"Ours is not to reason why, son. Let's just say it's a little added insurance policy."

The youngster thought this over before responding. "I hear you, Pete. And I'm with you all the way."

* * *

Back in the *Bokken*'s control room, Bill Brown, Chris Slaughter, and Benjamin Kram were tightly gathered around the sonar console. Jaffers was the star of the moment as he explained the latest sounds being picked up by his headphones.

"They're diesels, Captain. And I'd be willing to bet a month's pay they belong to another Romeo."

"Admiral Walker did mention that Ishii had two Romeo-class subs in his fleet," said Slaughter.

"What better vessel to hunt us down with?" commented Bill Brown.

Jaffers was quick to interject. "I don't believe that's the case, sir. They're currently heading due south, straight for the mouth of the inlet."

"They're making a run for it!" exclaimed Benjamin Kram. "All we have to do is hide in their baffles, and follow them through the sub net and out into the open sea."

"But can we catch up to them in time?" asked Brown.

Chris Slaughter reacted forcefully. "There's only one way to find out. Mr. Foard, bring us crisply around to course one-eight-zero, at flank speed! We're going to have to shut down all unnecessary systems, and have Mr. Roth and his gang squeeze out every last bit of juice left in our batteries. We won't be able to surface and initiate a recharge until we're well past that net."

Yano Sumiko was not having a good night. It had started to go wrong after he'd called in his usual evening report. As was his habit, he'd been sitting down for a light meal of dried mackerel and rice when the phone began ringing off the hook. The assistant director himself was on the line, and he gruffly instructed Sumiko to relate the exact details concerning the submarine allowed entrance into the bay earlier. Sumiko did his best to satisfy his inquisitor's stern request, and when he eventually hung up the phone, he thought he had succeeded. Yet he'd no sooner returned to his table than a loud knock sounded on his front door, and in walked a trio of stern-faced, white-smocked technicians. They went directly to the sensor console and began a comprehensive systems analysis that took over an hour to complete.

Sumiko was in no mood for this unwelcome disturbance. He was tired and hungry, and his back hurt from shoveling mulch for most of the day. Besides, the system had been thoroughly checked less than three days ago, so this whole thing was nothing but a waste of time.

The technicians departed as abruptly as they had arrived, with absolutely no explanation as to what they had found. This was fine with Sumiko, who just wanted to be left alone in the first place.

To calm his nerves, he allowed himself an extra portion of sake, which he made certain to thoroughly warm before drinking. This did the trick, and not even bothering to clean out his rice pot, the old-timer headed straight for his futon. The firm canvas mattress had never felt so good, but just as he was about to nod off, the first muffled blast sounded outside.

He supposed this was a byproduct of the construction project. During the days when the complex was being excavated, such explosions were a common occurrence, though seldom did they take place after sunset.

Several more blasts followed, and Sumiko found it hard to hide his annoyance. A fellow needed a sound night's sleep if he was expected to rise at dawn and put in a full day's work. He was so upset that he was even thinking about calling in a complaint. But such an act would only serve to call attention to himself, and this was something that wasn't the least bit desirable.

Sumiko had determined to make the best of this noisy business when four successive blasts were followed by a thunderous explosion that actually threw him off his mattress. He landed on the floor with a rough jolt, and it took him several painful minutes to stand fully upright once again. Well aware that the blast he had just heard was strong enough to bring down half a mountain, Sumiko stiffly made his way outdoors. He couldn't believe the scene that awaited him.

It seemed the entire northern horizon was filled with towering flames and billowing smoke. The majority of this inferno appeared to be centered in the very heart of the complex. This surely meant the tragedy would be most costly both in property and human lives.

As Sumiko watched the spreading flames turn the night sky into a hellish panorama, he heard his telephone ringing. In the hope that the caller would be able to explain what had precipitated this disaster, he returned indoors.

The phone was mounted beside the sensor console, and Sumiko picked up the receiver and put it to his ear. Once more, he was greeted by the stern voice of the assistant director. Without giving Sumiko a chance to ask about the fire, his superior relayed a series of strict instructions. Sumiko was to open the net immediately to allow the *Katana* access to the open sea. Once the submarine had safely transitted the inlet, he was then to instantly reseal the bay and arm its CAPTOR mines so that they would respond to contact detonation only. Sumiko was asked to repeat these orders, and after he did so, the line went dead.

Realizing he still didn't know the cause of the fire, the old-timer got on with his duty. He pulled out a chair, sat down before the console, and, after rubbing his arthritic hands together, slowly began to address his keyboard.

Aboard the *Bokken*, Jaffers was the first to hear the sounds of the opening of the sub net. Since he had also been tasked to carefully monitor the position of the other Romeo-class submarine, he hastily rechecked his data before sharing it with his superiors.

"Mechanical sounds dead ahead indicate the sub net is in the process of opening," reported the senior sonar technician. "As it looks now, our twin is going to beat us through by a good couple of minutes."

"Let's just pray that the net keeper takes his sweet time resealing the bay," said Bill Brown, whose glance shot to the control room's ceiling as a shrill, metallic screech suddenly filled the compartment.

"Sounds like we could be rubbing up against a mine's mooring cable!" warned Jaffers.

Both Bill Brown and Chris Slaughter hurried over to sonar, where Jaffers readjusted his sensors to get a definite identity on this unexpected disturbance. By isolating several of their hull-mounted hydrophones, he was able to determine that the sound was coming from the port side.

As the sickening screech intensified, Benjamin Kram rushed over to join them.

"Shouldn't we stop and reverse course, Captain?" he questioned.

"We can't, Ben," replied Slaughter. "If that net closes with us on the wrong side, we'll be stuck in this bay for all eternity."

"But what about that mine out there?" asked Kram.

"Don't forget that as far as the CAPTOR is concerned, we're still a friendly," reminded Bill Brown. "As long as we don't snag it, and it's not set to detonate on contact, we've got more important things to focus on, like getting a couple of more knots out of this rust bucket."

The screech seemed to be getting even louder, and the veteran's worst fears were realized when Jaffers excitedly called out. "The cable appears to be stuck in the crease of our port hydroplane! We're currently pulling down whatever it's attached to."

"Captain, you've got to stop this submarine!" insisted Benjamin Kram.

Chris Slaughter struggled to hold firm to his decision as Jaffers added.

"The sub net's closing, sir! That other Romeo must be through."

Slaughter looked at Bill Brown and expressed his deepest fears. "I hope to God you're right, Bill, and if it's really a mine we're dragging down on us, it hasn't been reprogrammed to explode on contact."

Since he really didn't know how the mine was programmed, Bill Brown realized this was a gamble that couldn't be taken as long as there was an alternative, even though this alternative was untested. He turned to the helm and forcefully shouted out.

"Mr. Foard, engage that stern hydroplane, full rise!"

"But at this depth we could breech," countered the helmsman, who was used to taking orders only from his OOD.

Brown looked to Slaughter for support, and without bothering to even question the veteran's motives, Chris Slaughter firmly called out. "Just do it, Mr. Foard!"

This was all the helmsman had to hear. He yanked back on his control column. In response, a surge of hydraulic fluid caused the stern hydroplane to angle sharply upward, and the rusted mooring cable that had been caught between the hydroplane and the hull snapped. This sent the now rearmed contact mine, which had been only inches from the *Bokken's* upper deck, bobbing harmlessly to the surface.

"We've cleared the snag!" observed Jaffers, who wasted no time in turning his attention to the waters directly in front of them.

Though still concerned about the race with the closing net, Chris Slaughter took the time to express his gratitude to the veteran who stood beside him. "That was a hell of an idea to clear that snag, Bill. Since it's not in any manual I ever read, how did you think of it?"

Brown grinned. "I guess you can indirectly thank the Naval Submarine League for that one, Chris. I was at one of their symposiums when I overheard a World War II vet discuss a mine incident much like the one we were just involved in. Though it was never officially chronicled, he used his sub's hydroplane to cut a snagged mooring cable."

"We're less than fifty yards away from the net, Captain," interrupted Jaffers. "Mechanical sounds indicate that it's still continuing to close on us."

Both Brown and Slaughter looked to the bulkhead-mounted speed indicator. The arrow showed that they were traveling at nearly thirteen knots, which was about the best submerged speed they could hope to attain. Unless they were somehow able to increase it, it appeared they would be caught short.

Realizing this, Slaughter reached out for the intercom handset, to personally ask Chief Roth to see what he could do about squeezing out another knot or two. Meanwhile, his gray-haired companion continued staring at the speed indicator.

"Come on, *Bokken*. You can make it," urged Brown. "Move!"

* * *

Stanley Roth patiently listened to the concerned voice on the other end of the line. Even though the young officer was asking for the impossible, Stanley replied, "I'll do my best, Commander. Just hold on and pray that it's good enough."

Stanley hung up the handset and scanned the adjoining console. The majority of the gauges that monitored the internal condition of the sub's engines were well into the red danger zone. This included the all-important tachometer.

With the steady grinding hum of the vessel's twin shafts in the background, Roth solemnly reached for the throttle mechanism. The way he saw it, it was now a choice between two evils. They could either continue at their current speed, and lose the race with the closing net, or risk overloading the engines by opening the throttle wide.

Stanley Roth had never been a truly religious man. Nevertheless, he silently mouthed a prayer to the god he was just now rediscovering as he put his hand on the throttle and pushed it all the way forward. In response, the tach jumped far into the red, the needle all but touching the extreme right side of the dial.

Bill Brown was also saying a desperate silent prayer as the speed indicator his gaze was locked on gradually moved to the right. He could hardly believe his startled eyes when it increased by a full half-knot, and still continued edging upward.

"We can't be more than fifteen yards from the opening," observed the strained voice of Jaffers. "Damn, this one is going to be right down to the wire!"

Chris Slaughter also saw the increase in their forward speed, yet he didn't express himself until they'd passed fourteen knots.

"We're going to make it, gentlemen. I just know we're going to make it!"

His words of encouragement were tempered by the next update from sonar.

"Mechanical sounds continue," reported Jaffers. "I believe our bow should be just about crossing the line."

Bill Brown visualized the net closing, the *Bokken* sandwiched in between. Even if it did close on them, they could still make it as long as the net didn't snag on their stern hydroplanes like the mine's mooring cable had.

The next thirty seconds would be critical, so Brown returned to his prayers. Most of his shipmates in the hushed control room did likewise. And when the half-minute had finally passed, and the *Bokken* continued on unhampered, the veteran knew his divine petition had been answered.

"We're through!" cried Jaffers triumphantly. "Wow, talk about your heart-stopping photo finishes!"

The control-room crew celebrated with a muffled cheer, and Brown exchanged handshakes with both Chris Slaughter and Benjamin Kram.

"I'm getting too old for all this excitement, gentlemen," the relieved veteran admitted. "My ticker's

318

still beating away in double time."

"Join the crowd, Bill," replied Slaughter, who addressed his next remark to his XO. "Ben, you'd better inform Chief Roth to ease off on that throttle. And please pass on my compliments on a job well done."

"Aye, aye, Skipper," returned Kram, as he left them to pick up the nearest intercom handset.

"Old Stanley and his boys really came through," said Brown. "It would have been hell to pay if we'd gotten tangled up in that net. Now what's on the agenda?"

Slaughter looked over toward sonar. "I guess that depends on what Jaffers has to say concerning that other Romeo. Though I'd like nothing better than to head back home, as long as that vessel's on the loose, our mission's not over."

"Does that mean you're thinking about taking them out?" asked Brown softly.

Slaughter hesitated a moment before answering. "I don't know, Bill. But if there's the slightest possibility they might be carrying biologicals on board, we've got to stay on their tail until they show their cards."

Brown nodded in agreement. "I hear you, Chris. Just too bad we can't contact Admiral Walker and get some help out here. Though your men have done a hell of a fine job getting the most out of this antique, now we really need the high-tech ASW capabilities of a vessel like the *Hawkbill*. I don't even think Pete Frystak could figure out how to take out a submerged sub with the outdated fish we're carrying."

"I don't know about that," countered Chris Slaughter. "From what your weapons officer showed me back in the bay, I'd say he's capable of doing just about anything. Brother, did we ever surprise the hell out of the crew on that patrol boat!"

"That sure must have been some hellish sight," reflected Bill Brown, following Slaughter over to sonar.

Jaffers was monitoring the sub's forward hydrophones, and Slaughter questioned him while gently massaging the tight muscles of the senior sonar technician's neck.

"What's the latest on our fellow Romeo?"

Jaffers cocked his neck backward to get the most out of this greatly appreciated massage, then answered. "We're smack in their baffles, Captain. They continue to head due south, though as we approach the one-hundred-fathom line, I wouldn't be surprised if they soon initiate a course change."

"You did some fine work back there in the bay, Jaffers," complimented Slaughter. "We couldn't have made it without you."

"I was only doin' my job, Captain," replied the humble sonarman, who tried his best to stifle a yawn.

"When was the last time you were relieved?" asked his CO.

Jaffers shook his head. "I really couldn't say, sir."

"Well, I'll call someone in to watch this console while you go and stretch those long legs of yours," Slaughter promised. "Grab a cup of coffee and some chow while you're at it. And don't even think about coming back until you've gotten some well-deserved rest. You're going to be doing me no good if you pass out from exhaustion."

Jaffers readily replied. "I believe I can handle that, Captain."

Slaughter looked over to Bill Brown and smiled. The veteran winked in response, knowing full well that the quality of men who served in today's Navy easily equaled that of those who'd seen active service in his time.

Twenty-one

Unbeknownst to the crews of the two Romeo-class submarines another submerged warship was present in the open waters due south of Takara Bay. Silently loitering at a depth of seven hundred and fifty feet, she was approximately the same length as the Romeos but with double their displacement and a vastly more modern design.

The *Nadashio* was the latest Yuushio-class submarine belonging to the Japanese Maritime Self-Defense Force. It sported a sleek, rounded, teardrop-style hull in the manner of the newest US Navy attack boats, on which it was patterned. Unlike its American counterparts, however, the *Nadashio* was of double-hull construction, its externally framed pressure hull formed from high-tensile NS-90 steel. This gave the ships of the Yuushio class an unprecedented diving depth of over 1,000 feet.

Packed within the *Nadashio*'s inner hull was the very best Japanese technology. The powerful electric motor, designed by Fuji, could produce underwater speeds of up to twenty knots. The ZQQ-4 passive sonar array occupied the entire bow, with three circular transducers stacked one above the other. This served to reduce the vertical beam of the sonar and to drastically reduce the signal-to-noise ratio, allowing for unparalleled detection capabilities. Directly tied into this array was an advanced weapons-control system designed by Hitachi.

Nowhere was the level of the *Nadashio*'s high-tech design more apparent than in its combined control-and-attack center. Set immediately abaft the six forward torpedo tubes, this all-important compartment was filled with flashing digital read-outs and glowing computer screens. Highly automated, the attack center was manned by only three sailors and a single officer. Two of these highly trained enlisted men now sat before a large attack screen on which was projected a complete readout of the sub's vital engineering functions, along with a constantly updated, three-dimensional bathymetric chart of the surrounding waters. In place of the standard hydraulically powered control columns, each technician had a heavy plastic joystick mounted into the console before him. As was the case on the latest generation of fly-by-wire jet fighters, the slightest movement of this device controlled the sub's depth, bearing, and speed, and could launch its weapons.

Seated between these high-tech helmsmen, securely harnessed into a high-backed leather command chair of his own, was the *Nadashio*'s present CO, Captain Osami Nagano. The thirty-seven-year-old Annapolis graduate had his gaze centered on the attack screen, which showed their position and that of their two targets. The *Nadashio* was represented as a flashing blue star, lying motionless in the chart's southeastern quadrant, while the arrows corresponding to the two Romeos were red, one closely following the other, both headed due south.

"So that appears to be the extent of the underwater flotilla we've been tasked to eliminate," Nagano observed almost nonchalantly. "Very well, target them both, and let's be done with it."

As the technicians he sat between went to work on their keyboards, Nagano sat back, his eyes still locked on the attack screen. By merely shifting his line of sight to the left-hand portion of the screen, he could read their exact depth, and determine precisely how much charge they had left in the batteries. This was certainly more convenient than the latest American subs he had sailed on. They still relied on outdated monitoring systems whose level of technology was more suited to the 1970's.

Nagano often found himself wishing he could show off his current command to his contemporaries in the US Navy. How very proud he was of the advanced hardware that surrounded him! His schoolmates back at Annapolis would be amazed by the *Nadashio's* futuristic design; it was years ahead of any comparable American vessel.

Though rich in tradition, the US Navy put too much emphasis on wasteful backup systems and old-fashioned, manually powered valves and switches. Not only did their cluttered bureaucracy keep new equipment from being introduced, their leaders lacked the foresight to break from the past and try something radically different.

Yuushio-class warships were designed totally

324

around the computer. Whereas Americans were reluctant to put their complete trust in a machine, the Japanese had long ago learned to rely on and value automation. The *Nadashio* was living proof of the superiority of the Japanese way of life.

"We have a solution for both targets, Captain," the senior technician seated to his right reported.

Nagano hastily surveyed the attack screen to recheck the positions of both Romeo-class submarines before delivering his next instructions.

"Prepare to fire torpedoes one and two at the lead boat, then three and four at the one that follows."

The senior technician efficiently entered this request into his keyboard and responded. "Firing solutions are confirmed, sir. Tubes are flooded, outer doors open."

"Fire one and two!" ordered Nagano firmly.

In response to this command, the senior technician slid the cover plate off the top of his joystick and depressed the red button that was hidden inside twice.

"Firing one . . . firing two," he matter-of-factly said.

The deck below them shuddered twice, as a powerful blast of compressed air sent the torpedoes on their way.

"Fire three and four!" instructed Nagano.

The senior technician once more pressed the red button inside the top of his joystick.

"Firing three . . . firing four," he said.

Again the deck trembled, and as Nagano noted the exact time of this launch, he addressed the young technician seated to his left.

"This is an historic moment, Hiroshi. Your first cruise with us is turning out to be an interesting one, isn't it, lad?"

"That it is, sir," replied the wide-eyed sailor.

"Well, relax and enjoy the show," Nagano added as he pointed toward the four flashing white dots representing the torpedoes, now visible on the screen directly in front of the *Nadashio*. "Because as Toshiki here can attest, we don't see real action like this very often."

As Jaffers began his well-deserved rest, Seaman Second Class Jed Potters found himself assigned to be his replacement. This was a great responsibility, and Potters somewhat nervously settled himself in behind the relatively unfamiliar console and followed the instructions Jaffers had left with him.

No stranger to the workings of the *Hawkbill*'s sonar, Potters found the *Bokken*'s sensor array simply archaic. It fit in perfectly with the rest of the sub's antique operational systems, though they had proved their ruggedness during the recent depth-charge attack.

The fair-skinned, Floridian tried hard to forget about that terrifying bombardment as he scanned the waters surrounding them with the boat's hull-mounted hydrophones. Jaffers had emphasized the importance of monitoring the status of the other Romeo-class sub they were following. It was extremely important that they remain silently tucked away in this vessel's sound-absorbent baffles, and it was up to Potters to inform the OOD the second he sensed a course change.

His headphones presently conveyed a constant, muted throbbing that was emanating from the other Romeo's battery-powered electric motor. Potters had been instructed to readjust the hydrophones every couple of minutes, to listen for the approach of any other vessels that might be in the area. Yet this sweep was only of secondary importance. His primary responsibility remained the other Romeo.

Because his knowledge of the Fenik array was extremely limited, Potters didn't dare attempt to experiment with its various dials and switches. He was content to concentrate his attention solely on the unit's passive capabilities, which in reality was much like listening to the input from an underwater microphone.

The monotonous throbbing tones of the vessel they followed were enough to put a fellow to sleep, and Potters looked forward to his occasional sweeps of the surrounding seas. It was during one of these impromptu scans that an unusual buzzing sound caught his attention. Barely audible at first, it continually intensified, until it dawned on the startled sonarman that he had heard a similar racket before, while listening to a tape at sonar school.

"Captain . . ." Potters pressed the right headphone up against his ear. "I believe I'm picking up the sound of high-speed screws. I think it might be coming from a torpedo."

This tentative warning brought an immediate response from the two senior officers who had been gathered around the nearby chart table. As Chris Slaughter looked up from the bathymetric chart he had been immersed in, Bill Brown rushed over to sonar and put on a set of auxiliary headphones. It took the veteran a couple of seconds to sort out the variety of sounds now streaming into his ears. And though it had been years since he had last heard the characteristic buzzing whine of an approaching torpedo, this was a sound a submariner never forgot.

"They're torpedoes, all right!" warned Brown as he searched the console to determine which portion of the sea this scan was coming from. "I count two fish, coming in on bearing one-three-zero, maximum range."

There was a tension in Chris Slaughter's voice as he loudly cried out. "Right full rudder! Flank speed!"

A similar scene was taking place aboard the *Katana*, where Saigo Yoshino coolly monitored the unexpected attack from the boat's sonar console.

"There are two of them, Captain, on bearing one-three-zero."

Satsugai Okura stood calmly beside his seated helmsman.

"So, Mikio, this was a clever ambush all along," observed Okura, who was dressed in a white martial-arts robe. "I should have expected as much. Initiate evasive maneuvers! We shall see our way out of this trap, then take the offensive ourselves!"

328

"Fish continue to close!" informed Bill Brown, who remained at sonar, frantically attempting to make some sort of sense out of the console. "Though I still can't give you an exact range."

The deck was canted over sharply to the right, and Slaughter tightly gripped an overhead support bar as he answered. "Hang in there, Bill. At last word, Jaffers is on his way back to spell you."

"Without a decoy or any noisemakers on board, how are we going to shake those torpedoes, Skipper?" asked a very concerned Benjamin Kram.

Slaughter looked over at his XO and somberly shook his head. "I guess all we can do is try to lose them with a knuckle in the water."

"Mr. Foard!" he added to the helmsman. "Bring us up crisply to six-five feet. Then take us back down to maximum depth, full power!"

As the helmsman pulled back on his control column, the deck angled sharply upward. An assortment of loose debris went sliding up against the aft bulkhead, where a single black sailor could be seen struggling to make his way through the hatch.

"Jesus!" exclaimed Jaffers, as he fought the upward slope of the deck, like a mountaineer in the midst of a steep ascent. "I leave you guys alone for a couple of minutes, and just look at the mess you get us into!"

Meanwhile the *Katana* was headed in the opposite direction, while negotiating a series of extreme underwater turns. Okura held onto the back of Chief Mikio's chair, watching as the muscular helmsman expertly rotated the control column from side to side. This unorthodox tactic left an agitated surge of confusing turbulence in their wake, and it soon proved effective.

"We've lost one of the torpedoes, Captain!" Saigo called out from sonar.

"As we shall lose shortly the other," replied Okura confidently. "Mikio, bring us around hard to course one-three-zero."

"But, Captain, such a bearing will lead us right into the path of our attacker!" countered the confused helmsman.

"Precisely, Chief," said Okura, whose eyes glistened as he added. "Every samurai knows that the only way to successfully ward off an attack is to initiate one. And we shall do just that with a four-shot salvo on my command!"

Aboard the *Bokken*, all eyes were on the depth gauge that continued to drop until the seventy-foot level was passed. This prompted Chris Slaughter to firmly order.

"That's enough, Mr. Foard. Now take us down, like a bat out of hell!"

With an intense effort, Foard pushed forward on his control column, and the sub momentarily leveled out before beginning a steeply inclined dive into the depths from which they had just ascended. A bevy of loose equipment slid across the deck and smashed into the forward bulkhead, and for those not constrained by seatbelts, it was an effort merely to remain standing. These men included Bill Brown, who held onto the side of the sonar console for dear life. Immediately beside him, Jaffers had just secured himself to his chair and already had his headphones on.

"The fish are coming down with us," he breathlessly observed. "Range is four thousand yards and closing."

"How deep are we going, Skipper?" asked Benjamin Kram from his position beside the chart table.

"The chart says we've got nine hundred feet before we hit bottom," replied Slaughter. "And that's where I'd like to leave those fish."

"But can this old lady make it?" added Kram.

Slaughter answered without taking his eyes off the depth gauge. "I guess we're all gonna learn the answer to that question soon enough, XO."

It wasn't retreat that Satsugai Okura had in mind as he addressed his sonar operator. "Recheck that firing solution, Saigo."

The *Katana* angled over hard to port, like a jet fighter in a dogfight, and Saigo found himself thrown up against the right portion of his harness.

"Firing solution confirmed, Captain," he managed, while grasping the canvas belt.

Having only the back of the helmsman's chair to keep him balanced, Okura ordered. "Fire one, two, three, and four!"

Inside the high-tech environs of the *Nadashio's*

attack center, the *Katana*'s torpedoes showed up on the elevated screen as four miniscule white dots in the process of leaving the lead Romeo.

"Four high-speed torpedoes headed our way, Captain!" reported the junior technician unnecessarily.

Osami Nagano watched as this tightly grouped salvo turned to the southeast and calmly replied. "So I see, Hiroshi. Prepare to launch mobile submarine simulator and initiate quick-stop procedure."

With a lightning-quick flurry, the young sailor addressed his keyboard, and seconds later he responded. "Decoy ready to launch, sir."

"Launch decoy!" ordered Nagano.

It was the senior technician who depressed the red button recessed into the top of his joystick, and the entire deck shuddered. On the attack screen, a white dot appeared beside the blue star, representing the *Nadashio*. As the dot began flashing and headed to the northeast, the junior technician spoke out clearly.

"Captain, the decoy is emitting."

"All stop!" instructed Nagano. "Sound a condition of ultra quiet throughout the ship. For all effective purposes, the *Nadashio* will now become invisible."

With no high-tech attack screen to show them their position in the undersea battlefield, the crew of the *Bokken* depended upon constant updates from their senior sonarman.

"Torpedo range is now down to two-thousand yards," said Jaffers, whose strong voice did not waver.

Chris Slaughter listened to this report, while fighting back the forward slope of the deck from his position behind the helm. The depth gauge had just passed the six-hundred-and-fifty-foot mark, and as they continued their descent, the hull welds began to creak.

"I don't know what's going to get to us first, sir," remarked the tense helmsman as he continued to push down on his control column, "this depth or those torpedoes."

Slaughter's reply was curt and to the point. "I'd much rather die trying, Mr. Foard. After all, that's what life is all about."

In the *Bokken*'s forward torpedo room, the loudly creaking hull ominously moaned, and those in the compartment now had something besides the torpedoes to be concerned about. Tightly holding onto the torpedo pallet to keep from tumbling forward were Pete Frystak, Adie Avila, Miriam Kromer, and the SEALs. Not having the benefit of Jaffer's constant updates, they could only visualize the worst, and of those present, Old Dog appeared closest to losing it.

"This rust bucket's gonna split wide open!" observed the frightened commando, as the deck violently shook beneath them.

"Easy son," advised Pete Frystak. "These boats are built incredibly strong. She'll make it, sure enough."

A small trickle of water began streaming from the edge of the brass cap of the number two torpedo tube. Adie Avila was the first to notice it.

"Pete," he said as calmly as possible, "I think we could have a problem with—"

His words were cut short by a loud bang, as the cap sprung open and a torrent of seawater gushed in.

"We've got to cap her or we're goners!" exclaimed Pete Frystak.

This was all the SEALs had to hear to charge into action. Cajun was the first to let loose of the pallet and attempt to reach the ruptured cap. The slippery deck caused him to lose his footing, and he sprawled on his backside. Yet because of the steep angle caused by the sub's descent, he slid forward to the very point he'd been trying to reach. Both Warlock and Traveler made the best of his example; they merely sat down on the wet deck and allowed gravity to pull them forward.

This put the three soaked SEALs immediately beside the open cap. Seawater was pouring in as if from a high-pressure fire hose, and it was apparent that it would take a combined effort to stem the flow.

"Damn it, Old Dog!" cried Warlock. "Are you just going to stand there?"

The tall Texan's grasp had frozen on the iron rim of the torpedo pallet as he'd watched his teammates vainly attempt to push the cap closed. The onrushing seawater poured inside with a deafening roar, and Old Dog seriously doubted they had any hope of surviving.

"Come on, Adie!" said Pete Frystak. "They're going to need all the muscle they can get."

Old Dog watched as the veteran pulled a two-foot-long iron crowbar from the pallet's tool locker. Frystak then sat down on the deck and allowed the slope to pull him to the bulkhead. His lanky assistant followed, and Old Dog briefly looked over at Miriam Kromer, who tightly gripped the pallet beside him.

"Can I help?" asked the concerned toxicologist. There could be no hiding the fear in her eyes, and Old Dog suddenly felt ashamed of himself.

"Don't worry, Doc," he said with gathering confidence. "You just hold tight, and we'll get this whole thing over with real quick."

He loosened his grasp, and the pull of gravity caused him to fall hard on his right side. His big body rapidly gained momentum as it hit the cold, wet deck and tumbled straight toward the bulkhead. It proved to be Traveler who alertly intercepted him before he crashed into the steel partition headfirst.

"What kept ya', big guy?" Traveler quizzed as he helped Old Dog stand.

Old Dog was in no mood to answer this question. Instead he joined the individuals gathered about the sprung cap. They had already managed to position the crowbar behind the cap's brass head, and without waiting for an invitation, Old Dog grabbed the tool's topmost portion. Pete Frystak also gripped it, along with Cajun.

"We'll give it a try on the count of three," ordered the veteran. "Adie, you and Traveler stand by to tighten it down the second we get it closed."

Miriam Kromer could just hear these instructions from her position beside the pallet. The water continued relentlessly pouring in, and was well over a foot deep in the compartment's forwardmost portion. Amazed by how quickly it seemed to be accumulating, she realized that it wouldn't be long before the whole torpedo room was completely flooded.

Her panic intensified as claustrophobia possessed her. The walls suddenly seemed to be closing in, and it was an effort merely to breathe. Once more she was carried back to her childhood, to that traumatic afternoon when she'd almost smothered beneath her collapsed bed. Yet it was the powerful voice of Pete Frystak that snapped her back to reality.

"One . . . two . . . three!"

As her gaze focused on the men assembled around the open torpedo tube, she found herself desperately projecting her will in an effort to help them in this life-and-death struggle with the onrushing sea. The stiff crowbar they held seemed to flex under the strain of their combined pressure, and in response, the cap bit into the torrent of gushing water. Like a solid wall, the flood resisted their efforts, and a momentary stand-off ensued.

Not to be denied, Old Dog let loose a powerful war cry inspired in equal parts by fear, frustration, and willpower. An almost superhuman effort followed, the big Texan almost single-handedly utilizing the crowbar to nudge the cap forward until the now disrupted flow began wildly spraying in all directions. Both Traveler and Adie Avila rushed in at this point to push forward on the cap, and as they redogged the tube's fittings, the raging torrent became but a mere trickle, this opening to the sea successfully resealed.

In the *Bokken*'s control room, the worried crew members were preoccupied by a drama of a different sort.

"Torpedo range is down to nine hundred yards and closing," said Jaffers.

The tense voice of the helmsman followed. "Captain, we're coming up on eight hundred feet. Should I pull her out?"

Chris Slaughter looked at the depth gauge and icily replied. "Hold it just a little longer, Mr. Foard."

"Torpedo has capture!" exclaimed Jaffers.

This was all Slaughter had to hear to change his mind. "Pull us up, Mr. Foard. Emergency ascent!"

Foard yanked back on the control column, and as the vessel's hydroplanes bit into the surrounding water, the *Bokken* leveled out and began gliding upward like a lumbering jumbo jet at take-off. It took almost a full minute for Jaffers to sort out the cacophonous mixture of sounds in their wake. But as he did so, he was quick to report.

"Both torpedoes just went active again. If we only had some way to further mask our signature, I think we could beat them."

This innocent remark suddenly struck the white-haired man who stood beside him.

"The bubbler!" exclaimed Bill Brown. "We almost forgot about the masking device we're outfitted with!"

Stanley Roth was at the alternator, doing his best to squeeze as much battery power as possible from their already vastly depleted store, when the call arrived from the control room, ordering him to engage the bubbler mechanism. He wasted no time in implementing this request.

"Hey, Orlovick!" he shouted. "Start up that bubbler on the double. And pray it works, son, because we've still got two fish on our tail that don't know the word quit."

From his vantage point on the catwalk, Roth could see the young reactor specialist acknowledge this order with a wave and rush over to the bubbler's compressor. This was the heart of the device, where the millions of sizzling bubbles would be created and then projected out into the surrounding waters, from the thousands of pin prick-sized holes that completely encircled the vessel's pressure hull.

Orlovick had to get on the tip of his toes to reach the metal box in which the power switch was located. Yet when he did so, he couldn't seem to get it started. He jiggled the switch up and down for several frustrating seconds before taking a step back and smacking the side of the switch box with the open palm of his hand. Instantly, the compressor coughed to life, and Stanley Roth smiled.

"That's my boy," he said to himself with a satisfied sigh as he turned back to the alternator, to get on with the task of pulling the very last bit of power out of their badly depleted batteries.

The sounds made by the bubbler device caught Jaffers by surprise. Hissing, sizzling bubbles filled his headphones with an alien commotion that all but overshadowed any other audible signatures. For a moment, he completely forgot about the torpedoes he had been closely monitoring, and then he realized that their nerve-racking race with death was finally over.

"They're gone!" he joyously observed. "We lost the damn torpedoes!"

Inside the *Nadashio*, a celebration of a much more low-key nature was taking place. Osami Nagano appeared smugly confident as he peered up at the elevated display screen and watched the four torpedoes the lead Romeo had shot at them head to the northeast, hot on the trail of the flashing decoy.

"If we can penetrate a US Navy carrier task force and outrun one of its Sturgeon-class subs, escaping this feeble attack is nothing for the *Nadashio*," he bragged. "Yet now we must turn our attention back to our prey. What is the exact progress of our attack?"

There was a momentary pause as the technicians addressed their keyboards. Nagano impatiently looked to his right.

"Well, Toshiki, how soon until our torpedoes hit?"

The senior technician scanned the data visible on the screen and hesitantly replied. "I don't understand it, Captain. Both Romeos seem to have disappeared."

"But that's impossible!" exclaimed Osami Nagano. He looked at the screen to confirm this report.

The red arrows corresponding to the two Romeos were nowhere to be seen, and for the first time Nagano's expression displayed a hint of uncertainty.

"Could our torpedoes have hit their targets?" he offered.

"Unless there's been a major malfunction in the fire-control feedback loop, that's highly unlikely, sir," answered the senior technician. "Because I still show no indication that any of the warheads have yet detonated."

"Then where are the two Romeos?" asked the *Nadashio's* captain.

His senior technician's only response to this was a confused shake of the head as he furiously queried the sub's computer in an attempt to find an answer to this perplexing situation.

A solemn, funereal atmosphere prevailed inside the *Katana's* control room, where Satsugai Okura stood behind the sonar console, looking grim and dispirited.

"The torpedo continues to close, Captain," reported Saigo heavily. "We just can't seem to shake it."

"And the vessel that launched it?" quizzed Okura.

The sonarman checked his display before answering. "It remains directly above us, sir, on the other side of the thermocline."

Okura thoughtfully looked up to the pipe-lined ceiling and softly whispered, "If in his mind the warrior doesn't forget one thing, that being death, he'll never find himself caught short."

"Excuse me, sir?" said the sonarman, who thought these barely audible remarks were meant for him.

"It was nothing that concerns you, Saigo," responded Okura, directing his attention to the sonar console. "How much longer until impact?"

"Two minutes at the most, Captain," answered Saigo.

Okura squared his shoulders and inhaled deeply before speaking out loudly for all to hear. "If it is indeed our time, we shall go as true samurai warriors. Take us straight up, Chief Mikio! For the glory of the Emperor!"

Spiraling out of the black depths, the persistent torpedo close behind, the *Katana* shot upward, its V-shaped bow headed straight for the rounded underbelly of the unsuspecting *Nadashio*. As the Romeo-class vessel penetrated the thick layer of cold water that had masked it from its attacker's sen-

341

sors, the torpedo attained capture. And at the exact moment its contact warhead detonated, the *Katana* sliced into the *Nadashio*'s reinforced hull, causing both vessels to instantly implode in a white-hot mass of swirling seawater.

Twenty-two

Dawn was just breaking as the *Bokken* safely reached the sea's surface. Quick to make their way up onto the sub's sail were Chris Slaughter, Bill Brown, Pete Frystak, Stanley Roth and Miriam Kromer. As this group squeezed onto the crowded bridge, they were met by a spectacular sunrise and a warm, gently gusting breeze richly scented with the clean smell of the sea.

"Oh, this fresh air smells divine!" observed Miriam Kromer as she gratefully stretched her arms over her head.

Chris Slaughter pointed north, where the sky was still aglow from the burning remains of Ishii Industries. "It appears our explosives took out much more than that BW lab," he reflected.

"I wonder if we'll ever know the identity of the sub that took a potshot at us?" Bill Brown said.

"Right now, all we can assume is the other Romeo took it out, sacrificing itself in the process," offered Pete Frystak.

Stanley Roth looked over at Chris Slaughter and grinned. "You sure gave us a hell of a roller-coaster ride, Commander."

Slaughter turned away from his inspection of the

343

glowing northern horizon to scan the faces of those assembled before him. "Though we left a bloody trail in our wake, our mission was accomplished, and that's the bottom line in this business. We'll be heading back to Alpha Base now, and I'll never be able to thank you all enough for your assistance. I imagine you're quite anxious to get back to your lives."

"I don't know about that," said Pete Frystak. "Speaking for myself, I'm going to miss all this action, though I've got plenty of work waiting for me back in Florida. By the way, you're all welcome to visit us down on Big Pine Key. And don't even think about paying for your rooms."

"It looks like I'll be shipping back to New London," said Stanley Roth. "I've got a new class of potential bubbleheads waiting for me there, and I sure wouldn't want to disappoint them."

"What are your plans, Bill?" asked Slaughter.

Brown was pulling his corncob from his pants pocket as he answered. "I've got a date with a very special lady back on Sarasota Bay."

Traveler suddenly appeared on the sail behind them, having just climbed up the forward access trunk. He ran the Stars and Stripes up the sail's flagpole.

"This one's for you, Doc, compliments of the men of SEAL Team Three!"

Five-thousand feet above them, from the cramped cockpit of his Mitsubishi Zero Dr. Yukio Ishii peered through a pair of binoculars to the sea

344

below. A single submarine lay motionless on the surface, and Ishii did his best to identify the faces of those assembled on the vessel's open sail. Though he was still too far away to make them out, he couldn't miss the red, white, and blue flag that fluttered in the wind at the rear of the bridge.

"So, it was the Western barbarians all the time!" he exclaimed, his voice filled with rage. "They may have won yet another battle, but the struggle to free Nippon shall continue—for all eternity if necessary!"

Ishii angrily lowered the binoculars and readjusted the fit of his hachimaki headband. It was only too obvious that the clever Americans had somehow stolen the *Bokken,* and had then used it to penetrate Takara Bay and put an end to his great dream. It was thus only fitting that he answered this cowardly act of treachery in the traditional way of the warrior.

"Banzai!" he screamed as he pointed the nose of the Zero downward and began a steep, kamikaze dive straight for the exposed sail of the surfaced submarine.

"Air contact, Captain!" the amplified voice of Ray Morales broke through on the sail's intercom. "Bearing zero-nine-zero and rapidly closing!"

This report caught the sail's occupants by complete surprise, and all eyes went to the east, where the sun was already climbing in the morning sky. Oblivious to the blinding glare, Pete Frystak scanned the heavens with his binoculars and excitedly pointed high into the heavens.

"I see it!" he exclaimed. "Shouldn't we dive?"

"We can't!" answered Stanley Roth. "We're in the midst of a battery recharge."

Chris Slaughter swept the eastern sky with his own binoculars, and did a double take upon spotting the red Rising Sun decals visible on the prop-driven plane's fuselage.

"Either I'm seeing things, or we've got a Jap Kamikaze headed straight for us. Clear the bridge!" he firmly ordered.

This sent the group scrambling for the hatch that was set into the sail's floor. Stanley Roth was the first to reach it, and when it failed to budge, Pete Frysak bent down to give him a hand.

"I'm afraid it's jammed shut." Stanley vainly continued to attempt to pull it open.

"It must have gotten damaged during that depth-charge attack," offered the veteran weapons officer.

Miriam Kromer overheard them. "Do you mean that we're stuck up here?" she asked.

Traveler briefly met her worried gaze. Then he looked to the open, aft access trunk. It invitingly beckoned on the sub's foredeck. Doubting that they'd have the time to make it to shelter here, the SEAL reached out instead for the intercom. His voice was strained as he instructed the quartermaster to patch him directly into the forward torpedo room. Once this connection was made, he firmly addressed the handset's transmitter.

"Cajun, sixty-second drill! We've got an airborne bandit coming down at us out of the sun, and if you ever want to see that beloved bayou of yours again, you're going to have to be the one to take it out!"

Warlock acknowledged receipt of this frantic message, and then Traveler turned his glance back to the eastern sky. He could clearly see the approaching plane now, could hear the distant roar of its engine.

"What was that call all about, Traveler?" Miriam stood right beside the commando, her eyes also locked on the diving Zero.

The SEAL replied as calmly as possible. "When I left Cajun, he was in the process of field-stripping his weapon. I instructed him to reassemble it, and with a little good luck, that plane up there will soon be history."

"But how in the world can you take out a plane with a mere rifle?" she asked.

Traveler coolly grinned. "Hey, Doc, have you already forgotten who you're dealin' with here?"

Standing at Traveler's other side, Bill Brown peered up into the eastern sky in utter disbelief. "That son of a bitch is really coming straight for us! What kind of fool would even think of doing such a thing?"

"Have a look and see for yourself," suggested Chris Slaughter as he handed the veteran his binoculars.

Bill Brown had to readjust the focus before he could get the fuselage of the Zero into clear view. Seated beneath its canopy was a single, elderly pilot with long, shoulder-length silver hair and a tapering, Fu Manchu-style mustache. Brown's thoughts flashed back to the photograph Henry

Walker had shown him, and he knew without a doubt that the kamikaze was none other than Dr. Yukio Ishii.

Just as this startling realization dawned in Bill Brown's consciousness, Cajun popped out of the forward access trunk. The Louisiana-bred SEAL was the perfect picture of coolness as he sighted his target and then balanced the long barrel of his rifle against the lip of the open hatch, calmly peering into the scope.

The Zero was less than six hundred yards away from the *Bokken* when a single 7.62mm shell exploded from the Heckler and Koch's black barrel. With an ear-shattering crack, this armor-piercing round instantly went supersonic. As it tore into the Zero's 14-cylinder radial engine, the fuel pump shattered into a shower of red-hot fragments that immediately ignited the volatile petroleum fumes, and the entire engine subsequently blew apart, tearing open the wing-mounted fuel tanks and causing the aircraft to disintegrate in a blinding ball of fire.

The great heat created by this explosion could be felt even on the sub's sail, and its occupants were forced to duck for cover to escape the shower of smoking debris that rained from the sky. The bulk of this wreckage fell harmlessly into the sea, and as the last torn piece of metal clattered onto the deck, Traveler rose and called out, "Way to go, Cajun! SEAL Team Three strikes again!"

Yet before the rest of the sail's occupants could join in the celebration, the intercom crackled to life.

"Captain, radar shows another airborne contact approaching on bearing one-eight-zero." It was the voice of Ray Morales.

"Now what?" asked Miriam as she looked disgustedly into the southern sky.

"Relax, Doc," advised Bill Brown, who scanned the sky with his binoculars. "This is one of ours."

The veteran's observation proved true as a lone Sikorsky Seahawk helicopter came into view. The shiny white chopper swooped in low from the south and completely circled the *Bokken* before hovering directly above it. The chopping roar of its twin turboshaft engines reached an almost deafening pitch as the Seahawk descended to a mere 100 feet above the sub's sail.

"Dr. Miriam Kromer?" The powerfully amplified voice came from the chopper's open fuselage door.

The toxicologist appeared genuinely puzzled as she spotted the helmeted individual responsible for this query. She waved a hand overhead to identify herself, then listened carefully as the Seahawk's air tactical officer once more spoke into his megaphone.

"Dr. Kromer, we've been ordered to transfer you back to the *Enterprise* at once. There's been an explosion at a pharmaceutical plant in Vladivostok, and the Russians have asked for your help in containing the damage. Air transport to the mainland awaits you on the carrier."

Speechless, Miriam Kromer watched as the chopper began dropping a cable-mounted transfer sling.

"You certainly earn that paycheck of yours," remarked Bill Brown as he caught the harness and then began securing it around her.

"We're sure gonna miss that pretty face of yours," said Stanley Roth. He checked to be sure the harness fit tightly beneath Miriam's shoulders.

Chris Slaughter also double-checked the harness's fit before giving the chopper's ATO a thumbs-up. "Thanks again, Doctor," he said.

As the cable tightened, the stunned toxicologist struggled to find words to express her feelings. "It was a real pleasure working with each one of you," she got out. Then her goodbye was cut short as the chopper's winch began lifting her skyward. She was soon dangling high above the sail, and as she peered downward, Traveler issued her a crisp salute and loudly shouted. "Don't forget to keep your cool, Doc. See ya' round!"